HOW TO GROW AN ADDICT

HOW TO GROW
AN ADDICT

A NOVEL

J. A. WRIGHT

swp

SHE WRITES PRESS

Published 2015
Printed in the United States of America
ISBN: 978-1-63152-991-7
Library of Congress Control Number: 2015939986
Cover Photo credit: Henry Hargreaves and Caitlin Levin

For information, address:
She Writes Press
1563 Solano Ave #546
Berkeley, CA 94707

She Writes Press is a division of SparkPoint Studio, LLC.

To those

who trudge the road to happy destiny,

so they don't have

to drown in a sea of despair.

PROLOGUE

I still can't figure it out. How the therapist persuaded me to stay in rehab. Maybe it was her smile or the way she motioned for me to sit down, or perhaps it was the way she put her hand on my shoulder when she introduced me to the group. Most likely it happened when I saw her wipe a tear from her cheek after I lied to the group about my black eyes and broken nose.

I sat and listened to the others talk about the trouble they were in, the kinds of drugs they used, what they drank, and how they liked to party because I felt I owed her something for making her cry. I also felt like she wanted me to talk, but I couldn't. I wasn't like them. I didn't drink or take pills so I could party all night. I used alcohol and drugs to help me feel okay, to calm me down, to shut off the voice in my head that told me I was nothing. That's what drugs and alcohol did for me. But I wasn't about to tell that to them.

I was going to get up and run when I heard one of the guys say, "Hey Teach, how many sad shit stories am I sup- posed to tell you before you sign my court paper and let me out of here?"

"As many as you got," she replied. "And if you're thinking some judge is the reason you're here, you're dead wrong. Drugs and booze are why you're here, why you're all here, and I hap- pen to know a lot about both. I also know things will run a lot smoother if you understand your treatment plan doesn't include me hearing about your favorite color, your astrological sign, or the TV shows you like to watch. What I want you to talk about are your secrets. How about we start with the three that got you here? Everyone has at least three."

Only three things? I thought to myself. I have way more than three.

I'd never heard a woman talk like her, and I'd never considered that just three things could be responsible for all the trouble I was in. She was scary, but kind of nice. And I was curious. So I stayed.

CHAPTER 1

I know a lot about trouble. Mostly about causing it and not much about staying out of it. It all started when I was seven and began taking things. At first it was just money and candy, but as I got older, and better at stealing, I began to take things just for the sake of taking things. I tried to be careful about what I took and who I took it from, and I hardly ever got caught. But every once in a while I made a mistake and took something that caused a problem. Like the time I took my brother Robbie's backpack from the players' bench and he had to walk home in the rain from baseball practice because the bus driver wouldn't let him ride without paying. A few days later he came down with a bad cold and almost died from an asthma attack. I wasn't there to witness the attack, but I heard about it for years. Mom got all choked up every time she told the story of how Robbie was suffocating right in front of her, and she couldn't find his inhaler because some school bully had stolen his backpack. She never knew it was me who took it. Because after I got the money out I threw the backpack in a dumpster.

I didn't mean for Robbie to get sick; I just wanted to buy a cherry Slurpee on the way home from school, and I didn't have any money. Robbie always had money because Dad gave him some almost every day. Dad never gave me money, said a little kid didn't need any, and the one time I got mad about it and told him it was unfair he said, "Men need to have a bit of money on them in case they get a chance to buy a girl a drink."

I thought that was a stupid answer and asked Robbie if he would share his money with me, but he just laughed and said, "You heard what Dad said." I decided from then on to help myself. At first it felt wrong, but once I got started it was hard to stop, and pretty soon I was taking money from Dad's wallet or Robbie's gym bag at least once a week. After a while I began to feel good about it. Mainly because it was unfair that Robbie got money and I didn't. Not only that, I hated that he didn't have any chores except mowing the lawn on Saturdays and sometimes helping Mom in the garden. I seemed to have lots of chores, including washing the breakfast dishes, emptying the dishwasher, and starting loads of laundry—all of which had to be done before I left for school. Once, after I read *The Adventures of Pippi Longstocking*, I made a nametag for myself that said "House Slave" and wore it until Dad noticed and made me take it off. "You're about as far away from being a 'house slave' as you are from being a 'house genius,'" he said.

We all knew the only "genius" in our family was Robbie. Not only was he smart, he also, as he got older, got better looking and popular. He became a goody-goody, the type of person who could do everything really well. He dressed well, spoke well, wrote well, and looked better than most people. I used to wonder how he got that way and if it would happen to me too.

When I was about five I loved him more than I loved anyone else, and I think he loved me too. Even though he was eight years older than me, he was my best friend. He took care of me and taught me how to do things like make toast, tie my shoelaces, tell time, ride a bike, and hit a tennis ball. He even cut the manufacturer tags out of my shirts and pants because they scratched me. I didn't just like him; I wanted to *be* him. I used to sit at the bottom of our front porch stairs and wait for him to get home from school to play catch, or to make macaroni and cheese and watch TV with me. When I was finally old enough to go to school, Robbie walked me to Bradford Elementary every day. It was about four blocks out of his way to his junior high, and sometimes his friends would walk behind us and tease him about being my babysitter, but he didn't seem to care. He wanted to make sure I got to school okay. And I know Mom appreciated it because I'd heard her tell people how helpful he was. I thought Robbie and I would live together forever, and he often told me he'd never leave me alone with *Dem*.

Dem was the code word we used for our parents when they were fighting, or if one of us could see Dad had been drinking. We'd warn each other with a quick *Dem* to let the other one know to stay away. The way Robbie said *Dem* was funny. It sounded like he had a mouthful of mud, and it always made me laugh. Just as funny were the times he'd write it out after he huffed on a cold glass window or used his food to spell *Dem* on his dinner plate.

● ● ●

I had a great time hanging out with Robbie, and I got to do lots of stuff I wasn't supposed to. Mostly things like climbing trees or shooting BB guns at the neighbor's fence. And if I was with Robbie no one ever said a word to me about going into a PG-13 movie. I even got to see *Poltergeist* when I was six because Robbie's friend worked at the theater and let me in for free. Afterward, Robbie swore he'd never take me to another movie because I insisted on sleeping in a chair next to his bed for almost a week. That's how long it took until the little girl with long white hair stopped appearing in my head every time I closed my eyes.

Besides being a great brother, Robbie was especially good at baseball, probably because he was tall and thin and could run super fast. I liked to watch him play from the backstop area, just behind the umpire and catcher, because it was a good distance from Dad. Dad always stood on the left field sideline because he said the umpire, coach, and players could hear him best from there. I hated it when Robbie's friends, or their parents, would look over at Mom or me when Dad was yelling at someone. It made me feel bad and sometimes Mom and I would leave because we were embarrassed.

If Robbie had had his way, Dad would never have been allowed to attend any of his games. Dad thought the coach was a "moron" and that the umpire "didn't know shit about shit," and one time he called Robbie's coach a "fucking pussy" and got into a fight with the umpire, who'd stopped the game and walked over to Dad.

"You're gonna have to shape up or leave," he said.

Dad grabbed him by the neck and pushed him to the ground. He was just about to kick him when Robbie's coach ran over and told Dad to back off. Dad said a few nasty things about the umpire's wife, and then told Mom and me to follow him to the car. I was happy we were leaving, but instead of getting in the car, Dad got a hunting knife out of the trunk and slashed the coach's tires. He mumbled something about "showing him" as he got into the driver's seat, and I heard Mom say, "I don't understand why you have to ruin things for everyone."

I didn't see him slap her, I only heard it and then heard Mom scream. I wanted to get out of the car and run away, but I couldn't make myself open the car door, so I slid down onto the floor and covered my head with my sweatshirt.

● ● ●

I figured out real early that it was best to stay out of Dad's way, especially if he was mad at me. I also figured out I'd have to get real good at playing baseball if I wanted to keep hanging out with Robbie, because other than school, that's the only thing he liked to do. So I got good at pitching—so good that Robbie let me play on his team once. I was happy about it, but the other kids weren't, and they complained I was too little and not a boy. I thought they might change their minds if I got perfect at pitching, so I kept practicing and going to their games until they let me be a batboy and help some of the guys warm up before games. With my baseball skills and short hair, a lot of people thought I was a boy. A couple of times, when Robbie's team was short a player and didn't want to forfeit a game, they let me take right field, but only after I'd put on a baseball cap and one of their team shirts.

I must have been about eight when an official-looking guy took Robbie aside after a game and told him that girls can't play baseball. On the walk home, Robbie told me I couldn't play or practice with them anymore. I'd have to join a girls' softball team—a bunch of crybabies who complained about everything and got hurt a lot. I joined the Shopgood Lassies softball team because Robbie said I should, and even though most of the girls on the team weren't very good players, we took first place in our division anyway. I pitched a couple of no-hitters my first year thanks to Robbie coming along and cheering me on. He even gave me his old baseball glove at the end of the season.

● ● ●

The year Robbie started his junior year in high school something weird happened, and things changed between us after that.

I'd gotten out of school early one day and run all the way home to see my cat, Rascal, who was pregnant and had been meowing in a strange way the night before. I was worried about going to school and leaving her alone, even though Mom said she'd be okay. That morning I'd helped Mom make a bed for Rascal out of a cardboard box and old towels. We put the box in my closet because Mom thought she'd be more comfortable there, and she wasn't too happy about the thought of Rascal giving birth on my bed. I was late leaving for school because Rascal wasn't interested in the box, and I had to get her out from under my bed three times before she finally stayed in the closet.

When I got to my room after school that day I opened the closet hoping to see Rascal, but she wasn't there. I looked under my bed to find her with five little black-and-white kittens all snuggled into her belly. They were the cutest things I'd ever seen. Rascal looked tired. She was lying on her side, and when she saw me she licked the kitten closest to her and then meowed a couple of times, as if to tell me how happy she was.

I was so excited about the kittens I could hardly keep my hands off of them. I wanted to tell someone the good news, so I went to the kitchen and called Mom at work, but the receptionist said she was with a customer and couldn't come to the phone. Then I noticed Robbie's coat and book bag on the dining room table, so I headed down to the basement to his room.

Robbie's door was slightly open—enough for me to see that something unusual was going on. And the closer I looked, the more I could see that something bad was happening to Robbie.

Robbie was being murdered by a guy who was straddled over him, pushing something into his behind. I could tell from the strange sounds Robbie was making that it was bad, like the noises I imagined someone would make on their way to being dead. I ran back to the kitchen and dialed 911. I told the operator my brother was being murdered and that she should send the cops right away. Then I went to my bedroom and crawled under the bed next to Rascal and the kittens and waited for the police.

By the time they arrived, Robbie and the guy were in the kitchen eating toast and drinking chocolate milk. I realized right away that whatever had happened between them must not have been the horrible thing I thought it was, because they were joking around and laughing.

When the doorbell rang, I sprinted from the kitchen to the front door and told the policeman I'd made a mistake, that nothing bad had happened and that he should go away. I was whispering and holding the door slightly ajar so Robbie wouldn't hear what was going on, but he came to the door anyway, asking the policeman why he was at our house. Both the policeman and Robbie looked at me and I felt I had no choice but to explain what I'd seen and why I called. When I got to the part about seeing a naked, sweaty guy on top of Robbie, he interrupted me and told the policeman I was imagining things and what I'd seen was a couple of guys practicing wrestling moves. I mentioned, under my breath, something about the other guy sticking something up his butt and Robbie yelled out, "She's a retard, a fucking retard! She wouldn't know a slick wrestling move if it hit her on the head!" The policeman must have believed Robbie, because he left without further questions.

After the cop car drove off Robbie chased me all the way to my bedroom, shouting that I was about to regret the day I was born. I scrambled to get under my bed, but he was close behind. That's when he noticed Rascal and her kittens. Robbie pulled me out by my feet and then reached over to Rascal. I thought he was going to pet her but instead he picked up one of her kittens, stood up, and started walking real fast down the hallway. Before I knew it, he was in the bathroom and I arrived just in time to see him drop the kitten into the toilet bowl and flush. When I started hitting him and screaming he turned around and squeezed my chin so hard I thought he would crush my mouth.

"If you ever mention a word to anyone about what you think you saw, I'll flush all the kittens down the toilet."

He had a crazy look on his face, the same face Dad got when he was pissed off, and I was scared. I couldn't believe Robbie had turned into a monster. I was worried he'd kill the rest of the kittens, so I got a sleeping bag out of the hall closet and put it under the bed next to Rascal, planning to stay there until I was sure Robbie was done killing kittens. While I was in the closet, I helped myself to a few other things: a flashlight, a canteen, and a big hunting knife. I told Mom I wanted to sleep with Rascal and the kittens; I didn't say anything about the hunting knife I'd hidden under my pillow or that Robbie had turned into a crazed killer. Mom said it was okay, but I shouldn't play with the kittens or bother Rascal too much.

● ● ●

The next morning, on my way to the kitchen I heard Robbie say, "Hey Dad, yesterday I saw Randall in the park smoking."

I yelled out, "That's a big fat lie, you were the one smoking."

Dad called me over to the table and asked me about it. I told him Robbie was the smoker, not me. He made me hand him my school bag. On the outside pocket, he found a half-empty pack of Marlboro Lights and a pink Bic lighter. He looked at me and said in a low, quiet voice, "You're nothing."

"Robbie put those in there, I swear to God," I screamed.

"Should I bother looking through the rest of your bag?" he replied.

I didn't know what to say so I said, "I don't care."

I watched Dad unbuckle the inside pocket, reach in, and pull out a ribbon with his purple-heart medal attached to the end, the one he got for helping soldiers in Vietnam. He held it up and read out loud a word Robbie had obviously written on the ribbon with a black felt marker: "yellow."

Dad's face turned red and purple at the same time and I thought veins in his neck were going to explode. I moved slowly backward until I was sitting on the living room couch. I looked over at Robbie and saw him smirk. I looked at Mom and she motioned for me to leave the room. I got up and ran to my bedroom, climbed under the bed, and moved to the very end, by the wall.

I waited until I heard Dad's car leave before I went out to the kitchen to talk to Mom. She said she found it hard to believe I would have cigarettes and even harder to believe I would take Dad's Purple Heart. "Maybe you forgot you put them in there? You do that kind of thing sometimes. Besides, I can't believe Robbie would do something like this."

I shook my head side to side until she told me to sit down and eat some breakfast.

A few minutes later, as I headed to the front door, I heard her say, "Do you know what the word 'yellow' means?"

"Sure I do, it's a color—like a lemon or a banana."

"Actually it can mean 'cowardly' too. I'll have a word with Robbie about all this tonight," she said.

Robbie spent the next year threatening to have a few of his friends beat me up if I ever said a word to anyone about what had happened in his bedroom. He also spent a lot of time in his room with the guy who ran the bowling alley, but only on Tuesdays and Wednesdays, when Mom worked late. That guy was spooky, and I didn't like him. I wondered why Robbie wanted a friend so much older. After a few weeks, though, I got used to the guy coming over and hearing them grunt and moan.

After Mom came home early from work one day and saw Robbie walk from the kitchen to the bathroom with hardly any clothes on, I began to offer my lookout services to Robbie in exchange for five dollars each time. I promised to knock three times on his bedroom door if our parents called or came home. I made a bunch of money that year, more than sixty dollars.

That was also the year I met my half-sister, Tammy, and the year Dad went to jail for trying to kill his brother Bill.

CHAPTER 2

I don't know if my Dad really meant to kill his own brother, but it sure looked like it. It happened when I was eight, on one of the days between Christmas and New Years in 1983. I'd spent most of the morning helping Dad clean up his car garage and putting screws and bolts in the colored glass storage jars Mom bought him for Christmas. He wanted the place to be spic-and-span.

"I've invited some of my family over for dinner and I don't want them to think we live in a dump, so make sure you sweep the driveway and the porch," he told me when I was helping him carry his shopping from his truck to the garage bar: four bottles of Canadian Club, two bottles of Beefeater Gin, and a six-pack of tonic water. We had two garages: a two-car garage connected to our house, and a much bigger garage, big enough to fit six of Dad's classic cars inside, behind our house.

I mopped his big garage floor and swept the driveway and sidewalk like he asked me to, all the while trying to remember what I'd heard from Aunt Flo about their family.

Aunt Flo was Dad's twin. She and Uncle Hank lived in a big cottage house about a mile from us. It was a lot more fun being at their house than mine and they didn't seem to mind having me stay, so I did, every chance I got. Aunt Flo was always busy with her garden and Uncle Hank was always busy talking to his friends and neighbors. I liked to listen to him talk. He sounded a little like Latka on the TV show *Taxi*.

I often heard Uncle Hank and Aunt Flo talk about their families, so I knew that my Dad went to a Catholic high school, that Aunt Flo once considered becoming a nun, and that their mother was Irish and very sweet and their father was Dutch and Scottish and didn't like kids. I also knew they'd grown up on a cattle farm just outside of San Bernardino and that Dad had joined the Marines when he was eighteen to get away from his father.

I was excited about meeting Dad's other sisters, my aunts, and wondered if they'd be anything like Aunt Flo. I think Mom was excited about them coming over as well because she got up really early and cleaned every room before she started making dinner.

Dad didn't seem happy about the dinner or about seeing his sisters or brother. He was grumpy and asked me to make him a drink at about 3 p.m., just after I finished cleaning the dirty shot glasses he'd left on his garage workbench. I mixed his whiskey and water "kind of weak," the way Mom always told me to.

"This isn't a drink, it's water," Dad said. "Leave the bottle on the bench and go get changed into one of those dresses your mom is always buying for you. My sisters are snobs and you need to look presentable. And keep your fingers out of your mouth—got it?"

I went to my room to put on my new red velour jumper, and to put Band-Aids on the all the fingers I'd bitten that morning.

Four of my six aunts arrived in the same car at 5.30 p.m., and Dad started yelling at them before they even got into the house. He thought they'd parked too close to our garage door and he wanted them to move. He was also pissed off about the little poodle they'd brought along.

"Why can't you leave that mutt at home, Gert? It doesn't need to go every goddamn place you do," he growled at Gert who'd driven and who had a beehive hairdo that was so high she had to hold it in place as she got out of the car.

Since it was their first time at our house and they didn't know Dad's rules about parking, I told the tallest one I could move the car for them. They all looked at me, and one of them asked if I knew how to drive. That's when Dad yelled out, "Damn right she knows how to drive! She can hit a baseball out of the park, too."

They each took my hand and introduced themselves as they got out of the car and headed toward our front door. It was easy for me to remember Gert (the one with the beehive and the little black poodle) and Violet (the shortest one), but I got Ivy and Angelis mixed up. " Don't worry, I have a hard time remembering all of our names myself," Ivy laughed as she squeezed my hand.

I moved their car a few feet back and then went into the house to help Mom. "It's weird how much they all look alike. I can see Aunt Flo in each of them, but not much of Dad," I told Mom.

"Wait until your Uncle Bill gets here, he's the spitting image of your Dad," she said.

● ● ●

The sisters were all tall, thin redheads. They walked the same way, they all spoke alike, with a low tone that was familiar to me, and they had a unique cackle-laugh that I sometimes heard in myself. They were all beautiful, but none of them was as glamorous as Aunt Flo.

I was happy to meet them, and I made them all a Harvey Wallbanger before I left them in the dining room with Dad to go help Mom in the kitchen. I was mashing potatoes when Dad came in and poured himself a tall glass of whiskey.

"That asshole brother of mine is late as usual. Let's not wait for him. They're all hungry and I'd like to get this over with as soon as possible."

"You shouldn't drink like that today," Mom said to him.

"Don't tell me what I shouldn't do," he sniped.

My aunts said all kinds of nice things when Mom and I brought the fried chicken and mashed potatoes to the table, but no one said anything while they ate, which made me wonder if they'd noticed the gravy was burnt. We were almost finished eating when Dad said, "Listen up, I've waited long enough for my share of Mom and Dad's house. I've got a son signed up for Cal State and it's expensive. Don't you think it's time for Gert and Rose to move out and get their own place so we can settle up?"

Gert put her fork down and made a big huff sound before she called him a greedy, selfish crackpot. "If I'd known you were inviting me over here to bully me into moving out of my home, I wouldn't have come," she said.

"It's not your home. Mom and Dad left the house to all of us. Why do you need to live in such a big place anyway? Christ, if we sell it, you'll get enough money to buy a nice condo that doesn't need all the maintenance of Mom and Dad's house," Dad replied.

"It's not about the money. Mom wanted Rose to stay at home for as long as she could and you know it," Gert said.

"Jesus Christ . . . Mom's been dead for ten years!" Dad yelled.

"You're still as mean as ever," Gert snapped.

I could hear their youngest sister, Violet, crying—we all could—but they didn't seem fazed by it, didn't even offer her a tissue, and I was too scared to do anything, so I just kept my head down and picked at the Band-Aid I'd put on my left thumbnail earlier.

I was grateful when Mom walked into the dining room a few minutes later with a large bread pudding in her hands and broke up the argument. "Let's not talk about this right now. I've made your mom's bread pudding, and my little helper here"— she winked at me—"made a nice vanilla custard."

We ate dessert in silence, and when Uncle Bill arrived, just after we'd finished, Dad went outside to meet him. That's when things got loud. I heard Dad's truck start up, so I went outside to see what was going on, and it looked to me like Dad was trying to run over Uncle Bill as he was running back down the street to his car. It also looked like Genie, the secretary of Dad's car club, was sitting in the front seat of Uncle Bill's car.

Dad missed Bill, but not by much, and the truck kept going and didn't stop until it hit the house across the street. It smashed the Kendricks' living room window and only came to a stop when the top of their porch fell down onto the hood of the Dad's truck.

I watched Dad try to reverse the truck, but it wouldn't move. The wheels just spun and smoked, and pieces of grassy lawn flew everywhere. Mr. Kendrick came out of his house with a baseball bat. He knocked out Dad's front and back lights, smashed what was left of the windshield, and dented the hood and the doors, all the while screaming at Dad, "I'm gonna knock your fucking block off!"

My aunts stood on our driveway with my mom, Robbie, and me, all of us watching. And I'm pretty sure the entire neighborhood, including my friends the twins and their parents, were out on the street watching as well.

"Oh shit!" I heard Mom say really loud at the very same moment I heard the sirens. One fire truck and two cop cars arrived in the next minute and parked right in the middle of the street, blocking our view of Dad's truck and the Kendricks' porch. We all walked down the sidewalk until we were almost to Uncle Bill's parked car. That's when I noticed how much Uncle Bill looked like my Dad, but with hair. It's also when Mom noticed Genie in the front seat next to Uncle Bill, watching the action in the Kendricks' front yard.

"Of course. It's all about her!" Mom screamed as she turned and ran into the house.

The cops spent a while trying to convince Dad to unlock his door. "Sir, you need to unlock the door now," I heard one of them yell out.

After a few minutes of waiting, the cop signaled a fireman over to Dad's truck, and I was more scared than ever as I watched him break the door lock with an axe and pull Dad out of his truck.

They pulled his arms back, handcuffed him, and pushed him into the backseat of their squad car. One of the firemen had to hold Mr. Kendrick back because he took a swing at Dad when the cops were handcuffing him and almost hit him. I wished he hadn't missed; I really wanted Dad to get clobbered, just once, real hard.

Robbie took off with one of his friends who'd arrived in time to see Dad get arrested, and everyone else (except the Kendricks and the firemen) went back to their homes or cars, except for Uncle Bill. He got out of his car and came into the house to tell Mom he was going to press charges. I was at the door when he arrived on the porch.

"Where's your mom? I want to talk to her," he said.

"I'll see if she wants to talk," I replied as I turned around to see if she was in the kitchen.

"Why'd you bring her to my house? You know better," Mom yelled out from the kitchen.

Uncle Bill walked into the kitchen, so I leaned against the sink and pretended I was getting a glass of water.

"We're getting married," Bill said.

"Ha! Give me a break. She's not going to marry you. She's just using you—and I wouldn't have minded one little bit if you'd both been run over," Mom replied.

From my place in the hallway I could see my uncle smirk and then I heard him say, "You know, Susan, you've always been dumb as dirt."

Mom fired back, "Dumb enough to know a Nothing when I'm looking at it."

He turned to walk out the door, and she threw her beer bottle at him, hitting him on his left shoulder. I thought Uncle Bill was going to turn around and clobber Mom, but he kept walking. He didn't even slam the door on his way out.

I brought Mom another beer like she asked me to. She drank most of it in one go. "I just don't know what to do anymore," she cried out.

I was scared, so I called Olive, Mom's best friend since junior high school, and told her about Dad and asked if she could come over.

"I can't come over right now, honey, but hand the phone to your mom and go find her bottle of Xanax, probably in her bedroom or in her purse," she said.

I gave the phone to Mom and then sprinted down the hallway to get her medication. After Mom had finished talking to Olive, she looked at me with sad eyes and said, "I'm sorry about today," then swallowed two Xanax. I sat next to Mom on the couch while she dozed off, all the while thinking about Uncle Bill and Genie and wondering why Genie hadn't told me she was going to marry my uncle. It had only been about a week since I'd helped her with the decorations at the annual Classic Car Club Christmas party, the same party where I saw Dad kiss her under a piece of mistletoe. I thought about calling Aunt Flo to ask her about Genie, but I was afraid I'd wake up Mom.

 CHAPTER 3

In my opinion, if my dad had just been a bit nicer, everything would have been perfect. But he didn't have much niceness about him. I used to think it was because of his age. He was forty-five when I was born on June 1, 1975, and I don't think he really wanted me. Robbie was born just after my parents got married in 1967, and it was pretty obvious they wanted him, because his baby pictures were all over the house.

Dad worked for a big company as a salesman and traveled a lot, sometimes for a week or two. If he wasn't at work, at a car auction, or at one of his club shows, he was in his big garage restoring one of his cars. I was allowed to be in the garage, but only if I kept myself busy and didn't ask him "stupid" questions. He said I specialized in asking stupid questions, so I'd do my best to keep my mouth from moving and stay out of his way unless he needed me to hold something or hand him a tool.

I became a really good helper. I was especially good at polishing hubcaps, oiling tires, and cleaning leather car seats with toothpaste and old T-shirts, just the way Dad's friend Mike from the car club showed me. I also swept the floor, kept both of the garage fridges stocked with beer, and taught myself how to siphon gas from one gas tank to another with a garden hose Dad had cut up for just this purpose. Although it took me a few months to get it right, and I got myself drenched a few times, I didn't mind because I loved the smell of gasoline. Sometimes, when I thought I could get away with it, I'd put a little bit on a rag and take it to bed with me.

Dad's garage had several workbenches, two old leather recliner chairs, a mechanic's pit, two beer fridges, and a bar with every type of whiskey in the world, as he used to tell everyone. His friend Mike gave him an old jukebox and helped wire its speakers into the ceiling of the garage. It only had fifty songs on it, and they were mostly Glen Campbell tunes, but Dad always let me choose which one to play. We both knew the words to every song, and it was fun to sing along with Dad while he sang along with Glen. I told Dad he had a much better voice than Glen Campbell and he agreed, but he said Glen was one hell of a bagpipe player, and his guitar playing wasn't bad either, "and that's why Mr. Campbell is so famous."

Restoring cars and country music weren't the only things Dad liked; he also liked "Bourbon, Cigs, and Big Tits." I know this because it was written out on a blackboard sign hanging on the only wall of his big garage not decorated with *Playboy* centerfolds. He had every one from the years 1972, 1973, 1974, 1975, 1976, and 1978, and a few from the olden days, 1967 and 1968. I knew all "his girls" pretty well and I liked the dark ones best, the ones with the rounder boobs. It seemed to me they had friendlier smiles, nicer than the cute little smiles of the blondes or the smirky grins of the redheads. Dad liked his blondes the best, and the bigger the boobs the more he liked them. "No use having great tits and hiding them under clothes," he told me one day when I was about eight and Mrs. Benson had just driven her 1972 red Chevelle up to the open doors of Dad's big garage to get see if he would check her oil before she drove to San Francisco to visit her sister. It was the first time she'd ever seen the inside of the garage, and when she saw Dad's collection of centerfolds all over the walls her mouth dropped open. She put her hands on her hips and in a real scary voice said, "What the hell is all of this? Are you crazy?"

"Those are Dad's posters, not mine," I said, really fast and really loud.

Dad just laughed and took a long drag of his cigarette. After he put some oil in her car, he said, "When you wanna get rid of this thing let me know. I'll give you a decent price."

"When you wanna get rid of those disgusting pictures on your walls let me know. I'll do a decent job," she replied.

"They're just boobs. We all got 'em." He grinned as she pulled away.

He told me after she left that I should pay more attention to what I ate and get lots of exercise because it might help me develop a "decent rack."

"A good set is the ticket into the Playboy mansion, and even if you don't become a centerfold bunny, I hear the tips at the club are pretty good," he said.

● ● ●

I found out that I had a half-sister, Tammy, by accident when I was in third grade. She was Dad's daughter from his first marriage, and she was twenty-three when I was born. I met her when our teacher, Mrs. Hodge, left to have a baby, and she substituted for our class. The first day back at school, after Christmas break, we all had a bag of jellybeans on our desks and a little note explaining that our teacher's baby had come and she wouldn't be back the rest of the school year. When the substitute teacher wrote her name on the blackboard I thought it was interesting that we had the same last name. On my way out to recess I stopped by her desk.

"My last name is Grange," I said.

She smiled at me and said, "Is your dad's name Randall too?"

"Yes," I replied.

"Well, Randall, we're half-sisters. It's nice to finally meet you." She smiled big as she put her hand out to shake mine.

I thought she might be teasing me, but I shook her hand anyway and smiled right back at her. I stared at her the rest of the day, and the more I did the more I saw how much she looked like Dad—and when she laughed while reading a page from *Charlotte's Web*, she sounded just like him.

When I got home from school that day, I asked Robbie if he knew anything about Dad having other children, "Yeah, I think I heard something about Dad being married before he met Mom and having a kid. I don't know for sure, though. You should ask Mrs. Benson, 'cause she's the one who told me," Robbie said.

"Why would she know about Dad having another wife?" I asked.

"I was mowing her lawn one day a couple of years ago when she came home with some lady who she introduced as Mrs. Grange. Then she said something about me meeting my half-sister someday."

Mrs. Benson lived right behind us in an old house that Dad called a "fucking dump." It had lots of overgrown trees and bushes, and the front porch was stacked high with old furniture and appliances, but Mrs. Benson didn't care. She didn't like my dad, either, but she did like me and I could always count on her to tell me the truth about things. I headed to her house to speak with her about Tammy, but no one answered the door.

I couldn't wait for Mrs. Benson to get home to get more information, so I called my Uncle Hank and Aunt Flo. When Uncle Hank answered I blurted out really quick, "Do you know if my dad had another baby before Robbie, because my substitute teacher says we might be half-sisters."

"Oh, my. You've met Tammy, have you? I'd better put Flo on the line, honey," he said.

I asked Aunt Flo the same thing, and she hesitated for a few seconds before she said, "Yes, she's your sister. Well, half-sister, but I'd better not say anything else. Your dad wouldn't appreciate it. You know how he is."

She also said I should keep Tammy a secret. "There's no reason for you to tell anyone about her, especially your dad. He's probably not in a very good mood after going to jail and I just don't think he needs to know." I promised I wouldn't mention her to Mom or Dad, but it was going to be pretty hard since Tammy was going to be my new teacher until the end of the school year. And I didn't for a long time, but I did look through a photo album that Dad kept on a shelf in his big garage to see if I could find a photo of Tammy. There weren't any. The album was full of car photos, plus a few from Vietnam and one of Dad at the beach holding hands with Uncle Bill's fiancée, Genie.

After I put Dad's photo album away, I went to my room and wrote a few things in my poem diary. Nice things about Tammy, because I knew I couldn't mention her to anyone and I needed to tell someone how happy I was about having a sister.

I wondered if there were other sisters or brothers of mine somewhere, and I thought about my parents and how they never talked about their parents or siblings. I asked my dad about it once, on the drive home from a car event. "My parents are dead and the rest are pretty useless," he told me. "If you want to know about Mom's you'll have to ask her because I can't remember their names. Now stop talking."

● ● ●

A few weeks after Tammy started as my third grade teacher, I told Mom I'd gotten an A on my math and history test, and while I was at it, I told her about my teacher-sister. I told her everything I knew, including what she looked like and how she had a nose like Dad's and a little snaggletooth like mine.

"How do you know for sure that she's your sister?" Mom asked in a very quiet voice.

"Aunt Flo said it was true."

Mom pinched her lips together. "I wish she'd mind her own business."

"I made her tell me, Mom, she didn't want to," I replied.

"Well, I'm happy that the cat's finally out of the bag on this one, and I'm glad she's nice to you, but let's not tell your dad."

Mom was much better at keeping secrets than I was.

She had lots of them, including things about her family that she rarely told anyone. What I knew about her family I learned from eavesdropping on her phone calls with Olive. Mom often called her at night after a few glasses of Ernest and Julio, and that's how I knew Mom's parents lived in San Diego, that her younger sister, Evelyn, was married to a preacher, had four girls, and lived in Utah, and that her brother, Tony, taught high school in Boston and had three boys.

Mom could talk to Olive for hours, and I often hung out in the kitchen pretending to do my homework so I could hear what she was saying. Sometimes she talked about work or her family, but mostly she complained about Dad and how she hated his car club buddies and the amount of time he spent in his garage building cars. And once I overheard her tell Olive she thought Aunt Flo was a royal bitch. "I just don't get why he doesn't talk to anyone in his family except for her. Sure, they're twins, but have you ever noticed how he'll argue with me until the cows come home, but not Flo—whatever she says goes."

That was the truth. Dad never fought with Aunt Flo, and he just about went crazy when he found out that his other sisters who came to dinner at our house had also gone to the police station with Uncle Bill the next day to make official statements about Dad trying to run him over. Dad spent days on the phone yelling at them.

Aunt Flo was pretty mad about what had happened too, but she didn't go to the police to complain. In fact, she helped Dad by sending Uncle Hank down to the jail to bail him out because Mom didn't have enough money. A few days later, a letter arrived at our house, from Aunt Flo and addressed to Dad. I didn't read it, but I was in the kitchen when he did, and it must have said something bad about his drinking because after he squished up her letter and threw it in the trash he took all the booze out of the house and his garage and poured it down the laundry room sink. I think he drank more that day than he poured out, though, and Mom and I had to clean up his mess after his tirade was over.

• • •

I was proud of myself for keeping Tammy a secret for so long. For five months I didn't tell anyone about my sister except for Mom, Uncle Hank, Aunt Flo, Mrs. Benson, and a few people at my Saturday arts and crafts class. I felt like I'd found a big treasure and I didn't want anyone to take it away.

Then one day toward the end of school year, for no good reason, I spilled the beans and mistakenly told Dad. I was sitting at the breakfast table reading Mom the list of people I'd invited, or was planning to invite, to my ninth birthday party at the roller rink, and I don't know why I said her name but I did. Dad stopped reading his newspaper, reached over, grabbed the list out of my hands, and re-read the names. When he got to my teacher's name he said, "Who the fuck is Tammy Grange?"

"She's my teacher, and I think she's my sister, too," I said. "I've already invited her to my party."

I knew before I'd finished talking how Dad was going to respond to this news. I watched him get up and walk to the hall closet. He took out his overcoat and then in a low voice he said, "Absolutely fucking not. She doesn't exist."

This is the same thing Dad said about lots of people he didn't like, including our mailman, the guy who took care of the lawns at the park down the block, the principal of my school, and our neighbor, Mr. Kendrick, and once he said it about me after I accidently scraped some paint off the back door of his Falcon at a classic car exhibition. Dad's friend Mike walked over to me when I was climbing into the backseat to get away from Dad and said, "Don't pay attention. He's drunk, and drunks say dumb things." I didn't tell him that Dad was more or less drunk all the time, and it was hard not to pay attention to him.

I felt like I'd ruined everything by telling Dad about Tammy, and I didn't know what to do. On my way into the classroom that day, I stopped at my sister's desk and told her I'd mistakenly mentioned her to Dad and he wasn't happy about me inviting her to my party. I couldn't help but cry when I said it.

"Oh sweetheart, don't be upset. I wouldn't have been able

to come anyway. I'm going to be out town that weekend."

I felt so much better after she said that.

A few days before my party, she gave me a cupcake and a small photo album with about twenty pictures in it, and she marked the one she liked best—a picture of her and Dad at a beach when she was just a baby. Dad was holding her up in one hand and holding a beer in the other, and they were both smiling. There were also a few pictures of her as a little girl, without Dad, and she sure was cute.

She looked a little more like Robbie than me, except her teeth, which were exactly like mine. In the back of the album, there was a picture of her and her mother swimming at a lake and another photo of them sitting on a dock holding hands and laughing. The last picture in the album was a photo of Dad from a long time ago. He was wearing a military uniform and standing in front of a car kissing a blonde woman. I guessed the woman was Tammy's mother. He looked so young and happy in the picture, happier than I'd ever seen him. When I finished looking through the photo album, my sister told me our dad got hurt in Vietnam and had to stay in a special hospital for a long time. "I was only eleven and I really didn't understand what had happened to him, but he never came home and I never saw him again," Tammy said.

I felt bad for her, especially because she seemed so sad about it. I wondered why Dad went to a hospital and never went home to Tammy and her mother.

That night, when Mom and I were at the kitchen table making up gift bags for my party, I told her about the photo album and what my sister had said about Dad being in a hospital after the war. I hadn't noticed that Dad had come in the back door and could hear us until he said, "If you know what's good for you, you'll mind your own fucking business and keep your trap shut." The glass of whiskey he threw barely missed my head before it smashed against the wall.

"You're gonna cut yourself," Mom said as I bent down to pick up pieces of broken glass. "I'll clean it up. Why don't you take your list and the birthday bags to your room and get ready for bed?" she offered gently.

I cried all the way to my room. I really wanted to slam my door shut but I didn't because I could hear Dad in the kitchen arguing with Mom and I knew I'd get in big trouble if I did.

Mom knocked on my door just as I finished putting the magic trick cards in each of the birthday gift bags. When I didn't answer she opened the door and stuck her head in. "I really don't know why your dad acts like that. I do know he's got a lot going on at work and he's worried about money. Robbie's college is going to be expensive and he owes Mr. Kendrick thousands for the damage to his house."

I stared at a gift bag.

"Can I come in?" she asked.

"I guess," I said.

Mom handed me a glass of water and a piece of one of the blue pills she usually took at night. "Here, swallow this. It'll help you forget everything and sleep. I'm about to do the same thing." She shook her head up and down slowly and walked backward all the way out to the hallway.

While I waited for the pill to work I wondered if my sister would still like me even though my dad didn't want anything to do with her.

CHAPTER 4

Olive and my mom's hairdresser and friend, Ken, came over the night before my birthday party. They brought me a new pair of roller skates and a big chocolate cake. They also brought a few bottles of champagne to celebrate Olive getting a new job.

After we'd eaten cake and they'd finished the second bottle of champagne, Olive looked at me and said, "Hey, I hear you've got a secret sister."

I looked over at Mom and frowned. She grinned and said, "Sorry."

"I guess she's not a secret anymore, and she's only my half-sister and my teacher for another week. But she can't come to my birthday party tomorrow because Dad hates her," I said.

"Oh honey, try to remember that your dad hates almost everyone, not just your sister. He can be awful sometimes. Absolutely awful!" she shrieked.

Ken rolled his eyes and nodded in agreement.

Mom smiled at me in a way that told me she agreed with Olive, all the while doing her best to pull the cork off the top of the third champagne bottle. "Ya know, he wasn't always awful, and he never used to drink much," Mom said.

"In your dreams." Olive laughed.

"He used to be such a gentleman, and I don't think he drank at all when I first met him," Mom said.

"Ya know, I've been doing your hair for years, and I've heard about your house, your kids, and your boss, but you've never told me the story of how you two met," Ken said.

Mom sat down at the kitchen table, filled her glass to the rim, and told a story I'd never heard before: "I was a senior in high school and working part-time as a waitress at the officers' club in San Diego. He arrived with his wife and little girl one day for the brunch buffet. He was so charming and handsome, and he looked at me like I was the only person on earth. I had an instant crush on him. One Sunday I served him a stack of pancakes and dropped a bottle of syrup right in his lap, and when I reached to get it he grabbed my arm and didn't let go until I looked him straight in the eye. Then he slid his hand away so slowly I got goose bumps all the way up my arms and my legs went weak. It was a good thing his wife and daughter had gone to the bathroom and didn't see us, because I would have died of embarrassment.

"He showed up most Sundays for brunch from then on, always with his wife and little girl, who must have been about eight or nine. But one Sunday, he arrived alone and asked me to his house for dinner. I thought he was offering dinner with him, his wife, and daughter, so I said sure. But they weren't at his house when I got there, and I told him I couldn't stay but then he kissed me and I couldn't make myself do anything but kiss him back. By the end of the night I was in love," she said.

"My god, girl, what did your parents think?" Ken laughed as he threw his head back and finished off his glass of bubbly.

Mom said her parents were angry with her for getting involved with a married man, but she didn't care and would sneak out to meet him whenever he called. "It took a lot of careful planning to avoid his wife and her friends, but we managed. I found out I was pregnant a few weeks after I turned nineteen, and a week after he'd left for his second tour of Vietnam. I didn't write to tell him until I was eight months along because my parents didn't want me to. They begged me to forget about him, but I couldn't."

"When my baby died, a few hours after she was born, I sent a telegram to him to let him know and thought he'd call or write, but I didn't hear from him again for more than two years. He showed up at my house one day with a bunch of flowers and a story about getting shot and getting a divorce."

Even though I had to go to the bathroom, I didn't move an inch. I felt glued to my chair as I listened to my mother talk about another sister that I never knew of.

● ● ●

"We eloped a few months later and moved here to Huntington Beach because he was raised out here and had enrolled in a college to get a business degree. We were happy but we didn't have much money, so I worked at a department store and he worked part-time as a mechanic. That's where he met his car club friends and got interested in classic cars. He also spent time with his mother, who didn't live far from our apartment. He drove her to church every Sunday, and we often had dinner with her on Sunday nights. She liked me, told me she was glad her son married me and hoped we'd have a happy life together. I think we did—for a while, anyway, especially when Robbie came along. He was a different man then, a nice guy," Mom said.

"I don't remember him ever being a nice guy, and I've known him almost as long as you have," Olive said.

Mom looked up at Olive, shrugged her shoulders, and started to cry. Olive apologized for what she'd said about Dad, but that didn't stop Mom's tears.

I'd never heard the story of my parents meeting before, and I had a feeling Mom wouldn't have told it if she hadn't drunk so much champagne. I didn't know what to say to her because it sounded unbelievable, like the story of someone else's parents, not mine. "What was the baby's name?" I asked.

"Her name was Casey, and she was a beautiful baby—just like you, sweetheart," Mom said, and she smiled at me in a way that let me know everything she'd said was true.

• • •

When I went to bed that night I tried to think of what Dad was like way back then, the way she described him, but I just couldn't imagine it. I didn't know much about a dad who brought flowers to Mom or drove people to church. I only knew the dad who sold engine supplies to airlines, liked cars as much as he liked whiskey, said there was no God, and was mean to almost everyone.

As mean as Dad was, he didn't look mean. He had a nice, friendly face and really blue eyes. He wasn't fat or thin, but he was tall—a lot taller than most of his friends and my mom, at least. He had a little bit of hair, mostly in the back of his head, and his skin was tanned all year round. I would say he was just about perfect- looking, and when he slept he even looked peaceful.

There was a time when I couldn't get enough of my dad. I used to follow him everywhere, even to the bathroom. I was five or six then, and would often sneak into my parents' bedroom late at night when they were asleep because I liked to listen to him snore. His snore had a whistle sound to it, like a train in the distance. What I liked to do even more was to touch the little hollow space at the front of his neck. I liked to put my finger on it and feel it move up and down. I knew from experience I had to be careful and not press too hard or keep it there too long because if I did he would wake up and yell at me or tell Mom I was being creepy, and she would tell me to get back to my room. I really just wanted to crawl into bed with him and snuggle up, and I thought one day he would wake up and tell me to, but he never did.

My mom was a lot younger than Dad and almost his total opposite. She was just five foot two and had long dark hair, pale skin, skinny legs, and tiny feet but with big toes and nails that she painted a shade of orange she called coral. She looked pretty all the time and she was rarely in a bad mood, and except for when she was arguing with Dad, she was pretty quiet. She could sit in a chair for hours reading without moving or saying a word, and she loved romance novels. She had a whole bookshelf filled with them. Dad said she was sick in the head for reading that shit, but he always brought a couple home with him if he'd been out of town.

It wasn't like she just sat around all day reading; she'd had a job at a bank for as long as I could remember. She told me once she worked at the county courthouse but she quit that job after a case about a man who murdered his wife with a hammer. She said it was too upsetting to be in the same room with criminals all day so she took a job at an insurance company after Robbie started school, as a claims processor, but then she quit because her boss was "a nasty piece of work." She started working at the bank when I started second grade but I don't think she liked it. "My job is very boring but it pays the bills and I don't mind working ten-hour days Monday to Thursday because I love having Fridays off," she said.

That was the day she'd get her hair and nails done and do the weekly shopping.

Every Friday, for years, until I was about fourteen, she'd pick me up after school so I could go shopping with her, and we'd drive all the way across town to the Piggly Wiggly. It was the most expensive store in town, but she said it was the best store in town and refused to go anywhere else. When Dad questioned her about it, she said, "It's clean, their fruit is fresh, and you can't get better service from a butcher than the one at Piggly Wiggly."

Shopping with Mom was always a big chore for me and a good time for her. Before heading for the back of the store to see the butcher, she'd hand me a list and a pen, all the while touching up her makeup and straightening her clothes. I'd spend my time running from aisle to aisle filling up the cart with the things she wanted, and just about the time I'd head for the checkout counter Mom would appear with a big smile on her face. "Okay, I'm ready to go, hope we got everything," she'd say.

I followed her once to see what was so interesting about the butcher. I hid behind a display of Fig Newtons so I could listen to them without being seen. He was a lot younger than Dad, and not as tall or handsome. When he saw Mom walking his way he stopped what he was doing, stood up straight, put his hands on his hips, and said, "Wow, you're exceptionally lovely today."

She giggled and waved her arm in the air. After that, their conversation never moved past questions about different cuts of meats and his new meat slicer. I felt weird listening and watching them, mainly because she acted so silly, playing with her hair, swaying to the elevator music coming from the walls of the store, and leaning on the glass cabinet like she was a movie star.

She really liked the butcher. She even brought him gifts, including a cassette tape of one of her favorite singers, Barry Manilow. She was so excited about giving it to him. "Do you think it's the kind of music a butcher would listen to?" she asked on the drive to the Piggly Wiggly.

"I don't know, Mom. It's not the kind of music Dad would listen to, but he's not a butcher," I replied.

"We don't talk about Dad on Fridays, remember?" she said, gently slapping my leg a few times.

"Oh yeah, forgot!" I laughed.

 CHAPTER 5

I started the fourth grade with a cast on my ankle because I fell into Dad's mechanic pit when I was helping him rotate his truck tires. It only hurt for a few days, and I had a nice new pair of crutches. I think the attention I got from my new teacher and the other students helped to distract me from thinking about Tammy when I was at school.

Having a cast and crutches didn't stop me from doing things like shopping with Mom. I liked helping her; it made her happy, and when she was happy she was especially nice to be around. Besides, being able to shop unattended had its advantages. I could eat candy while I shopped and I could easily put things in the cart that weren't on the shopping list without Mom noticing. That's how I got my collection of extracts and flavorings.

I came up with the idea—chewing on flavored toothpicks instead of biting my nails—at the beginning of fourth grade. It only took a few weeks to get a collection started. I began with the usuals—vanilla, brandy, maple, orange, and rum—and by the time Halloween rolled around, I had twenty-six extracts in various-size bottles and different brands. I kept them in a small sideboard cabinet Mom bought from Mrs. Benson's garage sale and put in my bedroom because it didn't fit in the hallway. I usually added a few drops of an extract flavor to a can of 7 Up when I got home from school, but mostly I liked to soak toothpicks in extracts for a day before I would chew on them. Coconut and maple were my favorites, and I learned not to chew on rum or brandy toothpicks at school after my teacher thought I smelled funny one day and took me out into the hall to talk to me.

"You smell like you've been drinking rum," she said.

"I haven't," I replied, and I pointed to my locker. "Here I'll show you."

I opened my locker door so she could inspect it. I showed her my Tupperware container and opened it so she could see my ten toothpicks soaking in the rum extract I'd poured over them that morning.

"Why do you need to chew on toothpicks, Randall?"

I reluctantly put my right hand out, palm down, so she could see my fingernails.

"Oh, well I guess chewing on toothpicks is better than doing that to your nails. But try another flavor, one that doesn't smell like booze, and just bring one or two toothpicks to school, not a whole bowl of them," she said.

I walked back into class and everyone grumbled. "Did you get a whack on the butt?" I heard Katie snicker.

Dad didn't like my toothpicks either. When he saw me in the living room watching TV with one in my mouth he said, "Why are you doing that? You look more stupid than ever."

"My teacher said it was okay," I replied.

"Your teacher is a dumbshit!" he said.

He told Mom she'd better get a handle on me before it was too late. "It's better than watching her chew her nails all day," she argued. "I'm sick and tired of trying to get the bloodstains out of her shirtsleeves and off the living room furniture."

I was always grateful that Mom kept a supply of Band-Aids in the bathroom and that she never yelled at me about using so many, especially when I went through a particularly bad phase and had to put two Band-Aids on every finger before I went to school. Occasionally, when I wasn't paying attention to hiding my hands and my fingers were visible, she'd have a quick look at them and say something like, "Those must hurt pretty bad, huh?" I usually got embarrassed and pulled my hands away real fast. But sometimes I'd nod in agreement. "Yeah, they hurt a lot," I'd say.

A week after I got the cast off my ankle, Dad discovered two chewed-up toothpicks, and a few bloodstains, on the backseat of his Mustang. At the car show the next weekend I heard him tell his friend Mike he was going to break me of my bad habits once and for all. He made me get rid of all my toothpicks and extracts and started inspecting my hands every morning at breakfast. If he could tell I'd been biting them, he'd yell at me until I cried, and then he'd yell at Mom, which always made me feel bad because she was getting in trouble for something I couldn't stop doing. Mom usually stuck up for me, even though she thought nail biting was a gross habit and wanted me to make more of an effort to stop.

"If she had some motherly direction and a few constructive things to do, I bet she'd stop doing it," he said.

Mom agreed with him and invited Olive over to show me how to knit, crochet, and hook a rug. All of those things did keep my hands busy, and I didn't bite my nails for two whole weeks. But after that I started biting them again for some reason, and in no time at all I figured out how to crochet or knit and bite my nails at the same time. The blood was pretty noticeable on the scarf I made for Olive, but I gave it to her anyway.

After Dad noticed I could knit and bite at the same time, he took me to the doctor. "You need your head examined," he said.

When the doctor came into the exam room Dad stood up, shook his hand, and said, 'Listen, Doc, the girl's had ants in her pants and fingers in her mouth since she was born. She's a bit slow."

The doctor crinkled up his nose and forehead. "Why don't you have a seat, Mr. Grange, and I'll have a little talk with Randall," he said.

He turned around to face the examination table where I was sitting, "I know you probably don't want to show me, but can I have a look, please?" he asked, motioning to my hands.

I pulled my hands from my jacket pockets, and I was glad he didn't ask me to take all the Band-Aids off. He looked at my left middle finger and said, "Do you bite them more in the morning or night?" he asked.

"In the afternoon," I replied.

"Why do you think that is? Are you hungry in the afternoon?"

I was going to tell him I wasn't sure when I heard Dad say, "Look at her, she's twelve years old and a little pig, she can't be hungry."

"I'm not twelve, Dad; I'm nine," I said, really softly so he wouldn't get mad.

The doctor turned to Dad really quick and in very flat, calm voice he said, "She's not slow, she's not fat, and she probably bites her nails because she's scared. Millions of people bite their nails, and she might grow out of it or she might not. Maybe she'll learn to paint or draw instead? I'd stop making a big deal out of it if I were you," he said as he looked over and smiled at me.

The doctor took a pen out of his jacket and a piece of paper from a folder he brought into the room with him that had my name on it. "This guy is great with kids, and I'd be happy to set up an appointment for Randall," he said as he handed the piece of paper to Dad.

Dad stared at the paper for a minute while the doctor wrote something else in my folder. "I could give her something to calm her down but I really think it would be better if she saw the doctor I just gave you the number for," he said.

"I'll think about it, but if she's not slow then she's just plain lazy, and no shrink can do a thing about lazy," Dad said.

• • •

The drive home was scary. We were in Dad's Falcon, and he drove like a maniac. I didn't talk. I just sat still in the backseat and tried not to look up at the rearview mirror because I knew he was looking back at me to see if I had a finger in my mouth.

I stared at the floor and thought about Dad telling the doctor I was lazy. It was the same thing he said about Mom all the time. He didn't like the way she kept the house, and he was always complaining about her cooking. He had lots of ideas about what she should do and how she should think, and he was always saying mean things about her friends and her boss. Dad hated her boss, and ever since the day he found out Mom got a ride to work with him after her car broke down he wouldn't stop talking about it and asking her to find a new job. He'd go on for hours about her 'faggy' boss and how much mom liked fags. I'd get so angry with him for being so mean to her but I couldn't do anything except go to my room and play music or cover my head with a pillow.

I don't know when I started wanting him to die, but it had become my daily, sometimes hourly, prayer by the time I'd met my sister Tammy. "Go, please go, die, please die." Just saying it over and over in my head made me feel better.

I liked what the doctor said about me taking up painting. So when Dad pulled the car into his big garage, I said, "Maybe you could help me learn to paint, you're always painting cars."

"That's not painting. And I'm not an artist or your teacher," he replied.

"What about your tattoos?" I asked.

"They're not art. They're tattoos," he said as he got out the car.

Dad had five tattoos. He got them all in Saigon. Three of them were the names and dates of his buddies who died in the war and the largest was an American eagle on his left shoulder. But the most interesting was his tattoo of a naked woman, posed like one of those women you see on the mud flaps of semi trucks, on his right bicep. When Dad flexed his arm her boobs got bigger. Mom didn't like that tattoo, but I thought it was cool and he seemed to get a kick out of showing it off.

A week after the doctor's appointment Mom enrolled me in a Saturday art class at a little school a few miles from my house. I knew a few of the kids in the class; they were all about my age. The school was too far to walk, so Mom took me and picked me up for the first two weeks.

The third week it was Dad's turn for pickup. He had to come into the classroom to get me because we were running late and he didn't want to wait outside in the car for me any longer. It was a warm day for November, and Dad was wearing one of his sleeveless T-shirts. One of the girls in my class said something about how many tattoos he had, and that's when he flexed his bicep so that she could see the boobs on the woman get bigger. She thought it was cool, but the teacher didn't.

"Why would you show that to anyone, let alone a group of kids? You should be ashamed of yourself," she told him.

I was embarrassed and Dad was pissed off. On the drive home he said I should quit the class. "You're in real danger of becoming a moron, just like that teacher of yours," he said.

"I don't want to quit. I like the teacher and the other kids, and they like me. Besides, I'm in the middle of making something really cool," I replied.

"Not possible," he grumbled under his breath, as he lit a Pall Mall.

I didn't tell him the something I was making was his Christmas present.

I'd made a few gifts before, but nothing as good as the hooked rug I was working on in my art class. I spent weeks thinking about it, got Uncle Hank to help me copy the Ford Mustang logo design I found in one of Dad's car magazines, and bought a dark, tan-colored yarn for the base and black yarn to spell out the word "Mustang." I finished it a week before Christmas and was so pleased with myself that I showed everyone I knew, including Mrs. Benson.

"It's perfect," she said. "I sure hope your dad appreciates

all the hard work you've put into it."

On Christmas morning I was the first one up. After I got my cereal and started a pot of coffee for Mom and Dad, I went out to the living room to see if there were any gifts on the fireplace mantel for me. We never had a Christmas tree, Dad wouldn't allow it, so Mom and I used the fireplace mantel to put gifts on and we usually decorated it with lights and Christmas ornaments.

There were only three presents for me, and four for Robbie, but I didn't care because mine were big and I knew I had a few more waiting for me at Aunt Flo's and Uncle Hank's—and besides, I was more excited about the presents I'd made for Mom and Dad.

Robbie opened his presents when he got up at about eleven, and then he took off with his friends. It was almost noon when Mom and Dad walked into the living room; I'd already unwrapped, examined, and rewrapped all my presents. I tried on my new boots, played around with the cassette player/recorder, and wondered if Mom realized she'd bought me Barrel of Monkeys the year before. I'd thought about it for a couple of hours and decided not to say anything to her, and that I'd act surprised and happy about it because I could always give it away to someone at school.

After Mom and Dad got their coffee and sat down in the living room, I handed them their gifts. I watched Mom open hers and hold up all four of the silk-screened dishtowels I'd made for her. "These are beautiful honey, thank you," she said.

Dad opened his, too, but only after he finished his coffee and cigarette. He looked at the front and back of the rug. "Did you make it or buy it?" he asked.

"Made it all by myself. Sketched out the design, picked out the yarn colors and hooked the entire thing. It should fit perfectly in the back window of your Mustang," I replied.

"Think so, do you?" he said, and then went outside to his big garage.

We drove to Aunt Flo's and Uncle Hank's for Christmas

dinner at about 4 p.m. in Dad's Mustang. Uncle Hank was in the driveway wearing a Santa hat and a beard when we arrived. "Ho, ho, ho," he said as we pulled up. With his accent it sounded more like "Hi, hi, hi." Both Mom and I laughed.

I gathered up my gifts for Uncle Hank and Aunt Flo and had just started to get out of the car when I noticed Dad pointing to the back window and Uncle Hank leaning in to have a look. "Wow, that looks really nice there in the window, perfect fit. She did a great job," Uncle Hank said as he leaned in a bit further so I could see his entire face smile at me.

"Best present she's ever given me," Dad replied.

CHAPTER 6

Robbie got an acceptance letter in the mail from the college Dad had picked out for him a few weeks before he graduated from high school. Mom and Dad made me go to his graduation ceremony even though I told Mom a few times I shouldn't have to go because Robbie had refused to attend my tenth birthday party the week before.

"Boys don't like birthday parties, especially girly ones with pink cupcakes and screaming ten-year-olds," Mom said.

Even though only four of my friends came, it turned out okay, especially after Olive and Ken and Ken's friend Ron showed up at the skating rink. They brought their custom made white leather skates and taught my friends and me how to turn around and skate backward.

The next day we went to Robbie's graduation, and because he was class president and had to give a big speech, we had to sit in the front row. I must admit, Robbie did look handsome when he walked up on stage, and I felt proud of him for a few minutes. I didn't understand much about his speech, though. It was something about life being easier for losers than winners because winning hurts. At the end of his speech he told everyone he was off to college to get a degree in "poli sci" (whatever that was) so he could become a congressman or the state's attorney general.

Mom was the first one to stand up and cheer. "I've never been so proud of anyone!" she yelled in my ear.

Dad turned around and shook the hands of other fathers, all the while saying things about Robbie being a genius. I couldn't think of anything nice to say, so I didn't say anything.

Afterward, about a hundred of Robbie's friends showed up at our house for a party and Dad was right in the middle of it, pouring shots of tequila and whiskey for anyone who wanted to "drink like a motherfucker."

I don't know if I drank like a motherfucker, but I did drink enough to make it impossible for me to walk from Dad's big garage to my bedroom. I crawled on the grass for a while before I stopped to rest. Someone must have found me sleeping on the lawn and put me into bed that night, because when I woke up later, I was in my room.

The next morning, when I threw up on my way to the bathroom, Dad yelled out from his room, "Go get yourself one of those light beers your mom drinks and sip it. That'll make you feel better."

He was right. It did.

I think Robbie had a party every Saturday night that summer from then on. Dad let him use his garage, bought kegs of beer for him and his friends, and even let them drink his whiskey. Mom made me stay inside. "Robbie's friends might think it's funny to get you drunk and watch you fall down, but I don't. You stay inside and watch TV," she said.

She brought her portable TV into my room, along with all my favorite 'tos—Cheetos, Fritos, and Doritos—and I stayed up past midnight for weeks watching horror movies and old reruns. I also played softball that summer for the Lassie's team, but I quit the last week of July so I could go with Aunt Flo and Uncle Hank on a road trip to the Grand Canyon. While I was used to spending time at their house, this was the first time they'd invited me to go with them on a monthlong road trip.

Uncle Hank once told me that I was a blessing, and I knew both my aunt and uncle thought I was better off at their house than at home, especially if my Dad was around. I sometimes overheard Uncle Hank saying things to Aunt Flo like, "That brother of yours is a hurricane headed straight for a tornado, and his son isn't far behind."

The Grand Canyon trip was the first time I'd ever been out of California, and the time I learned about the interstate highway that connected all the states together. I had a hard time remembering all the state names until Uncle Hank made up a game where I had to find all the letters in the name of every state on road signs as we drove by them. When I started school that year, my teacher was impressed with my ability to name, and spell correctly, all the states. When I told her Arkansas was really Kansas again, with a small addition, she said she'd never noticed that before and was impressed that I had.

We did something fun every day on our trip, including swimming in rivers and fishing for our dinner. Aunt Flo cooked whatever we caught. Mostly trout, because the salmon hadn't started heading back to where they were born—to die—yet. I thought the story of the salmon was the saddest thing I'd ever heard and couldn't believe anything would go to so much trouble to have babies.

On our way home, in late August, we stopped at an Indian reservation so Uncle Hank could buy a box of cigars and Aunt Flo could buy a bottle of gin. They also bought a box of fireworks, beaded earrings, and a matching hair clip for me, and a pair of soft leather moccasin slippers for Aunt Flo.

I had a great time, didn't get into any trouble, and had a full set of fingernails when they dropped me off at my house. Uncle Hank helped me take my stuff up to our front porch, and Mom met us at the door and gave us both a big hug.

"She's a great traveler, and just so you know, she's welcome at our place anytime," Uncle Hank said as he winked at me.

I walked with him back to the RV so I could say good-bye

to Aunt Flo, and then I stood on the street and waved good-bye until I couldn't see their silver bullet RV any longer.

● ● ●

Robbie didn't even last a year at Cal State. Something to do with him and a couple of guys taking drugs and getting drunk and one of them choking on puke and having some type of fit. It took the police four days to find Robbie because he got lost in the desert around Palm Springs. When they finally found him he was only wearing an undershirt and boots, and he was too sick to walk. He spent a whole week in the hospital because of his bad sunburn (on his privates too) and a few broken ribs. Then he came home for the summer because Mom wanted to make sure he was taken care of properly.

Dad was sure Robbie had been the victim of spiked drinks given to him by a group of "fraternity homos." He even wrote a letter demanding the school investigate the incident and contacted his lawyer because he was considering suing. Then he called his friends and visited all of our neighbors to tell them Robbie was home for the summer because a drunk driver hit him at a crosswalk. He made me promise to tell people, if they asked, that Robbie had been run over.

Robbie was released from the hospital the day I turned eleven. I was supposed to have a birthday dinner with an ice cream cake from Baskin-Robbins, but Robbie needed peace and quiet, so Mom took me to McDonald's instead. On the drive home, she said I'd be spending the summer with Aunt Flo and Uncle Hank.

"Thank you, God," I said quietly and then put my hand over my mouth so Mom couldn't see how big my smile was.

Aunt Flo was seventeen minutes older than my dad and the only person I ever heard tell my dad to shut up without getting into trouble. I know this because I used to listen to them talk about grown-up stuff, and every so often, when Dad would start in about the Democrats or what a messy pig I was and how he thought kids needed a good smack now and then, Aunt Flo would tell him to "shut up." But sometimes she'd say something like, "We all know what a good beating will do for a kid, don't we?" instead, and that would stop Dad from saying another word too.

Besides her ability to stand up to Dad, Aunt Flo was glamorous and beautiful. She was tall and thin, with a squeaky voice and straight white teeth that stuck out a bit. She also had long fingers, a long nose, and vibrant orange hair that she wore in a bun on top of her head. She told me one day, when I was visiting for the weekend, that she achieved the special orange tone by mixing red and yellow food coloring with her Nice and Easy hair dye. Uncle Hank loved her hair color and often told her so. Sometimes he'd say nice things about my hair too. But I think he was just being kind, because my hair color was a mousy brown and not very nice—not like his. He had lots of dark brown, wavy hair and he looked just like the guy on *Magnum, P.I.*, which Aunt Flo wouldn't miss for anything in the world. Mom didn't see the resemblance to Tom Selleck; she thought Uncle Hank looked more like Robert Goulet, whom she said she once danced with at an LA nightclub.

I'll never forget the time she told me about it. We were up late watching TV one night because everyone in my second grade class had come down with chicken pox and I seemed to have it the worst. They were even in my nose and ears, and I couldn't keep myself from scratching. Mom wanted to make sure I didn't scar my face, so she made a little bed for me on the living room couch and held my hands while she watched *The Late Show.* When she heard Johnny Carson announce that Robert Goulet was his guest she practically screamed, "Oh honey, stay awake for this!"

She got a chair from the kitchen and moved it right up to the TV screen. When Robert Goulet started singing she put her face against the TV screen and sang along. Later, before she walked me to my bedroom, she told me the story of how she'd gone to a nightclub a couple of years before I was born to celebrate her birthday and was sitting alone at the bar, waiting for my dad to arrive, when Mr. Goulet sat down next to her, tapped her on the shoulder, and said, "Can I buy you a drink?"

"I said no because I expected your dad to arrive any minute and I didn't want him to see me talking to another man. I waited for more than an hour for your dad, but he didn't show up. I was going to leave, but instead I leaned into Mr. Goulet's shoulder and said something like, 'If the offer still stands, I'll take a dry martini.'"

Mom was both laughing and crying when she told me how Mr. Goulet bought her a couple of drinks and danced with her a few times before he told her he was an actor and then asked her to meet him for a drink the next night.

I had to try hard to stay awake and act as if I was interested in what Mom was telling me, but I really didn't get it. The only thing I understood was that Dad didn't show up for her birthday and she was mad at him so she danced with the guy who'd sung on TV.

After she tucked me into my bed and put a pair of her white gloves on my hands to keep me from scratching, she said, "Just so you know, I thought about Mr. Goulet's invitation the rest of that night and all the next day. Even after your dad explained how he'd missed his flight and couldn't get another one, I was still tempted, but I just knew I'd fall in love with Mr. Goulet, and I wasn't up for a broken heart or a broken home."

The next time I saw Aunt Flo I told her about Mom and Mr. Goulet, and she said it didn't surprise her one little bit. "Your mother is the most provocative fly in the cage, that's for sure," she said.

Even though I wasn't sure what she meant, I guessed it had something to do with the way Mom acted when men were around. Mom had a baby-talk voice that she only used with men. I thought it was funny and kind of silly, but Aunt Flo said it was neither of those things. She said it was flirty and dangerous. "Women who act like your mother only cause concern for other women," she said.

It took me a few years before I realized what Aunt Flo meant when she said that.

Most of the men who came to our place seemed to like the way Mom spoke to them, and Dad didn't seem to care, or even notice. The only time I ever saw him get mad at her for giggling and talking silly was the time we went to one of his office dinner parties. I had to go along because Robbie had a high school function and they couldn't find anyone else to babysit, and because Dad said taking a little kid along would give him a good excuse to leave early.

The dinner took place at a French restaurant, and we sat with five people who all seemed to know Dad, and what to do with the fondue pot in the center of our table. Everything was going pretty well until suddenly Dad reached over my plate and grabbed Mom's wrist really hard. "For Christ's sake, stop harassing the man and order something," he said.

Mom had been using her best baby-talk voice to try to persuade our waiter to explain the menu in French; even though he'd told her a few times he didn't speak French well enough to explain the menu. I felt the heat of embarrassment move all the way from my belly to my face, so I looked down at my plate and prayed Mom wouldn't yell at Dad and make it worse. Mom jerked her arm free of Dad's hand, buttoned her blouse all the way up, and drank her entire glass of wine in one go. She didn't talk to anyone the rest of the night and didn't eat any of her dinner.

The drive home was horrible. Dad imitated Mom's baby-talk voice the entire time, and I stared out the window and tried to pretend I wasn't there.

● ● ●

Mom wasn't the only grown-up I knew who spoke in a baby voice. Ken and Ron did it too, especially when they talked to their poodles Bitsy and Itzy. Ron owned a dog-grooming salon right next to Ken's hair salon in the middle of town, and they often came to our house when Dad was away. Dad said they were cross-dressers and queers and he didn't want anything to do with them.

Ken and Ron were nice and I liked them okay, but it was Mom's friend Olive who I liked the most. She was nice to everyone, especially my mom. They met on their first day of junior high, and Olive told me once that Mom was her idol. She moved from San Diego to Huntington Beach after Robbie was born because she missed my mom so much. I don't think Mom felt the same way about Olive—mainly because she was fat and didn't have much hair, and Mom didn't think women should allow themselves to get fat. Ken and Ron were both a little fat, too, but that didn't bother Mom.

"Men look better with a little meat on their bones," she told me one night when Ken and Ron were over playing gin rummy and after she'd handed Ken a second piece of lemon cake. Ken liked to play cards and fix hair. He even tried to help Olive with hers. He bought her a hairpiece once, but she said it was too hot and made her head sweat, so she only wore it a couple of times before she threw it away.

One weekend, when I was about seven or eight, they all spent an afternoon at our house drinking wine coolers while Ken gave Olive an Afro perm on the little bit of hair she had, which was mainly around the sides of her head. Olive hated the Afro, said she looked like a clown. A few weeks later, after Mom and Olive rented a video called *10*, Mom bought Olive a blonde cornrow wig and she wore it for years, until she got her Cleopatra wig.

Olive lived in a housing development not too far from us, and sometimes, when Mom got one of her headaches, I had to ride my bike over to Olive's so she could take care of me until Mom felt better. I never knew what kind of sickness Mom had that gave her headaches, but I once overheard Aunt Flo talking on the phone, and she told the person on the other end she believed Mom got so many headaches because she was out of her mind. She said Mom did things that only crazy people do, including painting our living room maroon and wearing a black lace bikini at Aunt Flo and Uncle Hank's annual Fourth of July barbecue and then kissing all the men, including Uncle Hank, in a "more than friendly way."

It wasn't just my mom who Aunt Flo thought was more than friendly with Uncle Hank, though. She thought most women were after him. If we were out in public and a strange woman spoke to Uncle Hank, Aunt Flo would get between them and interrupt the conversation. Uncle Hank thought women were friendly to him because of his accent, but Aunt Flo didn't. She thought they were trying to get him interested in them. If they spoke to him for more than a few seconds, she'd move in close and pretend to translate, or she'd change the subject and ask the woman about her church. Uncle Hank and I both knew she wasn't interested in hearing about their church.

I really didn't care what Aunt Flo said or thought about my mom—didn't care if she said things about her that weren't very nice or referred to her as a tart—because I liked Aunt Flo and Uncle Hank more than I liked Mom and Dad. They did things I'd never seen my parents do, like kiss for no reason and hold hands when they were watching TV. Sometimes, when he didn't think anyone was watching, Uncle Hank would pat Aunt Flo's bottom, especially if she was wearing stretch pants, and then he'd grin from ear to ear.

When I heard from Mom that Robbie was going to need all of her attention now that he was out of the hospital, and that I'd be staying at my favorite place for the whole summer, with the people I loved the most, I was so happy that I stayed up late packing my bag and thinking about the fun I'd had the summer before with Aunt Flo and Uncle Hank on the Grand Canyon road trip.

Mom and Dad stayed up late fighting. And because my bedroom was right next to theirs, I heard everything. Mom was mad because Dad was going away for two weeks on a business trip, and she thought he should stay home to help with Robbie. Dad was mad at Mom for spending too much money on new clothes and too much time with her weird friends. After Dad told

Mom she'd let herself go lately, I heard her cry for a few minutes and then say, "Are you sure you're going alone this time?"

Before I fell asleep, I heard Mom tell Dad to call my principal and let him know I was going to miss the last week of school.

The next morning, Mom won the fight over who would drive me to Aunt Flo and Uncle Hank's house. It was only a mile away, and I was prepared to walk, but decided to get a ride with Dad because I'd put just about everything from my dresser into my suitcase, and it was heavy. I got into the backseat of Dad's yellow Falcon with my suitcase and a picture of Rascal. He dropped me off at Aunt Flo's front gate.

"Don't cause any trouble, and keep your goddamn fingers out of your mouth," he said.

He drove off so quick I'm sure he didn't hear me say, "See ya later, alligator."

I knocked on the front door for a long time before Uncle Hank answered. He invited me in and asked what I was doing there.

"Is it okay if I stay here until school starts in September?" I asked.

He grinned, motioned for me to come into the house, and said, "I don't see any reason why not. But why, have you run away?"

I wasn't too surprised that Mom and Dad had forgotten to call Uncle Hank and Aunt Flo about their plans for me to stay with them for the summer.

I followed Uncle Hank to the kitchen and watched him put two pieces of bread in the toaster before I blurted out, "I have to stay with you because Robbie's in big trouble and the police had to take him to the hospital and now he's all messed up and at home with Mom and she said she can't take care of both of us and sent me over here."

"Oh, that doesn't sound so good. I'd better wake up Flo. She'll want to hear this."

I ate my toast and watched *Good Morning America* while I

waited for Aunt Flo to get up and get dressed. When she finally appeared, she asked me what was going on at home. I tried to explain it all accurately, and when I finished Aunt Flo said, "Hmmm . . . I think a little Bloody Mary is on the breakfast menu today."

Uncle Hank laughed, looked at me, and said, "It's fine sweetie. Of course you can stay with us. Why don't you go to your room and unpack your things and I'll give your Mom a call and let her know you've arrived safely."

● ● ●

I had my own room at my aunt and uncle's house, decorated just the way I liked it, with paintings Uncle Hank and I made on the wall and a white bookshelf full of books I sometimes read out loud to their cats. My room was big, with its own bathroom and a walk-in closet that was almost the same size as my bedroom at home. When I was five, they bought me a little bed with a Cinderella headboard. Then the very next year, they bought an even bigger bed for me after Uncle Hank noticed how much his cats liked me, which was around the same time I learned to operate their electric can opener and could feed them all by myself. When that happened, the cats stopped sleeping in the living room and began sleeping with me, and at first it was okay, but after a few nights in a little bed with a bunch of cats it got uncomfortable and made it impossible for me to sleep. The one with the loudest motor slept on my pillow, up against my head, and a couple of the others crawled under the covers and snuggled next to my feet. One night there was a big fight and I had to get up and remove three cats from my room. After I put them out, though, they scratched the floor, meowed, and stuck their paws underneath the door until I couldn't stand it any longer and got up to let them back in.

So I was really happy about the big new bed Uncle Hank bought for me, because it was roomy enough for me and all the cats, and I really loved his cats, even though I didn't like their names: Helga, Thor, Alena, Vlad, Natasha, Olga, Edita, and

Boris. I renamed them, and for convenience I referred to them as A, B, C, D, E, F, G, and H. Short for "Are We Happy," "Better than Baby," "Cuddle Up Quick," "Dizzy Girl," "Every Little Kiss," "Funny You Asked," "Gimme a Paw," and "Heavenly Fur Ball." It took a while for both me, and them, to learn their names; it would have helped if Uncle Hank had cooperated and learned their letter names too, but he didn't. He continued to call them the names he liked and they continued to respond to him.

Within minutes of Dad dropping me off for the summer, I was in my room at Uncle Hank and Aunt Flo's, unpacking my bag and getting things just the way I liked them. I couldn't wait to go to sleep that night in my big bed, in my very own room, a room that was just a small part of a great house—a large, cottage-style house that Uncle Hank had designed and built before I was born. It was painted pale yellow with a lilac-blue trim, and it had an orange clay tile roof and a porch that went all the way around it. I heard it was just like the place Uncle Hank grew up in, complete with squeaky floors and doors that didn't always close. The front yard was huge, with a rose garden on one side, including every rose imaginable—even the purplish gray ones that don't smell like anything. On the other side, the garden was filled with all kinds of flowers, like lilies and petunias and daisies.

Because the front door to the cottage was a long way from the front gate, visitors had to walk through a field of flowers (and bees) that spilled over onto what Uncle Hank said was a mosaic pathway, designed and built by him from old dinner plates and colored glass he got from friends, flea markets, and garage sales. He made a lot of stuff and he often carried a notebook and pencil in his shirt pocket to write down his ideas.

● ● ●

There was so much going on at Uncle Hank's and Aunt Flo's that it was hard for me to keep up. Uncle Hank was busy all the time, and so was Aunt Flo. She kept busy with her various hobbies—sewing, knitting, embroidering, and fashion design. But the thing she liked to do the most was take care of her garden. She loved growing things, and sold her flowers and vegetables from the front gate using an honesty box that Uncle Hank made from an old wood ladder and attached to the bottom of the gate with a big chain and lock. Nothing went to waste in Aunt Flo's garden, not even old flower petals. She picked them up off the ground and pressed out the juice and oil with a special machine. With the juice and oil she made her own brand of floral tonic. How she made it and what she added besides flower juice was her secret. Uncle Hank swore it was lemon juice, but I knew it wasn't because one time I watched her add a few drops of apple cider vinegar to the pot. Aunt Flo would spray her tonic on almost everything, including on me first thing in the morning. She also sprayed my face and my hands at night before I went to sleep to help keep them soft and to help me remember not to chew my nails. I wasn't the only one getting sprayed; Uncle Hank usually got a thorough spray, and sometimes the cats did too.

Growing up, I didn't always catch what Aunt Flo and Uncle Hank were doing around their house and garden, but as the years went by and I spent more time at their place, I noticed more about them and their home. By the time I came to visit that summer, I could see it all. There were six colorful pathways (with different flowers represented in each) that began at the front gate and swirled around the front yard until they met at the beginning of Aunt Flo's rose garden. I also noticed the mosaic wall behind the bathtub (made with small stones and pieces of red plates sanded until the edges were smooth); and the very best thing of all—a large swimming pool with a beautiful mermaid on its floor.

"When did this pool get here, Uncle Hank?" I asked.

"We finished her about six weeks ago. Isn't she beautiful?" he replied.

He had it built after their neighbor agreed to sell a piece of land behind their houses so the pool would fit.

"It took me twenty years of thinking about it and less than six months to make it," Uncle Hank said as he bent over and splashed some of the water to scare off his cat Olga, who was about to drink from the pool. "She shouldn't drink this water; it's got chemicals in it."

I couldn't wait to get into the pool, but Uncle Hank said I had to know the rules first. He took my hand and walked me around the pool. "This pool isn't a regular swimming pool. She's got two ladders on each side and one beneath the diving board. She's more than eight feet deep for the first thirty feet. After that she gradually gets shallower, with the last ten feet being four feet deep. What that means is that you need to be very careful and head for a ladder if you're ever in trouble," he said.

"Okay," I replied.

We walked around the entire pool while he explained the reasons I shouldn't run or leave my stuff lying around. I nodded my head, but I don't think I was paying much attention. I was too distracted by the mermaid. She was beyond beautiful. Her body spanned the entire pool, and her tail, which was various shades of blue and green, went all the way to the edge of the shallower end. Her flowing, wild orange hair reminded me of octopus arms. It extended up the inside wall of the pool and overflowed to just beneath the diving board. Her eyes were wide open, her mouth was smiling, and her arms were spread out like she was waiting to hug me.

"How'd the beautiful lady get in there? I mean, who put her there?" I stammered.

He chuckled and said, "She's more than a beautiful lady. She's a mermaid, a merry maid also known as a goddess."

Uncle Hank said he had created the mermaid at the bottom of the pool with small and large pieces of turquoise, crushed carnival and bottle glass, broken marbles, and amethyst crystals.

"Can I swim with her now—can I, can I?" I asked.

"Hold your horses. I haven't finished. The most important thing for you to know about swimming in this pool is that you must tell us when you're going in. We need to know you're in there, okay?"

"Cross my heart. Now can I swim?"

"Sure you can," he laughed.

From above the water, the mermaid looked completely smooth, but I discovered on my very first swim that she had a few rough spots on her face. Her eyes and cheeks were made from violet and yellow crystals that Uncle Hank chiseled from the large crystal rock he bought from the same Indian guy who gave him bags of old glass marbles and turquoise pieces. Later that night, when I asked about her sharp glass eyes, he said he was afraid the rock tumbler would zap the energetic light from them and she wouldn't be able to work her magic, so he'd left them sharp. "Venetian eyes" is what he said they were. But other than the rough spots on her face, the merry maid was perfectly smooth—even her tail. Everyone who saw her wanted to be with her, wanted to swim with her, but no one more than me.

● ● ●

It was obvious to me, because of her flowing red and yellow hair, that Aunt Flo was the inspiration for the merry maid. When I asked her about it, she said, "I posed for hours in the blazing sun for Hank, and that mermaid doesn't look a thing like me."

She also said she was used to sitting still and posing, as she'd worked as a model for years before she married Uncle Hank. She'd stopped modeling because he asked her to. She said he told her he didn't want his wife to work, but really he was more concerned about other men touching her the way some photographers needed or wanted to. After a few years of not earning her own money, she took a job at the local art school as a life model, and she also let a photographer take photos of her holding vitamins and other things for a monthly leaflet promoting specials at the local drug store. Those little modeling jobs provided her with enough money to buy things she didn't feel like discussing with Uncle Hank, like her perfume and a special kind of gin the man at the liquor store kept in stock especially for her.

Gin and tonic was her favorite thing to drink, and usually

after she made the first one she'd let me take over. I learned to mix them just the way she liked, which wasn't very strong. Uncle Hank didn't drink gin, but he did like whiskey, and by the time I was ten I knew how to mix up the perfect whiskey sour: ice cubes, juice from an entire lemon, a shot glass of whiskey, and a teaspoon of powdered sugar.

One day after swimming for hours above the merry maid, I was sure I heard her say *Mayadelsa*. It was like she was introducing herself to me. When I spoke the word out loud it felt like I was speaking a foreign language. I told Uncle Hank about it at dinner and he said it was a good name and he thought it suited his merry maid perfectly. From then on she was known as Mayadelsa. For short we called her May or Delsa, and sometimes we yelled out to her before jumping in, "May I?" and then one of us yelled back, "Delsa!"

Her glow was reliant on the sunshine, and I thought she looked her best on a sunny morning around 7:30 a.m. If you saw her then you couldn't help but notice how she lit up the whole backyard with a glow that seemed to have every color in it. At those times, I'd sit on the diving board and stare at her until I couldn't resist her call any longer. Then I'd let my body roll off and sink to the bottom of the pool so I could run my fingers over her orange lips and rosy chin. But I rarely got to swim with her that early because I wasn't supposed to be in the pool until Uncle Hank said it was okay. He liked to swim laps in the mornings, and I often watched him from the side of the pool so I could count how many laps he swam. He could do a lot more than I ever could, but he never bragged about it. In fact, he never even counted; he just did it because he could.

My summer visit was going very well, and by the end of June I could pretty much do all the swimming styles, except butterfly. I couldn't make my body move well enough to do the butterfly. Uncle Hank said once I developed upper-body strength I'd be able to do it easily. "Why don't you get up early and exercise with me?" he asked.

Getting up before the sun was up didn't sound very

appealing to me, so I pretended I didn't hear him. He told me plenty of times that he wanted me to be a competitive swimmer, and even took me to the beach so I could learn to swim through big surf, saying it would help me build stamina. But I wasn't strong enough to get past the surf and he usually had to help me.

One afternoon, after a day of nothing but defeat and a belly full of saltwater, I told Uncle Hank I didn't want to swim competitively and he said, "Fine, fine, fine—what about the diving, then? I'm sure you'll make a good diver."

Even though I told him I wasn't sure diving was my thing, he insisted I learn about it and taught me what he knew, including correct positions and procedures and where to find the sweet spot on a diving board. This was the place I had to hit with the balls of both feet, at the same time, to ensure I got the right amount of lift for the front somersault or the pike or whatever dive I was doing. He told me once, after a bad belly flop, that diving was all about willingness. "Be more willing, okay?"

What I especially liked about the back somersault was how powerful it made me feel and how at the end of it I would be face to face with Mayadelsa. What Uncle Hank liked about my back somersault was my timing and how tight I could curl up. It took me a while to learn how hard I needed to bounce to get high enough to curl and uncurl so that I wouldn't make too big of a splash when I entered the water. Uncle Hank liked my form but he didn't think it was a good idea for me to hang at the top of my somersault as long as I liked to, "You're showing off with that trick and it doesn't make your dive any better. Pay attention to your technique instead."

I decided to take his advice only after hitting the water head first, or chest first, one too many times. Once I hit the water flat on my back and knocked the wind out of myself, and Uncle Hank jumped into the pool—with his good clothes on—and carried me out. When I got my wind back, I swore I'd never dive again. He laughed a little bit when I said that and told me a story about him hitting a diving board so hard once that he broke his nose. He wouldn't let me go into the house and get ready for bed until I did a double back somersault three more times, and he stayed in the center of the pool, fully dressed, for all three. I didn't need his help, but it was sure nice to have him there.

CHAPTER 7

Aunt Flo said I was as good a student as Hank was a teacher. She often sat by the pool to watch me dive, and even made me a one-piece navy blue bathing suit because she'd noticed I was always pulling my suit bottoms up. But it was too tight and uncomfortable, so I only wore it a couple of times before going back to wearing the red and yellow floral two-piece Mom had bought for me at Sears. I told Aunt Flo I had plenty of time to pull my bottoms up when I was down talking to Mayadelsa.

I liked to be close to Mayadelsa and watch her face glow when the sun hit her the right way. Some days I could stay down with her to the count of one hundred before I'd have to pop up for air. Aunt Flo was impressed but said I spent too much time in the pool and she'd like it if I could make some time to help her out in the garden because "it takes a lot of hard work to keep a garden looking good."

It wasn't like she did all the work herself. A couple of Mexican guys were at the house every morning with rakes and blowers, and they'd sometimes be there until lunchtime.

Aunt Flo liked to be outside with the gardeners so she could tell them what to do. She was also particular with the way she looked and wanted us all to be dressed and ready to face the day by the time the gardeners arrived. I hated to get up early and I often tried to pretend I didn't hear Uncle Hank knock on my bedroom door at 7 a.m. But it never worked, mainly because he knocked so hard the cats would wake up and want me to open my bedroom door so they could get out.

I could wash my face, brush my teeth, get dressed, make my bed, and feed the cats in fifteen minutes. And since we couldn't eat breakfast without Aunt Flo, Uncle Hank and I had to find things to do to keep us busy while we waited for her. Sometimes I'd watch TV and other times I'd sit outside in a lawn chair and watch Uncle Hank swim laps

I once asked Aunt Flo if it would be okay to sleep in until she was up and ready and she said, "Why? Are you sick? Have you broken your leg or something?"

Uncle Hank laughed when he heard her answer and said, "Why don't you tell her the reason we all have to be up and ready so early, Kitten?"

"Because it's never okay for the help to see you in a dressing gown. If you let them see you at your worst they will take advantage of you," Aunt Flo said.

Her answer didn't make much sense to me, especially since I didn't know what a dressing gown was, but I shrugged my shoulders in agreement and decided never to ask again.

Uncle Hank said it took Aunt Flo a long time to get ready in the morning because she had a personal style, especially when it came to her hair. "It's her signature piece," he said.

She told me once when we were out shopping that I wasn't old enough to worry about having a style. "No one your age ever has style. Wait until you're thirty and then you'll know what suits you. What suits you in your thirties becomes your style," she said.

Aunt Flo never went anywhere, even outside, without looking like she was going somewhere important. When she swam, she tried her best to look glamorous and wore a dark red bathing suit that looked like the one Marilyn Monroe was wearing in a photo Aunt Flo kept on the refrigerator (to remind her not to eat ice cream). She also wore a white bathing cap with one white plastic flower on the top and a chinstrap to keep it from sliding off when she dove off the board. She was a good swimmer—"Very graceful," Uncle Hank said—and I was always surprised to see her emerge from under the water with her makeup perfect, even her lipstick.

Looking good and looking young were Aunt Flo's favorite things to talk about. She had a friend named Helen who sold Avon and they had lunch every Tuesday in the garden and talked about the latest everything. They didn't mind that I hung around because I was a good bartender and a willing model. Helen wasn't as attractive or talkative as Aunt Flo, but she liked to discuss makeup just as much as Aunt Flo did. One afternoon, after they'd both had a few "G and Ts" and Helen had finished putting almost everything from the new Avon product line on my face, she told Aunt Flo she should update her style because it was "so 1960." Aunt Flo went quiet for a minute, and then told Helen she might think about matching her foundation with her skin tone because she looked like an orange. I looked up at Helen, who was rubbing blusher on my cheeks, and made a sour face. I wanted her to stop so that I could leave because I was sure they were going to argue. But the very next moment Aunt Flo let out a big snorting laugh, and a few seconds later Helen laughed too, and then they both laughed so hard they could hardly breathe. I got up and went into the house after Aunt Flo fell off her chair.

I told Uncle Hank about it later because I didn't understand what had happened and he said, "Your Aunt Flo can be very snappy when someone hurts her feelings. But she usually gets over it pretty quickly. She just wants to be helpful, that's all. Good thing she has a sense of humor or she'd be miserable to live with. Maybe their drinks were too strong, huh?"

"Maybe they were, but only because Aunt Flo sent me back to the kitchen twice to remake hers. Sometimes I think she doesn't like me very much," I said.

"Of course she likes you. She just doesn't show it very well. Try saying nice things to her and asking her for advice. She needs to be needed, maybe more than she knows."

So I decided to try it, and once I did she responded by offering to help me with all kinds of stuff. She taught me how to use hairpins to keep my bangs back, how to wear a bathing cap so it didn't pinch my ears, and how to pluck out the little brown hairs from what she called my "middlebrow." She even started taking me to the beauty place she went to every week. I liked how they steamed my face and massaged in different creams. And they always sent me home with face cleansers and lotions that I was supposed to use every morning and night.

● ● ●

My new skin ritual added a few minutes to my morning routine, but it didn't eat up enough time to make me feel better about waiting so long for Aunt Flo. Most mornings it took her almost an hour to get ready, and by the time she appeared in the dining room I was so hungry it was almost unbearable.

When she was dressed and ready for the day, she'd make an announcement from the bedroom, and Uncle Hank would take his seat in the living room on his favorite chair, which had a good view of the hallway, and yell out something corny like, "Come to Papa," or "Here, kitty kitty." Only then would Aunt Flo begin her stroll down the hallway, pretending she was a model in a fashion show. She never broke a smile or stepped out of character until the finish, when she'd land on Uncle Hank's lap. They'd get all romantic before they'd join me at the dining table for breakfast.

I didn't like to watch Aunt Flo's walk as much as I liked to watch the cats run down the hall with her. It didn't matter where they were or what they were doing, when they heard Uncle Hank call out to Aunt Flo they'd run right to him and most of them would arrive on his lap before Aunt Flo did. Then he'd do his best to get them off because Aunt Flo wouldn't sit down if the cats were on him. I don't know what was funnier, the cats jumping on Uncle Hank's lap or his shooing them away.

Aunt Flo would get so mad at the cats that she'd threaten to buy a dog just to get back at them. But we all knew that would never happen, and we also knew the cats were really Uncle Hank's. Aunt Flo was more of a small dog person but was too allergic to have one in the house.

"Cats are my favorite animals," Uncle Hank told me on our drive to the Grand Canyon after I saw a few deer on the side of the road and told him how much I liked them. "I suppose I like cats because my mother had three and I grew up in a small village where everyone had animals and homes so close together you could have a conversation with the neighbors without leaving the house," he said.

Uncle Hank's hometown was near the sea in Lithuania. He lived there until he was thirteen, and by then he'd learned to swim so well his parents thought he'd become a national champion.

"World War II changed everything. My parents made me and my little sister Liora leave the country with some people they knew. I was barely thirteen and my sister was ten. It was a dark time," Uncle Hank said. They ended up in Brooklyn and lived there until Liora got married and moved to California.

Uncle Hank moved to Los Angeles in 1951, when he was twenty-four, and met Aunt Flo at a housewarming party he attended with Liora and her husband. "Your Aunt Flo was there with a friend, so I only had a few minutes with her, but they were the best moments of my year," he said.

He was interested in Aunt Flo, but he also had dreams of being in the movies. He trained to be a Hollywood stuntman and got lucky from the start because he could ride a horse well and knew a few tricks. He said he worked pretty steady for years and got lots of jobs because of his abilities and flexibility; Aunt Flo said it was also because of his good looks.

After four years of working hard and getting tired of being alone, Uncle Hank mustered the courage to call Aunt Flo and ask her out on a date. He said he knew she was available because Liora was friendly with Aunt Flo's sister Violet. He also said he knew he'd marry her one day but needed to know he could make enough money to keep her happy. They started dating a few weeks after he finished working on a big horror movie, and got married the summer of 1956.

Night Scream was his first "big" movie, and I got to watch it, but only once, because it took a long time to set up the projector and film reels, and Aunt Flo said it was too much work just to watch Uncle Hank fall out of a tree and land on top of a crazed bimbo zombie. Uncle Hank said she didn't like the movie because he'd dated the actress who played the bimbo zombie before her.

He quit working as a stuntman when he was forty, after "some asshole" screwed up and gave a signal to a driver to turn right instead of left. He hurt his back real bad and it took him years to be able to move the way he used to. Dad said he made more money from the insurance payout after the accident than he'd made in his entire career as a stuntman. He thought the settlement was in the six figures. At least, that's what I heard him tell his mechanic.

After he gave up the movie business, Uncle Hank took up writing jingles for radio advertisements and copy for greeting cards. According to Aunt Flo, Uncle Hank was pretty good with words and she often helped him because she had great advice to give. "It ain't doing anyone any good just sitting in my head," she said.

The Pretty Good Card Company bought most things Uncle Hank sent them, and I thought writing must pay pretty well because he and Aunt Flo never seemed to worry about money. But I found out the real story the summer I stayed with Aunt Flo and Uncle Hank. Just after their Fourth of July barbecue (which my parents weren't invited to), Dad called their house and I answered the phone. My stomach got all twisted up when I heard him say, "Put Hank on the phone will ya?" because I had been hoping I wouldn't see or hear from Dad that summer.

A few days later, he showed up in his blue convertible T-bird because he was selling it to Uncle Hank. "He needs money for Robbie's tuition," I'd heard Uncle Hank tell Aunt Flo earlier in the day. I went out to the driveway with Uncle Hank when Dad arrived and said hello but Dad didn't say anything back. After a bit of discussion, Uncle Hank handed Dad a big envelope and I stood next to the fence petting one of the cats and watching Uncle Hank slowly walk around the car, looking at the tires and fenders and even the mirrors.

Dad stood on the driver's side counting the money out on the hood of the car. "You must make some big bucks from selling those secrets of yours to the commies, huh Hank?" Dad laughed.

Uncle Hank's eyes went wide for a second and he took a big step toward my dad and stuck his hand out. Dad stopped counting and reached out to take Uncle Hank's hand and I could tell from the way my dad's face crinkled up when Uncle Hank grabbed his hand that it hurt. The handshake went on for a long time before Uncle Hank said, "I have no secrets and I'm not a communist."

Dad pulled his hand away and stepped back. "Well, if you ask me, only a spy or my mother would have that much money stashed away," he said.

"But no one asked you," Uncle Hank said in a calm and matter-of-fact way as he reached over and took the Thunderbird's car keys off the hood of the car.

I could feel myself starting to laugh a little so I turned and walked toward the house so my dad couldn't see me. For as long as I could remember, Dad had been telling my mom and his buddies at the car club that Uncle Hank was a communist spy, and now Uncle Hank had let him know he was wrong in a way I'd never heard before and it was kind of funny—but I had a feeling Dad didn't think so.

I'd never seen Uncle Hank behave like that before, and I'd never seen that much money, either. If I hadn't gone with Uncle Hank to his garden shed earlier that day, I might have sided with

Dad. But Uncle Hank had been telling me for a few days about a special surprise he had in store for Aunt Flo and how he wanted my thoughts on it, and I was curious about the surprise, so when he waved me out of the pool to go to his shed that morning, I didn't hesitate.

The shed was next to the garage, not too far from the pool. It was full of Uncle Hank's stuff. I often helped him with the rock polisher he kept in one corner of the shed, below the shelves of wine bottles that he labeled himself and stored by year. I watched him push an old steamer trunk from its place near the back wall, opposite the rock polisher. He pointed to several floorboards and asked me to lift them up. They were loose, so it wasn't hard at all. Once they were up, I saw a large red metal toolbox sitting on top of a big wooden chopping block, similar to the one Uncle Hank made for their kitchen. I let out a sigh of excitement and Uncle Hank laughed.

He lifted the box and set it down on one of the several tables that lined the back wall. The box had a small combination lock on it, and he told me the code was the same as their street address: 22123. Uncle Hank's red box was filled to the top with colored paper money he called pounds, and other bills he said were francs. Underneath the foreign money there were piles of US hundred-dollar bills stacked on top of shiny gold, rectangular bars.

"Is this yours? Where did you get it?" I asked with excitement.

He chuckled and told me it was all his, and then he picked up a gold bar and handed it to me. "I bought eight of these in 1970 when gold was cheap. They weigh ten ounces and they cost me three hundred and fifty dollars back then. They're worth more than two thousand dollars now. It was a good investment," he said.

The gold bar was cold, hard, and smooth, and it felt good in my hand. I held on to it while Uncle Hank sorted through his things and pulled out a small black box. He smiled when he put it up to my face and opened it really slow. I heard myself gasp when I saw what was inside: a large, beautiful green stone, and two round diamonds almost as big as the green one. They were sitting close together, as if they were attached.

The gems and the foreign money had once belonged to his mother and father, he said, and he'd been saving hundred-dollar bills for years. "Make sure you save a little something from every paycheck. That's how people get rich."

I nodded in agreement and then sat down on a wood stool Uncle Hank pulled out from under the table for me. I somehow knew I needed to slow down and pay attention, but I was so excited I kept wiggling around and almost dropped the gold bar. Uncle Hank took it from me, smiled, and said, "You don't need to be nervous. These are my treasures, and I want you to know about them."

He placed the gems in the center of my left palm and I immediately put my right hand underneath to support it. Then he opened a small piece of paper and put it down on the table in front of me, "This is the ring I'm having made for Flo. What do you think?" he asked.

The drawing wasn't in color, so I just guessed that the green emerald would be in the middle and the diamonds on each side. Under the drawing of the ring were the words, *Hank always loves Flo.* I felt myself blush when he noticed I'd read it.

"Oh, she'll love it, Uncle Hank, that's for sure. It's almost as big as her wedding ring," I said.

"Not quite. Flo's wedding ring has a very big rose cut diamond in the center. I wore it and a few other gems in a small hidden pocket my mother stitched into my coat before I left Lithuania. Liora had gems sewn into the hem of her dress, but we had to sell most of those in New York so she could afford to move to California. When she passed away last year her husband sent me one of the diamonds I'm using for Flo's new ring," he said.

"I'm sorry about your sister," I said.

"Me too," he replied.

Uncle Hank spent the next few minutes organizing the gold bars and money before he spoke again. "My jeweler friend from the community center is going to make Flo's new ring, and he promises it will be ready by August 15—our thirtieth wedding anniversary."

After he put the gems back in the black box, he took a picture frame out of a purple velvet pouch that he'd pulled from underneath the stacks of American money. He introduced me to his mother, father, two older brothers and two sisters, all standing close together in front of a fireplace and looking very serious. Uncle Hank was about six or seven in the photo, and Liora was standing next to him holding his hand. When I asked him where his family was now he shrugged his shoulders, looked down at the floor, and said, "Gone, all gone, all of them."

I sat quietly and watched him kiss the photo before he put it back into the velvet pouch and laid it gently on top of a gold bar. He picked up a few stacks of US hundred-dollar bills and put them in his shirt pocket before he put his treasures back in the red box and the box back under the floorboards and pushed the steamer trunk back where it belonged. When we were walking back to the house, I asked him why he didn't keep the money in the bank, and he told me he didn't trust banks or bankers or anyone else with his things. "You shouldn't trust others with the things that are most important to you, okay?"

I nodded yes before I told him I wanted to go for a swim. He patted my head and said, "Go for your swim, but promise me you'll keep the box our secret. Don't breathe a word about it to anyone, especially your brother, and don't say anything to Flo because I'm planning to surprise her with it one day; I just haven't decided when."

"Not a word, Uncle Hank, I promise."

He reached over and wrapped his arm around me. "You're the most important person in my world—next to Flo, of course—and I sure hope when we're gone you can raise your family here."

No one had ever told me I was important. I felt so good about it that I didn't care about Dad not talking to me that afternoon.

I stayed awake much longer than I wanted to thinking about Uncle Hank's reaction to my Dad accusing him of being a spy. Uncle Hank had been so serious, almost angry, and it scared me a little. I also thought about what Dad always said about Uncle Hank, that he was a spy and a millionaire. I'd overheard him tell his friends at the car club how Uncle Hank's greeting card racket was a cover for his spying, and how he wrote jingles containing codes and secret messages.

It did seem to me that Uncle Hank had a lot more money and stuff than my parents had, and I wondered what type of special information Uncle Hank might have that someone would pay a million dollars for. Other than his hidden box and his plan to make a ring for Aunt Flo, he'd never told me anything especially secretive, maybe how to do a good poker face and master the game of cribbage, but I was sure others knew what 15-2, 15-4 meant.

The more I thought about it, the more I became convinced that Dad was wrong about Uncle Hank. Especially after I recalled how much Aunt Flo helped him with his jingles, and how I'd even helped him once with a greeting card message and he'd given me thirty dollars—ten dollars for each word I contributed. He even showed me the card when it was printed up and it didn't look to me like there was any secret code in it.

I think my contribution of "you hate peas" really made the card special:

> *I can't wait and you sleep late.*
> *You like opera and I dig the blues.*
> *I love cooking and you hate peas.*
> *I drink coffee and you like tea.*
> *Though we don't always agree;*
> *I know you're the one for me.*

CHAPTER 8

Uncle Hank wasn't just good at writing jingles; he was good at lots of other things too, including cooking. They had a kitchen that reminded me of a restaurant, complete with a big gas stove, a double wall oven, and three stainless steel sinks, one for washing, one for rinsing, and another one for rinsing again. There was a large work counter next to the sinks, and another they used as a breakfast counter. I loved everything about their kitchen, especially the card table–size butcher block in the middle and the rack of copper pots and pans hanging above it. Uncle Hank spent a lot of time in the kitchen cooking and cleaning. He often wore a large white chef's apron around the house, even when he wasn't cooking.

Every cupboard and drawer was full of utensils, and their walk-in pantry was stacked from floor to ceiling with boxes and bags of food. They had a large spice rack on the inside of the pantry door and a bunch of herbs growing in a dirt box on the back porch. And because Uncle Hank loved tomatoes, there were four hanging baskets just outside the back door that provided tomatoes all year round.

On the few days it rained the summer I stayed with them

I awoke to the smell of baking and knew that Uncle Hank had gotten up extra early and used the sourdough starter he kept in the back of the refrigerator to make a loaf of chewy bread. He told me that he'd given pieces of his gooey sourdough starter to more than forty people since he got it in 1963 from an old lady he used to pick up and take to church. "A few months before Mrs. Kulis passed away she invited me over to see photos of her family, and while I was there she gave me a glass jar with a ball of dough in it. I spent the next couple of hours with her learning to care for it and making the best loaf of rye bread," Uncle Hank said.

I loved Uncle Hank's sourdough toast just about as much as I loved his blackberry jam.

Besides bread, Uncle Hank also made cheese, yogurt, juice, and wine, and he even had a meat smoker he used to make a special type of ham. But the biggest source of food at their house was the garden. All year round it produced fruits and vegetables. What they didn't eat, Uncle Hank gave away to neighbors and friends at the community center. The same community center where he took cooking and pottery classes and played bridge on Fridays.

I felt like Uncle Hank's food guinea pig. He was always trying to get me to eat something and I often had no idea what it was. I was about five the first time he served me shredded kale, red cabbage, garlic chives, and toasted pecans over baked peaches sprinkled with cumin and cinnamon. I remember sitting at the dining table and crying because I didn't want to eat it and Uncle Hank pleading with me to try a bite or two. I finally did, but only after he poured some Hershey's chocolate syrup on the peaches.

It took time, but I eventually got used to eating his unusual dishes, and sometimes I'd even ask for his mashed honey-glazed carrots, parsnips, and leeks with roasted pumpkin slices and fried shallots. Occasionally Uncle Hank would drizzle dark balsamic on top to give it a little tang.

Over dinner one night, just after I arrived, Uncle Hank

and Aunt Flo told me about a month-long cooking competition they were about to begin. "I read an article in *Reader's Digest* about a couple in Rhode Island who have a cooking competition every year and I convinced your uncle that we should do it too," Aunt Flo said.

They wanted to know if I'd be willing to give them a hand in the kitchen when they needed help. "What we need is a reliable and honest kitchen assistant. One who doesn't offer advice or play favorites, and one who would never do anything to sabotage a meal," Aunt Flo said.

I knew she was referring to Uncle Hank when she said that, because he was always offering her cooking tips, but I pretended I didn't understand and so did he.

"What do you say? Do you think you're grown up enough to handle the responsibility of being our assistant?" she asked.

"I suppose so," I replied.

Uncle Hank laughed and promised they wouldn't be too tough on me. "You might even enjoy our little project," he said.

I hated competitions, especially between adults. They scared me, probably because of my Dad's competitions. Every so often he'd hold a poker game in his garage and invite his car club buddies. They'd shout and argue and compete about who could drink the most whiskey or pee the farthest. One time, Dad took a "Tom Bradley for Governor" sign off of our neighbor Mr. Kendrick's front lawn and nailed it to our fence. Then he challenged his poker friends to drench the sign with their pee. Mr. Kendrick came over and told Dad to return the sign or he'd call the police. Dad laughed and said, "Take your black ass back to your house before I kick it there."

When one of Dad's poker friends pointed out that Mr. Kendrick wasn't black, Dad just said, "He might as well be."

Robbie and I had to wait until my dad's friends left, and our parents finished fighting, before we could sneak outside to take the sign down and clean the fence.

While Dad's poker games and competitions didn't always go that badly, I'd also seen competitions go south between

Uncle Hank and Aunt Flo. It had only been six months since their last one, a Christmas decorating competition. I was staying with them over Thanksgiving weekend, so I was there for the beginning of it.

There weren't any rules, except about money. My aunt and uncle agreed not to spend more than one hundred dollars each. Aunt Flo got the front yard to decorate and Uncle Hank worked on the outside of the house. They had so many people drive by to see their winter wonderland that the community police had to put a sign up warning drivers about delays. Everyone wanted to see Aunt Flo's snowwoman and her seven snow children. The local newspaper even put a photo of them on the front page.

The snow children were made from several large bushes she had her gardeners dig up and move from the backyard to the front yard the day after Thanksgiving. It took them an entire day to transplant the bushes and another day to shape them using a hedge trimmer, garden scissors, and the hair clippers Aunt Flo took from Uncle Hank's bathroom drawer. When they finished, Aunt Flo gave her gardeners, Carlos and Jorge, forty dollars and a bottle of whiskey each. Carlos said it wasn't enough money and he'd have to add the extra hours to the monthly bill. That's when Uncle Hank stepped in.

"Sorry guys," he said, "but this is between you and Flo."

I thought I should go to my room for a while so I left my wheelbarrow on the rose path and got to the front porch just in time to turn around and see Aunt Flo stomp her foot, throw Uncle Hank a vicious look, and say something under her breath that I didn't catch. But Uncle Hank must have because he put his tools down, wiped his hands on a rag, and walked to his car. He got in and drove off pretty quickly, but I don't think Aunt Flo noticed, she was too busy pleading with the gardeners, "Come back tomorrow and help me spray them with fake snow and string lights around them. I promise I'll make it worth your while."

"You still owe us for the forty extra hours we worked last month, and besides, we don't work on Sundays. We go to church," Jorge said.

"I know, I know, and I'll pay you, I promise. Just come back tomorrow. Maybe after church," Aunt Flo begged.

They left without promising to come back, and Aunt Flo went to the kitchen to make a drink. I stayed outside and tried to keep busy and out of sight because I knew she was angry. I could hear her mumbling mean things about the gardeners, the kind of mean things my dad would say about Mexican people. I was relieved when I saw Uncle Hank pull up and get out of his car with a bag from Mickey's Burger Barn.

Aunt Flo was already sitting at the dining room table when Uncle Hank put the bag of burgers and fries down. I got the ketchup out of the fridge and joined them.

"How much money do you have left in your decorating budget?" Uncle Hank asked her.

"I haven't got a cent left, and I owe the gardeners money for the extra work they did last month too," Aunt Flo said. "But it's okay. I don't need your help. I'm taking a live modeling job at the art school and I'll be able to pay my own bills in no time at all."

Uncle Hank's face went blank, and he removed his glasses and stood up. He left the dining room table and returned a few minutes later with his checkbook in one hand and a pen in the other. "How much do you owe the gardeners, Flo?"

"At least eight hundred, but pay them nine so I have a credit. I'm going to need their help to put the bushes back when Christmas is over."

That was it. They didn't say another word to each other about it, and before I went to bed that night, I saw them hug and kiss and knew everything was okay.

I stayed awake for hours thinking about them, wondering why Uncle Hank paid Aunt Flo's bill and didn't seem too upset with her for breaking the competition rules. I finally decided that he loved her so much it didn't matter if she followed the rules.

We waited for hours the next day for Carlos and Jorge to arrive, but they didn't show, and they didn't answer when Aunt Flo called to tell them she had a check waiting for them. I had to help her with the lights, but I wasn't tall enough to string them over the top of the snowwoman bush and I was too big to crawl underneath the snow children to wind the lights up the middle the way she wanted.

After a couple of hours of getting it wrong, Uncle Hank took over. He said he had concerns about the electrical extension cord we were using, but I knew it was because he wanted Aunt Flo to stop bossing me around. He did a great job, and even though his Santa sleigh display on the roof of the garage was just as good as Aunt Flo's snowwoman and children, Aunt Flo said the photo of her work on the front page of the newspaper was the winning vote and he agreed.

● ● ●

While the Christmas decorating competition seemed like a cool thing to do, especially since so many people enjoyed the results, I couldn't figure out why Uncle Hank and Aunt Flo now wanted to hold a recipe competition in the summer. It seemed to me they were too busy to do much more than take care of their house and garden. I thought perhaps they had money riding on it, because the night we all sat down to go over the rules I noticed they both had the same crazy look in their eyes that my dad got when he watched a horse race.

I asked them why they were doing the competition, and Aunt Flo said there was absolutely nothing wrong with competitions. "Everyone should participate in competitive activities. It keeps the creative juices going and helps a person learn about being a good loser, and there's nothing better in this world than a pleasant loser, in my book, anyway."

Uncle Hank looked up over his reading glasses and said, "Nothing better in this world than a pleasant winner, darling."

The competition would run from June 20 to July 19, and they would alternate cooking days. The only day they wouldn't cook was Wednesday because *Magnum, P.I.* and *Dallas* were on that night. On Wednesday nights we'd eat burgers, fries, and strawberry shakes from Mickey's Burger Barn.

They agreed not to use, or even look at, cookbooks, or to ask advice from anyone, even each other. They could use anything they found in the pantry, could spend up to thirty dollars on a meal, and could use discount coupons for supplies. The coupon thing was a big deal, and they discussed it for hours before Aunt Flo finally came out and told Uncle Hank she wanted the coupon collection for herself because she found them, cut them out, and sorted them into categories. "I spend hours every week clipping coupons and writing to manufacturers for their free stuff, so I shouldn't have to share," she said.

"And I'm the one who goes to the store to buy the newspapers and magazines, and I'm the one who takes your mail to the post office. If I didn't, there wouldn't be a coupon collection," Uncle Hank replied.

Later on, after *Dynasty* was over and Aunt Flo had finished her drink, she handed him a bunch of coupons and kissed him on the forehead.

It was pretty tense around the house for the first week, and I thought they were going to have a big fight the day Uncle Hank found a Betty Crocker cookbook in the bathroom, hidden under a stack of towels. Aunt Flo swore she didn't know a thing about it, and I was surprised to hear Uncle Hank say he believed her. I knew he didn't, and I also knew he pretended not to see her when she took four copies of *Good Housekeeping* magazine out to the garbage can.

Neither of them ever wrote down their recipe until after we'd eaten and voted. If it was a worthy recipe, Aunt Flo wrote it out in longhand in a book she kept under the Yellow Pages—a book she'd been writing recipes in since before I was born. My vote was often the deciding one, especially when it was Uncle Hank's night to cook (Aunt Flo rarely voted to keep his recipe), and because I didn't want to hurt anyone's feelings, I always voted yes, even for Aunt Flo's poached grape and albacore tuna pasta bake. It was terrible. Neither Uncle Hank nor I could eat it. I filled up three napkins with the dish and put them in my back pockets to flush them down the toilet later. I watched Uncle

Hank fill his mouth with pasta and grapes, then get up and leave the room, returning a few minutes later drinking a glass of water and smiling.

Aunt Flo agreed it wasn't her best work, but she claimed the grapes she used were too bitter for the tuna and that Uncle Hank was to blame for that. "By the time I got to the vines, all the juicy ripe grapes were gone," she said.

"I didn't know you were planning to use grapes. If I had, I wouldn't have harvested any last week," Uncle Hank replied.

Two weeks into the competition, it was pretty clear to me that Uncle Hank was winning. The night he made a roasted four-cheese (Havarti, mozzarella, Gruyère, and Gouda) and five-onion (red, white, yellow, green, and leeks) casserole, Aunt Flo was visibly upset, and after taking just one bite she said it was way too rich for her and she wouldn't be eating any more. Instead, she ate a piece of the pine nut, zucchini, and whole meal cracker loaf she'd made the night before. Uncle Hank and I finished off the cheese dish the next day for lunch. I still think it's one of the best things I've ever eaten. A few days later Uncle Hank served curried cod with grilled prawns; avocado, tomato, and celery salad; a side dish of string beans; and green salsa topped with fried sage leaves (in sesame oil); and a dessert of cornbread pudding that had a warm cinnamon cherry relish inside and topped with orange curd. It was so good I asked for seconds and thirds.

Before I went to sleep that night, Aunt Flo came into my room, sat on my bed, and said, "I want you to go to the store with Uncle Hank from now on. I need to know who he's talking to, and what they talk about, because someone is helping him, that's for sure. Can you do this for me, please?"

She gave me a little notebook and a pen so I could write down the things I noticed. I didn't want to spy on Uncle Hank, but I took the notebook and pen because I didn't want Aunt Flo to be upset with me either. I was so worried about what to do that it was hard to stay asleep that night.

I went to the store with Uncle Hank the next day and

explained to him on the way what Aunt Flo wanted me to do, and when I finished he just chuckled, threw his head back, pounded the steering wheel, and said, "Oh, she's a real piece of work, my Flo. God, I love her. Do whatever she wants you to and don't tell her I know. It will ruin it for her if you do."

I felt so much better after that, and I tried to do what Aunt Flo asked, but it was hard because Uncle Hank spoke to everyone about everything, and I couldn't tell if they were talking about cooking oil or motor oil or the weather. When I gave her my first report, she told me I hadn't been very helpful. "You should've written more about what the butcher told him rather than all this stuff you wrote about the shopping cart's broken wheel," she said.

Uncle Hank went to the store almost every day and he always invited Aunt Flo, but she didn't like to go with him. She said she didn't want him to see what she was buying because he'd spend the entire drive home trying to guess what she was planning to make. A couple of times she got a ride to the store with their neighbor, and even though she had to sit in the backseat with two little kids, she said it was better than getting the third degree from Uncle Hank. I asked her why she didn't drive herself to the store and she said she didn't like driving a stick shift. "It makes me nervous and I miss gears all the time," she replied.

Uncle Hank told me she wasn't a very good driver. "She gets the driving jitters pretty bad," he said. He told me Aunt Flo quit driving a few years after they got married, after she was pulled over by the state patrol for driving twenty miles per hour on the freeway and changing lanes without signaling.

I suggested we take the bus once, so she didn't have to ride in a backseat with little kids, but she just made a face and told me she didn't like buses. "They're so dirty," she said.

The one time we took a taxi to the grocery store she asked the driver to wait while we shopped, and he charged her fifteen extra dollars for the time he spent waiting. When we got home Uncle Hank had to come outside and pay the driver because

Aunt Flo didn't have enough money with her. From then on Uncle Hank drove us to the store and waited in the car while we shopped. She was happy about that because she liked his driving and he didn't nag her about wearing a seat belt (she never did). She also stopped worrying about him seeing her purchases after she sewed herself a couple of black canvas shopping bags with drawstrings at the top, which she pulled closed before Uncle Hank put them in the trunk.

● ● ●

There was a lot to do around the house with the competition going on. I was in charge of several things, including clearing the cats from the dining room chairs (one of their favorite places to sleep) and using masking tape (rolled around my hand like a mitt) to pick up whatever they'd shed that day so it wouldn't get stirred up and contaminate the food. It was also my job to set the table, which I'd try to avoid doing until the last minute, usually when I'd heard either my aunt or uncle say, "Final call or no dinner for you." Only then would I crawl out of the pool, change into something appropriate for the dinner table, and make my way to the kitchen to hear from Uncle Hank, or read (if Aunt Flo was cooking), the list of items to be put on the table for the meal. I appreciated Aunt Flo writing it down because I often forgot the soup spoons and could never remember the kind of mustard she wanted, Dijon or American.

Aunt Flo's specialties were pasta with cream sauces and almost any type of dessert. She was big on using flower petals and lavender blooms in or on her cakes, pies, and custards. She was also messy, took over the entire kitchen, and listened to loud music when she cooked, mostly soundtracks from Broadway— shows like *Westside Story* and *Man of La Mancha*. I liked the music; I'd even sung "Dulcinea" at my school's talent show. My teacher thought it was an odd song for a kid to sing but she said I sang it pretty well.

When Uncle Hank was cooking he liked silence and he only used one counter and the butcher block. He always had the doors and windows open, even if it was raining, and he cleaned up as he cooked. He was big on garlic, onions, herbs, and mustard. He also liked fish, but he didn't serve it too often because they both hated the smell of it in the house. Overall, his meals were more flavorful, while hers were always better looking, though I never got used to eating rosebuds and pansy petals in my desserts.

Dinner was served every night at five minutes past six, and we had to be seated by six. Once the food was on the table, my aunt and uncle would spend too much time, in my opinion, asking each other questions about the meal, or smelling different components to try to guess what spices were in it. I didn't have many questions, I just wanted to eat, but I wasn't allowed to until they were done talking and we'd given our prayer of thanks. Uncle Hank loved God and tried to do good things every day because he said God wanted him to. He knew my family wasn't godly because neither of my parents would close their eyes and bow their heads and pray when we had Christmas dinner at their house.

I was probably in the third grade when I noticed my dad eating while Uncle Hank was saying a prayer of thanks. I thought it was odd, so when I was helping clear the table I said to Uncle Hank, "You know, my dad and mom don't think there is a god."

"It doesn't matter if your parents believe in God or not because God believes in them. God is here to help everyone and everything."

"Really? He wants to help me?" I replied.

"Of course he does. You only need to ask Him," he said.

The more I prayed before dinner with Uncle Hank, the more I got to like it. It felt good when Uncle Hank, Aunt Flo, and I held hands, closed our eyes, and said thanks to someone (somewhere) for helping us. It was peaceful, and when we all smiled afterward it felt like we were connected in some nice way. I once tried to get my parents and brother to hold hands before dinner and pray but Mom just looked at me with a squished-up nose and said, "Sweetheart, we don't pray and we don't believe in God."

Dad looked over at me and said, "There's no God. God is just a fantasy of lazy people with no ambition."

I got a sick feeling in my stomach and excused myself without eating any of the awful spaghetti Mom had made.

I found the God thing confusing and wished my parents were more like Uncle Hank. I liked the idea of someone out there who wanted good things for me, who would help me if I asked and didn't care if I ripped my new shirt or left a mess in the bathroom; it sounded good. I wondered why my parents didn't believe in God and if my dad was right about God being a "fantasy for lazy people." But Uncle Hank wasn't lazy. And if there was no God, why did I feel so good when I prayed along with Uncle Hank but felt bad when I was around Dad?

● ● ●

A few days after Uncle Hank paid me for helping with the greeting card jingle, the three of us went to the mall and I bought a few pieces of floral material, elastic ribbon, sequins, felt pens, and a bottle of Hawaiian Tropic dark tanning oil because I'd read about the benefits of suntans in one of Aunt Flo's beauty magazines and decided I should go for the "deep dark glow" mentioned in the advertisement. Aunt Flo wasn't convinced that I needed a tan, or a big bottle of suntan oil, but after I promised to keep the lid on it, and to wipe it off before I got into the pool, she gave in and let me buy it.

On our way out of the mall, I tripped over a man who was asleep on the pathway, fell down, and scraped both of my knees. I didn't see him because I was busy reading the instructions on the bottle of suntan oil. Uncle Hank helped me up and asked me if I was okay. Then he leaned down and asked the man if he was okay. I looked at the man and wondered why he was wearing a coat. It was a very hot day—too hot for a coat, I thought.

Aunt Flo whispered to me that he was a homeless man, "a hopeless, good-for-nothing drunk."

I'm pretty sure the man heard her because she whispered it pretty loud. I was shocked and embarrassed. Especially because a few people had come out of the mall to see if I was okay and I think they heard Aunt Flo too.

I told everyone I was fine and tried to cover my bloody knees with my hands so they'd stop looking. "We should get her home and take care of her knees, Hank, and we should do it now," Aunt Flo said.

She opened her purse, took out a Kleenex, and handed it to me. Then she took a dollar out of her wallet and put it down next to the man, all the while pulling at Uncle Hank's shirt so he'd stop talking to him.

Uncle Hank said, "Stop it, Flo, I'm not done here." He took his hat off and handed it to the man.

Aunt Flo rolled her eyes and said, "Holy smokes. Next thing ya know he'll be giving him his shoes."

I followed her out to the parking lot, because she told me to, and we waited for Uncle Hank for more than twenty minutes. Once he started the engine, he asked Aunt Flo why she'd given the man one dollar. "Why not five or ten dollars?" he said.

"One dollar is more than enough for a person who did nothing to earn it," she replied.

"Why not give him enough to make him feel better instead of just enough to make you feel better?" Uncle Hank asked.

"Why did you only give him your hat and not your pants and shoes?" Aunt Flo asked.

"That's different," Uncle Hank replied.

It was a quiet drive back to the house; Aunt Flo didn't say a word until we pulled into the driveway. Then, in a very calm voice, she said, "I presume you're speaking about yourself, Harold Matanich, because I am certainly not stingy."

That was the first time I'd ever heard his real name, and I wondered why he was called Hank when his real name was Harold, and why he used the last name of Mann instead of Matanich, but I decided to save my questions for another time.

I was out of the car and in the house first, and thought it would be best if I swam the rest of the afternoon and stayed out of their way. Uncle Hank headed to his garden shed and

Aunt Flo went to the kitchen. I heard the ice cube tray crash into the sink when I walked to my room to get my bathing suit on, and I wondered if Aunt Flo knew I'd moved her tonic water to the fridge on the back porch to make room for the chocolate pudding she'd made the night before.

After swimming for a while I got my new purchase out and slathered the suntanning oil on my arms and legs. Then I dragged one of the lounge chairs to the side of the pool with the most sunshine, which happened to be where the cats were sleeping. Aunt Flo was right: the suntan oil was sticky and it made the loose cat hair cling to my legs. I dove into the pool a few times to get it off. Then I tried to soak up the oil and cat hair I left floating on top of the water with a towel, but I didn't do a very good job.

It was after seven when I went looking for Uncle Hank. I was hungry and wanted him to drive to·the Burger Barn; it was Wednesday, after all. I looked everywhere for him—or at least I thought I had, and then I heard their bedroom door open and Uncle Hank yell out, "I'm starving, let's go get some burgers!" When I met him at the front door I was going to say something about the lipstick on his cheeks and neck but he was in such a good mood and looked so happy I didn't want to spoil it.

● ● ●

On Aunt Flo's last night to cook for the competition she served fresh penne pasta with a garlic, tomato, chicken, bacon, and mushroom cream sauce and a salad of avocadoes, yellow tomatoes, minced red onion, cilantro, anchovies, and grated Romano cheese. Her meal was so delicious that both Uncle Hank and I had thirds. But it was the dessert that sealed the deal: a lemon butterscotch chiffon cake that was almost a foot tall and covered with vanilla bean butter cream icing that Uncle Hank raved about until she said, "Okay, okay, enough already. Eat up."

All three of us agreed that Aunt Flo was the winner, and not just because of her last meal. She'd caught the essence of the competition better than Uncle Hank because everything she'd made was unique and "new." Uncle Hank seemed happy about her winning, and he wrote down her chicken and bacon pasta recipe in her black book of good recipes, which she promised she would publish one day.

● ● ●

A few days after the competition ended, Aunt Flo told me that two of her sisters, my aunts Rose and Gert, were coming over for lunch because their birthdays were July 24 and 26 and Aunt Flo wanted to do something nice for them.

We made a special cheesecake birthday cake. I grated the skin off a pink grapefruit, a tangerine, orange, lemon, and lime, and put a tablespoon of each in a bowl of chopped up lavender blooms with a pinch of rock salt. Aunt Flo added it all to a whipped cream cheese and egg mixture before she poured it into a pan she'd lined with a crushed gingersnap cookie and butter mix. Just before her sisters arrived, she poured a tangerine glaze over the top of the cake and put pink rose petals around the plate. It was beautiful.

They were a little late, which upset Aunt Flo because she had plans to watch *General Hospital* that afternoon and she wanted to watch it alone. Worse than being late, though, they brought three dogs with them, even though they knew Aunt Flo was allergic to dogs. Gert's corgi Missy was the mother of the other two, who were only about a year old and really cute. The dogs ran right into the living room and immediately started chasing the cats. There was a lot of sneezing, hissing, and barking, followed by a chase around the kitchen and dining room and a few cat slaps. After one of the cats bit one of the dogs on the ear, and the dog let out a cry that was terrifying, Uncle Hank said, "Enough of this," and asked me to help him take the dogs out to Gert's car. He re-parked her car under a big tree on the street and rolled down the windows so the dogs wouldn't suffocate. Then I went back into the house, but Uncle Hank stayed outside to talk to the mailman.

Gert and Rose lived about ten miles away, in the same

house they'd grown up in. I'd never been to their house, and I'd only met Gert once before, on the night Dad had tried to run over Uncle Bill. Rose didn't come to our house that night, and after meeting her I was glad she didn't because I don't know how she would have made it up our front stairs. Rose was a bit hunched over and wore metal braces on both of her legs. Other than that she looked just like her sisters, except her hair was completely white. "You have nice skin, just like our mother had," she said when I introduced myself.

"That's because Aunt Flo bought me some Noxzema skin cleanser and has me using it day and night," I replied.

Noxzema made my skin glow but it also made me smell like one of Uncle Hank's dresser drawers, the bottom one where he kept his sweaters and mothballs.

Once the dogs were in the car and the cats were out of sight, Aunt Flo told Gert, Rose, and me to have a seat at the dining room table while she finished a few things in the kitchen and took something for her allergies. I sat down in the chair next to Rose because I was curious about her braces and the crutch she used to move around. I wondered why she was so crooked and had to bend in such a weird way when she walked. It looked to me like she was going to fall down every time she took a step. I couldn't take my eyes off of her. "Do those things hurt your legs?" I asked.

"Oh, not really, honey, I'm used to them," Rose replied.

"What happens if you take them off? Do you fall down?" I asked.

Before she could answer, Aunt Flo called me into the kitchen and told me to stop asking questions. "Rose had polio when she was a little girl and it almost killed her. I don't think she likes to talk about it, so how about you ask her about something else, perhaps about those badly behaved dogs they brought with them?" she said.

It was a very hot day, and the cheese soufflé Aunt Flo made fell flat. "This goddamn oven always does this!" she screamed as she dropped the soufflé pan into the kitchen sink.

We all laughed when we heard the scream and Gert said, "I'd rather have one of your tuna sandwiches, to be honest. You make the best tuna."

Aunt Flo smiled, took a bow, and said, "I sure do. But it's going to take a few minutes and I need to toast the bread because the sourdough loaf is frozen."

That's when Uncle Hank walked into the dining room and invited my aunts outside for a tour of the garden and a taste of his homemade wine. I followed closely behind Rose, just in case her crutch sank into the grass and she needed someone to pull it out, and because I thought I might get a glass of wine too. Uncle Hank loved his wine, and he showed Rose and Gert how he smashed the grapes with a special mallet he'd made and what he did with the juice after squeezing the grapes. He even made them inspect the wooden barrel he kept the juice in until it turned into *vino*, and then showed them the special light blue wine bottles he bought and labeled himself: *Fino Vino 1980s*. When he finished telling them everything he knew about winemaking, he poured us all a glass of his *best* and made a toast to good health and good wealth. My aunts sipped and smelled and asked questions about the wine but I drank mine real fast then put my empty glass out for more, only to get a sour face from Uncle Hank and a request that I go back to the house to help Aunt Flo.

I hid behind a flowering bush outside the kitchen door to watch them walk back from the garden shed and told Aunt Flo how nervous I was about Rose. I thought for sure she was going fall over and I wasn't sure I'd be able to help her up because she was much larger than me.

But they made it back to the dining room table just fine and I set the table for lunch while they talked about relatives I'd never heard of. It probably wasn't a good idea for Uncle Hank to keep refilling their wine glasses during lunch, and I heard Aunt Flo tell him to cool it a couple of times, but he just laughed and said the wine wasn't very strong: "It's more grape juice than wine," he said.

About the time she finished her fourth glass of wine, Rose said the room was spinning and asked me to help her to the couch so she could lie down. After she was comfortable, I went back to the table. I was about to ask Aunt Flo if I should make a pot of coffee when Gert asked me to pass her the wine bottle Uncle Hank had left on the kitchen counter. Even though Aunt Flo told her coffee was on the way, Gert insisted on having another glass of wine. She poured every last drop into her glass and asked me to sit down next to her. "You look a lot like your dad, not a thing like your mom. Your mom's good-looking but she's a bit of a ditz. Why else would she stay with your Dad all these years while he carries on with Bill's wife Genie?" she said.

I saw Aunt Flo throw her a look, but it was too late. I'd heard it and I was interested to hear more. Then Rose yelled out from the couch, "Not only that, I think your mom was pregnant for a year with you!"

Aunt Flo stood up. "Enough, you two. Let's change the subject."

But Gert just talked louder and faster. "You know, your parents were separated when your mom fell pregnant with you. Your dad was living with Genie but he went back to your mom because she said she was pregnant, and your dad's not the type to avoid his responsibilities."

"After you arrived, Genie started dating Bill, and that made your dad meaner than ever!" Rose yelled out from the couch.

Aunt Flo got up and walked over to Gert. She put her hands on Gert's shoulders and said, "Come on, Gert, let's go outside and get some air. You're drunk."

Gert squished up her face and let out a loud burp and said, "It's the God's honest truth, Flo. Everyone knows it, and the girl's old enough to know it too."

"She's barely eleven," Aunt Flo said.

"Is Genie really married to Uncle Bill?" I asked. "My mom said he's lying about it."

I didn't get to hear the answer, because Aunt Flo put her hand over Gert's mouth about the same time I felt Uncle Hank's hand reach under my arm and pull me up. When I looked up, he smiled and asked if I could help him out in the kitchen, so I followed him. I was filling the sink with soap and water when he told me in a very serious voice that Rose and Gert were gossip girls and I shouldn't believe everything they said. I told him I knew about Genie because my parents fought about her all the time. Uncle Hank said he was sorry I had to listen to my parents fight and then he rustled my hair, rubbed my back, and whispered in my ear, "Don't worry about these things; they're not important in the big picture."

He poured cups of coffee for everyone while I washed the lunch plates and thought about how much I wanted to stay with Aunt Flo and Uncle Hank forever. When I offered to carry out the cream and sugar for him, he said, "I'd better tend to the dragons on my own. I think you'd have a better time watching TV or working out how to use the zoom on your new camera."

I was glad I didn't have to go back into the dining room because I could hear Gert and Rose talking about my dad and how much money he had to pay our neighbor Mr. Kendrick for wrecking his front porch.

● ● ●

Aunt Flo and Uncle Hank had bought me a camera for my birthday and I'd already used six rolls of film, mostly taking pictures of the cats. I liked to dress them up with the flower chains I made from garden flowers and take their pictures. A few of the cats were okay with it, especially if I gave them a drink of milk or shared my lunch with them first.

Aunt Flo thought cats had germs and told me several times, "Don't let them eat from your plate or you'll get sick." I didn't care about getting a cat sickness because those cats were my best friends. They let me carry them around and pose them in all sorts of positions for photos.

Just the week before our lunch with Gert and Rose, I'd made all the cats jumpsuits using the material and elastic string I bought at the mall. I also used a little sewing machine Uncle

Hank got from a garage sale and a roll of tape from Aunt Flo's desk. It took a long time to put the suits on the cats, and two of them protested and scratched me pretty bad. Then, when I finally got them all dressed and ready for a photo shoot, they wouldn't stay still and look into the camera like I wanted. They wouldn't do anything but lie down until Uncle Hank brought a cube of butter out to the garden and put a little bit on their ears, and then they got up and starting licking each other.

"Be quick," Uncle Hank said. "This won't last long."

I clicked away as fast as I could and got eight good photos of them all dressed in jumpsuits, flowers taped on their heads and licking each other's ears. Uncle Hank took my roll of film to the drugstore and when we got the pictures back he told me they were the best photos he'd ever seen.

We didn't have a cat at our house until I was seven. That was when Aunt Flo left Rascal in a box on the front porch with a note that said, "This cat needs a home and you have one." I had already met Rascal before Aunt Flo dropped her off. I was at their house when Rascal snuck into the kitchen looking for something to eat. Uncle Hank said she was a stray, and they tried for months to make Rascal feel at home, but she didn't get along with their other cats, so Aunt Flo decided she should live at my house.

When I found Rascal on our front porch, I hid her in my room and put Aunt Flo's note in my diary. It took Dad almost a week to notice her. He spotted her on the kitchen counter one morning, and by the time I got to the kitchen he was trying to catch her. I managed to get to her first and refused to hand her over because I knew he was going to toss her out the back door. I ran to my room with Rascal, got the note Aunt Flo had left, and walked it back to Dad. He read it and then picked up the phone. I pretended to go back to my room but I really just stood out in the hallway while he spoke with Aunt Flo. He started off with, "You know how I feel about cats; they're just rats with furry tails." He got quiet for a second, started to say something, and then stopped midway through. Then I heard him say, "I did not run over Tiger. That rag shouldn't have been sleeping under my car."

He slammed the phone down and I never heard him say another thing about getting rid of Rascal.

I got a few good close-up pictures of the cats that afternoon and finished a whole roll of film by 6 p.m., about the same time I saw Uncle Hank helping Aunt Rose and Aunt Gert walk to their car. I waited for them to drive away before I went into the house. I looked in almost every room for Uncle Hank and Aunt Flo before I found Aunt Flo on the patio outside the dining room, sitting in a lawn chair, smoking a cigarette, and drinking a cup of coffee.

"Come over here for a second, honey," she said.

I sat on the grass next to her chair and looked up at the almost invisible half moon making its way toward us. "Hank took my two very silly and drunk sisters home. Forget what they said if you can."

I wasn't sure if I could make myself forget, so I just told her I'd try.

"He's taking a taxi home and he promised to bring burgers and strawberry shakes back with him, so I hope you're hungry," she said.

"I'm starving," I replied.

CHAPTER 9

A couple of weeks later, on August 11, 1986, Uncle Hank had an accident. The police said it was likely he slipped and hit his head on the side of the pool before he fell in. Aunt Flo found him floating facedown above Mayadelsa. I heard her screaming and rushed to my bedroom window to watch her jump into the pool. I knew something was really wrong because she'd never screamed like that before, and she'd never gotten into the pool with her pajamas on. I ran outside in my underwear to get the gardeners and they ran to the pool to help Aunt Flo pull him out.

"Call for help!" Aunt Flo screamed as she held Uncle Hank's head above the water. I ran to the kitchen, grabbed the phone, and tried to dial 911, but my hands were shaking so much that I misdialed the first two times. When I finally got through to an operator, all I could say was, "*Please.*"

Aunt Flo and the gardeners got Uncle Hank out of the pool and took turns doing CPR until the firemen and ambulance arrived. I stood next to the pool and watched a fireman pound so hard on Uncle Hank's chest that he practically sprang off the ground. But nothing worked. He was gone.

When they put him in the ambulance and covered his face with a sheet, Aunt Flo screamed so loud the neighbors from all the way down the block heard her and came over to see what was wrong. It was awful. Everyone was crying, even Carlos and Jorge. I was so scared I thought my body was going to fall apart, like my arm would fall off or my eyes would pop out.

Mom and Dad arrived just after the firemen left but had to leave early the next morning to go to work, so I was on my own with Aunt Flo for a few hours. I called Mom at work a couple of times to ask if I should make Aunt Flo breakfast or do the laundry and she said, "It won't hurt to keep busy, honey. I'll come over straight after work."

I fed the cats, put some towels in the washer, and made Aunt Flo some toast and a cup of coffee, but she wasn't interested and didn't look up when I sat a tray next to her. I didn't know what else to do so I sat on the couch and watched TV while she sat in Uncle Hank's lounge chair and sobbed.

I was relieved when Aunt Gert showed up at 2 p.m. and said she could stay for a few days, because no matter how hard I tried, I couldn't get Aunt Flo to eat, drink, or stop crying. I was afraid she was going to faint or die from a broken heart.

Aunt Flo's face was red and her eyes were so swollen they were barely slits. I told Gert that I'd tried to get her to eat and I'd made up a few ice packs for her eyes and put them in the freezer, just in case she wanted them. Gert tried to talk Aunt Flo into taking a bath, but Aunt Flo wouldn't talk and wouldn't look up at either of us until Gert asked her if she'd like a drink. "Make it a double," Aunt Flo said.

I filled her favorite highball crystal glass almost halfway up with gin, dropped in two ice cubes, poured tonic to the top, and took a few sips before I handed it to her.

When Mom showed up after work to take me home I told her I wanted to stay one more night. "Gert doesn't know anything about the house or what to feed the cats and I think she's gonna need my help to get Aunt Flo to bed," I said.

"Oh, I suppose one more night won't hurt. But don't make her drinks so strong. She's a little too wobbly," Mom replied.

● ● ●

The next morning, after Gert and Aunt Flo drove off in Uncle Hank's T-bird to the funeral home to pick out a casket and take some clothes for Uncle Hank to wear, I threw my half-empty bottle of Hawaiian Tropic oil away and spent an hour scrubbing the diving board with hot water and Joy dish soap. My swim with Mayadelsa afterward was hard. I tried to stay under until I went to wherever Uncle Hank had gone, but I couldn't do it.

Aunt Gert and Aunt Flo got back from the funeral home about an hour before my mom drove up. They each ate one of the sandwiches that a few nice ladies from the community center had dropped off earlier. I made Aunt Flo another G and T and told her I'd cleaned the suntan oil off of the diving board. "I'm sorry Aunt Flo, I should have cleaned it off the other day when I noticed it but I forgot," I said.

She looked down at the drink in her hands and almost whispered, "You're always on the move, aren't you? A very busy child. Too busy."

I felt my insides sink and thought she was saying it was my fault that Uncle Hank was dead. I was about to say, "What's that mean?" when I heard Gert say, "Accidents happen all the time, and this was just an accident. You didn't mean for anyone to get hurt."

Uncle Hank's funeral was held the day before his thirtieth wedding anniversary in a small church not too far from their home, and so many people showed up there wasn't one place left to sit or stand. The casket was open, and I got to walk up with Aunt Flo to see him before they closed the lid and put him into the hearse. He looked peaceful, and his hair was combed back just the way he liked it, but someone had put red blush and lipstick on him and it made him look like an old woman. I tried to wipe some of it off with a tissue Mom had given me earlier but Aunt Flo told me to leave him alone. "He's perfect, so perfect," she sobbed.

After they lowered his casket into the ground at the cemetery, a guy from his church got everyone, including my dad, to say a prayer, and then we went back to Aunt Flo's because her sisters had made a big lunch. I think everyone from the funeral arrived to eat and talk about Uncle Hank. I hated it.

Mom was the first one to mention Aunt Flo's ring. It was an emerald and diamond ring I'd never seen before, but I did recognize the design and the gems from Uncle Hank's hidden box. When Mom asked about it, Aunt Flo looked at the ring on her right index finger and told us she'd found it in Uncle Hank's drawer when she was looking for a good pair of socks to send over to the funeral home. "It was in a little silver box next to a card with my name on it. The card says *Hank always loves Flo*, and I'm going to sleep with it for the rest of my life," she sobbed as she caught the tears off the end of her nose.

I decided to stay with Aunt Flo after the funeral because Gert had to get back home to help Rose, and because Aunt Flo needed someone to feed the cats and take out the trash, but mostly because I knew it was my fault that Uncle Hank was dead and I didn't want Aunt Flo to hate me. I knew that if I'd been more careful with my suntan oil like Aunt Flo had told me to, Uncle Hank would still be alive and no one would be heartbroken. And I thought if I stayed I could somehow find a way to make Aunt Flo feel better. I couldn't, and it all got to be too much when she drank an entire bottle of Uncle Hank's wine late one night and I found her sitting on the diving board cursing at Mayadelsa for taking Uncle Hank away. I had to call Mom and Dad to come over to help me get Aunt Flo into the house and into bed. After she dozed off, Mom said, "I think you've had enough of the grief scene for a while. You'd better come home and get some rest."

It was hard to leave Aunt Flo, and before I got into Dad's car I woke her up to say good-bye. She took my hand and squeezed it. "I'm sure it's going to be okay one day, but it might take a while," she said.

Then she pulled me to her chest and hugged me for the

longest time. It scared me and made me cry almost as hard as she was crying.

I called Aunt Flo every morning for weeks after the funeral to see if she was okay. She was never okay, and even though she'd answer the phone, she wouldn't say much, just a quiet "hello" and then nothing. So I would say "hi" or "good morning" and then read her something out of the newspaper, the headlines mostly, and eventually she'd ask what the weather forecast was and how many more days it would be before she stopped seeing him in the hallway or hearing him call out to her in the middle of the night. I always cried when she said things like that. I didn't have an answer, and besides, I missed him too.

● ● ●

I started the sixth grade a month after Uncle Hank died, and I rode my bike to Aunt Flo's after school every day until Christmas. Sometimes Aunt Flo would be in a good mood, and sometimes she'd be cranky or sad. When she wasn't feeling good, she'd hand me a grocery list and some money. It always took me at least an hour to ride to the store to get her groceries and back, and when I returned it would be time for me to go home. If she was in a good mood, the front curtains would be open, the sprinkler would be going, and I'd spend my time petting the cats or cleaning the leaves off the top of the pool or watching TV. Visiting her was a good thing for me. I felt much better being with her and around Uncle Hank's things than I did at home. Plus, Robbie was still at home recuperating from his accident.

Robbie didn't go back to college until January 1987, five months after Uncle Hank died. Dad's boss helped him get into a private university because his old school didn't want him back. When Robbie got the news that he was accepted, he packed his bags and told us he was leaving right way. Mom thought his initiative was admirable and told me if anyone could bounce back from a bad situation, it was Robbie. "He's special and determined, not to mention handsome, just like your father."

He took off a few days after New Year's without saying

a thing to me, which kind of bothered me because I'd made a special effort to be nice to him since Uncle Hank died. A few days after he left, on my way home from Aunt Flo's, I saw him in a car with his bowling alley friend. They stopped the car in the middle of the road, honked, and waved me over. I got off my bike and took my time walking over. When I reached the car, I asked Robbie why he lied about going to college and he started laughing and said, "Everyone lies and everyone dies. You know that."

I just looked at him.

"You gonna tell Dad?" he asked.

"I might," I replied.

His friend said he'd give me ten dollars to keep my mouth shut. I told him I wanted his pack of cigarettes and lighter and the bottle of beer he'd just opened, too. He handed all of them to me and I took the long the way home, down a couple of alleys so I could drink the beer and smoke a cigarette. About the time I finished the beer, I felt so good I didn't care if I ever saw Robbie again.

● ● ●

It was almost Easter before Aunt Flo started feeling better, but finally she did. She even started gardening, which was good because her yard looked like a forest and the pool had a layer of dark green slime and dead leaves on top and I couldn't see Mayadelsa. I felt great the day I arrived at her house and found Carlos and Jorge working in the garden. They were happy to see me and didn't seem bothered by Aunt Flo, who was giving them orders about what to do with every tree and bush.

When I told Mom and Dad about Aunt Flo feeling better, Dad said, "It must be Valium or vodka, because Flo will never get over Hank. She'll probably die soon herself from lack of attention. Hank did nothing but pay attention. It was pathetic."

So we were all pretty shocked when Aunt Flo had us over to dinner on Memorial Day and introduced us to her new husband, Reverend Bob. She told us they were married the week before in Las Vegas.

I thought Reverend Bob was a religious man, but Dad said he wasn't anything close to godly. "He's a small-time 'Nothing' with a stupid name," Dad said.

Aunt Flo was the happiest I'd seen her since Uncle Hank died. She even called me "sweetheart" about ten times. After dinner she invited me to stay the next weekend with them, "I'll make dinner and a strawberry sponge finger cake for your birthday. Twelve, right?"

"Yes, I'll be twelve in two days, and yes to staying," I replied.

I was excited about spending time with Aunt Flo and the cats and about being able to swim with Mayadelsa. The next Friday, after school, Mom and I went shopping and then she dropped me off at Aunt Flo's place. Mom didn't go inside because she was in a hurry to get home. "I hate it when the frozen peas thaw out and get the other groceries wet," she said.

Aunt Flo met me at the front door and told me she had big plans for us. "You probably want to go swimming first though huh?" she said.

Boy, was she right. I raced past the cats lounging in the living room to get to my room to change into my suit and then ran as fast as I could to the pool, only to find Reverend Bob floating on an air mattress, hovering over Mayadelsa.

I was going to say something, but it looked like he was asleep, so I headed for the diving board and played around on it, hoping he'd notice me and move out of the way. After what seemed like an hour, he looked up and said, "I would hope you'd have the good sense not to dive in when the owner of the house is trying to relax in his own pool."

"Hardly your pool," I fired back before I could stop myself. I dove in, making a smooth entry, and shot all the way under his mattress to the end of the pool. As I emerged I heard him say something about a smartass kid. Two more dives were all it took to get him out of the pool. I stayed and swam until Aunt Flo insisted I come in and get ready for dinner. "I've made a special birthday meal and a cake, so get your behind in here now," she said, laughing.

Aunt Flo and I ate our meal and birthday cake at the dining table while Rev Bob ate his from a TV tray in the living room so he could watch *Jeopardy*. "Don't be too upset with Bob. He's no Uncle Hank, but he loves me and I need him," she said.

I slept with all of the cats that night and it was so cuddly and nice that I decided I would have eight cats of my own one day.

● ● ●

At breakfast the next morning, I noticed Aunt Flo's hair was different. It wasn't in a bun on top of her head; it was hanging past her shoulders and parted in the middle, and it looked like she'd had a perm.

"Your hair is different," I said.

"Oh, it's a new style I'm trying out. Bob thinks long, wavy hair makes me look younger."

She also said she had a surprise for me in the living room, so I put my cereal bowl in the sink and headed over to see what it was. It was a big bag filled with all kinds of stuff to make a scrapbook, including colored construction paper, glitter, felt pens, ribbon, and what seemed like a hundred photos of Uncle Hank and me, some I'd never seen before. I stared at the photos for the longest time and could tell that I was happy, even as a small baby, to be with Uncle Hank. Aunt Flo continued to hand me photos even though she knew I was crying. When I looked over at her I could see she was crying too, but I didn't feel like she wanted to stop looking so I got a box of Kleenex from the bathroom. We spent most of the morning cutting and pasting photos on pages of my new scrapbook.

The next day, when Aunt Flo arrived home from a Mary Kay party, she walked into the bathroom while Reverend Bob was washing my back. She called me a "nasty girl" and she called him a "child molester."

I jumped out of the bathtub and grabbed my towel. "I

told him to stay out, Aunt Flo, but he wouldn't leave me alone!" I cried after her.

"She's a liar. She begged me to wash her back," Reverend Bob said as he looked down at me, a mean grin on his face like the Joker from Batman.

Aunt Flo must have believed him, because she told me to go to my room and get my things. I sat on my bed and tried to think of the right words to say to make her believe me. I also tried to think of what I did to make Reverend Bob think I wanted him to come into the bathroom.

Aunt Flo drove me home an hour later. I was thankful for the radio, even though it was on the country music station and they were playing a Tammy Wynette song that I didn't like. Just before she turned the car onto my street, Aunt Flo turned the radio off and said, "I'm sorry about what I said earlier. I didn't mean it."

I told her it was okay, that I didn't want to cause any trouble. "I just didn't know what to do," I said.

She squeezed my hand. "I hope I haven't made a mistake with Reverend Bob."

Before I got out of the car she handed me an envelope. "I'll call you soon, honey, I promise," she said.

I took the envelope, got out of the car, and watched her drive away. I waited until I was in my bedroom and Mom and Dad had gone to bed before I opened the envelope. Two twenty-dollar bills and a note: *Buy yourself something nice. Love Aunt Flo.*

● ● ●

A few weeks after the bathroom incident, Reverend Bob showed up at my softball game. He pulled up next to me as I was walking to the bus stop. "Hey, your aunt sent me to get you. She's not very well and wants to see you," he said.

I was worried about her, so I got into the backseat and closed the door. Reverend Bob didn't drive to Aunt Flo's, though. Instead he drove the other way and stopped the car in an empty part of a hardware store parking lot. Then he reached over the seat to hand me a shoebox. "I got you this present because you're so young and so pretty. Try it on. I want to make sure it fits," he said.

"You said we were going to see Aunt Flo. I want to see her," I demanded.

"Just open the present and try them on and then I'll take you back!" he yelled.

The present was a bra and underwear set and I was scared when I saw them.

"Put them on," he insisted, "or I'll come back there and put them on you myself."

The bra was way too big and the lace on the underwear was hard and scratchy. He wasn't too happy with me because I refused to lie down so he could take my photo. He yelled at me to pose the way he wanted me to, but all I could think about was how mad Aunt Flo would be if she ever saw a photo of me in lace underwear, smiling like I was something special. He finally gave up and told me to get out of the car. I grabbed my coat and slammed the door as hard as I could. I ran until I was out of breath. It took me almost an hour to get home, and the scratchy lace underwear I still had on was so painful I had to stop at the library to use the bathroom so I could take it off and leave it in the garbage. I don't know when I started shaking; I think it was when I noticed how dark it was and how far I still had to walk before I got home. I really hoped Mom would be there when I arrived so I could tell her what happened. But no one was home, so I toasted a couple of Pop-Tarts and went to my room.

When I heard Mom's car in the driveway, I went to the door to meet her. I think I told her everything about Reverend Bob before she had a chance to put her purse down.

"Are you hurt? Should I take you to the doctor? Oh god, wait until your Dad hears about this, he'll kill him."

"Aunt Flo will hate me. Please don't tell Dad," I pleaded.

When Dad got home from Seattle the next night I heard him and Mom in their room talking about what Reverend Bob did, and a few minutes later I heard Dad walk to the kitchen.

I met Mom in the hall on my way to the living room and she reached over and rubbed my head. I stiffened up and pulled away. "Why'd you tell him?" I asked.

"He's got a right to know," she replied.

I pretended to watch TV in the living room while Dad screamed on the phone to Aunt Flo, "Who the fuck goes to Las Vegas for the weekend and comes back with a loser like Reverend Bob? He's a child molester and you're an idiot for marrying him!"

That was the first time I'd ever heard Dad talk to Aunt Flo that way, and something inside of me was happy about it. After Dad slammed the phone down, he came out to the living room and told me I should've locked the bathroom door and I had no business getting in a car with anyone. I looked over at Mom, and she shrugged her shoulders and gave me a big frown that let me know she agreed with Dad. When Mom knocked on my bedroom door later that night, I told her to go away.

"I know you're upset, but Aunt Flo shouldn't have married anyone so soon after Uncle Hank's death, and especially not that pig Reverend Bob."

I pretended I didn't hear her and pulled the covers over my head. I waited for her to go to bed before I got up and took one of her pills from a bottle in the bathroom cabinet. I broke it into four pieces, swallowed one piece, and put the rest in my sock drawer for later.

No one mentioned Reverend Bob or Aunt Flo to me for weeks after Dad's phone call, and then one day in August, two days after the first anniversary of Uncle Hank's death, when Dad and I were driving home from a weekend car club exhibition and after he had drunk all five beers from the cooler in the backseat, he said, "You're sure it was Reverend Bob?"

I didn't answer, because I wasn't sure what he was asking.

"The bathtub, the bra. Was it him?" Dad asked about a minute later.

"It's the truth, Dad, I promise."

He drove straight to Aunt Flo's, got out of the car, and

stomped past the gate and to the front door. I followed because I didn't know what else to do. Dad didn't knock, he just opened the door, and we both could see Reverend Bob sitting in Uncle Hank's favorite chair watching TV. Aunt Flo was in the kitchen, but when she heard Dad yell at Reverend Bob to get up and get outside, she came right out and told Dad to leave him alone. "It's none of your business," she said.

Dad fired back, "Touch my fuckin' kid and it's my fuckin' business."

Dad picked Reverend Bob up out of his chair with one hand, and I watched in amazement as he put him in a headlock, dragged him out to the front gate, and threw him down on the street curb. He kicked him really hard right in the stomach and told him to "get the fuck out of Dodge." Aunt Flo yelled at Dad to leave him alone, and I ran to the car, got into the backseat, and covered my ears. It was all over by the time the neighbors got to Aunt Flo's gate, and I peeked through my fingers to see the taillights of Uncle Hank's T-bird, with Reverend Bob in the driver's seat, disappear down the road. Aunt Flo was standing by the front gate crying.

"He's a fucking bum, Flo, and you know it," Dad yelled as he got into the car and took off so quickly that I slid clear across the seat and hit my head on the door handle.

Even though it was a Sunday and Dad had to work the next day, he drove home the long way so he could stop at the Mic Mac Tavern. I was happy to stay in the car and wait because I'd never felt safer or more loved by my dad.

 CHAPTER 10

Just after I started the seventh grade, Mom told me that Aunt Flo had kicked Reverend Bob out for good, but not before he stole a lot of the money she got from Uncle Hank's life insurance. I remembered Uncle Hank's hidden box and wondered if Reverend Bob had taken that too. I knew that Uncle Hank would be angry if someone stole his things and I really wanted to go over to the cottage and have a look in the shed, but I wasn't sure if Aunt Flo would want to see me. She'd stopped calling me after Dad beat up Reverend Bob.

I spent most of the year leaving notes and cards in her mailbox. I even knocked on her front door a few times. She never answered and she didn't respond to my notes or phone messages, either. I'd just about given up on ever seeing her again when a box arrived at my house on June 1, 1988.

> *Happy 13th Birthday Honey. I'm passing these on because*
> *I know how much you like them and Hank and I talked*
> *about giving them to you on your 13th*
> > *—Love Aunt Flo and Uncle Hank*

Inside the box I found the little gold and sapphire hoop earrings Aunt Flo used to wear all the time, the ones Uncle Hank gave her when they got married.

Mom was surprised. "She hasn't been in touch for almost a year and now she sends you a gift like this? It's too much," she said.

Dad said they were too expensive. "You're just gonna lose them like you lose everything else," he said.

I put the earrings on anyway and left a long message on Aunt Flo's machine about how much I loved them and how much I missed her. This time she called back and we talked for hours.

● ● ●

Aunt Flo got married again in February of 1989, only this time she married a man with "real money," according to Dad. Arnold Smythe and Aunt Flo had a Valentine's Day wedding at a fancy yacht club not far from his house in Malibu. It took an hour and a half for us to get there. That's an hour and a half of Dad driving while swigging from a fifth of Jack Daniels and listening to his favorite Waylon Jennings cassette so loud that it was almost impossible for me to talk to Mom about why I shaved my legs even though she'd told me not to. I'd been asking her for months about shaving because I knew lots of girls who were thirteen who shaved their legs and underarms, and some who even shaved their privates. I begged Mom to let me shave and even made her have a close look at my legs one day, outside in the sunshine, but she said there wasn't enough hair on them to shave off. She told me to rub my legs with lotion.

I tried the lotion but it didn't do much to hide the hairs, and although I did my best to ignore it, I found myself thinking about it all the time. Sometimes at school I'd sneak off to the bathroom just to have a look at what was happening with my leg hairs. On the morning of the wedding, I found ten new little black hairs on my right shin. I thought about plucking them out, like I'd done to the ones on my left leg, but there wasn't time, so I used Dad's razor while I was in the bathroom. I'd watched Dad shave a few times, so I knew I was supposed to put shaving cream on my skin first, but the shaving cream can was empty so I just used water. It took forever for the bleeding to stop, and even though I put flesh-colored Band-Aids on the seven or eight places where my skin had come off, red was showing through them. Mom noticed right away. She yelled at me most of the morning. "I went to a lot of trouble and spent a lot of money on that beautiful dress you have on. Now no one is going to notice because they'll be too distracted by your bloody shin."

The outfit Mom bought for me was a bright yellow satin midi dress, complete with shoulder pads and puffed sleeves. She got it because she thought it matched the purple satin minidress she'd bought for herself. Dad was supposed to wear the tuxedo she rented for him but he didn't. Instead he wore his black jeans and cowboy boots and put a brown suit jacket on, but only after Mom insisted he wear one. Aunt Flo gave Dad a dirty look when she saw him and mentioned something about his bad dress sense and bad manners. She loved my outfit, though, said it was a nice style for me. "Not many people can wear lemon yellow as well as you. And with those beautiful earrings you look like a princess." She also liked my red headband and lip gloss, and she didn't mention my Band-Aids.

A few people did ask me about my leg, and I told them about a stray dog that had attacked me when I was taking the garbage out the night before. I think they believed me. Even if they didn't, after my second glass of champagne, I didn't care.

I was dancing by myself next to the bar when I saw Mom motion me over to the reception hall kitchen area. "You promised to help me pass out wedding cake, remember?" she said.

"Sure Mom, I'm only here to serve," I laughed.

I winked at Mom as I picked up two plates of wedding cake and tucked little forks under the cake like she suggested. I was about to walk out to the reception hall to pass them out when I heard her say, "Don't forget the napkins—and why are you so happy? Have you been drinking?"

"Just the glass of champagne Aunt Flo gave me for the toast," I lied.

Mom gave me her half-grin, eyebrows-up stare, the one she always gave me when she was upset with me, but I didn't respond. Instead, I picked up a third plate and placed it a bit higher up on my forearm and pretended I was one of the Denny's waitresses I often admired—the ones who could carry four or five plates at one time, cradling them all the way up their arms. I was doing a pretty good job passing out cake until I slipped and dropped a piece at the feet of Aunt Flo's maid of honor, Helen, and it got all over her silver shoes. While I was stooped over trying to pick up the cake, I heard Helen tell Aunt Flo that I was either drunk or a complete spastic and that I shouldn't be allowed to hand out anything.

"I'm sorry, Helen, the plate just slipped out of my hand," I said.

The next second Mom came running out from the kitchen with a dishtowel and bent down to wipe the icing from Helen's shoes. Helen told her to stop and took over cleaning her own shoes. "You should attend to your daughter. She doesn't look well," Helen said.

Mom pushed me into the ladies' room. "What's wrong with you? No one gets drunk from one little glass of champagne. You'd better not let your dad see you in this condition," she said.

"He's too wasted to notice," I replied.

"He might be, but I'm not," she said.

She made me splash water on my face and said I needed to get something in my stomach, including a cup of coffee.

● ● ●

The buffet table had so many different types of food on it that I couldn't decide what to eat, so I just stared at the chicken until Mom jerked the plate from my hand, said something about hating being a mother sometimes, and then piled as much food as she could onto it before handing it back to me and telling me to eat every last bite. I took a seat at a table occupied by a really old man who seemed to be asleep. A few seconds later, Mom walked up behind me with a cup of coffee.

"I put three sugars in it, so drink it all. I'll check on you later, but I need to get back to your dad before he drinks the bar dry," she said.

It took me a while to eat the potato salad, corn on the cob, prime rib, and roasted chicken, but I did. I also finished the half bottle of beer someone had left on the table. Aunt Flo came over to see if I was okay but she only stayed for a minute. "I've got a gorgeous new husband waiting for me and I'm gonna find out if he can dance," she squealed.

I sat and watched Arnold and Aunt Flo swirl and twirl around the dance floor for two or three songs before I took my empty plate into the kitchen and grabbed a piece of cake for myself.

That night I discovered drinking and dancing must go together, because the more people drank, the more they danced, and some of them were really bad at it. I didn't hit the dance floor until the band started playing my favorite song, "We Belong," and that's when I first met Arnold's grandkids, Tyler and Sissy.

After watching me dance alone for a few minutes, Sissy *Soul Train*–danced over to me and introduced herself. "I'm Sicily, but everyone calls me Sissy. I'm Arnold's granddaughter, and that's my brother Tyler walking out the back door."

I tried to catch a glimpse of Tyler, but there were too many people in the way. "I'm Randall," I replied.

"Really? Someone named you Randall?" she asked.

"Yeah, I think it was my dad," I replied.

"It's a great name, much better than Sissy," she said.

I didn't know if it was okay for two girls to dance together, but since no one was looking at us and no one yelled out for us to stop, I pretended she was a boy and danced away. When the band started playing "Boogie Wonderland," I showed Sissy my best version of the hustle. She got it right away, and so did a few of the other guests, and pretty soon there were about ten of us doing the coordinated steps all together.

I was having the most fun I'd had since Uncle Hank died, so I stayed and danced with Sissy until we were both exhausted and thirsty. When the band started playing a Kenny Rogers song we headed to the punch bowl to get a glass of what tasted a lot like Hawaiian punch. Sissy was the one who suggested we only fill our glasses halfway so we could top them up with the pink wine from the kitchen. She drank her glass of wine punch in a few swallows and poured another, so I did the same.

We stood next to the kitchen door waiting for the band to play a good dance song but it took so long that we had time to refill our glasses two more times with the punch and wine. We also had time to talk about our parents. I didn't want to talk or even think about my dad, but it was hard not to, especially because he was running and jumping around the dance floor doing some type of weird jig.

As my dad followed up his jig with his version of the alligator, Sissy asked, "Hey, what's with your dad? Is he wasted or what?"

"Yeah, but he's wasted a lot," I replied.

"Sorry about that. I know how it is. My dad was like that too," she said.

"Where is he now?" I asked.

"In a prison somewhere in Texas, I think. He doesn't stay in touch and Arnold thinks we're better off without him."

"How come he's in jail?" I asked.

"He ran over a woman, and since he'd been in trouble for drunk driving a few times they sent him away," she said.

I was surprised to hear this story. I thought kids weren't supposed to talk about the bad things their parents did.

"Yeah, my dad did something like that once and he had to go to jail for a weekend," I replied.

"Too bad they didn't keep him, huh?" She laughed.

I laughed too.

Sissy told me her mother hadn't been around for years.

"She lives in Idaho in a commune, or something like a commune. Anyway, she never calls or writes, but it doesn't matter." With that she changed the subject abruptly and suggested we go see what her brother was up to.

Sissy didn't seem too sad about not having a dad or a mom around. Maybe it was because she was fifteen, two years older than me, and so mature that she didn't need parents. I thought she was interesting, cute, and the coolest girl I'd ever met. She had light brown freckles all over her nose and forehead and reddish-blond, curly hair that she wore in braids tied together in a messy way with six different-colored ribbons. She also had the greenest eyes I'd ever seen, and when she smiled you could see all her teeth and they were big, white, and perfectly straight. Not like mine, which were small and yellowish and a bit crooked, but not crooked enough to get braces, according to Dad.

I followed her outside to the parking lot, where a bunch of kids about Sissy's age were hanging out. Sissy introduced me to everyone, including Tyler, who was leaning on the front of Arnold's shiny black Lincoln Town Car smoking a cigarette and drinking a beer. Tyler was even better looking than Sissy, and I was feeling so strange and so good that I thought I should kiss him, but I knew that was out of the question. I didn't want him to think I was a loser and laugh at me. Besides, I could feel Sissy tugging at my sleeve and pulling me away and I heard her whisper, "Stop making goo-goo eyes at him."

I moved to the other side of the car with her so she could talk to a girl she knew, but I didn't hear a thing they said to each other. I was too busy listening to Tyler, who was talking to a couple of guys about a car he was thinking about buying. It was hard not to interrupt and ask him questions. I wanted him to know that I knew a few things about cars, but I kept my mouth shut because he was talking about Fiats and Triumphs and I only knew about American-made cars with V8 engines because that's all my dad and his car club friends owned.

Sissy and I were just about to go back into the reception

hall when Tyler lit up a joint, took a drag, and walked right up to me. "You wanna hit?" he asked.

I wasn't sure what to do, so I looked at Sissy, and she said, "You can stay and smoke if you want, but I'm going."

I took a step back from Tyler. "No thanks," I said. All the while I was thinking about the lecture Robbie had given me at Christmas about the evils of marijuana and how it leads to heroin addiction in 99 percent of all cases. Robbie's talk was pretty scary, and although I usually didn't listen to a word he said, I knew he'd joined a few groups at his college, including the new one called D.A.R.E., Drug Abuse Resistance Education, which was all about spreading a message that drugs are dangerous. "Pushers, druggies, and potheads are ruining this country, and something needs to be done about it," Robbie had said.

I whispered in Sissy's ear that I didn't like to smoke pot. Not that I ever had—but I wasn't about to tell her that.

"I hate that shit too. Just makes ya hungry and stupid," she replied.

● ● ●

We made it back into the reception hall just in time to dance to "American Pie" and to help ourselves to a couple of half-empty beers we found by the bar. Sissy and I hiked our dresses up and did the cancan, and I thought we were looking good, but Mom didn't seem to think so. When I boogied my way over to her table, picked up her beer, and took a swig, she grabbed my arm and the beer and told me to knock it off.

"You're almost as bad as your dad," she said. "Stop that crazy dancing and go get yourself and your Dad a cup of coffee."

Dad had his head down between his arms on the table. "Is he passed out?" I asked.

He lifted his head. "Who the fuck's asking?"

We had to leave soon after that because Aunt Flo told us to. I threw up on a bush on my way to our car. Mom didn't say a thing. Probably because she was so mad at Dad for grabbing a big blonde woman and putting his face right into her cleavage and then making a loud blubbery sound. Everyone saw him do it, including the woman's husband, who was much taller and bigger than Dad. I thought he was going to punch him, but he didn't. I think he knew Dad was wasted, because he just walked him over to a table, sat him down, and said, "Next time you die, you dumb son of a bitch."

I saw and heard the whole thing, and so did Aunt Flo and Arnold. But I wasn't going to let Dad ruin my good time, so I did my best to ignore him and pretended not to hear him when he yelled, "Those are some tits, man!" Instead I put the coffee cups I'd gone to get down next to Mom and went back to the dance floor until Sissy said, "Looks like Flo and your mom are trying to carry your dad out of here."

I thought about Sissy and Tyler the entire drive home, which was hard to do because Dad wouldn't let Mom drive and he was all over the road. Sissy and Tyler were the luckiest kids I'd ever met. They didn't have parents telling them what to do all the time and they both seemed so grown up. Sissy said they went to private boarding schools and spent holidays and every other weekend with Arnold.

"I like Flo. She's got a colorful aura and good energy around her," Sissy had said. She'd also said she wasn't planning to get to know Flo too well because she was wife number five, and Arnold's last wife had only moved out of the Malibu house a few months ago. "Tyler and I are still pretty pissed off about it. We liked wife number four a lot."

● ● ●

The day after the wedding, I woke up with a horrible headache, and so thirsty I drank four glasses of milk. I also took a couple of aspirin and decided to make breakfast, as I'd read an article in one of Mom's magazines about hangovers and it said eating and drinking water is the best thing to do.

I knocked on my parents' bedroom door at noon to ask if they wanted some of the pancakes and scrambled eggs I'd made. "Can you bring us some coffee and an ashtray? Make your dad's coffee a special one, please. He's not feeling too good," Mom said.

I put a little half and half in Mom's and two shots of Wild Turkey in Dad's and put both cups on a serving tray with a pancake for Mom.

I sat down on the bed next to Mom and told her how much I liked Arnold and Sissy and Tyler and how much fun the wedding was. "It was the best time I've ever had," I said.

"I thought it was a beautiful service, and the food was delicious. I even liked Arnold's black-and-white-checkered tuxedo," Mom said.

"I liked it too. Almost as much as I liked Sissy's lavender poncho dress," I replied.

"Arnold will be good for Flo. He certainly is good looking enough for her. He's got the *Miami Vice* style down perfectly," Mom said, half giggling.

Right about then Dad sat up, coughed a few times, took a big drink of his coffee and then lit a cigarette. "Don't get too friendly with them, girls. Arnold's too young for Flo and he's gonna get sick of her pretty soon. Another fucking fancy-pants, pot-smoking, draft-dodging liberal with a trust fund. He'll never go the distance," he said.

Mom rolled her eyes at me and I rolled mine right back.

The more I thought about it, the more I wanted to be like Sissy and my mom. I wanted people to notice me the way they noticed them. They were both cute and they both had big boobs. I thought I could probably find a way to become cute, but without big boobs I couldn't imagine getting a boyfriend or having men whistle at me when I walked down the street or hand me a business card in an elevator the way a man did to Mom when we were out shopping for dresses to wear to Aunt Flo's wedding. Mom smiled real sneaky-like at that man and he said softly that he thought she was the best-looking broad he'd seen in a long time.

"How about I make you happy for the next forty minutes," he whispered in her ear.

"Only forty, huh?" Mom laughed as she grabbed my hand and pulled me out of the elevator.

I didn't know what he was talking about, but Mom obviously did because she smiled at him and put his card in her coat pocket before the elevator doors closed. After that she seemed to transform into the happiest woman alive, and we spent the rest of the day together shopping and laughing. She even bought me lunch at a nice cafe and let me order a large hot fudge sundae instead of a sandwich. I realized, as I watched her read the business card and sip her ice tea, that our great day was made possible because some strange man said a few strange things to her.

I made a plan. I bought a plain Jane–style white cotton bra at the Goodwill store for a dollar. (I wasn't about to buy a lacey thing like the one Reverend Bob made me try on in his car.) It was one of those push-up bras with a couple pieces of what felt like coat hanger wire sewn in. I thought if I started wearing it, it might send a signal to my body to fill it up. Until then I thought it would be okay to put balled-up toilet paper in the bra cups to keep them from looking all wrinkled under my shirt.

I wore my new bra to school right after spring break, and everyone mentioned my new, mature look. When my friend Katie saw me she said, "Holy shitballs, what the hell happened to you?" and then tears started rolling down her face. I didn't ask her why she was crying because I figured she was just jealous. She so wanted to beat me at becoming a woman and really thought she was going to start her period any day. It was all she talked about. She'd been carrying a schoolbag around since the beginning of eighth grade that contained just about every type of tampon and pad you could ever imagine. She'd often go into the girls' bathroom when other girls were in there and rummage through her bag, pulling out a tampon or pad and announcing something stupid like "The monthly uglies are with me again" before disappearing into a stall.

Earlier in the year she'd even convinced me to try a tampon on for size, just so I would know what to do when the time came. I went into a bathroom stall with one of her tampons and she stood outside the door and told me what to do. I told her I didn't need her help because I'd read the Tampax instructions leaflet at least a million times. But I hadn't really read them; I'd only looked at the pictures and wondered if the map was accurate and whether I had all those things inside me. I got the whole thing wrong and didn't pull out the cardboard inserter, and boy was it painful when I walked. Katie insisted it would get better and told me to wear it through gym class. But after the first cartwheel I was pretty sure I was going to die from the pain and had to get a bathroom pass from Mr. Ronald, who asked if I was okay. It took me five minutes to dig the tampon and cardboard wrapper out of me. I was sore for days, and pretty mad at Katie for making me do it in the first place.

So I wasn't really concerned about Katie being upset with me and my new boobs, but I couldn't take her crying about it, either, so I decided I'd tell her the truth. This was a big mistake, because later in the day I got to the cafeteria just in time to overhear her tell the best-looking boy in our school to have a look at my chest and tell her if he thought my boobs were lopsided or not. I gave her my "hate you" look and then had a quick look down to discover she was right: the wad of pink toilet paper I'd stuffed into the left bra cup had slipped out and crawled all the way up to my neck. I was going to have to find an alternative to toilet paper.

I used pantyhose for the next two weeks, until I had a dentist's appointment that gave me a brilliant idea. In the waiting room, I noticed a woman pulling a large white cotton pad from a small box she had in a diaper bag. She put the pad in her bra after she fed her baby. After a good ten minutes of staring at her to make sure the pad wasn't visible through her shirt, I took note of the box and decided I'd have a look for those pads the next time I was at the store. I figured a pad like that would be better than toilet paper because it wouldn't get loose and crawl up. I went shopping with Mom the next day, and after I ate a Snickers bar and hid the wrapper behind a box of Apple Jacks, I headed for the baby supply aisle to see if they carried nursing pads.

I discovered the store carried a variety of pads, so I picked the smallest box because I thought I could easily hide it under other things in the shopping cart. I was used to hiding small things under bigger items, but the box was a bit larger than the things I usually hid, so I grabbed a twelve-roll pack of toilet paper instead of the four-roll pack Mom had requested, and then I got an extra loaf of bread. With these two items placed on top of the nursing pad box I was sure no one would notice. But someone did. The woman stocking the shelf with baby food looked at me like I was up to something and I thought she was going to tell me to put them back, but she didn't. After walking up and down the aisle for a few minutes, thinking about what I should do, I decided not to risk Mom or anyone else catching me with a box of nursing pads, so I put the box under my shirt, parked the cart in a safe place, and headed for the bathroom.

It took me a while to get all twelve nursing pads into my bra, six on each side, and I was a little concerned that my boobs looked noticeably larger than usual, but I was willing to take my chances. I tore the box up into the smallest pieces I could and flushed them down the toilet. It took a few flushes to get it all down but I did it.

The additional padding made my Goodwill bra feel tight, almost too tight to breathe, so I had to take short little inhales and exhales as I headed to the makeup aisle to get a few new nail polishes. I'd just started on my way to find Mom when I almost ran the cart into my half-sister, Tammy, although I didn't recognize her at first because of her real short, blond hair. I was so surprised and happy to see her that I forgot about my padded bra until she hugged me.

I could tell from the look on Tammy's face that she knew something was up, but she didn't make a big deal about it. She just smiled and said, "Nice developments, sister."

I blushed and said, "They're not real, ya know."

"I figured that out," she joked as she looked over the

contents of my grocery cart. "How are you gonna get out of here with three six-packs of Miller Lite?" she asked.

"Those are Mom's. She's getting something from the butcher," I said.

She turned her attention to the five bottles of nail polish I'd put out on top of the bread.

"I'm looking for the right color for my skin tone," I explained. "Mom's *Cosmo* says women with blue undertones look best with pinkish purples, and not so good with melons or orange shades, and since I can't tell what my undertone is, I'm getting a few different colors to try." I held my hands out so that she could see my glue-on nails.

"A rainbow of nails might be a good idea for me, too," she said, laughing.

It was about then that I saw Mom walking up the aisle struggling to carry something wrapped in butcher paper. My sister practically sprinted to help her with what turned out to be a leg of ham Mom had mistakenly ordered the week before and was too embarrassed to tell the butcher she'd meant to order a ham hock, not a ham leg. Mom said thanks as they dropped the ham into the shopping cart.

"Aren't you going to introduce me to your friend?" Mom said and then, looking at Tammy more closely, whispered, "Oh, you're the schoolteacher, aren't you?"

My sister smiled and said, "Yes."

No one said anything for the longest time, and then Mom said we had to go and started walking toward the checkout line. I wanted to stay and talk to my sister, but she said she had to go too. "Bye, Tammy!" I yelled out as I ran after Mom.

Mom didn't say anything at the checkout stand. She didn't even answer when the checker asked her if she wanted the ham in a double bag, so I said, "Yes, please." I thought Mom would notice and say something about the nail polishes or the three bottles of maple extract and two packs of toothpicks I'd put in the cart earlier, but she didn't. She didn't even notice my overstuffed bra; she just looked straight ahead, wrote a check, and handed it to the checker without saying a word. She walked like a robot all the way to the car.

I followed her with the cart. When we got to the car, I watched her unlock the door, get in, and pour the contents of her purse out on the passenger seat. I had to knock on her window three times to get her to hit the trunk release button, and when I did I could see she had two small yellow pills in her hand, the new ones she'd recently got from her doctor. With the car trunk open I was able to take the nursing pads out of my bra without Mom, or anyone else, noticing. I put them in one of the shopping bags and took a few deep breaths. I took my time moving the grocery bags from the cart to the trunk and rearranged them a few times to kill time, hoping Mom would snap out of her weird mood and drive us home.

By the time I climbed into the passenger seat, she was leaning on the steering wheel, crying and mumbling some pretty nasty things about Dad. A few minutes later her hiccups started, and that seemed to make her mad and sad at the same time. We stayed parked long enough for me to finish an entire bag of Fritos and a half a bag of Cheetos, and for her to finish the two beers she made me get from the trunk.

She guzzled those beers down so fast it made her burp about ten times. I couldn't help but laugh about that, and she started laughing too. It went on for a few minutes, and then she suddenly stopped giggling and asked me if I had a cigarette. She hadn't smoked for years, and while I'd gone through a phase where I helped myself to Dad's Pall Malls, I hadn't smoked in months.

"I don't have any cigarettes Mom, I don't smoke," I said.

"Sure you don't. I've seen both you and Robbie smoke, so don't give me that story. I don't think I'll be able to drive home without a cigarette. In fact, I'm sure of it," she said.

She opened her door and, using it as a support, she stood up and steadied herself for a few seconds before she headed to the store's front door, returning a few minutes later with three packs of Winstons and a lighter. She coughed and cried her way through her cigarette and didn't start the engine until she'd finished the first one and lit a second.

I was going to say something about her raccoon face—the smeared and runny eyeliner and mascara—before she went into the store to get cigarettes, but I didn't because it had only been a few weeks since she'd had a meltdown about Genie bringing her car to our house for Dad to fix. I didn't want to make it worse. Once we were driving, I saw that her make-up had run completely down her cheeks but pretended I hadn't noticed because she wasn't driving very well. I knew if she tried to clean her face we'd likely end up in a bad accident.

After what seemed like a week we pulled into our driveway and Mom drove right into the back bumper of Dad's truck.

"Take that, you asshole," she said under her breath.

She told me to carry the groceries in because she was too tired and needed a nap. I put the groceries away, shoved the bra pads in my pockets, stuck the ham in the freezer, took a couple of wine coolers from the fridge, and went to my room to watch TV.

CHAPTER 11

Aunt Flo seemed happy with Arnold and excited about moving from her cottage house into his Malibu beach house. She called me one night, a few days after the wedding, to talk. "Did you have fun? Aren't Sissy and Tyler great? What do you think about my new dreamboat husband?' she asked.

"I liked everything about the wedding, especially the band, and I'm sorry I dropped cake on Helen's shoes," I said.

"Seems like you may have had a bit too much champagne," Aunt Flo replied.

"I guess I did. But I really like it."

"Try not to like it too much," she said before she told me she had to hang up because Arnold wanted her to swim with him.

I couldn't believe Aunt Flo had married someone who looked so much like a movie star. He wasn't an actor, though; Arnold was an illustrator, cartoonist, and animator who worked for a movie studio, it turned out. His houses, one in Malibu and one in Half Moon Bay, were filled with his paintings and posters. I heard him tell Dad, in the wedding reception line, that painting had never made him a cent; what brought in the big money were his original cartoon characters. Some were used in films, TV shows, and commercials. Although his most famous characters weren't well known in America, they were huge in Japan.

Aunt Flo had let Uncle Bill move into her house because he promised to repair the porch, take care of the cats, keep the place in good shape, and pay the property taxes. "You can go over anytime you want to visit the cats or to swim with Mayadelsa," she told me.

One hot Saturday afternoon in March, four weeks after the wedding, I asked Mom to drop me off at Aunt Flo's cottage on her way to visit Olive. She started crying and said, "You know that bitch Genie moved in there with your Uncle Bill."

"Oh," I replied.

I hardly ever saw Mom upset to the point of pulling her hair out, so I decided I wouldn't go over to Aunt Flo's cottage again until the "bitch" moved out. Besides, Arnold's beach house was pretty nice. It had a huge gate at the entrance that opened onto a long driveway, and a manicured garden with large statues of naked men and women in every corner. The house had sixteen rooms, including four bathrooms and a game room. There was a groundskeeper and a part-time cook who made orange cinnamon scones and a chocolate pie that tasted just like a candy bar. Even though the house was on the beach, it had a swimming pool shaped like a kidney bean and made from black-and-white marble. But swimming in the bean-shaped pool wasn't anything like swimming with Mayadelsa.

Aunt Flo said the only problem with the Malibu house was that it was too far away from the stores she liked; and since Arnold wasn't happy to drive her and wait in the parking lot like Uncle Hank used to, he bought her a brand-new automatic Mercedes Benz convertible for a wedding present. Aunt Flo still wasn't very good at driving, and she still refused to wear a seat belt, but she managed to get around okay.

It only took a few weeks of living with Arnold before Aunt Flo was transformed into a new person, someone seemingly younger and definitely friendlier than before. She started exercising with a guy she hired to walk with her, and to make her do sit-ups and lift weights. She stopped listening to show tunes and started listening to Paula Abdul and Madonna. She had her hair cut in a shag style, dyed it dark brown, and began to wear clothes similar to Sissy's—kind of hippie-like.

Music, exercise, and shopping became her new hobbies. She began phoning our house regularly on Thursdays to see if I wanted to go shopping with her. I always said yes and I always thought the long drive to pick me up was a big deal, but she didn't. We'd shop for hours and I'd often arrive back home with bags full of stuff that Mom thought was unnecessary or extravagant, like the leather fringe poncho and beaded moccasin boots Aunt Flo bought for me. Mom told me I had to return them, but I never did.

I liked the new Aunt Flo, and I loved her new home. I also missed Uncle Hank, but I only talked about him if she mentioned him first because I didn't want to make her sad. Aunt Flo said I was welcome at her new home any time. So just after school got out in June, a few days after I turned fourteen, I decided to stay with Aunt Flo rather than drive to a car convention in Texas with Mom and Dad. They dropped me off at the bus station a couple of hours before my bus was due to leave because they were eager to get on the road before the traffic got bad. Mom got out of the car with me and walked me to the ticket counter. "Here's some bus money and sixty dollars for you. Try to make it last, okay?" she said.

"Thanks, Mom, I'll make it last, I promise," I replied.

She kissed me good-bye before she got back into Dad's newly rebuilt, cherry red Mustang. I tried to get Dad's attention so I could say good-bye, but he was busy filling his flask from a bottle of bourbon and didn't look up.

After I bought my bus ticket, I found a seat on an empty bench outside the station and read the *Life* magazine someone had left behind. "Mind if I sit down?" I heard.

I looked up to see a strange-looking guy about my brother's age holding a stuffed unicorn under his arm. I scooted as far as I could to the other end of the bench. "Sure," I said.

I went back to reading, but he started asking me questions and wouldn't leave me alone, pestering me to give him ten dollars for a few pills he was selling.

"I spent all my cash on this present for my sister," he said, holding up the unicorn. "She's got it real bad and I'm trying to get to her place in Chicago before she kicks it."

I was sort of curious about his sister but decided not to ask any questions.

"Let me see the pills," I said.

He reached into his pocket, took out a plastic bag, opened it, and poured a few pills into his hand. I recognized them straight away as the same ones Mom kept on her dresser—the ones she used to give me small pieces of when I was little and couldn't sleep. I helped myself to them sometimes now; they made me feel good. But I couldn't take very many or she'd notice.

"I'll give you twenty dollars for twenty of them," I said.

"Sure thing," he said, and he counted out twenty pills and put them in my hand. I gave him a twenty-dollar bill and watched him stuff it in his shirt pocket and walk away.

I broke off a piece of one pill, swallowed it, and put the others in an empty Sucrets tin that had been sitting on top of the *Life* magazine. Then I shoved the tin deep down into the bottom of my bag.

About twenty minutes later I felt more relaxed than I had in months and was grateful that guy had shown up out of nowhere.

Once I got on the bus, I settled in for the ride. I wasn't expecting it to take more than four hours to get from Huntington Beach to Malibu, but it did. I'd never taken such a long bus ride before, and I didn't know about the three transfers until the first bus driver told me how I'd have to get off at the station in downtown LA and catch another bus west to another station to catch a third bus that would drop me off not far from Malibu.

Aunt Flo was waiting for me at the last bus stop. She

looked worried when she got out of the car. "I've been here for an hour," she said. "I thought something had happened to you."

"No, nothing much happened, but it takes a few buses to get here," I replied.

It was a ten-minute drive to her Malibu house. When we got there, I was surprised to see Sissy and Tyler walking down the stairs. I'd just put my bag down in the foyer when I heard Tyler say, "Hey everyone, the dancing girl has arrived."

My face turned red, my stomach did a complete flip, and when I tried to laugh nothing came out. I knew he was teasing me, and I liked it, but I wasn't sure how to respond, so I didn't look at him or say anything. I just kicked my bag to the side so that Sissy wouldn't trip over it as she reached in to give me a hug.

"We're gonna have a great summer," she said.

"I really like your hair, Sissy, how'd you get it so straight?" I asked.

"Flo has a little iron and she helped me take out the curls this morning."

I liked her long, straight hairstyle almost as much as I liked the braids she'd worn at the wedding. Sissy shook her head, turned completely around, and said, "It's grown a lot since you last saw it, hasn't it? Looks like you've been growing it out."

"I'm trying to, but it doesn't seem to grow very fast," I replied.

She reached over and tucked a piece of my hair behind my right ear. "It would look much better with a side part and some blond streaks."

"Blond streaks? My mom will have a total spaz attack if I do that," I said.

"She won't care, probably won't even notice. But then again, my mom's not around, so what do I know?"

"Just do whatever Sissy says," Tyler yelled out to me as he headed out the front door. "It will make your life easier."

Aunt Flo nodded her head in agreement and laughed.

I'd never thought much about changing my hair. I'd always worn it in a bob, just past my chin and parted in the middle, because Mom and Ken told me to. But I was willing to spend my first Saturday at Aunt Flo's Malibu home sitting as still as possible while Sissy gave me a new hairstyle. Not because I wanted one, but because I wanted her to like me.

"It'll hurt a little bit, but it's gonna be worth it, I promise," she said.

I tried not to complain about the pain as she pulled a tight rubber cap down over my head and used a crochet hook to pull strands of my hair through little holes, but I did say something about my head being on fire after she spread on a white paste that was supposed to turn those pulled pieces of brown hair blond.

I didn't think it was worth it at all. It took about three days for my head to feel better, and the strands of my hair she pulled out of the cap holes were too blond, almost white.

"I look like a zebra," I told her once she'd finished.

"No you don't. You look great—exactly what I was after," Sissy said.

It wasn't until Aunt Flo told me how beautiful I looked that I started to like it.

"Now about your makeup," Sissy said over breakfast the next day.

"I'm not allowed to wear any until I'm sixteen," I confessed.

"If you don't tell anyone, I won't. Besides, wearing a little foundation and concealer to cover up zits really can't be classified as wearing makeup."

That seemed like a good explanation, and I suddenly felt better about my sneaking into Mom's bathroom for the past few months to use her face powder.

Aunt Flo nodded her head in agreement with her. "Concealer is not makeup, it's a facial necessity. Are you still using Noxzema?" she asked.

"No. My mom won't buy it. She says it's awful, so I use Ivory soap."

Aunt Flo sighed and patted my head. Then she left

the kitchen and returned a few minutes later with twenty-five dollars and two coupons for Max Factor products. She handed the money to Sissy. "I just cut these coupons out of the newspaper yesterday. Why don't you two walk down to the drug store and get a few things? Don't forget the awful Noxzema," she added, laughing.

I said thank you to Aunt Flo about ten times before Sissy and I left for the store. I felt special that day, like I was something important, a project worthy of Sissy's time and Aunt Flo's money.

● ● ●

When Sissy and I got back from the drugstore with a whole bunch of stuff for my face, she invited me into her room to show me how to apply it all. "I have a big mirror in my room for one reason: so I can see what I'm doing," Sissy said.

It was when she was brushing the purple eye shadow onto my eyelids that she told me she was a witch. "I'm not an evil or dark witch. I'm a white witch, the type who helps people, animals, and other living things. Do you know anything about witches?"

"Only a little bit from *The Wizard of Oz*," I said.

She rolled her eyes, laughed, and said, "Perfect, a blank canvas makes the best student."

Sissy could read tarot cards. She owned three decks, all of them with different designs and shapes. She also had an old, round oak table in the corner of her room that she used as an altar to give praise and thanks to the Goddess. The altar had all kinds of stuff on it, including two rainbow-colored candles, photos of her friends (and enemies), and twelve strands of her brother's hair, seashells, driftwood, and a bunch of dried sage tied with twine. She lit her sage stick every time she entered her room—for "cleansing and purification purposes," she said.

"That stuff smells like burning grass," I said.

"More like burning pot," she replied.

She must have been right about that because one day when

I was in her room, learning to use a sage stick, Arnold walked in and asked, "Can you spare a doobie for your old grandpa?"

He seemed surprised when she replied that it was sage, not pot. I was surprised to hear that he smoked pot.

I asked Sissy at least a hundred questions about witchcraft and magic before she finally said, "You should become my student. You're someone who could really benefit from being empowered with the wisdom of the crone."

That sounded good to me, even though I had no idea what a crone was and didn't understand anything she said about witches or wisdom. I was just so happy about the idea of becoming something interesting that I told her I'd do whatever she asked.

My first lesson was learning numerology. Sissy handed me three books and told me I had a week to read through them. "If you pray to the Goddess for guidance, you won't have a problem figuring it out," she said.

All the number stuff was hard for me to understand, but I was determined to learn it. I spent two days in my room reading and working out my parents', Aunt Flo's, Arnold's, Tyler's, and my own numerological life path.

When I presented Sissy with what I'd figured out a week later, she was surprised but happy. "I didn't think you'd catch on so quick, but you proved me wrong." She gave me an orange altar cloth with a big yellow star in the middle of it, and talked to me about the waxing and waning moon as she shuffled a deck of tarot cards. "Women's bodies are always waxing and waning, just like the moon. The moon has no light of its own; it only reflects from the source of all the world's power, the sun."

"How do you know these things?" I asked.

"An old witch taught me a long time ago. She was from Ireland, and she took care of Tyler and me from the time we were babies until I was twelve and our mom left with her massage teacher for Idaho and our dad went to prison. She's the one who taught me about Pagans. They're people who worship the moon, sun, and Mother Earth rather than a man from the Bible."

I found it all hard to swallow at first. It didn't sound like anything Uncle Hank had taught me about God. But the more I thought about it, the more I liked the idea of God being a woman. It certainly made more sense than an old guy living high in the clouds and sending people to burn in hell for talking back to their parents or stealing a candy bar.

● ● ●

A couple of days after I became her official student, Sissy took me out to a clearing near the beach to teach me how to "bless clouds away." It was a sunny day with a few fluffy clouds floating high in a very blue sky. We put a beach blanket on a big sand dune and lay down to look at the clouds. She picked out a medium-size cloud for me to focus on. "See that one next to the big ribbon cloud, the one that looks like a beach ball with rabbit ears? That's yours. Now squint your eyes so that you can barely see, and in your mind make a large circle of gold and purple light and send it to your cloud. Ask your cloud, in a very nice way, to go away. Say something like this: 'Go away, go away, you needn't stay, we'll see you again another day.'"

It took a while for me to focus my colors on the cloud but I finally did it. "Okay Sissy, I'm doing it," I said.

"I'll time it," she replied.

It only took three minutes for my cloud to disappear. I was thrilled as I watched it come apart, and was delighted to learn I could do something magical. I stayed and made other clouds disappear. I only stopped when Tyler arrived with six of his friends. He had his guitar, and his friends were carrying a few lawn chairs and a keg of beer.

Tyler was looking better than ever. I could hardly bring myself to look at him if he was looking at me, but when he wasn't, I couldn't do anything but look at him. I wanted him to like me, and I'd been keeping track of things Sissy said about him and things I observed. He was left-handed, tied his shoes one loop over another, had two middle names (Whitmore and Julius), and, according to my numerology book, was an old soul (the total of his birth date was twenty-two). I even drew an illustration of him wearing his wiener on the right side of his pants, after Sissy made me look at a picture of a naked guy one day and then told me that if a man wears his penis on the left side it means he wants to do it with another man.

Tyler didn't do much all day except play his guitar and sing. His singing voice was much higher than his talking voice, and the first time I heard him I thought he was joking around and trying to sound like a woman or one of the Bee Gees. According to Sissy, Tyler wanted to be a musician more than anything and had already written a bunch of songs. He was even planning to record an album. "Arnold has friends in the music business and he got Tyler a meeting with a famous record producer," Sissy said.

When Tyler and his friends arrived at our cloud-blessing spot, Sissy wasn't happy. "Why can't you find your own place, Tyler?" she said.

"Free country, sister," Tyler replied.

Sissy wanted to leave, so I got up to go back to the house with her. "Hey, no need to run off, dancing girl," Tyler said.

"You can stay if you want, Randall. I've got better things to do," Sissy said.

When I told Sissy I was staying, she took off back to the house in a huff. I sat down next to Tyler and grabbed the beer he offered me. Then I drank it down pretty quick. All of Tyler's friends played the guitar. One of them offered to teach me, but I'd bitten my nails all the way to the skin the day before and they looked bad, so I said no. About an hour into their jam session, Tyler said he wanted us to hear his new song, even though it wasn't finished and he didn't have any lyrics for it. He played it on his guitar and I loved it. It sounded a little bit like Neil Young's "Old Man," only with an upbeat tempo.

I thought about Tyler's song all night, and wrote a few lyrics I thought might suit his music. The more I thought about his song, the more I was sure I could come up with the perfect words to match it, but I needed to hear it again.

· · ·

When I saw Tyler out on the back lawn with his guitar the next day, I went out to ask if he'd play the song into a cassette recorder I'd borrowed from Sissy. When he finished he told me about his voice lessons and that he might be getting a recording contract with a big company. It sounded so exciting, and he was so cool, that when he showed me his bag of pot and asked if I'd ever smoked before I lied and said yes. I'd never seen that much pot before. He pushed the bag into my face and said, "Here, smell it. This is good shit, you're gonna be smooth in ten."

I watched him roll a joint. "You wanna learn how to do this?" he asked.

"Not really," I replied.

"Ya know, there's nothing wrong with smoking pot. It's completely natural, and way better than smoking cigarettes."

I almost told Tyler what Robbie had said about people who smoked pot, but I didn't because I didn't want to ruin my chances with him. He put the burning joint right up to my mouth and insisted I take a puff. I didn't want to, but I did. I didn't inhale very hard, but it still burned my mouth and throat and made me cough. When I finished coughing he handed me the joint again, "One toke is never enough. Take a big puff and hold it in," he said.

I took a little puff and quickly handed it back to him. He smoked it until it was so small it barely fit between his fingers. I sat quietly and waited for something to happen—for some great feeling to arrive, like he'd promised it would. But nothing happened, and after watching Tyler sit still, like he was spaced out, for a few minutes, I got up and went into the house because I was hungry and I knew there were Oreo cookies in the kitchen.

I got a big lecture from Sissy that night about what a good student of the craft would and would not do. Basically she told me that I had to do whatever she asked whenever she asked it. "And stay away from my brother. He's seventeen. He's too old for you!"

It was a few days later that Sissy and I attended a midnight ceremony celebrating the first day of summer. She told me all about it when I agreed to become her student. Every June 21 an old hippie couple who had a huge farmhouse just down the beach from Arnold's place held a party to help guide in the new season—the "Solstice," Sissy called it.

"We're going to have a great time, and you'll be amazed by the drawing down of the moon circle dance. At least, I was the first time I did it," she said.

"What kind of dance is it?" I asked.

"The kind where everyone's happy," she replied.

● ● ●

Sissy packed a bag of stuff to take to the Solstice party, including a broom, a bag of salt, and four candles.

"Here, take your sweatshirt off and put this on," she said as she handed me a floor-length purple velvet robe that was too small for me and a head wreath of fresh flowers she'd made earlier in the day from an arrangement Aunt Flo had put on the dining room table the night before. Sissy put on a blue and pink robe. It fit her perfectly, and she looked great.

I felt silly walking down the beach path with a wizard robe on, but it didn't seem to bother Sissy one bit. And I don't know what I was expecting to find at the Solstice party, but it sure wasn't thirty adults, some of whom were naked and covered from head to toe with body paint, dancing around a bonfire and singing a song about coming from the goddess. Another group played the drums and howled. I stood way back from the huge bonfire and stared at them. It seemed to me I was living in a *National Geographic* magazine, and I felt scared.

"Let's go join them," Sissy said.

"Do we have to? They look so weird."

"Yes, you have to, it's part of the initiation—*so be it!*" Sissy yelled as she threw off her robe to display a little bikini made from sea grass. She pulled my robe off and pushed me toward the bonfire. Someone pulled me into the dance circle and I was glad I'd worn jeans and a T-shirt under my robe because I wouldn't want anyone to see me naked.

It only took ten or fifteen minutes of moving around the fire with the others before I began to feel okay about dancing with the naked strangers. I danced with them for a long time before a large woman with a large voice yelled out for everyone to stop dancing and give a gift. That's when everyone in the circle dropped to their knees and put their hands on the ground.

I did it too but I didn't know why. "What are we doing, Sissy?" I asked.

"We're giving the energy of our circle dance to the Goddess, to Mother Earth," she said.

When they finished doing the gift-giving thing most of them stood up and began to hug each other. I stood up too. I was sweaty and out of breath, but Sissy was radiant and kissing people, so I tried my best to imitate her and kissed the people she kissed. But only on the cheeks, until I saw Tyler. I hadn't noticed him until he was in front of me, putting his mouth on mine. Tyler's kiss made my legs weak and my insides feel like Jell-O. I thought I should move away, do something to stop it, but I didn't want to. I felt dizzy so I stepped back until I was away from the fire and away from the others. Tyler followed and he didn't seem to notice or care that we were suddenly falling to the ground. We rolled onto the ground still kissing, and I didn't stop kissing first.

Sissy and I left the Solstice celebration around 2 a.m., and she teased me the entire walk home about the red rash around my mouth, calling it a "passion rash." When we got home, she squeezed a little juice from the leaf of a big aloe vera plant she kept on the windowsill in her bedroom and smeared it on the rash, telling me it would help it fade.

● ● ●

For the next few days I tried to do whatever Sissy said and I stayed away from Tyler. But one morning, about a week after the Solstice celebration, Tyler caught me watching him brush his teeth from the hallway. He was getting ready to go into the city with Arnold for a meeting about college, and he looked back at me from his mirror. It was too late for me to pretend I was just walking by, so I froze and stared back at him. He smiled but didn't turn around, and didn't say a word until he spit the toothpaste out. As he held his brush under the water tap, he said, "Why are you always looking at me in that weird way?"

"I don't know. When I'm not looking at you, I'm thinking about you," I said.

"Good, I like that about you. I like a girl who knows what she likes. How about we meet tonight behind the house at eleven o'clock and take a little walk down the beach?"

"Should I invite Sissy? I asked.

"Hell no, that's like inviting the cops. I wouldn't mention it to her if I were you."

I nodded in agreement and went downstairs for breakfast. I was so happy I felt like I was floating. I spent the rest of the day thinking about Tyler and our date that night.

It took me hours to get ready. I took two showers, painted my toenails, put my new violet eye shadow on, shaved my legs, and sprayed myself from neck to knees with some perfume called No. 19 that I found in Aunt Flo's room. I also used her sewing machine to make myself a halter top. I created the pattern myself using a picture of a similar top I found in a *Cosmo* magazine. I had to use a piece of yellow gingham material I found in the laundry room because I didn't have time to walk down to the fabric store, but it turned out pretty good. I even included darts in it because the magazine article said that was one of the best ways to create the illusion of having a full bust.

I had to tell Sissy about my plan to meet Tyler because she wouldn't stop asking me what I was up to.

"You shouldn't go anywhere with Tyler until I read your cards," she said. "They'll tell you what the real story is."

We went to her room and she closed the curtains and lit her altar candles and some incense. Sitting on the floor, she motioned for me to sit cross-legged facing her. She said a

Goddess prayer and shuffled the cards. "Here, take them and shuffle them, but only three times," she said.

"Why only three?" I asked.

"I don't know for sure, but that's what I was taught," she replied.

Sissy took the deck of cards from my hand, divided them into three piles, and told me to choose one.

The first card was the fool; the second was the ten of swords; the third was the prince of swords; the fourth was the lovers; the fifth was the three of swords. Sissy stopped after the fifth card and said, "The message here is clear. You shouldn't go. It will be a romantic disaster, ending in despair for you."

"I don't believe it, Sissy. And even if it's true, I don't care about having a romantic disaster with the best-looking boy I've ever seen."

I knew deep down that my night with Tyler was going to be great, and I was going to go no matter what Sissy or the cards said.

"He's nothing special. He's my brother and I love him, but he's a stoner and a user. Maybe you should wait until school starts and find a boyfriend your age, huh?"

"He's only three years, two months, and six days older than me, Sissy," I said.

"Oh well, it's settled then. Blessed be." Sissy sighed.

Before I left her room she handed me a feather and anointed me with the special Goddess oil she told me she'd gotten from a head shop in Berkeley. "This might protect you from harm or it might not," she whispered.

● ● ●

Tyler was waiting for me at the beach, sitting on a small tree stump smoking a joint. He asked me how old I was and I told him I was fourteen and had been for a couple of weeks. "Cool," he said as he tried to hand me the joint he'd been puffing on.

I didn't take it. "I don't like the smell and I don't feel like being stoned," I said.

He stood up and took a big puff from the joint. Then he put his arms out like he was going to hug me. He put his hand on the back of my head and held me tight as he kissed me so hard I could feel his teeth on my teeth, all the while blowing pot smoke from his mouth into mine. I tried not to inhale, and I tried harder to push him away, but he was too strong. When he finally let go, I screamed, "Why'd you do that?"

"Why not?" he replied.

I thought maybe Sissy was right.

"I'd better get back to the house," I said.

He took another drag of the joint and said, "I kind of knew you were gonna be a cock tease."

I don't know if it was what he said or the way he said it, but I decided I didn't want to be a cock tease. I wanted him to like me, to be my boyfriend, so I sat down next to him. This time when he held up the joint and motioned for me to take it from him I took a drag and held the smoke in like he told me to. It burned my throat and made me cough so hard I had to relieve my throat fast. I drank almost all of Tyler's beer. He laughed at me, and his laughing made me laugh and I couldn't stop.

Somehow during our laughing session Tyler got his clothes off and was doing his best to get mine off too. He wanted to go for a swim. It was cold and dark and I felt like I was floating out of my body and needed to lie down, but I didn't want to come across like a little kid, so I took off my shorts, my new top, and my underwear and folded them nicely before I sat them down next to the beach path and followed him down to the shore. I was grateful it was a cloudy night and that there wasn't much moonlight because I didn't feel very good about being naked.

Tyler ran and dove into a big wave. I followed him but the water was too cold for me and I could only stand in the waves covering my chest with my arms and watching Tyler swim. "Dive in!" he yelled.

I couldn't, and I started to wonder what kind of make-out session we could possibly have in the freezing water with waves hitting us hard enough to knock us over. The good feeling I'd gotten from the pot disappeared, and I turned around and headed up to the beach to get my clothes.

I was about twenty feet from where I'd left my clothes when I noticed a shadow of a person and thought Sissy had come down to the beach to spy on us. I was wrong, it was Arnold, and he was standing in the pathway holding my clothes in one hand and a bottle of whiskey in the other. I could tell by the way he was swaying that he was drunk.

"Can I have my clothes please?" I asked.

"Oh, are these yours?" he said, laughing.

"Give them to me," I demanded.

He chuckled before taking a swig of whiskey and moving a couple of steps closer to me. Close enough for me to catch a whiff of his booze breath. I adjusted my right hand and arm to make sure it was covering my boobs and spread the fingers of my left hand over my crotch. "Can I please have my clothes?" I begged.

I was getting more scared and embarrassed as the minutes passed, so I decided to run and grab my clothes out of his hand. As I got closer to Arnold he put my clothes up to his face and said, "They smell like you—like a little bit of trouble," and then lifted his hand and my clothes over his head. "Would you like a drink?" he asked.

"No, and can I have my clothes, please!" I yelled.

"Girls like you are poison for men like me," he said.

I couldn't go anywhere or do anything, so I closed my eyes and begged him to give me my clothes. When I heard his zipper open, my knees went weak and my heart dropped. "Stop crying, I'm not gonna touch you. I just want to have a look, so move your hands away from your pussy, will ya?" he said.

Suddenly, and without really wanting to, I heard my own voice yell out, "Okay, okay, but give me the bottle first!"

I put my hand out to take the bottle of whiskey, which freed up my right hand and gave him the view of my pussy he was after. I drank as much as I could as fast as I could, all the while knowing he was looking at me and moving his hand up and down on his penis. I wanted to run away but I couldn't make my legs move, and I wasn't going to open my eyes because I didn't want to see him looking at me or what he was doing. I took a few more swigs from the bottle before I heard him grunt and say, "Thank you, sweet thing."

I asked him for my clothes and he threw them at me, zipped up his pants, and didn't once avert his eyes while I got dressed.

Tyler arrived just as I was slipping on my sandals, "What's going on?" he asked. I think he had a pretty good idea, but then again, maybe he was too stoned to notice. "Nothing," I said.

"It doesn't look like nothing," Tyler said, and then looked me up and down like he didn't care about me.

"I thought you two might want a little drink so I brought a bottle. Not much left, I'm afraid, your girlfriend's a bit of a lush. How 'bout a little smoke, Tyler? I've got some nice bud back at the house," Arnold said.

"Sure thing, Gramps."

I kept Arnold's bottle of whiskey and finished it off as I watched the two of them walk off together. I wanted to go home, wanted my mom, wanted to run away, but I was too scared to do anything. I found a big driftwood log in the grassy sand dunes and lay as still as I could, on my back, up against the log, wondering what I should do.

Later, when I thought they were all asleep, I made my way to the house and let myself in through the kitchen door. I took a big knife from the silverware drawer and went to my room. I shut the door and stuck the knife between the door and the jamb, and went looking for the Sucrets box I'd stashed in the bottom of my bag at the bus station. I took one of the pills and tried my best to fall asleep, but I was too upset to sleep. I couldn't do much more than stare at the ceiling and think of what type of lie I could tell Aunt Flo so I could go home without her suspecting anything.

• • •

In the morning, I told Aunt Flo and Sissy that Mom had phoned the night before. "They had a good time at the car convention, and Mom wants me to come home to help paint the fence," I said.

"I didn't hear the phone ring," said Aunt Flo.

"The cards never lie," Sissy whispered, just loud enough for me to hear.

Aunt Flo said if I hurried and got the fence painted she'd drive in to collect me for their big Fourth of July party. She'd invited just about everyone in the neighborhood and was sparing no expense on the party. She'd even booked the same band that played at their wedding. I promised to do my best, but I knew I wasn't ever coming back.

I phoned my Mom and told her I was coming home. "Can you pick me up at the bus station?" I asked. "I think it gets in at 3 p.m."

"Is something wrong?" she asked.

"No, I'm just kind of homesick, and I miss Rascal," I replied.

"Rascal and I were talking about you last night, and I think she'll be happy to hear you're on your way home. Me too," Mom said.

Tyler had to drive me to the bus station because Sissy only had a learner's permit and Aunt Flo had a hair appointment. No one mentioned anything about Arnold driving me, which was a relief. As we pulled out of the driveway, Tyler said, "Hey, about last night. I was going to fuck you but I'm glad I didn't. Arnold says you're nothing but trouble."

"No, I'm not. I would've let you if you'd asked," I said.

"Is that right? How about now then?" he said.

"Now? Sure, okay. Where would we do it?" I replied before I had a chance to think about what I was agreeing to.

"I know a place, a dead-end road no one else knows about. But are you sure? You're not gonna chicken out, are ya?

You're not gonna scream rape or do something stupid like tell me to pull out? It's not a trick, right?" he said.

"No, no trick," I said.

I felt sick to my stomach right away and wanted to back out of having sex with Tyler, but I felt obligated to go through with it. I wished I'd just kept my mouth shut.

We parked at the end of the dead-end road and got our pants off. I really didn't like the way he kissed me. And the sex hurt so much I couldn't help but cry. When Tyler finally stopped moving his body into mine I thought he'd get off me, but he didn't move or do anything for the longest time, and I didn't say anything—even though he was heavy and I felt squashed—because I thought it might be part of the sex thing. Like when dogs got stuck together. So I just breathed lighter and tried not to cry too hard.

I was just about to start wiggling out from underneath him when he lifted himself up on his hands, kissed me, and then picked up my hand and put it on his wiener, which felt hard and rubbery. He put his hand over mine and moved our hands up and down for a little while until his body got rigid and his wiener got really stiff and then he moaned and rolled off onto his side. I watched as he wiped snot from his upper lip and wondered if it was his snot or mine. He helped me put my underwear back on, and then put his wiener back in his underwear and pulled his jeans up. I didn't know what to do about the goo on my leg and noticed some of it had gotten on my shorts as well. I just did my best to pretend it wasn't there.

When we finally got back on the road, Tyler slipped off one of his shoes and his sock, handed me the sock, and told me to use it. I just held it in my hand because I didn't want to wipe myself while he was watching, and I especially didn't want to have to hand a gooey sock back to him or to mention anything about the sex. So I didn't do or say anything and neither did he. I think we both knew we'd done something we weren't supposed to. I stared out the window and prayed we'd get to the bus station before I started crying again. When he pulled the car into the station parking lot, I reached into my bag and took out the song lyrics I'd been working on. I handed him the piece of paper and he looked at it, and read it quietly out loud:

"Shot off your big mouth, some pretty mean stuff.
She's walking away, just had enough.
Been too many times that you've been unkind.
If you think she's staying—boy, you're blind.
It may not get better; probably get worse.
You'll be alone with your old friend remorse.
You get what you gave and since you can't behave.
Don't wait for her call or plead for a hug.
Best to forget, but you can still bet.
You'll sleep lonely with your new friend regret."

He smiled at me. "Hey, I really like that. Did you write it?" he asked.

"Yeah, I wrote them for your song," I replied.

I was doing my best to get the passenger door open before he said anything else, but it wouldn't open. When he reached across me to unlatch my door I thought he was going to kiss me so I pulled back. But he just said, "It gets stuck sometimes," and pushed the door open with one hit. I jumped out, took my travel bag from the backseat, and walked away.

Two days later Aunt Flo called and asked if I wanted her to come and get me. "I hope you're done helping your mom, because my Fourth of July party is going to be a lot of fun and I'd really like it if you'd come. I think Sissy needs the company. She's bored."

I was about to tell her that I had other plans for the Fourth when Mom motioned to me, clicking her fingers in front of my face, to give her the phone. Aunt Flo got an earful about my zebra hairstyle and my makeup. "She's not your kid, Flo. You don't get to make decisions," Mom said just before she slammed the phone down.

I went to bed that night feeling relieved that I didn't have to create any more excuses for not going to Aunt Flo's.

• • •

I started the ninth grade the same week I started my period. I didn't tell my mom about it until she asked me, and she only asked because I'd used all of the pads in her bathroom drawer.

"I was wondering if you were going to get your period," she said. "You've been so moody these past few weeks, and it's about time you got it."

I agreed with her about my period causing me to be moody because I didn't want her to know I was mad about what I'd done with Tyler. I really wished I hadn't had sex with him. I never thought I'd hear from him again but I did. Tyler and Sissy both sent me Christmas cards in the same envelope later that year. In Tyler's card I found a piece of Arnold's engraved letterhead and a check for two hundred dollars made out to me from Arnold. The note said, "Thanks for helping out with my song. Your lyrics were perfect. Tyler."

I first heard Tyler's song on the radio just after New Year's. The singer sang the words almost exactly how I'd written them. I really liked the song, and was excited about it, so I called Arnold's house to talk to Sissy. I wanted to know who the singer was; I couldn't imagine it was Tyler. The guy's voice was too low. Aunt Flo answered the phone and said Sissy had gone to Ireland as an exchange student and that yes, it was Tyler singing on the record. "Isn't he great?" she said.

"He is, and I'm so happy he used the lyrics I wrote," I replied.

She didn't respond for so long I thought the phone had gone dead. I was just about to hang up when I heard her say, "You must be mistaken. I was there when Tyler sat down at the piano and wrote that song."

"I wrote the lyrics, Aunt Flo. I gave them to him when he drove me to the bus station last summer," I replied.

"What kind of game are you up to, missy?" she asked in a very serious voice.

I tried to explain how I'd heard Tyler play the song and then recorded it so I could write some words. I even told her about the check for two hundred dollars I got from Arnold and the thank-you note I got from Tyler at Christmas. But she said, "No, you didn't. That's a lie and you know it."

I didn't know what to say. I felt my face turn red and my stomach turn sour, so I hung up.

CHAPTER 12

I hated that Aunt Flo didn't believe me and I thought about sending her my original copy of the lyrics, but after buying and listening to Tyler's recording of "Your New Friend Regret" and noticing he'd changed a few words, I decided to not send her my copy or call her for a while.

I was pretty busy with schoolwork anyway, which was good because I didn't have time to think about Tyler and Aunt Flo too much. I'd been working on a two hundred–word short story for my English class since before Christmas, and only found the time and inspiration to write it after my awkward phone conversation with Aunt Flo and after I'd spent a week sorting through my poem and lyric notebooks. I had close to five hundred poems and lyrics to songs in folders and notebooks hidden in my closet and under my bed. I even had a shoebox full of poems I'd written on bar napkins I'd found in the glove boxes of Dad's cars. And once I had to tell the school librarian that I lost the copy of *Ramona and Her Mother* I'd checked out because I wrote a poem about Ramona learning to air burp on pages 2 and 3 in pen and I didn't want her to see it.

I wasn't sure why I wrote poems, or what they meant, but

I was pretty sure everyone in my school would laugh at me if I ever read "Should've Been a Boy" or "Nice to Be Dead" to my English class. I rewrote my writing assignment at least fifteen times before I threw it in the garbage and decided to tell my English teacher I'd lost it. I couldn't bring myself to hand in my short story, "When You Breathe I Sneeze, When You Grunt I Jump," about a boy who knows a girl who loves him and doesn't care.

My classmates already called me "weirdo," and though I hated it, deep down I knew it was true. It seemed to me other kids my age knew the right things to say and the right way to act. They never looked like they felt out of place the way I did, and I would bet my life most of the girls in my class wouldn't have agreed to have sex in the front seat of a guy's car like I had.

I was tired of being the girl everyone avoided. I wanted to be one of the girls who everyone admired and wanted to be like. So I decided to quit spending my spare time at school writing poetry and instead work on trying to be popular. I even convinced my mom to let me buy the type of clothes the cool girls wore, and I spent the last few months of the ninth grade shopping for new clothes at the mall on weekends so I'd have something new on every Monday, just like the popular girls did. But dressing and talking like the cool girls didn't help me with things like sitting still in class or knowing what to do with my hands. I'd always found it hard to keep my hands quiet and harder still to not wiggle around in my chair. "If you could just sit still like the other kids, you'd be fine," my mom said after attending a parent-teacher meeting at my school.

My math teacher told her how I played with my hands, chewed pencils, made church steeples with my fingers, and constantly doodled on my desk and in my schoolbooks during class. She even showed her my math Pee-Chee—the one I'd written "It's not the bite, it's the chew that I like" all over in red pen.

"Your teacher told me you don't pay attention in class, that you spend your time wiggling around and writing strange things," Mom said.

My moving around too much not only bothered my homeroom teacher, it bothered my other teachers, too—everyone except for my PE teacher. I thought she hated me, but I was wrong. One day, after our school's softball tryouts in March, I found her standing by my locker when I went to get my coat. She smiled at me and said, "Where'd you learn to pitch like that?"

"My brother taught me," I replied.

"This school hasn't had a good girls' softball team for years, so I'm glad you've tried out. Would you be interested in playing on a summer league team as well? I know of a team that's looking for a few new players."

"Sure," I replied, while trying to keep still so she couldn't tell how excited I was about her asking me.

She drove me to the summer league tryout a few weeks later and talked to the coach while I pitched for their practice game. Afterward, the summer league coach said he'd be happy to have me on his team.

I was thrilled and thanked her a couple of times on the drive back to school.

"You don't have to thank me, it's my job to help. And besides, the team needs you as much as you need them," she said.

● ● ●

Everyone on my new summer softball team could play pretty well, and I joined as a relief pitcher because they already had a pitcher who'd been with them for years. She came up to me after my tryout and said, "Get used to riding the bench, 'cause I ain't giving up the mound."

I didn't care too much that she didn't like me because the rest of the team seemed to, and even though I knew I wouldn't get to pitch too often I was happy to be on a team and to have something to do that summer other than help Dad with his cars.

When I told Dad I'd joined a summer league team that already had a steady pitcher, he hit the roof. "Who told you to do that? You'll waste the entire summer sitting on the bench and never get to pitch. And why didn't you ask me about getting on a team? I could have found one for you."

"I wasn't even thinking about playing softball this summer until my PE teacher brought it up," I replied.

"Your PE teacher? Who the hell is your PE teacher?" he yelled.

"She's nice. I like her. She drove me to the league tryouts last week and told my new coach she thought I had talent."

"Talent? Jesus Christ, now that's something I haven't heard before," Dad said as he stomped through the kitchen on his way out the back door. "And haven't you learned your lesson about getting in cars with strangers?"

I could feel my insides turn to mush and felt like crying, but I didn't. Instead I snuck a beer from the fridge and went to my bedroom.

After listening to Mom and Dad fight about me playing softball later that night, I thought Dad was going to call my PE teacher and yell at her, but he didn't. He didn't come to any of my games that summer, either, which I was pretty happy about because I don't know what I would've done if Dad yelled at my coach the way he used to yell at Robbie's.

Whenever I got a chance to pitch, most of my team encouraged me to do it as hard and fast as I could. The only girl who didn't cheer me on was the team's steady pitcher. She was kind of snotty, and I'm sure it was because the coach (to my surprise) let me pitch at least two, sometimes three, innings every game.

● ● ●

A few weeks into the summer season, my coach told me about a softball camp in July. "It's a good camp, a week of practice games and team building. I think everyone on the team is going this year. You should too," he said.

I took the information sheet home to show my parents. Mom thought it was a great idea, but Dad wasn't so sure I'd learn anything at camp that I couldn't learn from him. "Sixty bucks is a lot of money for a week of goofing around. I wonder how much practicing there really is."

After he called my coach to ask about the training plan and the parental supervision at the camp and discovered the coach happened to be his boss's son, he got off the phone and said to Mom, "Make sure she's got a pair of decent shoes and a proper softball mitt. Don't let her take that old thing of Robbie's with her."

The first few days of softball camp were a lot of fun. The weather was perfect, and I liked training and playing all day. I also liked a couple of my teammates, especially the catcher and the second baseman. I shared a cabin with them and they showed me around and introduced me to everyone they knew. It was on the fourth night of camp that the snotty team pitcher showed up at our cabin after dinner with a bottle of vodka and poured some into our cans of soda. She didn't drink a thing, just kept refreshing our drinks until there wasn't any soda or vodka left. The three of us got "totally wasted," according to the rest of the team. We ended up in the same bed together. I don't know for sure but I'm guessing it was me who peed the bed because my jeans were wet; I don't know whose vomit it was on the floor.

What I do recall about that night was how they all talked to me about sex and what they called my "strangenesses."

"If you really want to get a decent boyfriend you're gonna have to stop talking and moving around so much, biting your nails, cracking your knuckles, and smelling everything before you eat it," the catcher said.

I knew she was right, especially about talking so much. Sometimes I'd catch myself talking a mile a minute, for no reason at all.

The four of us got kicked out of camp and suspended for the rest of the season. I was glad the pitcher got kicked out too.

The other three girls' parents came and picked them up by noon, but I had to wait outside on the road until 5 p.m. for Dad to arrive because Mom was home in bed with a bad headache and couldn't drive. Not only did he have to leave work early, he missed an important work function where he was supposed to get an award for selling more stuff that year than anyone else.

He was fuming mad. "Get in the fucking car and don't say a fucking word."

I got in the backseat and sat as low as I could. I prayed we'd get home before he finished his six-pack of beer.

● ● ●

Things got worse between Dad and me after the camp incident. I got kicked off the team and Dad apologized to my coach, on my behalf. "Good-for-nothing brat" was his new title for me. I tried my hardest to keep busy and out of his way the rest of the summer. I even paid him back the sixty-dollar camp fee with money I made from sweeping up hair on Friday and Saturday afternoons at Ken's beauty salon. The rest of the time I was home alone, and it didn't take long for me to discover that two beers made cleaning, ironing, and washing windows kind of fun.

Just before I started the tenth grade my parents got into a huge fight about school clothes for me. Dad said I didn't deserve anything new. "She's old enough to get drunk and make a fool out of me, so she's old enough to get a job and buy her own goddamn clothes!" he yelled.

Mom took me clothes shopping anyway. "You've grown so much these past few months, and I'm not going to make you start your sophomore year wearing old clothes and shoes that are too small, no matter what your dad says."

I hugged mom so hard I thought I'd cracked one of her ribs, but she smiled at me anyway.

● ● ●

Things calmed down at home after I started school. Dad wasn't home much, and Mom had to work extra hours because her department was merging with another one, so I was home alone after school. I usually goofed around and watched TV for a while before I started my homework, and sometimes I helped myself to a wine cooler, but only one. I did my school work every night, and I even went to the library, checked out *Lord of the Flies* and *To Kill a Mockingbird*, and read them all the way through.

When I brought home my report card, four A's and two B's, both Mom and Dad seemed kind of proud. They even invited me along to see *Dead Poets Society* the next weekend because Dad had won free movie passes at his office raffle.

A few days after the movie, Mom took me out to dinner and asked my advice about her plan for Dad's sixtieth birthday present. She'd arranged for him to drive one of his cars in the opening parade of the national classic car convention in Las Vegas and wanted to know if he had a car ready or not. "He's got two cars ready and both are really nice," I told her.

She kept her plan a secret until the morning of his birthday, November 17. That morning she put the car show tickets under his coffee cup, and when he picked them up and saw what they were he put his paper down and grinned from ear to ear. "You've got about thirty minutes to get ready. If we don't leave here by eight thirty we won't make it in time for the parade," Mom said.

"I can be ready to go in ten minutes," I said.

"No fucking way! She's not coming!" Dad yelled out as he walked down the hall and into the bathroom.

I looked at Mom and tried to hold back my tears but I couldn't.

"Hey honey, it's his birthday and you're fifteen, old enough to stay home alone. Be good and I'll take you shopping for those boots you want next week," Mom said.

Dad had been talking about driving in a classic car parade for years, but he never did because he said it was too expensive. I think he never went because he didn't think he had a car that was good enough. But things were different that year. He'd finally finished restoring the two cars he'd been working on for years. Both were in pristine condition and worthy of turning a few heads.

It took Dad less than fifteen minutes to shower and dress, but much longer to decide which car to drive. After calling a few of his club buddies, he finally decided on his yellow-green 1965 Ford Falcon because he'd recently given it a complete overhaul, including new tires and wheels, tinted windows, and lime-green vinyl upholstery on both the front and back seats. It looked great. "It's not as smooth-driving as my Mustang, but it's the one I want people to see," he said.

I thought he should have taken the 1965 Mustang because it was cherry red, with two orange flames on each fender and a white leather interior. It was my favorite car, and on rare occasions when he took it out for a drive, he'd let me go too. But only if I washed my hands first and promised not to bite my nails, chew gum, pick my nose, or stick my hands out the window.

While I was helping Mom put her suitcase in the trunk and fill up Dad's beer cooler for the drive, she said, "We'll be back Monday. Stay home and do your homework. I know you have some because I saw it on your bed."

I let out a big huff and said, "What if someone breaks in and kills me?"

"Oh honey, no one's gonna break in and kill you. It's only for two nights, and I told Mrs. Benson you might stop over if you got scared or lonely," Mom replied.

I took a deep breath and said, "Sure, I'll do my homework, I promise." But I didn't mean it. I didn't plan on doing anything that weekend.

After they drove off I went back to bed and slept most of the day.

● ● ●

When I woke up I was hungry for ice cream. I knew I wasn't supposed to leave the house, but we didn't have any ice cream in the freezer, so I walked down to the corner store the next block over.

I was picking out my ice cream when my neighbors, the

twins, walked up behind me. The taller one said, "Yo, get the Neapolitan, then all three of us can eat it." Then they both started laughing. They laughed so hard the potato chips they were eating flew from their mouths and onto the front of the freezer door.

I hadn't talked to either of them since school started that year, ever since they'd gotten cars and started driving to school. They lived five houses down the block from us. For a few years when I was little I thought they were deaf.

"They're not deaf. They're just shy, and maybe you talk so much they can't get a word in—huh?" Mom said.

I used to walk home from school with them or behind them and I never got to know them very well, but I did know that they were a year older me and they both played on the high school tennis team and smoked pot.

I put a half-gallon of Neapolitan in my cart and told them they could come over and have some, and that my parents were away for the weekend. "I wouldn't mind having a close look at your dad's Mustang," said the cuter one.

"Sure, come on over and look all you want," I replied.

After we finished the ice cream, and a fifth of Dad's Southern Comfort, the taller twin suggested we take the Mustang out for a little ride. I thought it was a bad idea at first, but the more I thought about Dad and how much he hated me, the more I thought taking his precious car out for a drive was an okay thing to do, especially after the cute twin kissed me and asked me if I had a boyfriend.

It was two local fishermen who found the car. I don't remember too much except a little bit about getting stuck in the sand and walking down the beach with the twins to find someone to help us get the car unstuck. It was awfully dark and we were really drunk. I guess we got lost because I woke up on the side of the highway under a bush. The twins were nowhere to be found. I walked to a gas station, about a half a mile down the road, to ask for help, but a couple of fishermen had already pulled the car out of the sand and towed it to the gas station. I guess the tide had come in overnight because the Mustang was saturated with sand and water. The guy at the gas station happened to recognize the car—and he knew my brother—so he called Robbie to tell him what was up and he gave me a ride home.

It was Robbie who told Dad about his Mustang when they got home from the convention, and it was Dad who broke my nose.

When we arrived at the emergency room, they stuffed my nose with cotton gauze and asked me what had happened. "My dad hit me," I said.

When two policemen showed up a few minutes later and asked me where my dad was, I told them he was at home. Mom was standing behind them, facing me, and shaking her head. "I didn't mean that my dad hit me," I retracted. "It was actually my brother, but it was an accident. He was teaching me to hit left-handed and a ball went right into my face."

"Thank you," Mom mouthed.

I guess the police believed me because no one ever followed up with Dad or Robbie. It didn't matter, though, because Dad stopped speaking to me after I ruined his Mustang.

CHAPTER 13

D ad died on Thursday April 25, 1991, at the end of my sophomore year. I got home at 5 p.m. after a day of hanging out with Wade, a new kid from St Louis who told me I was cute and asked me to ditch school with him. We'd spent most of the afternoon at the beach park, in his car, drinking beer and smoking pot. We also made out a few times, and I let him give me a couple hickeys on the front of my neck because he wanted to.

When I got home, I knew I smelled like pot smoke, so before I did anything else I took a shower and used lots of Mom's apple-scented shampoo, hoping it would wash the smoke smell out of my hair. Then I tried to cover my hickeys with face powder and concealer, but neither of them did a very good job so I put on the orange turtleneck Olive had given me for Christmas.

It was almost 5.30 p.m., time for Mom to get home, when I went into the kitchen to start dinner. I usually didn't make dinner but Mom had asked me that morning if I would.

"Hey, your dad's stuck in Seattle for a few more days, so why don't you make us fish sticks and fries for dinner?" she'd asked.

Dad hated fish sticks and fries. He said they'd make me fat, and that they made the house smell like a sewer. I didn't care, and neither did Mom, so whenever he was out of town we ate nothing but fish sticks and fries.

I'd put an entire box of fish sticks on a cookie tray and turned the oven to 400 before I noticed the light flashing and the number three lit up on our phone message machine. I hit the button to hear Robbie yell, "Where the fuck are you? It's 10 a.m. and your school said you didn't show up today. Dad's dead, Mom's a mess, and I'm driving there right now. Call me on my car phone! I mean it!"

Robbie was the only person I knew who had a phone in his car. It came with his new Oldsmobile, the one Dad had helped him pick out and probably paid for. I listened to the next two messages, both from Robbie, the last one at 4 p.m.: "I'm at the hospital with mom. Call me back."

I hit the replay button a few times and listened to the messages again. I wanted to make sure that I understood what Robbie had said before I dialed his number. When he didn't answer I felt relieved. I wasn't going to leave a message on his phone but I did. "Got your message. I've been home all day in bed with bad cramps. How can Dad be dead? I thought he was in Seattle?"

I hung the phone up, put the cookie tray in the oven, and sat on the kitchen floor thinking about how angry Dad had been with me for the past six months, ever since I ruined his Mustang. I felt pretty bad about it, and I'd tried to apologize at least one hundred times, but Dad had just ignored me and never once mentioned his Mustang or my broken nose. The one time I tried to explain what had happened, he put his hand around my neck like he was going to strangle me and said, "If you know what's good for you, you'll stay out of my way." From then on, whenever I asked him a question he'd act like he didn't hear me and say something to Mom like, "Tell the girl to stop talking at me, will ya?"

As I stared at the kitchen ceiling I prayed really hard that

Dad had died from some type of accident and not anything to do with his high blood pressure. Robbie had told me at Christmas that I was the reason Dad had high blood pressure. "All you've ever done is cause trouble. Dad's blood pressure is through the roof thanks to you," he'd said.

After thinking about things for a while I began to wonder if Robbie was playing a trick on me just to be mean. *Why would he drive all the way from Sacramento to Huntington Beach if Dad was in Seattle?* I wondered. I phoned Olive and when she answered I told her about Robbie's messages. "Is it true? Is dad dead?" I stuttered into the phone. "Oh honey, I don't know if he's passed away or not. Your mom is at the hospital. You could try to phone her there," she replied.

I felt my legs melt into Jell-O and my stomach turn sour. I was more frightened than ever and could see my hands shaking as I picked up the phone book to look for the hospital's number. When I finally found it and called, the switchboard operator transferred me to a nurse. When I asked her about Dad, she said, "He is here, but I can't give you any information about his condition."

I felt like something inside of me was fading away. My throat tightened and I could barely say, "Is my mom there?"

"She left a few minutes ago with your brother, I believe."

I looked at the oven clock and saw that it was after 6 p.m. I wondered how long it would take Mom and Robbie to drive home. I took the fish sticks out of the oven and paced around the house. I tried to watch TV, folded laundry, and dusted Mom's Hummel collection (which could only be done with Q-tips) before I realized how much trouble I was probably in. I couldn't stand the way I felt. I wanted it to go away, but I knew if I helped myself to a beer my brother might smell it on me, so I decided to have a look in Mom's room for something else. She always had pill bottles on her dresser, and I'd been helping myself to them for years. She never seemed to notice, probably because I was careful not to take any if there were only a few left in the bottle.

After reading the labels on three of her prescription bottles, I found the one I wanted. I was only going to take one, but then I remembered Mom saying, "Why do I only take one of these when I know I'm going to want another one in an hour?" So I swallowed two pills, lay down on the couch, and waited for the calm to arrive.

It was just after seven when Mom and Robbie walked in the door. I really wanted to get up and ask what had happened to Dad, but I could hardly open my eyes, and my head was too heavy to lift. When I tried to speak, I couldn't make any words, only weird sounds.

Robbie yelled, "So you've really done it this time, haven't ya loser?" as he slapped me on the side of my head so hard I thought he might have broken my skull.

I slept all night on the living room couch and didn't get up until noon the next day. I was still groggy from the pills, and it took me a while to make it from the couch to Mom's bedroom, only to find she wasn't there. I called out to her and then to Robbie, but no one answered, so I heated up a can of soup, ate it with an entire box of Ritz crackers, and wondered when I was going to get the chance to ask Mom about Dad.

It didn't take long: Robbie and Mom arrived home about 3 p.m. and Mom headed straight to her room, so I followed.

"How did he die? Where did he die? You told me he was in Seattle, so how did he get home?" I practically screamed.

"He lied to me. He was with Genie in a hotel room down the road. The doctor thinks he had a stroke," she said as she took her coat off and let it drop to the floor.

I watched her look over her prescription bottles for a few seconds and then pick up the one I'd helped myself to the day before. I thought about telling her to only take one pill because I was still a bit stoned from the two I'd taken, but she'd popped two in her mouth before I had a chance to say anything. "God, I needed those," she said as she reached out and grabbed me around the top of my shoulders.

I snuggled into her. "Do you think we'll be okay?"

She hugged me for the longest time. "Sure I do. We'll be fine," she whispered in my ear before she released me and fell back onto her bed, the same way I used to when I was little and happy about something. I tried not to stare at her as she flung her arms over her head and grinned from ear to ear. I was confused about her smile and more confused about the emerging smile on my face. "I'm not worried about us, Mom. I'm worried that Dad died because of me, because of the high blood pressure I caused him to have."

"That's ridiculous. You didn't cause his high blood pressure. He didn't take care of himself and he drank too much." She got to her feet and told me she needed a long bath and some time to think.

I went to my room and threw myself on my bed the same way Mom had thrown herself on hers. I put my arms over my head and thought about Uncle Hank. I wondered if Dad had gone to the same place as Uncle Hank and if they were together, talking about me. It was hard for me not to replay the scene from the day Uncle Hank died. I knew it so well. I also knew he'd still be alive if I'd just cleaned up the suntan oil I'd spilled. Now it seemed that I might have killed Dad, too, even though Mom said I didn't. Everyone, including my mom, knew how red Dad's face and neck would get when he was around me. One time, a few months before I ruined his car, he yelled at me for leaving the back door open all night and got so dizzy he had to sit down.

I guess if I'd just been a better person, or maybe a boy, he might not have hated me so much, or had high blood pressure.

● ● ●

I couldn't take thinking about Dad and Uncle Hank any longer, so I got up and went to the kitchen to sneak a wine cooler. Robbie was sitting at the kitchen table drinking Dad's Crown Royal from his favorite whiskey glass. When he saw me, he got a dirty coffee cup from the sink, poured some whiskey in it and handed it to me. Then he raised his glass over his head and said,

"Here's a toast to the best old man a guy could ever ask for." Robbie downed the contents in a couple of swallows and threw the glass in the sink, smashing it to bits.

I sipped my whiskey for a few seconds before I finished it off, all the while wondering how my brother could think Dad was the best father ever.

"Hey, if you've got anything stored in my room get it out now or I'll throw it out, 'cause I'm moving back in for a couple of weeks and I don't want to look at your shit."

"I'm not moving my craft table and stuff just so you don't have to look at my shit. Move it yourself! Why do you have to stay here, anyway? We don't need your help!"

"Someone's gotta help Mom make the funeral arrangements, and it certainly ain't gonna be you, so move your shit!"

I flipped him the bird, took a wine cooler from the fridge, and went back to my room. Later, I overheard Robbie talking on the phone telling someone he was staying around because he wanted to make sure no one, including Dad's brother Bill, took any of Dad's things, because it was all his.

Robbie left with his bowling alley friend around 8 p.m., just as Olive and Ken arrived with two bottles of wine and a bag of M&M's. I had to knock on Mom's bedroom door four times before she called for me to come in. When she finally got dressed and joined us in the kitchen, Olive handed her a glass of wine and said, "I don't know if I should cry or laugh, but I'm sorry this is happening, honey."

"Me neither. I feel like crying and laughing at the same time," Mom replied.

I sat at the kitchen table eating M&M's while they talked about funeral arrangements and Ken wrote an obituary for the newspaper. Dad's funeral was set for the next Tuesday (five days after he died) because the funeral home was booked up until then.

Before I went to bed, Mom gave me a hug and said, "You look tired, honey. I'm worried that you're worried. So stop worrying." She smiled and then told me that Robbie had called my school and told them that I wouldn't be back until after the funeral. "So please make an effort to get along with Robbie. He's being very helpful," she said.

"I will if he will," I replied as I walked away.

● ● ●

Robbie spent all day Saturday sorting through Dad's belongings in the house and in the garage, editing the obituary Ken had started, and reading over Dad's will and life insurance policy. When I asked him if we were going to have to sell the house, he said, "Hell no. This house is officially paid off, and Mom's going to get some serious cash too. Don't get your hopes up about getting anything, though. You're not mentioned in Dad's will."

"Big surprise there," I replied as I headed outside to water Mom's hanging flower baskets like she'd asked me to.

Robbie insisted on buying a stainless steel casket and contacting someone at the Marines about getting a flag for the coffin and a uniform for Dad to wear. I heard Mom tell him a couple of times that Dad wouldn't want a military service. "He hated that war, Robbie," she said.

But Robbie wouldn't take no for an answer and even polished Dad's military medals so he could put them on display at the funeral parlor. He also arranged for several of Dad's friends to follow the hearse to the cemetery in their classic cars and hired a catering company to bring sandwiches and salads to the house for an after-funeral lunch in Dad's garage.

I wanted to help, to contribute in some way, but I couldn't think of anything I could do until after I went out to the garage to sit in Dad's lounge chair on Sunday afternoon and think. I helped myself to one of Dad's Pall Malls, and halfway through it decided to turn on some music, which was when the idea hit me. I remembered that Dad's best friend, Mike, a really good guitar player and sound technician, had convinced Dad a few years earlier to record two of his favorite Glen Campbell songs. Mike had made copies of the recordings and had given one of the cassettes to Dad and another to me.

Dad thought his version of "Hey Little One" sounded almost perfect, but he didn't like his rendition of "Less of Me." He said he sounded too dramatic and that his pitch was off. I liked both and had almost worn out my copy of the cassette. I looked all over for Dad's copy but couldn't find it. I did find Mike's phone number on the wall behind Dad's workbench, though, so I called him. After Mike told me how sorry he was about Dad I explained my idea to finish off the funeral service by playing Dad's version of "Less of Me." Mike thought it would be a nice tribute and said he had a spare copy of the recording.

"Mine's probably in better shape than yours," he said. "I haven't played it once. I'll call the funeral home and make arrangements to bring in a small sound system, okay?"

I know Mike could hear me crying because he said, "Hey kid, it was just his time to go. He was a tough guy, but I'm sure he loved you."

● ● ●

Even though I knew I was supposed to feel really sad about Dad dying, I didn't. I was actually kind of happy that he was dead, and that confused me. I lay on my bed with Rascal for the next couple of hours biting my nails and wondering how life was going to be without Dad around.

That same night, while I made dinner, I listened as Robbie told Mom that Dad's company had a small pension fund that she was entitled to, about forty thousand dollars. He wanted her to help him pay off his student loan with it, but I don't think Mom wanted to because she didn't answer him when he said, "He'd want me to have it, Mom, right?"

I finished making all of us grilled cheese sandwiches before I interrupted their conversation to tell them about Mike bringing a recording of Dad singing to the funeral.

"What a great idea. It'll be perfect. Your dad was such a good singer," Mom said.

"We're not having any honky-tonk country-bumpkin

music at Dad's funeral. He was a Marine, for god's sake!" Robbie shouted.

"I've already arranged it," I replied, and ran off before Robbie could say anything else.

Mom came into my room while I was getting ready for bed and asked me if I would clean up Dad's garage the next day. "Can you please take those awful centerfolds off the wall and move a couple of cars out to the yard so that people have a place to sit and eat their lunch?" she asked.

"Should I keep the centerfolds or put them in the garbage?" I asked.

"I vote garbage," she replied.

"So do I."

She also asked me if I wanted to say something at the funeral. I knew Robbie had been writing a eulogy, and that he planned to talk for ten minutes before introducing some guy Dad really didn't like to say a few words about the local classic car club and how Dad had been a founding member. I also knew Aunt Flo planned to say a few words because I'd heard Mom talking to her on the phone, but I hadn't thought of saying anything.

"It might be nice, but only if you want to," she said.

"I'll sleep on it and let you know tomorrow."

● ● ●

The next morning I dug through my poem box looking for something I could read. I didn't find anything so I spent the afternoon taking Dad's playboy girls off the garage walls, cleaning oil off the floor, setting out chairs, and thinking up a new poem I could read:

> *Hey Dad*
> *You can search a million miles and never find me.*
> *I can say a thousand words and we'll never agree.*
> *You can blink a hundred times and never see.*
> *I can love you ten ways but you'll still leave.*

• • •

Robbie made me read what I'd come up with to him the night before the funeral. I didn't want to because I knew he was going to laugh, but he insisted, so I did.

"What kind of poem is that? It's crazy mumble-jumble and you sound like a deranged psycho when you read it!" he yelled.

"It's nice. I like it," Mom said.

"It doesn't make any sense. It's stupid, and if she reads it everyone's gonna know she's a mental case," Robbie said.

"Listen, Robbie, he was her father too and she can read it," Mom replied.

That was enough to set Robbie off. He freaked out, yelling at me about being a loser before announcing he was going out to get fucked up, because that's what Mom and I were, and storming out of the house.

He was still drunk when he got home the next morning, and even though Mom made him drink three cups of coffee and eat some dry toast, it didn't help. He was still slurring and stumbling around when the limo from the funeral home arrived. The driver had to come in to help Robbie.

"Would you happen to have any beer and tomato juice in the house?" the driver asked.

"Yes," I replied.

"Would you mind pouring some beer into a glass and topping it up with tomato juice? I think it might help," he said.

I did exactly what the driver asked and watched Robbie sit on the front porch steps, sipping and gagging, until Mom said, "We'd better go. We can't be late for the funeral."

On the drive to the funeral home, Robbie threw up into a bag the driver had given him, and when I started to laugh he looked at me and said, "You're the reason Dad's dead. No, wait . . . Dad probably died the day Mom found out she was pregnant with you. I remember being in the kitchen when Mom told him she was expecting and Dad yelled, 'Worst news I've had in my life!'"

Mom looked over at me and said, "I'm sure he didn't say anything like that, honey. Robbie's drunk. Don't pay attention to him."

I told her it didn't matter, that I didn't care, and I spent the rest of the drive picking at the cuticles on my thumbs.

I did care, though, and I believed what Robbie had told me. Even on the drive to Dad's funeral I felt unwanted, like I wasn't welcome. So when we arrived, I found a chair in the back row with a nice cushion on it and sat down until Mom motioned for me to take a seat in the front row with Robbie, Aunt Flo, and Olive.

When the time came to start the service there were only about twenty people in the room, mostly friends of Mom's from the bank, a few guys from the car club, and my sister, Tammy, who was standing by the door. Mom asked the funeral director if he could wait fifteen more minutes because she was expecting a few of his sisters. He agreed, but they didn't show up.

Then, just about the same time the funeral director started to speak, I heard a commotion coming from the back of the room. Mom heard it too, and she whispered to me to see who it was. Sure enough, it was Genie, wearing a big black hat with a veil over her face. Uncle Bill was walking right behind her with his head down. I told Mom I couldn't tell who it was because I didn't want her to get upset. She figured out I'd lied just as soon as Genie started sobbing. It was so loud that Robbie got up and went to the back of the room. Everyone heard him tell Uncle Bill to take her outside, and I started to turn around so I could see what was going on, but Aunt Flo took hold of my arm and told me "never mind." A few seconds later, I heard the sound of high heels walking on a tile floor, a door closing, and then no more crying.

With Genie out of the room, I focused my sights on Dad's casket. From my seat in the front row I could see Dad's entire face and most of his body. It was spooky. He looked like a creepy ghost, and I kept thinking he was going to sit up and start yelling at me. Aunt Flo and Mom thought he looked distinguished and said they were glad they'd decided on an open casket. I thought it was weird and excused myself to go to the bathroom, but instead I found a seat a few rows back and sat next to Mom's friends Ken and Ron.

I didn't pay too much attention to Robbie's speech about Dad being a dedicated father and husband, as well as a loyal and brave Marine who was willing to give his life for his country, or to the car club guy who spoke about Dad's great contribution to the club and his remarkable talent for restoring cars. But I did listen to Aunt Flo talk about how Dad struggled as a boy to please their father, an impossible task in her opinion. "Don't get me wrong, my brother had his faults and they were too often the most obvious things about him, but in spite of them he still managed to give life to a few of the loveliest people in the world," she said.

I knew I was one of the people she was talking about, and I felt good for the first time in a long time. I went up front when Aunt Flo finished and said my poem from memory without coughing or having to stop and start again. When I finished, I looked over at Mike and he started the music. Suddenly, the entire room was filled with Dad's voice singing "Less of Me" and I couldn't help but cry, and neither could Mom or anyone else, even Robbie.

 # CHAPTER 14

Only a few of Robbie's friends showed up for lunch after the funeral. And they only stayed long enough to drink all the beer, eat all the food, and help Robbie take the wheels off of Dad's Ford Falcon and put it up on blocks. The next day Robbie sold Dad's truck and his partially restored Corvette to Dad's used car dealer friend and split the money with Mom.

"Why'd you put the Falcon up on blocks?" I asked Robbie when he showed up in the kitchen just in time to eat a couple of the tacos I'd made for Mom and me.

"What do you care?" Robbie replied.

"I'm gonna be sixteen pretty soon and I'm getting my license. I want to drive it."

"You're not driving the Falcon . . . ever. We all know what you can do to a car, don't we dumb-dumb?" he said before he shoved an entire taco into his mouth and walked out the back door.

Robbie went back to Sacramento a few days later, but not before he took everything he wanted, including Dad's wallet and the US Flag someone from the Marines had delivered to the funeral home for Dad's casket.

Mom didn't care what Robbie took, and she seemed okay for the first week or two after he went home. It wasn't until we cleaned out Dad's dresser and closet that she got a little down in the dumps. It didn't take us too long to sort through his clothes, because he didn't have much: six suits, three coats, a few sweaters, and five pairs of boots. Mom let me keep the sixty-five dollars I found with Dad's gloves in the right pocket of his overcoat and I didn't say anything about the motel room key or the matchbook cover with a full mouth lipstick imprint on it that I found in the other pocket.

On Mother's Day, Mom and I took most of Dad's stuff to the Goodwill, except for his overcoat, gloves, and sunglasses; I kept those. After we put his stuff in the big donation bin behind the store we went inside and bought a teddy bear cookie jar and a patchwork cat bed someone had made.

"Your Dad would hit the roof if he saw us buying this crap," Mom said, laughing.

When we got home I put the cookie jar in the middle of the kitchen table and the cat bed next to the TV for Rascal, and Mom and I ate ice cream and watched TV until after midnight. It was the first time I'd ever felt peaceful at home; I spent more time hanging out with Mom in the living room and watching TV in the first month after Dad died than I had in my whole life.

As the weeks went by, I tried to be good and helped out around the house with chores and cooking. I didn't drink, skip school, or do anything I wasn't supposed to for the rest of the school year. I felt pretty good about myself when I placed second in a poetry competition my English teacher helped me enter and got an A on my report card because of it.

On my sixteenth birthday, Mom took me to Ken's beauty parlor and let him give me a shag haircut. Then we went to Kmart and she bought me almost every color of Maybelline eye shadow, eyeliner, and mascara we could find. "I think all females look better with eyeliner and blush. I never really cared if you wore makeup or not, but your dad hated the idea," Mom said as she was showing me how to put on black liquid eyeliner.

Later, after I'd drawn a perfect thick black line just above my lashes and put on as much mascara as possible, we went to the Sizzler for dinner. I noticed a couple of guys looking over at me when we were waiting to be seated, and I thought I saw one of them wink. It was exciting, and so distracting that I could hardly read the menu once we were seated.

"I know it's only been a couple of months since your dad passed but I'm feeling alright, not too sad or depressed like I thought I would," Mom said as she picked the croutons off her salad and put them on my plate. "Actually, I can't believe how good I feel. How 'bout you, are you okay?" she asked.

"I'm okay. I get little nervous when I hear a truck driving up our street, like it's Dad about to pull into the driveway, but other than that everything is okay." I didn't have the nerve to tell her that Dad's dying was just about the best thing that had ever happened to me, so I shifted around in my seat and looked down at the floor, hoping she couldn't see the big smile on my face.

● ● ●

I finished out tenth grade with a 3.5 GPA.

"I always knew you were smart," Mom said when I showed her my report card.

I'd planned to get a job at Mickey's Burger Barn that summer, but I didn't get my application in on time and they gave the job to someone else. I was a bit pissed off about it because I thought Mom might be mad. But she wasn't. "You've still got that little job at Ken's salon, don't you?"

"Yeah, but it's only four hours a week, and he only pays me four dollars an hour."

"That's probably enough huh?" She smiled as she reached over to move my bangs out of my eyes.

A few days later, when I told her I'd run into my old softball coach at Ken's salon and he wanted me to join his team even though the season was almost over, she said, "If you do, I'll promise to park my butt on the bench and cheer you on."

I felt a nice glow of happiness crawl from my chest all the way to my forehead. "That would be great, Mom—really, it would!"

I kept myself busy with softball practice on Tuesdays and Wednesdays and joined a summer reading club after the team's catcher gave me her copy of *Silence of the Lambs* and promised to lend me more books if I joined the club.

Mom was in a good mood most of the time, and that made me feel good too. She was happy to be back in touch with her family. The family Dad wouldn't let her talk to because he thought they were idiots. After Mom's sister called to say she was sorry to hear about my dad, they called each other almost every day and sometimes talked for hours. I'd never heard Mom laugh so much in all my life.

I went with Mom a few times to visit her parents in San Diego in June and July. Her mom, my grandma, was small just like my mom, and she called me "pretty girl" instead of Randall. My grandpa was real quiet and had a hard time talking because of a stroke.

"My dad wasn't always so frail and quiet. He used to be a fireman and a big guy with a big voice. It's hard for me to see him like this," Mom said on the way home from my first visit.

Sometimes Mom cried on the drive home as she talked about her family and how she'd pushed them out of her life. "I changed our phone number and sent them a letter telling them I didn't want to see them again. It was a horrible thing and I still can't believe I did it," she said.

"Why did you?" I asked.

"Your dad hated my parents, and my parents didn't like him, but they tolerated each other for a few years, until your grandfather refused to lend us money to buy a new Cadillac that your dad wanted. There was a big fight and afterward your dad told me I had to choose between him and Robbie and my family. It broke my heart to tell my parents to leave me alone, but I had no choice. I was pregnant with you, I didn't have any money, and there was no way your dad would have let me take

Robbie away from him. My parents tried to make contact with me lots of times. They sent cards and letters and they even came to the hospital after you were born. When your dad walked in and found them in the hospital room, he grabbed you right from my mother's arms and told them to get out. I should have stood up for myself but I was such a weakling. I let him control everything, God dammit."

Mom's story filled in a lot of questions I'd always had about my grandparents. I was sad to hear what my mom had to do to her parents because of my crazy dad, but glad to hear that my grandparents came to the hospital to see me when I was born.

I started my junior year with a whole new wardrobe, thanks to Dad's insurance policy and to Mom. Everything was going really well until two weeks before Thanksgiving, when my grandparents moved to Utah to live with Mom's sister. They needed someone to be with them full time and Mom couldn't do it. Mom and her sister got into an argument on the phone about their parents moving and Mom was pretty upset about it. She started drinking like never before and sometimes I'd have to help her to bed because she was too drunk to walk.

"I don't ever remember feeling this down," Mom said to me on Thanksgiving Day. She started seeing a shrink the next week, but as far as I could tell he didn't help her much. He gave her some strong sleeping pills and a new type of tranquilizer and she always took more than she was supposed to.

By Christmastime, Mom was in such bad shape that her boss sent her home from work and told her not to come back until she was feeling better. I was more worried than ever when I found Mom's purse, shoes, and car keys in the fridge one day after school. I called Robbie to tell him what was going on.

"I'm sure you're exaggerating," he said. "Put Mom on the phone."

"She's asleep," I replied.

"It's only 4 p.m., how could she be asleep?"

"Well that's the way it is around here lately!" I screamed as I slammed the phone down.

A few days later Robbie arrived home to spend Christmas with us, and he made Mom get up and get dressed so he could take her out to a nice restaurant for dinner on Christmas Eve. "Someone's got to cheer her up. Maybe if she had a decent meal she'd feel better," Robbie said, giving me a look that said he was disgusted by my mac and cheese and hotdog dinner.

They were back at the house within an hour, and Mom collapsed on the couch and rolled into a ball without even taking her coat or shoes off.

"She didn't want to get out of the car," Robbie explained. "I had to drag her into the restaurant. After one glass of wine she started crying and babbling about how much she misses her parents. Not a fucking word about missing Dad!"

After Robbie left to meet a friend for a drink, I put Mom to bed and gave her two of her new pills because she made me. I took one for myself, broke it in half, and took the first piece before I went to bed that night. I slept really well, and I guess Mom did too because she was still asleep when I went to the kitchen at 11 a.m. to get something to eat.

Robbie stayed with us for more than a week. He had no more luck getting Mom out of bed than I did. On New Year's Eve Robbie took me to the grocery store and he paid for everything. "You've got to get Mom to eat something. She's too thin," he said as he put two quarts of strawberry ice cream in our cart. "It's her favorite, so make sure she eats it."

Robbie drove back home to Sacramento later that day. Before he left he gave me twenty dollars and promised he'd call to get an appointment for Mom with a psychiatrist he'd heard about in Los Angeles.

I spent the next two days thinking about what I should do. I couldn't leave Mom home alone, so I decided I wouldn't go back to school when Christmas break ended. I'd stay home with her. But first I needed to hand in the four overdue library books I had in my bedroom and get my stuff out of my locker. I went to school January 4 with a letter I wrote and signed from my mom saying we were moving to Texas. I left it on the counter in the principal's office before I cleaned out my locker and headed to Ken's beauty parlor to tell him about Mom and her depression.

"I had no idea, honey," he said. "I'll give Olive a call tonight and we'll find a way to help. Don't worry, she'll get over it, I promise."

Throughout January and February, Olive called or stopped by almost every day to check on us. Sometimes she'd just sit on mom's bed and talk to her. "You are a good daughter and they know that. It wasn't your fault they didn't get to see you all those years. You've got to pull yourself together. There's more to life than taking pills and sleeping," I heard her tell mom one day when she stopped by after work with two pizzas and a bottle of wine.

Ken, Olive, and Mom all went to Utah to visit her parents the second week of March, and when they got back home Mom stopped taking her Seconal and Xanax and started eating several jars of banana baby food every day. She also went back to work the week after she got back from visiting her parents, so I started back at school again. I had to take Olive and Ken with me to explain to the principal why I'd been absent for so long. He wasn't very happy with me but let me come back when I promised to make up the schoolwork.

It was crazy to have missed ten weeks of school. I was way behind with everything and had to meet with the school counselor before I could go to class. I told her that I was absent all those weeks because I had to stay home with Mom or she would've died. She was nice to me and wrote notes to all my teachers so they wouldn't yell at me for being behind.

I felt glad to be back at school and to have something to do other than worry about Mom and watch soap operas all day.

Olive convinced Mom to eat three meals a day and join a walking class on the weekends and a salsa dance class on Friday nights. Mom didn't like the walking or eating but she seemed to love the dance class. She even made me dance around the kitchen with her one night when she got home. It was nice to see her happy again. It made me feel better about everything.

I came down with glandular fever at the end of April, about five weeks after I'd started back at school. I wasn't the only one who got sick. The four other kids from my cooking class got it too. I had to miss another three weeks of school. When I finally went back, in the middle of May, there were only a couple of weeks left in the school year and I was still so tired that it took me almost an hour to walk the one mile to my house. I missed sixty-eight days of school that year. That's what my homeroom teacher said on the message she left on our phone a week before the end of the school year. I deleted the message before Mom got a chance to hear it. I already knew I had to go to summer school to make up for all the missed days and I didn't want to discuss it with Mom or anyone.

The only good thing about being sick was that I lost twenty pounds and looked better than ever, but not even that seemed to make me happy. By the time I turned seventeen and finished eleventh grade I wanted to die. I didn't know why; it just seemed like it would be easier.

Summer school ran from June 20 to July 26, and I knew I had to go, so I did—for the first week, anyway. So did Wade and Crystal (two of the other sickies). But it was boring and the teacher always showed up late and left after he gave us a bunch of assignments to do, so we all stopped going. I hung out with Wade and Crystal until they became an item and decided to start hanging out in Wade's bedroom instead of the park.

● ● ●

Even though I told my mom I was going to school every day, I did nothing all summer. In August, when my summer school report card arrived in the mail, I discovered I'd passed both English and History and gotten an A minus on an algebra test I never even took. I was shocked and I didn't know what to do, especially since Mom had seen the report card first. She was so happy.

"Boy, you've really made an effort this summer. I'm so proud of you," she said as she hugged me.

I called Wade and found out he'd gotten almost the very same report card and his parents were so happy they were buying him a car. Wade made me promise not to say anything to anyone. "I won't get a car if they find out, so promise me you won't say anything and I'll give you a ride anytime you want," he said.

I agreed to not say anything to anyone about the report cards and I let mom buy me the new coat I'd been talking about for months as a reward for the good report. On our way out of the store she put her arm around me and said, "If you keep up the hard work you'll have a great senior year, and I might even help you buy that car you want."

"I hope so," I replied as I pulled away from her.

A week after the summer school report cards came out, when I was walking to the store to get cat food and a new toothbrush, one of the twins (the cute one) drove by and wolf-whistled at me. I smiled and whistled back and watched him turn his car around and pull up next to me. "Ya wanna come in for a little smoke?" he asked.

We smoked two joints in his car and then went to his house to make nachos and watch *Caddyshack*. Before I left to go home, he showed me the room in their basement where he and his brother grew weed. It was a big darkroom with purplish lights and little wood boxes nailed to every wall with plants growing in them.

After a few weeks of getting high together, the cute twin told me I could buy some weed from them to sell if I wanted. I thought it was a great idea. My first sale was on the first day of senior year. It was easy. I sold a couple of ounces to one of the local stoners and he told me to keep it coming.

By October I was buying and selling about a pound of pot each week. The twins used their profits to buy a motorcycle, and I used mine to buy my pills from an old guy the twins introduced me to. He sold just about every type of narcotic in existence, including the type of pills I liked, the ones that made my days okay.

Mom started dating Charles at the beginning of my school year. She met him at her dance class and made me swear not to tell Robbie or anyone else about him.

"What do you think about me dating a black man?" she asked.

"Well, Dad would spin in his grave, but I don't really care," I replied.

One night about two months after they started dating, just before Halloween, I got up in the middle of the night to go to the bathroom and saw Mom in the living room on her knees giving Charles a blow job. He saw me before she did.

"Hey, looks like someone likes to watch," he said loud enough for me to hear.

I was shocked and scared and turned around really quick to go back to my room. "Mind your own business!" I heard mom yell out in her drunk voice before I slammed my door shut. I put a chair up against my door, but I didn't go to sleep until I heard the front door close and a car drive away.

Mom didn't say anything to me the next day about Charles, and I was too embarrassed and grossed out to bring it up. Things got weird between us after that, and I stayed out of the house as much as possible. We had a couple of big fights, mostly about me staying out late on school nights. "We've got rules in this house, young lady. You'd better straighten up before someone makes you!" she yelled at me once when I slammed the front door hard enough to knock a few of her figurines from the shelf. But it was too late. I didn't know how to change and I didn't want to and I certainly didn't want to be anywhere near Mom and Charles.

● ● ●

My senior year of high school wasn't all that great. I was way behind in math and English because of my lousy junior year and I hated everyone and I knew they hated me too. Probably because I'd done such a good job at getting known around school as a slut. It seemed if I drank more than six beers (and

I usually did), I'd end up having sex—usually with someone I wasn't supposed to, like Katie's boyfriend Matt. Wade, Crystal, and I crashed Katie's Halloween party and I had sex with Matt after Katie passed out and Wade and Crystal took off. I don't actually remember having sex with him because I was pretty drunk, but I must have because we were both naked in her bed the next morning and my Catwoman Halloween costume was ripped all the way down the back.

Even though I said I was sorry and gave her a nice card with ten joints in it, she was so mad about me fucking Matt she wouldn't look at me and she told almost everyone at school what I'd done. It was a long, awful school year, made worse by Wade moving to Boston in December and Katie and her friends making fun of me, calling me a slut and spitting on my locker. I really hated Katie, so I continued to have sex with Matt, not because I liked him but because I knew one day Katie would find out and it would make her crazy. She did find out eventually, and it did make her crazy, and I didn't feel as good as I thought I would. When I saw her walking home from school crying after she saw Matt and me making out in the backseat of his car during lunch break, I felt bad and thought about walking across the street to tell her I was sorry, but I knew she'd hit me or spit on me, so I turned and went the other way. I stopped having sex with Matt after that, though he kept calling me and showing up at my house asking for it.

Mom and I kept our distance. It wasn't that she was mean or anything; she just ignored me, and I tried to stay away from her. She finally broke up with Charles when Robbie arrived a day early for Christmas and found Charles and Mom on the couch with their arms around each other. I went out the back door when I heard Robbie yell, "What the fuck's going on here?"

Mom didn't say Robbie was the reason she broke up with Charles, but I knew he was because I heard her crying on the phone to Olive a few times. "Robbie said he'd disown me if I didn't break up with Charles," she told her. "Sometimes he's just like his dad. It's scary."

We started getting along better after Charles was out of the picture, especially after Mom started dating the good-looking guy who owned the pharmacy she went to. I thought Nick was a "nice guy" but changed my mind to "perfect guy" after he arrived at our house on Valentine's Day with a dozen red roses for Mom and a dozen pink roses for me. He brought us gifts all the time from then on, and he even helped Mom fix the gate latch and hang a few flower baskets on our front porch.

I made a few attempts to cut back on my drinking and drugging after Nick encouraged me to try harder at school. But school was too hard, and I was way behind everyone else. Plus, I just couldn't stay away from drugs. I liked being high more than I liked anything else, and I was selling enough pot to buy all the pills I needed.

I don't think I was any worse than a few of my friends who got high every day. The only difference between them and me was that the school principal was on my case. He hated me and never missed a chance to say something mean, and he called my mom about everything I did. One day, just before spring break, he must have called her and threatened that I wasn't going to graduate because when she got home from work she was pretty mad.

"I hear you got five D's on your report card. I guess you're just gonna be a high school dropout, huh?"

"I probably will be, but I think I can get a GED, and that's almost the same thing as a high school diploma," I replied.

"No it's not!" she screamed before she grabbed her coat and slammed the door on her way out to meet Nick.

Mom and Nick started seeing each other about a week before Valentine's Day, and after that they met for drinks and dinner at a local cocktail lounge almost every weeknight. Sometimes, afterwards, they parked in our driveway and stayed in his car for hours. I knew they were having sex, and I knew Mom didn't want me to know. I think she was embarrassed. I spied on them a few times, though I couldn't see much since Nick's Lincoln Town Car had tinted windows

I could tell Mom had fallen in love with Nick the night he came in to use our bathroom. I was lying on the couch watching TV when she made him take his shirt off because she'd gotten her lipstick on his collar. She promised to wash it for him, and he left his shirt on the kitchen table before he went home. She didn't wash it until the next day, after she'd slept with it on her pillow all night.

They'd been dating for four months when she found out he was married, and that his wife was about to have a baby. She discovered this when she went to his store to surprise him with a birthday cake. It was toward the end of May during my senior year. I'd agreed to go with her—she wanted me to hold the lemon chiffon cake on my lap while she drove—but only after she agreed to buy me a long black cape so I could crash the senior prom after-party dressed as Morticia from *The Addams Family*. I was in the makeup aisle, waiting for her, when I heard someone walking toward me and sniffling. I looked up to see Mom holding a tissue to her nose with one hand and holding the cake in the other hand. She was very upset, so I took the cake from her and followed her out the front door into the parking lot. She grabbed the cake from me and threw it at Nick's car. Even though I was startled, I couldn't keep from laughing, and this made Mom laugh too. The cake made a big mess. Once we were in our car she told me what had happened.

"I opened Nick's office door singing 'Happy Birthday' in my loudest voice and holding the cake," she said. "There was a little girl sitting on his desk and Nick was kissing a very pregnant woman." She blew her nose. "I should have known!" she screamed.

Mom took the breakup pretty hard, and I did too—I thought Mom and Nick were good together, and I liked Nick. He was cool, and he always called me "Sexy Bird," which made my insides feel wobbly and weird, in a good way.

I tried to help Mom by listening to her talk about Nick, sometimes all day, and I didn't complain about the two weeks of driving by his store with her sitting way down in the passenger seat so she could watch him leave work. I even called him twice to tell him what a bastard he was like she'd asked me to. He just laughed and told me to tell her to call him whenever she wanted. "And you don't need to be a stranger either, Sexy Bird. Call me whenever you want," he said.

It was such a relief when a new salsa teacher started at Mom's dance class in June and used her as his dance partner the first night. She thought he was "dreamy," and she stopped crying about Nick after that.

● ● ●

I was surprised to learn I was going to graduate from high school. My grades were almost as bad as my attendance, and my principal had told me at least ten times that I'd be sitting in the audience on graduation day. So when I saw my name on the list of graduating seniors, and my homeroom teacher gave me a piece of paper with instructions about renting a cap and gown, I decided not to say anything about it, just in case they'd made a mistake.

Mom clapped when I finally told her the news. "The last time I spoke to your principal he said he didn't let kids graduate with less than a 1.8 GPA. You must have brought it up since then. Thanks," she said.

"Yeah, I think I did," I lied.

I'd been to the principal's office at least once a week that year, mainly for skipping school but sometimes for falling asleep on my desk. The last time I'd visited his office I'd been so stoned I'd dozed off while I was waiting and slipped off the chair onto the floor. He'd seen it happen. "I don't want you back here next year," he'd said.

I couldn't bring myself to respond, because I just didn't care.

● ● ●

I graduated a few days after my eighteenth birthday, and Olive and Mom came to watch. They took me to dinner afterward, and the only thing they talked about was dancing. I drank Mom's beer while she demonstrated how her new dance teacher did the samba. Everyone in the restaurant watched her. It was corny, and I tried to hide behind Olive. They dropped me off at home on their way to a dance contest, and I put a chair up against my bedroom door and snuck out my window. I hitchhiked to a big party on the other side of town and didn't get home until the next afternoon.

I was planning to work all summer at Ken's salon (and sell a little pot on the side) so I could pay off the little orange Ford Fiesta I had on layaway at a used car lot in town. The owner was a friend of my dad's, and he'd agreed to sell it to me for eight hundred dollars on a payment plan because he liked my dad.

I gave him a two hundred–dollar deposit at Easter (from my pot sales) and told him I'd get the rest to him by the end of June. I was thrilled when Mom gave me five hundred dollars for a graduation present; I gave the car dealer three hundred and told him I'd have the rest in a couple of weeks. I spent the other two hundred dollars on drugs because my old drug dealer friend gave me a really good deal on two pounds of pot and a hundred Percocets.

My plan was to ask Ken for a three hundred–dollar loan to pay off the car, but when I arrived for work at the salon the first Saturday after school got out he stopped me before I hung up my sweater and asked me to step outside.

"Honey, I've told you about a million times that you can't show up here stoned. The last time you worked you swept up the same pile of hair for twenty minutes and two customers complained. I've hired a student from the beauty college to replace you."

I cried all the way home from Ken's place. I was upset that he thought I was stoned when I was working. I wasn't stoned the day I swept the same pile over and over—not really stoned, anyway. Not stoned enough for anyone to notice. I didn't tell Mom about losing my job, and after a few days I began to feel okay about not working and figured I could make enough from selling pot to pay off my car.

I slept in and hung out around the house watching TV and eating nachos for a week—until Mom found out I'd lost my part time job at Ken's. She yelled at me about it for hours, and then made me write a résumé and go out to look for a job. I didn't want to work—I didn't want to do anything except watch TV, get high, and sleep—so I didn't make much of an effort to find a job. I just left my one-page résumé on the counter at a few stores and at McDonald's and went to the park to sell a few bags of pot afterward.

On the second day of my job search, I ran into my sister Tammy at the mall. I had seen her around, but we hadn't talked since Dad's funeral. I didn't know what to say so I just smiled at her and waited for her to say something.

"Fancy running into you here," she said and smiled really big at me.

"Yeah, I know. Mom's making me look for a job," I replied.

"Have you had lunch? Do you want a burger?"

She bought me a cheeseburger and Coke and we talked about why she hadn't been in touch. She said her boyfriend John was a good Christian, and she was doing her best to be one too. "We've both seen you smoking and hanging out with the wrong crowd, and John thinks you're a bit of a troublemaker. I think you're a lost soul."

I felt myself blush and looked away, hoping my face wouldn't turn beet red in front of her.

I'd seen John around, but I didn't know much about him except that he taught at the same private Catholic school that Tammy did and drove a brown Honda Accord. The school they worked at was only a block from my high school, so I often saw them driving to and from work.

When Tammy got up to go get us both a chocolate sundae I searched through my purse for a lifesaver so I could try to cover my smoke breath.

"I decided to keep a distance from you and pray that Jesus would put you on the right path, and it looks like he might be doing that now," she said when she got back with the sundaes.

I didn't know how to respond. I'd never thought I was lost, and I didn't know much about Jesus putting people on a path, so I kept eating and shrugged my shoulders a few times when she asked me about going to church with her.

"I'll have to ask my mom about church, okay?" I said after her sixth invite.

Tammy must have felt pretty bad about saying that stuff to me, because two days later she called.

"Hey, I've been praying and talking to John about you, and he said the recreation center is looking for someone to work at their front desk thirty hours a week and he's willing to put in a good word for you if you want. He's on the board and knows everyone there. Should I have him call and set up an interview for you?" she asked.

"I'll have to call you back and let you know because I have a couple of job offers already and I want to make sure I pick the best one," I replied.

"Well, don't wait too long," she said just before she hung up.

I don't know why I lied to her. I guess it was because I thought she was going to ask me to go to church with her and John, and I really didn't want God to know all the stuff I'd been doing. I waited a couple of days before I called her back to say I'd like to interview for the job. She didn't sound as happy and enthusiastic when I called, and told me I'd have to talk to John because she wasn't sure the job was still available.

I was pissed off with myself for disappointing Tammy. She'd always been nice to me. For a year or so after Mom and I ran into her at the grocery store, Tammy and I had gotten together every month to have dinner or go to a movie. She even took me to her mom's house once. I tried to convince her not to tell her mom who I was because I thought she might not want me in her home if she knew.

"Don't you think it will be harder to explain why I have a thirteen-year-old friend, not to mention someone with the same name as my father?" she asked.

"Yeah, I suppose," I replied.

"Honesty really is the best policy," she said, smiling.

I stood in the doorway with my eyes closed while she introduced me to her mother. Tammy was right about the honesty thing, because her mom said, "I knew who you were the second I saw you . . . even with your eyes closed," and laughed.

● ● ●

John talked the manager of the rec center into giving me the job but I don't think he was happy about it, especially after I asked him if it would be okay for me to get to work at 8:30 a.m. instead of 8 a.m. "I'll have to get up at 6:30 a.m. and that's too early," I said.

"No, it's not okay. Get an alarm clock. That's what everyone else does!" he growled.

I sold the rest of my pot and made enough to pay off and pick up my new car the night before I started my job as the front desk clerk. I felt pretty grown up driving my own car to my job that day. And it wasn't a hard job at all. I just had to answer the phone, hand out locker keys and towels, do the laundry, and sign people up for the classes the rec center offered.

I must have met at least a hundred people my first day, including Juan Perez. He came up to the front counter with a couple of other guys who practiced basketball there every afternoon. Juan was cute, and when I handed him his locker key he purposely touched my hand and mentioned how lovely my skin felt. He started hanging around the front counter, and I started to think he might make a good boyfriend. He was cute and he told some pretty good jokes.

We had sex for the first time five days after we met. I let him in my bedroom window after Mom and Olive left for the evening.

Juan had his clothes off within a minute of arriving. I couldn't believe how eager he was, or how big his dick was. He was all over me, kissing and pushing his hand down my pants and under my shirt. I told him to slow down because we had all night, but he just kept going. He didn't even get his dick inside of me before he finished. I didn't make a big deal out of it because he promised to do better next time, and the next time was about ten minutes later. He did last a bit longer, but not much. I had to get up to use the bathroom right afterward because I didn't like the goo in me or on me. When I returned he was dressed and putting his shoes on.

"I have to get home before my mom notices I'm gone," he said.

After he left I asked myself why I'd let it happen it again. Why did I let myself get a big crush on someone I hardly knew? I went downstairs and poured myself a vodka and orange juice. After I drank it, I went searching in Mom's room for her new script of Valium. I helped myself to four of them and slept most of the weekend.

Juan was waiting for me when I arrived at work on Monday morning. He brought me lunch and a little bunch of daisies. "I'm the happiest guy in the world," he said, smiling. "When can we do it again?"

I was surprised and happy to see him again and when he leaned over the counter and kissed me really quick I said, "We can do it in the laundry room during my lunch break."

And that's what we did, and we did it every day that week and the next week, too. It was toward the end of the following week when my boss opened the laundry door and found us. I knew I was going to lose my job because of it, but I didn't know I could be arrested too as well.

When my boss told me Juan was only fourteen years old I almost fell over. "Are you sure? He doesn't look fourteen," I practically screamed.

"Yeah, I'm sure, and I'm pretty sure you're eighteen, which makes your relationship illegal," he said.

How could that be? I thought to myself. Juan had a little moustache and a much bigger dick than any of the other guys I'd had sex with, and I was sure they were all much older than him.

John called my mom, and then Mom called Robbie. Robbie had just started his job in the office of a state senator, and even though he hated me, he told Mom he'd drive down the next day to sort it out.

Mom handed the phone to me.

"What?" I said.

"Listen, you worthless piece of shit. Just stay home and don't talk to anyone until I get there." He slammed the phone down.

Juan's parents, my mom, and Robbie weren't as upset about the sex as my boss, sister, and John were. After Robbie talked to Juan's parents, they agreed not to call the police, but only if I stayed away from Juan and the rec center. I wanted to say something in my defense, but I couldn't think of anything. I saw Juan sitting in his parents' car when I was walking with Mom to our car. I gave him a little wave but he turned his head and looked away.

I took 5 milligrams of Valium and drank two wine coolers before I went to bed that night. Mom saw me take the wine coolers from the fridge and I'm pretty sure she heard me crying too, but she didn't come into my room, and she didn't say anything to me about it the next day either.

CHAPTER 15

With no job and nothing to do, I slept in for an entire week. It felt good to do nothing, and I could hardly bring myself to get up at 3 p.m. to take a shower, do a few chores, and start dinner. When my paycheck from the rec center arrived in the mail, I bought myself twenty Xanax and I bought Mom a bottle of White Diamonds perfume and a small bunch of pink carnations.

"I love the perfume and the flowers," Mom said as she sat down at the kitchen table for dinner. "And I know you're sorry about what happened. But you've got to pick yourself up and get a job. You can't just hang out and hide the rest of your life."

We ate our fish sticks and fries in silence, and I promised myself I'd start looking for a job the following Monday. I even spent the weekend looking through my closet for something decent to wear. I finally decided on a plain blue blouse and black jeans. On Monday I was up before Mom left for work and spent the day handing out my résumé to anyplace I thought would take it, including McDonald's and Kentucky Fried Chicken, but no one had any work available. All the summer jobs were gone.

After I told Mom about my horrible day looking for work, I asked if there were any jobs at her bank that I could apply for.

"You don't want to work at my bank. That's not a good idea." She said it so quickly and quietly I hardly caught a word. From then on she stopped making employment suggestions and began leaving educational brochures on the kitchen table and talking to me about enrolling at the community college.

One night, toward the end of July, Mom put a pamphlet about a medical receptionist course under my dinner plate. When I picked it up she said, "I'd be more than happy to pay your tuition. What do you think?"

"It doesn't sound like me. I don't like school. I'm thinking about applying for a job with the state, on a road crew, as one of those people who hold up stop and go signs on highways."

"That's an old man's job," she said.

"So what? It pays well, and I wouldn't have to do much except stand on the road with a sign in my hand."

"I was hoping you'd have better plans for your life than standing on a road," she huffed before she got up and left the table.

The next day, a large envelope from Robbie arrived. It was full of information about the military. I read it over, filled in a few things, and left it on the coffee table with a note for Mom before I went to bed. "I'm going to sign up for the Navy. I'll go to the recruitment office tomorrow."

● ● ●

In the morning Mom bolted into my room and yelled, "You want to go to Iraq?"

"Well, no, but I could I suppose. Robbie thinks it's a good idea and I don't have anything else to do," I replied.

"It's not a good idea!" Mom replied.

She threw the Navy recruitment forms in the trash and called Robbie. "If you think the war is such a good idea, why didn't you sign up?"

I pretended to eat my cereal while Mom spoke with

Robbie over the phone. They went on talking for a few minutes and then I heard mom say, "Well, she's not your kid, so you don't need to worry about her."

Things calmed down a bit between Mom and me after that—until the next weekend, when Robbie arrived with his new girlfriend.

"How's it going, cradle snatcher?" Robbie said as he walked in the front door.

I didn't answer.

His girlfriend, Sam, walked over to the couch where I was sitting and stuck out her hand for me to shake. I didn't move. She pulled her hand away and introduced herself, all the while talking really loud, really slow, and in a very deep voice. I stared right into her face, trying to figure out if she was a boy or a girl. She was a dead ringer for the dark-haired guy on *Full House*, and I was pretty sure she was a man until I saw her red fingernails.

"Hey, no matter what Robbie told you, I'm not officially a moron or a retard, okay?" I said, smirking.

She turned around and looked at Robbie, but he only shrugged his shoulders and said, "She really is. She just doesn't know it."

They headed out to Dad's big garage and didn't come back in until Mom got home from work at 6 p.m. I was in the kitchen cutting tomatoes for a salad when she walked in with a loaf of French bread and carton of chocolate ice cream. "Thanks for making dinner, honey. I brought the dessert."

"Robbie is here with his new girlfriend—or boyfriend, I'm not sure. Do I have to make them dinner too?" I asked Mom just as the back door opened and Robbie and Sam walked in carrying bags of Dad's old car magazines.

"Sam's a bit of a car wizard and she wants these," Robbie said as he squeezed past Mom and me to put the bags down by the front door.

"That's weird, because that other girlfriend you had was some kind of mechanic too," I said under my breath, just loud enough for Sam to hear, but out of Robbie's earshot.

"Robbie says your car isn't running so well. I can have a look at it if you want," Sam said.

"That would be great. It's the starter, I'm sure," I replied.

"An easy fix. I'll do it tomorrow," Sam said as she grabbed a few plates from the counter and put them on the kitchen table.

I hadn't planned on making dinner for four people, but it was obvious they were staying, so I dumped a jar of canned tomatoes into my basil and mushroom sauce and took a few more chicken and parmesan raviolis out of the freezer as I listened to Robbie talk about a high school reunion they'd come to town to attend that weekend.

As soon as we were seated at the table, Mom poured herself and Sam a glass of white wine and Robbie started in about how lazy I was. "You'd better get yourself enrolled in school, because it's obvious you can't get a job. It's August 5th and you haven't done a thing all summer except become a criminal!"

Sam threw a surprised glance my way, and I put my head down and ate while Robbie went on talking. I heard Sam clear her throat a couple of times, but Robbie didn't pay her any attention. "She's a lazy cow, Mom, and you're not much of a mother for letting her get away with it," he roared.

That's when Mom kicked Robbie under the table, hard enough for him to yelp and to shut up. Both Sam and I let out a nervous laugh.

"We have a guest, Robbie, and she doesn't need to hear how you feel about me or your sister, so let's just eat," Mom said.

● ● ●

By Sunday afternoon, Mom was in tears and I was ready to kill Robbie. Before he left, I agreed to fill in the form for the medical assistant course at the community college, just to shut him up. I didn't want to be a medical assistant, didn't want to be around sick people or clean up anyone's puke or shit. But the only other course I could have signed up for was a three-year cooking course, and I couldn't think of anything worse than going to school for three years.

I made a beef stroganoff dinner for Mom and me after Robbie and Sam left, and I threw up a few hours later, and the next morning and evening too. I thought I had the flu until I remembered I hadn't had a period for a while. I helped myself to twenty dollars from Mom's wallet and went to the pharmacy on Tuesday morning to buy a pregnancy test. The instructions said it was best to get a urine sample first thing in the morning, so I had to wait all night and I didn't sleep a wink. At 6 a.m. I peed on the stick, and while I waited for the results, I vomited so hard I thought my guts were going to come out. *Pink equals pregnant. Fuck!*

There was no way I was going to have a kid, and there was no way I was going to tell Mom I was pregnant by a fourteen-year-old.

I counted the days from the last time Juan and I had sex and figured I could be eight weeks pregnant. I sat on the bathroom floor waiting for my stomach to settle and thinking about how I could make myself miscarry. I'd heard somewhere that taking three packs of birth control pills all at once would do it, but I didn't have any, and I didn't know where to get any. I called a Planned Parenthood help phone number that I found in the phone book and asked the girl who answered if it was true that poking yourself up there with a knitting needle would do it.

"You could injure yourself or even die from doing that. Don't do it! I can refer you to someone here who can help you," she said.

I said yes because I was too scared not to, but I didn't want anyone's help. I just wanted it to go away. I didn't know anyone who'd had an abortion, and I didn't know how to go about getting one, either, but I knew that was what I wanted. When the receptionist put me on hold, I hung up.

I decided to tell Mrs. Benson after she stopped by with a bag of lemons from her tree the next morning and asked me how my job at the recreation center was going.

"I lost it," I said.

"Oh, I didn't know. How come?"

I bowed my head and tried to hide my teary eyes from her, but she kept looking at me until I had no choice but to look up. "I'm in big trouble, as usual," I mumbled.

"I'm pretty familiar with trouble, so why don't you tell me about it. Maybe I can help?" she said.

"I'm pregnant," I replied.

"Oh, is that all? Well, don't cry, honey. It'll be okay. There are people in this world that can take care of that. I once had an abortion in the back room of an old doctor's house. I was scared and it hurt, but things have changed since then, for the better."

She told me she had a niece who worked at a women's health clinic and she'd go home and call her right away. "Save those tears. You'll need 'em later." She smiled as she grabbed my hand and gave it a big squeeze.

● ● ●

I got an appointment at the women's health clinic the very next day. I had to borrow five dollars from Mrs. Benson for gas, and I drove myself because I didn't want her to come with me, just in case they asked me about the father. I didn't want her to know I was a criminal.

I gave them some pee and blood and waited in the reception room for more than an hour before they called my name and took me to an exam room. "You're about seven weeks along, and you're a little anemic too," said the nice old lady doctor.

She asked if I'd thought about what I wanted to do or if I'd told the father about it. "I haven't told anyone and I'm not going to. I just want to get rid of it as soon as I can," I said.

"I understand," she said in a soft, calm voice.

She handed me a leaflet with information about termination. "You'll need to make an appointment to have the procedure done, and it's not likely you can get in until next Monday. The procedure costs four hundred dollars, and it would be good if you got someone to drive you home and look after you for a day or two."

I felt my chest clench and heard myself gasp when I heard that. "I don't have any money right now. It might take me a couple of weeks to find someone to borrow it from," I sobbed.

I felt like running away, and scooted off the exam table so quick I almost knocked her off the stool she was sitting on.

"Don't wait too long, and let me know if you have trouble raising the money," she said as she patted my arm and handed me a card with her phone number on it.

I went to the twins' house to talk to them about borrowing money. They'd stopped selling pot after they got busted just before graduation. I hadn't turned them in, but I think they thought I did because they both quit talking to me at the same time.

Their mom answered the door. She told me they'd left for Colorado the week before for college. Next I went to the car dealer who'd sold me my car and asked him to buy it back. "It's got a brand-new starter, two new tires, and the oil has just been changed," I told him.

"I don't want it. Wouldn't give ya fifty bucks for it," he said.

I couldn't ask Mom for the money because she'd given me money for the new tires the month before. Besides, if I asked her she'd want to know what I needed it for, and I wasn't about to tell her. I knew Mrs. Benson didn't have any money because she only got a little bit of a retirement from her job at the shirt factory. I thought about Aunt Flo. But I hadn't spoken to her in two years, since Dad died, and I thought she was still mad at me for telling her I wrote the lyrics to Tyler's song. I was afraid she'd hang up on me if I called, so I didn't.

The next day, Friday, on my way home from the pawn shop, where I got twenty dollars for Dad's Elvis Presley record collection, I got the idea to stop by Aunt Flo's cottage to see if there might be something in Uncle Hank's shed I might be able to sell. I'd often wondered about all the things in his garden shed, especially the box of money and gold he'd showed me when I was a little kid. I also wondered if he'd told Aunt Flo about it. She'd never mentioned it to me, and I hadn't spoken a word about it to anyone because my promise to Uncle Hank to keep it a secret was the only thing I had left of him.

I parked down the street and walked up behind the house and down a small pathway between the cottage shed and the neighbor's house. I had a look around the front garden, walked carefully onto the porch, and peeked in the front room window to see if Uncle Bill or anyone was home. They weren't; I was grateful, and glad to find that the shed door wasn't locked either.

Uncle Hank's shed was exactly like I remembered it. I didn't think Uncle Bill had cleaned up or cleared out a thing—at least it didn't look like he had. I had a quick look around, to see if there was anything that I might be able to pawn, before I headed to the back of the shed to check on Uncle Hank's old steamer trunk. I pushed it a few feet to the side, took a screwdriver from the drawer, and lifted a few floorboards. Uncle Hank's box was sitting in the very same place it had been the day he showed it to me, seven years before. I lifted it out and was encouraged that something might still be in it, because it was very heavy.

In the sunlight I could see the box was rusty and the little combination lock was almost completely orange, but after playing around with it for a while I was able to open the lock and the box. It looked like everything was still in place—well, almost everything. The gems were gone, of course. Aunt Flo had gotten them all in the anniversary ring he had made for her. I rummaged through the contents. The eight gold bars, the stacks of fifty US one hundred–dollar bills, Uncle Hank's velvet bag, and lots of foreign money were all there. I wondered, after all these years, why the box was still hidden. I didn't think Uncle Hank was the type who would keep a big secret from Aunt Flo but I guess he didn't have time to tell her before he died.

I felt sad looking through Uncle Hank's stuff, and tried to catch my tears before they dropped on his things. I had an awful feeling in my stomach about what I was about to do. How could I steal from him? I missed him as much as ever, and I had never wanted to let him down, but I couldn't ask Mom for abortion money. I knew she thought I was a loser, and the fact that I'd gotten pregnant by a kid would only make it worse. I decided the only thing I could do was to write an IOU and leave it in the box. I used one of Uncle Hank's drawing pencils, and a piece of draft paper I took from a notebook he used to draw in, and wrote, "I'm sorry, really sorry. I owe you four hundred dollars, and I promise to pay you back." I counted out four hundred dollars, stuffed it in my pants pocket, put the IOU in the box, and closed the lid. I tried to put the lock back on but it was too rusty. So I put it in my back pocket. I lowered the box onto the wooden chopping block, underneath the floorboards, and put everything back in place before I snuck out and drove home.

I called Mrs. Benson's niece later that same day and made an appointment for Monday morning. She told me a few things I needed to do before I arrived and asked if I had any questions.

"Can I use a fake name? And not to be gross or anything, but have you ever sucked out body parts by mistake? What do you do with the stuff you take out of me?" I asked.

"You can use a fake if you want, but we'd prefer that you didn't—and I'm not exactly sure what they do with the fetal tissue, but I've never heard of anyone's body parts getting sucked out," she said.

I was relieved and told her I liked the word "termination" more than the word "abortion." It sounded safer and cleaner. She agreed.

Before she hung up she reminded me not to eat any breakfast on Monday and asked if I had a friend or family member I could bring along for support. I said, "sure," because I didn't want her to think I didn't have any friends.

I went to visit Mrs. Benson the night before my appointment to tell her about my plan to get unpregnant and thank her for helping me. I didn't know why I cried when I told her. It wasn't like I was having second thoughts or anything.

"Oh, you're just crying because you got all those hormones racing around your body. You come over to my house tomorrow and I'll drive you to the clinic and make sure you're all right afterwards," Mrs. Benson said.

I hugged her for the longest time, and she hugged me back like she really meant it.

The termination was all a big blur, and I think I held my breath until it was over. Mrs. Benson got me home and in bed about an hour before Mom arrived home from work. I was glad Mom spent most of the night on the phone talking to Olive instead of checking on me. On her way to bed, she stopped by my room and asked if I was okay. I told her I had bad cramps and asked her if she had anything I could take. I'd already taken my last couple of Percocets, and the clinic had only given me four codeine pills, which I'd swallowed on the drive home. I didn't have any money to buy anything and I didn't have the energy to go out to Dad's garage and look for a bottle of booze, so asking Mom was my last resort.

Mom went to her room and came back with a Valium that I took right away. The next morning I found another one she'd left on the kitchen counter for me.

CHAPTER 16

O n August 28, two weeks after my termination and twelve days before I was supposed to start my course at the community college, Sissy called.

"I've been meaning to call you for ages," she said, "but I couldn't find your number until just now."

"Wow, I never thought I'd hear from you again," I practically squealed.

"Well it's really me, and I'm back from Dublin for good. My boyfriend Cian and I are going to get married next year, but that's not why I called. Do you want to go to Nevada for a couple of weeks? I've got a job at a big festival, and it would be great if you'd come along and keep an eye on Cian while I work. He's a bit of a party animal and I can't think of anyone better to keep him company than my one-time 'craft' student," she said, laughing.

"A festival? To hang out? Fuck yeah—I mean, yes please. When?"

"We're leaving from Arnold's tomorrow morning. Flo gave me your address and directions, so we should be there by 2 p.m. By the way, she said to tell you 'hello.'"

I was so excited to hear from Sissy, and to be invited somewhere, that I didn't even need to consider where we might be going or why. I spent the rest of the afternoon cleaning the house and thinking of what I should do about school. Going with Sissy and Cian meant I'd have to start school a week late. I decided to call the community college to tell them I couldn't start on time because my mom wasn't well.

The woman who answered the phone said she'd put a note in my file about starting late. "As long as you're here on the 16th of September it should be okay," she said.

When Mom got home from work that night I told her my medical receptionist course began on Sept 16th (instead of the 9th) and that I wanted to go away with Sissy for two weeks to a festival. After giving me an eyebrows-up stare and walking around the kitchen for five minutes, she said, "Maybe you should go. You've been kind of down these past couple of weeks, and I've been worried about you. Are you having a bad period?"

"Yes! I am. I've been bleeding for almost two weeks, but it's over now. Weird, huh?" I said.

"I used to bleed like that too. It's awful," she replied as she headed down the hallway and returned a few minutes later carrying a box of super-size tampons. "Try these next month. They're better than those regular ones you use," she said.

I took the box. "Thanks, I will."

She talked all through dinner that night about a new dating club she was planning to join. "I'm so sick of meeting loser men. The club guarantees high-class singles, and I've decided I'm high-class," she said, grinning.

"That's great, Mom." I smiled at her. "So . . . what do you think about me going away with Sissy and Cian?"

"Okay," she said, "but please call me every day or two so I know that you're okay."

I kissed her on each cheek, and then on her forehead, before I went to bed. When Sissy and Cian arrived at 2 p.m. the next day I was ready to go.

• • •

My trip with Sissy and Cian didn't work out the way I thought it would. Sissy's boss wasn't happy she'd brought two people along, as she was only allowed one guest, and he said he'd deduct thirty dollars from her pay for me to stay in her tent and eat in the staff cafeteria. Even though I promised to pay her back once I got some money, she was pissed off. She wanted to leave, but Cian talked her out of it.

Worse than that was that Cian turned out to be an even bigger drinker than Sissy had described. I tried to keep him from drinking so much the first day, but it was useless, so the next day I decided to try to keep up with him until we both got legless and passed out.

Sissy's job was to take tickets and give parking directions from 9 a.m. to 7 p.m. When she was done with her shift, all she wanted to do was eat dinner and go to sleep, and she wanted Cian with her. But Cian wasn't interested in sleeping, or in staying in the tent while she slept, so I followed him around like she asked me to.

On our fifth day at the festival Cian bought some mescaline and peyote from a guy he'd met at the communal bathrooms, and I took so much I thought I was walking on the moon. After I caught myself stepping over moon rocks, which were really people in sleeping bags, I got scared about losing my mind, so I went to the front gate to find Sissy and told her I was freaking out.

"I don't give a shit," she yelled. "Take a fucking shower and get over it."

After that, Sissy quit being nice to me.

On the ninth day, Sissy woke us up before she headed out to work the front gate. "Do you two have to get so wasted all the time? Can't you lay off for one day?" she screamed.

"We'll lay off today," Cian said in his Lucky Charms Irish accent. "I might even bring you some lunch later, but right now I'm sleeping."

I nodded my head in agreement and dozed back off.

Cian never got around to taking Sissy some lunch. Instead, he and I took off with a couple of guys we'd met at a huge drum circle the day before to drink the tequila they'd brought with them from Texas. The next morning I heard from one of the guys that I'd traded the sapphire earrings Aunt Flo and Uncle Hank had given me for a dream catcher and a pack of Marlboro lights. I looked around the festival grounds all day for the girl I'd supposedly traded with but I never found her.

I was so pissed off about losing my earrings that I took an offer from some biker guy to share his fifth of Jack Daniel's in return for letting him massage my feet with some homemade oil. I got shitfaced and he massaged more than my feet before he carried me to someone's tent and left me. I know I had sex with a couple of other guys, but I'm pretty sure Cian wasn't one of them. When Sissy found me two days later, sleeping outside of that same tent with a couple of my new friends, she shook me really hard.

"Wake up, Randall," she yelled. "Where's Cian?"

"He's in the tent, I think," I replied.

"Did you fuck him?"

"I don't think so. I'm pretty sure I didn't," I replied.

She practically pulled Cian out of the tent by his hair. "Did you fuck her?" she screamed.

"Fuck who?" Cian replied.

"Randall, you idiot."

"Don't think so. Can't recall," he said.

Sissy screamed at both of us for being fuckups, and she packed up and went home with Cian that afternoon. They even took the sleeping bag they'd brought for me.

I had to stay and help clean up the campgrounds to earn enough to eat and buy a bus ticket home, and I didn't get back until the afternoon of September 18th.

Mom was really angry with me for not calling her or coming home in time to start school. "I've been worried sick about you, and I didn't appreciate getting a call from the secretary of the community college asking how I was feeling and telling me that you hadn't shown up for school, which started on the 9th of September, not the 16th."

I tried to explain what had happened but she wouldn't listen. "They're not going to let you into the course, Randall. Either you get a job or you find another place to live," she screamed.

I hated that Mom was mad and I knew I'd screwed up, so I got serious about looking for a job. I went out the very next day and every day the following week with my résumé, and I filled out job applications every place I could think of, even the 7-Eleven. It was when I was at the mall, heading to JCPenney to fill out an application to be a cleaner, that I ran into Mom's old boyfriend Nick. He threw me a big smile and walked right up to me like we were good friends.

"Hey, Sexy Bird, I haven't seen you for a while. Where've you been?" he said.

"Mom and I don't shop at your store anymore. I guess you know why," I replied.

"Yeah, she was pretty mad. How is she anyway?"

"She's really good. She's got a new job and she's dating a real nice guy from her salsa class," I lied. "But I can't talk right now. I'm on the hunt for a job." I turned and started walking into JCPenney's service office.

"There's a part-time cashier's job available at my store. You can have it if you want it," he said.

Nick's offer of a job was a bit of good news. He had a store just outside the mall, and even though it was only a part-time position, I was pretty sure it would be enough to satisfy Mom.

On my drive home, after picking up my cashier smock from Nick's store, I decided not to say a word to Mom about Nick. I didn't want to cause any more trouble for myself. When Mom came home from work that night, I lied and told her I got a job at JCPenney's, in their phone order department, and she seemed happy to hear it, and happier to know I'd be paying her fifty dollars a week for room and board. Fifty dollars sounded a bit high at first, but then I realized I was going to earn almost two hundred a week and I'd have plenty of money to pay Mom, get new windshield wipers for my car, and buy a few pills.

● ● ●

I don't know how or why I got involved with Nick. I knew it was wrong, but I'd had a crush on him since the day he bought me and Mom roses for Valentine's Day. Of course, I never thought for a second he'd be interested in me. When he was dating Mom, he often arrived early to take her to dinner, and since she was always running late, he'd sit and talk to me about school and things until she was ready to go. Once or twice I'd caught him looking at me in a strange way—a way that made me feel good and bad at the same time. So when he kissed me in his office on my first day of work, and then invited me to his condominium for a drink, I was secretly thrilled. He had a place a few blocks from the store that he used to "get away from it all," and he said I could stay there any time I wanted to. "You'll have to invite me, though," he said, laughing.

I thought about taking him up on his invite, mainly because I didn't have anything else to do that night, but all I could think of was Mom and how I'd promised her I'd stop drinking. So I didn't go.

The next day at work he walked up behind me in the back room, while I was putting on my smock, and blew on the back of my neck. "You've got such a delicious-looking ass. One day I'm gonna take a bite."

I got a flush throughout my entire body and turned a hundred shades of red, but I didn't respond, and I tried my best to avoid him after that because I didn't want anyone at work to think there was something going on between us. It was hard, though, because every time he saw me he'd make a face like he was biting something, and it did make me laugh—for a few days, anyway.

I discovered a week later that Nick wasn't kidding about wanting to bite me after I woke up on his kitchen floor with two used condoms next to my head and bite marks on my butt and the backs and insides of my thighs. I couldn't remember too much about it. Didn't even recall how I'd gotten to his condo. The last thing I remembered was Nick handing me a beer in the back room of the store after work.

When I opened my eyes and discovered I was naked, I was more scared than I'd ever been. It took me a while to sit up, and that's when I noticed the blood. It was all over me, and all around me, but I couldn't tell where it was coming from. I didn't know how bad it was until I found the bathroom and looked in the mirror. Eight bites on my butt and six on my inner thighs (three on each). Some of the bites weren't very noticeable, but two of them were bleeding and I could see the imprint of teeth.

Nick must have known how bad he hurt me because he left bandages and an antiseptic spray on the bathroom counter. He also left a note on top of a black sweatshirt and pants that were on a chair next to the bathtub: "Sorry, but I couldn't resist. Have a bath and relax and I'll be around about noon to take you to get your car. PS: The stuff by the front door is for you."

I ran to the front door, hoping he'd left my clothes there, but instead I found a bag from his pharmacy with three bottles in it. I didn't look at the bottles. I was too worried about the time, thinking it might be close to noon and that Nick would be arriving to find me without any clothes on. I ran to the bedroom to look for a clock, but all I found was a wooden bed with leather straps tied to each of the four corners, and a big lamp. I looked down at my ankles and wrists to see if there were any marks and figured I must have struggled a bit, because my right ankle was pretty red and raw. I walked back to the kitchen and looked at the clock on the stove. It was eleven thirty; I needed to move fast.

I took a quick shower, just to get the blood off my face and out of my hair, and I tried to cover the bleeding bites, but it was hard to reach them and the bandages wouldn't stay on. I gave up after trying a few times and used a few paper towels from the kitchen instead. I found my purse and car keys in the kitchen sink, and even though I didn't know whose clothes were on the chair in the bathroom, I put them on anyway.

As I walked toward the front door, I thought about cleaning up the blood and flushing the condoms down the toilet, but I didn't plan on ever seeing Nick again, so I left everything as it was. I grabbed the two pharmacy-size bottles of Valium and Darvocet, and a small bottle of an antibiotic, and put them in my purse on my way out.

● ● ●

I was scheduled to work that day at 3 p.m., but there was no way I was going into Nick's store ever again. Besides, I could barely walk the three blocks from Nick's condo to the mall parking lot to get my car. I found a note on my windshield when I arrived and figured it must be from Nick, so I didn't open it. I drove home, took a long shower, and spent the afternoon trying to cover my bite marks with some big bandages I found in Mom's bathroom.

Just as I was heating up a frozen burrito, Mom walked in the front door. "What's with you not coming home and not calling, are you trying to drive me crazy?" she yelled.

"What?" I replied.

"Did you get the note I left on your car? I've been worried sick. I was gonna call the police."

"I didn't see your note. I'm sorry. I stayed with a friend last night and forgot to call. I'm sorry," I said again.

"When are you ever going to grow up?" she asked just before she went to her room and slammed the door behind her.

I took a Valium and a Darvocet from the bottles Nick had left for me and slept for fourteen hours. The next morning my entire butt and thighs ached so much that I decided the bites were infected and took a couple of the antibiotics and a couple more Darvocets and went back to bed. I did the same thing every day for three days.

Mom thought I had the flu, so she left me alone, and I didn't bother calling the store to tell the floor manager I was never coming back because I figured I was fired anyway.

Mom came into my room a few nights later and asked me about my job and when she could expect the fifty dollars for my rent. "How is it that your boss is okay about you taking time off when you just started the job?" she asked.

"Because I'm contagious and she doesn't want me to infect the others. I'm going back tomorrow, so I'll pay you this week when I get my check," I said.

She rolled her eyes and told me to clean up my room and pick up the wet towels I'd left on the bathroom floor as she walked out.

After a wine cooler and a Valium the next morning, I got the nerve to call the store and ask about my paycheck. Nick answered the phone. "Good to hear from you, Sexy Bird, how are you feeling?"

I couldn't respond. All I could do was cry, and I thought he would say sorry, but instead he said, "It's your fault, ya know. You've got a sweet ass and a way of walking that makes me hard."

I choked back the tears and said, "You hurt me."

"Hey, I left you some stuff. Just be happy I wore a condom, because it's not my policy," he replied.

He also said if I came back to work he'd give me my paycheck (without deducting the five days I'd missed) and let me have a few things from the store's pharmacy. "No charge, if you get what I mean."

I really needed my check, and I didn't have any other job prospects. And Mom was so pissed off with me that she could barely look at me. So I went back to work that afternoon and told the checkout manager that Nick had given me my old job back. "Oh yeah, we'll see about that," she barked.

She called Nick down from his office, and I listened as he sweet-talked her until she agreed to put me back on the work roster. He winked at me as he walked by, and for some reason I liked it. I also liked the card he stapled to the dry-cleaner bag he handed to me on my way out of the store after my shift. The bag contained the clothes that I hadn't been able to find after I woke up on his kitchen floor, and the card had my check in it and said something like, "I'm sorry we got off to a bad start, let's try again." It was sweet, and I wondered how he could be so nice after what he'd done to me.

The next day, when Nick asked me to come to his office, I told him I was still mad and my butt still hurt.

"I'll never hurt you again, sweetheart, it was just fluke. I don't know what got into me—besides you!" he said. "If it'll make you feel better and mend this fence, you can have something from the pharmacy—just name it and it's yours," he said.

I left the store that night with about six hundred pills, and from then on I met Nick at the condo whenever he wanted me to—for sex, mostly, because that's what he liked to do. After a few weeks of being tied to the bed while he did whatever he wanted, I kind of got used to it, and I think I even fell in love with him.

● ● ●

If it came as a surprise that Nick and I would be sleeping together, it came as more of a surprise that I'd fallen in love with him. I knew there were lots of reasons I shouldn't be with him. I thought about them all the time: he was my boss; I was eighteen and he was forty-eight; he hurt me; he was married; but the biggest of all was that I was pretty sure if Mom found out I was dating him, she'd disown me.

I met Nick's wife, Sharon, two months after I started working at the store, at the company Christmas party. She walked up to me and started telling me about her new house and how she was busy with her two little girls, ages three and six months. I was surprised, and also a little bit bummed out, that she was so friendly. I thought she might have noticed the look and the wink Nick threw my way when I walked into the room and was coming over to slap me around for flirting with her husband. Instead, she took a wallet of photos out of her purse and showed me pictures of her kids.

"Do you ever babysit?" she asked.

"Only once, for a neighbor, but the kids were asleep when I arrived," I replied.

"Great, we're always looking for a good babysitter. Can I call you?"

I didn't answer.

Sharon called me at the store a few days later to see if I had plans for New Year's Eve. When I said I didn't, she asked if I would babysit. She and Nick were going out for the first time since she'd had her second baby, and she couldn't find a sitter. "You're our only hope, can you do it?"

I could hear the desperation in her voice, so I said yes.

Sharon was nice, and we became friends, but not good enough friends for me to stop sleeping with her husband. By February I was babysitting for her at least twice a week.

But the more involved I got with Nick, the harder it was for me to see Sharon. So on my nineteenth birthday, after five months of helping her out, I told her I couldn't work for her anymore. She almost cried, and I felt bad, but I didn't change my mind.

Being with Nick also made living at home weird. I felt like Mom and I didn't like each other. She was keeping busy with work and a new man she'd met at the singles club, so we didn't see each other much—and when we did she was always drilling me about what I was doing with my life: "Are there opportunities for advancement at the call center? Are you seeing anyone? Where do you go after work? How come you stay out so late?"

I made up lies just to keep her off my back, and after a while I found myself lying to her all the time about everything.

I thought I could manage without the money Sharon paid me each week for watching her little girls, doing her laundry, and running errands, but I couldn't. After a couple of weeks I was broke, and I still hadn't paid Mom any rent for August.

I had to get more hours at the store or a find another job, so I asked my floor manager for another shift, but she couldn't give me any extra hours. When I asked the store supervisor about another position, all he had was cleaning the store after it closed, and I wasn't interested in that.

I put a card up on the mall notice board offering my (expert) babysitting services on Fridays and weekends for eight dollars an hour. Within a week I had two babysitting jobs, and each had just one kid. It was easy money, and I didn't mind working on the weekends because Nick didn't come around then, and I was lonely if I didn't have anything to do.

●　●　●

Nick and I celebrated our one-year anniversary on September 30th. He gave me a gift certificate to a department store in the mall, and I made him a spaghetti dinner at his condo. I was happy and everything was going well until the state carried out an audit on Nick's pharmacy just after Thanksgiving. From then on, it was hard for Nick to give me pills. He sent me to a doctor friend of his who was willing to write prescriptions for me, and that worked okay for a couple of months, but it cost me thirty-five dollars for every appointment, and I needed more pills than the doctor would write a prescription for.

On Valentine's Day, after we'd been out to dinner at the very same cocktail lounge Nick used to take my mom to, Nick went into my purse to get a pen and pulled out four prescriptions bottles, all with different names on them.

"Two of those are empty," I said as I grabbed the bottles and shoved them back into my bag.

"I was just checking it out. Seeing what my old doctor friend is supplying you with. Who the fuck is Vera Slider?" Nick laughed as he read the labels on the bottles.

"She's someone I babysit for once in a while," I said. "And your friend isn't supplying me with much. He's not worth the thirty-five dollars he charges to write a prescription for forty pills."

"Maybe you shouldn't take so many."

"And maybe you should go fuck yourself!" I snapped.

I was angry that Nick had discovered I'd stolen pills

from Vera Slider, the mother of the four-year-old I'd been watching on Saturdays. I was especially angry after he made fun of me because it was a bottle of phenobarbital. "It's an old lady drug, ya know. Not worth the effort of helping yourself to." He laughed.

He teased me about it all the way to his car, and I got so mad I slapped him. And then I did it again and again. I must have hit him ten times before he grabbed my hands and held them behind my back. I could tell he wanted to hit me back, but there were people standing by the lounge back door watching us, so he didn't.

It only took two weeks of me ignoring Nick before he met me at my car after my shift with a bottle of Darvon. "How about I make a trip down to Mexico and get you a barrel full of whatever you want? Then will you move into the condo?"

I moved into Nick's condo March 20th, a year and a half after I started working at his store, mainly because I didn't have to pay any rent and he promised to get me pills, but also because Mom's new boyfriend was just like my dad and was getting on my case all the time. Mom was, too, just like she used to when Dad was alive. One night she yelled at me about my shoes stinking up the living room and then looked right into my face and said, "I think I saw you and Nick walking out of his store together yesterday. Was it Nick?" she demanded.

"No, that was my friend Cory; he works at Nick's store, and I met him there after I got off work at the call center. We went out for pizza." I grabbed my shoes and headed for my room.

I wasn't making Cory up. He was a guy who stocked shelves at the store, and I knew he liked me, and I knew he liked pizza, too, because he often brought a pizza with him to work and he often tried to share it with me.

I didn't know if Mom believed my story, but it was clear that she was still hung up on Nick and driving by his store to see if she could catch a glimpse of him. I told her I was moving out soon after that. "My friend at work is going to New Jersey for a while and I'm going to housesit and take care of her cat for a few months," I said.

Mom seemed relieved.

● ● ●

Moving into Nick's condo wasn't such a good idea. He had keys and came and went whenever he wanted, and he got exceptionally mean once I was living there. After two months of being treated like a sex slave, just before my twentieth birthday, I made a plan to move back home with Mom.

When Nick found me packing my stuff and I confessed I was leaving because I didn't like the way he was using me, he said, "I'm not so sure I'll be going to visit my friend in Mexico if you're not at the condo when I need you to be. So think about that before you decide to leave, Sexy Bird."

So I stayed, hoping things would change and Nick would stop treating me like shit. He didn't, of course, and it seemed that I was making plans to move out every other month, until, before I knew it, a year had gone by and I was almost twenty-one.

I guess I just didn't care enough. And sometimes Nick was nice and gentle with me and I felt okay about being his mistress. Other times he was a crazy animal and I hated him. But I could never tell what he was going to be like from one day to the next, and maybe that's why I stayed with him—because it was exciting.

I felt stuck most of the time, and I continued to get high because it was the only thing that made me feel okay about my boring life and situation. I mostly took pills that Nick got from his friend in Mexico, but sometimes I used other drugs I bought from people I'd met at the mall.

After watching an episode of *Oprah* one afternoon a few weeks after my twenty-first birthday, I decided I'd try to get healthy and have better relationships. I wrote a list of things I would learn to cook and promised myself I would go visit my mom more often. I also figured out that sleeping pills were my biggest problem, because I couldn't fall asleep without them. So I flushed the four pills I had left down the toilet and bought a CD with gentle music on it. It didn't work, though, and after being awake almost all night for three nights I decided to buy some hash from a kid at work and smoke a little each night before I went to bed.

Smoking hash worked pretty well, and I was proud of myself for getting off the sleeping pills, but Nick wasn't. "Smoking hash and then eating a half gallon of ice cream isn't doing much for your figure," he told me.

I ignored him and kept doing it. In the first two months of my smoke-hash-to-sleep approach, I gained twenty pounds. Nick was pretty pissed about it. "When ya gonna stop eating everything in sight?" he asked me when he stopped by the condo on Labor Day morning to have sex and to give me a present before he left for New York with Sharon and his kids for a vacation. In addition to the bottle of Xanax I'd asked for, Nick gave me a bottle of Ritalin. "They might help you lose weight," he said, smirking, before he closed the front door.

I took the Ritalin and spent the rest of the week eating ice cream and wondering if Nick would ever take me to New York with him, or if I'd just be the fat girl he fucked in his condo on his way to work every morning.

By Christmastime that year I'd lost a few pounds. Not enough for Nick to notice, but enough to make me feel better about myself. I spent Christmas Day with Mom because she'd broken up with her boyfriend and Robbie wasn't coming home. It felt good to be at home with her. She made a ham, mashed potatoes, a green bean casserole, and deviled eggs, and after we'd eaten, I took a big plate of everything over to Mrs. Benson.

"Well, well, a miracle on my porch," she said, smiling as she opened the screen door to let me in.

I told her about my job at the store and my babysitting jobs while she ate her dinner. Afterward, we watched an episode of *Little House on the Prairie* without saying a word to each other. Before I left she said, "Thank you for the dinner. It was good to see you. I was thinking you weren't coming around 'cause you didn't want to talk about that bad situation you got yourself into a couple of years back. Come to find out, you just haven't thought about me," she said, chuckling.

"I'm sorry. I've just been busy," I lied. I stepped down off her porch feeling shattered and ashamed. Mrs. Benson had always been nice to me and I liked her. I guessed I'd been avoiding her because I didn't want her to know that I hadn't done much with my life.

"Don't be a stranger!" she called out as I stepped onto the road.

I turned around, waved good-bye, and waited for her to go back into her house before I ran home to Mom.

● ● ●

The next few months were filled with sleepless nights and various diets as I tried to stay off the sleeping pills and the ice cream. I was miserable, and on my twenty-second birthday, after mean and nasty sex with Nick, I told him he was treating me like a whore and that I didn't want him to come over anymore without asking me first. He grabbed my face, looked right into my eyes, and stared at me like I was nothing. Later on, when he was getting dressed to go home to his wife, he said, "I'll come over whenever I feel like it. If you don't like it, tough shit."

I wanted to punch him but he just laughed at me and told me to follow him out to his car if I was interested in the birthday present he had for me in his glove box. I followed, and even as I watched him get into his car and start the engine I thought I'd be able to resist, but when he rolled down the passenger window and held two prescription bottles up for me to take from his hand I only hesitated for a second before I reached out to grab them. When I did, he held on to the bottles for just long enough to let me know I could never leave.

CHAPTER 17

Nick went to a conference in Detroit in mid-June, a couple of weeks after I turned twenty-two. I was really happy about the idea of him being gone at first, but after two nights of hitting the local Hangout Bar alone, I started to miss him, and that confused me. I thought I'd be glad about being alone and not worrying about him or what mood he'd be in when he arrived to have sex with me in the morning, but I wasn't. I was sad and lonely and found myself taking more pills than usual, which hadn't been part of my original plan, as I needed to ration the pills I'd gotten from Nick for my birthday.

One particularly bad night, about ten days after Nick left, when I couldn't sleep and I didn't have any hash or pot and I didn't want to use any more of my pill supply, I drank almost an entire bottle of Nyquil. The next morning I was still pretty out of it, and I nodded off a few times on my short drive to work. The gritty high from the Nyquil stayed with me all day, and I vowed never to use that shit again.

I knew I had to find a way to stop obsessing about Nick, so when Cory asked me to go with him to the store's Fourth of July picnic I said yes. Cory was one of those guys who's almost too nice. He was twenty-three, six foot four, skinny, and had lots of blond, wavy hair and light bluish-gray eyes. He knew Nick and I were together because he'd seen us in the back room making out a few times. He also knew I was mad at him because he'd heard me tell him to "fuck off" a few times as well. I had to give him a lot of credit for asking me out.

I thought I was going to explode with anxiety as I walked from the staff room to my register. Was I cheating on Nick now? I knew if he saw Cory and me together he'd go crazy. But then I remembered that Nick wasn't due back until July 6th, so I stopped worrying about it and began to allow myself to think about Cory. Maybe dating him would help me feel better about myself. The fact that Cory often worked at night alone and might be able to get me something from the pharmacy was a bonus.

● ● ●

We were the first ones to arrive at the picnic. Cory wanted to get there early so he could drive us around the lake in the store's ski boat. It was fun, and I was having a great time until I spotted Nick and Sharon, right when we got back from our boat ride. They were standing in front of the store's display of US flags, next to a food tent. Nick smiled and whistled at me like he was calling a dog. I didn't respond, but I felt my insides whirl with excitement. I could tell Nick had noticed that Cory and I were together. That was too much for me to handle sober, so I headed to the picnic table that was hosting the open bar.

No one was at the beer tent when I arrived, which was great because Nick showed up just as I was deciding on what type of beer I wanted to drink and how many.

"What the fuck are you doing here with our stock boy?" he growled quietly as he walked up behind me.

"I didn't have anyone to go with and I didn't think you'd be back until next week," I replied.

"I cut it short. Good thing, huh? I leave for a few weeks and you're at it with anyone who'll have you!"

"I'm not 'at it' with Cory. We're just at the picnic together. There's nothing wrong with that. He's nice and he's not married," I sputtered, trying hard not to let him see how much my hands were shaking.

"What you need is a good fuck and a drug supplier, and I'm your man. As well as a nice guy!" Nick said.

"I can hear your wife calling you," I said, and I grabbed a couple of cold beers and went to find Cory. We sat with a couple of cashiers at a picnic table far away from where Sharon and Nick were sitting.

I was careful not to drink too much, or to let Cory see me look around for Nick, though I couldn't stop myself from doing it. When it came time for Nick to give a speech to the thirty or so employees at the picnic, he was so drunk he couldn't stand up, so Sharon did it for him. It would have been fine if Nick hadn't kept interrupting her with his slurry, "You tell 'em, honey. Tell 'em I'm a nice guy too, will ya?"

By the time I was ready to leave, Nick had peed on Sharon's chair and then fallen down next to the big barbecue pit. Cory and a few other guys tried to help Nick stand up, but he was too drunk to stand, so they carried him to his car and put him in the backseat.

I was glad Cory hadn't noticed me looking at Nick all day and that he talked about water skiing the entire drive back to the mall parking lot, where we'd met that morning, because I was afraid if I started talking I'd tell Cory something I wasn't supposed to.

"Thanks for the great day. Maybe we should do it again sometime, huh?" Cory said as he pulled up next to my Fiesta.

"Yeah, maybe," I replied and tried hard to give him a smile.

I had a feeling I was in big trouble with Nick, and I knew I'd never get any sleep unless I was drunk, so I stopped at the Hangout Bar and had a few rum and cokes on my way home. I can't remember driving to the condo that night, and I didn't hear Nick open the front door the next morning, either.

• • •

Nick shook me awake just after 6 a.m. "You're a fucking slut!" he yelled. He was on me before I could even react, slamming my head against the wall. I heard the thud before I felt it, and I screamed at him to let me go as I struggled to get away.

"You'll never get another thing from me!"

I wiggled out of his grip and ran to the kitchen, but he followed and knocked me down. I tried for a few minutes to get away, but he was getting meaner and I knew if I continued to resist I'd pay for it, so I gave up fighting. He made me have sex with him on the kitchen table with the blinds wide open so the neighbor guy could watch. I didn't struggle and I didn't say a word. I just kept my eyes closed until he was done.

I broke every plate and every glass in Nick's condo that day. I also took the thousand dollars he had hidden in the freezer and then left all the doors unlocked before I took all my things and drove to Mom's house.

I got there at noon and unpacked. I made a sandwich and watched *General Hospital* and then went to Mom's room to see if she had any pills on her dresser. I found a brand-new prescription of Ativan, so I helped myself to one and shoved another in my pants pocket for later.

Mom was happy to see me when she got home from work. She didn't even ask me why I was back, and when I told her I was planning to stay for a while she said, "Sure, honey, but remember you've got to pay me fifty dollars a week."

Fifty dollars didn't seem like too much of a price to pay to be away from Nick, and I was glad to be in my own bed. Rascal found her way onto my pillow that first night and purred all night long. I think I did too.

After two weeks of living at Mom's, and avoiding Nick and work, I began to feel better—not so down and not so worried. I even took my résumé around to a few stores in the mall, but I only got one interview, and it was for mall security and I wasn't qualified.

I found a note from Cory on my car window the same day

as my mall security interview. "Call me please," it said.

I crumpled up the note and put it in my pocket, a bit disappointed that it wasn't from Nick telling me how sorry he was. The next day I decided to take a part-time kitchen hand job at the Hangout Bar.

The Hangout was the hippest bar in town, and everyone who worked there was nice to me. I felt like a real grown-up sitting at the bar after my shift and drinking with people who had interesting jobs and knew lots of things about the world. Best of all was that I hardly ever thought about Nick when I was there. I was just too busy.

About six weeks after I moved out of Nick's condo and in with Mom, I found a note from Nick on my windshield, "Where the fuck is the thousand dollars I had in the freezer? Return it or else."

I was scared when I read the note, and shocked that Nick had only just discovered his money was missing. I thought he'd known it was gone since the night I moved out. I couldn't return it because I'd spent all of it. I'd used it to pay Mom two hundred for rent, buy rounds of drinks for some of my new friends at the bar, and score a bottle of sixty Valium from a guy who taught me to play pool.

I talked to one of the bartenders that night after my shift about what Nick had done to me and about the money I took. He said I deserved the money and that I should call Nick and tell him to go fuck himself and that he'd even dial the number for me.

Nick's mobile phone rang ten times before he answered. "Go fuck yourself, you asshole!" I yelled.

Telling Nick to fuck himself felt great, but it had the surprising effect of seeming to get him interested in me like never before. He left another note on my car the next day: "I don't care about the money. I miss you. Call me."

I was a little bit happy about the note, but also suspicious and scared, so I didn't call him. He continued to leave notes, pleading with me to meet him at the condo. The last one he left said, "You're fired, BITCH."

I was relieved, but a little sad, to read that note. When I showed it to my friends at the Hangout, two guys offered to kneecap Nick for me. I didn't want them to, but it was nice that they offered.

One night, at the end of August, almost two months since we'd gone to the picnic together, Cory came into the Hangout with a guy I recognized from the mall and sat down at the bar. He didn't know I worked there, and when I saw him walk in, my first instinct was to hide. It took about an hour for him to spot me playing pool and by that time I was just drunk enough to answer his questions about me quitting the store and not calling him.

"It was a bad time. I lost my apartment and had to move back in with my Mom. I've been meaning to call you but thought I'd wait until I got my own place," I lied.

"Okay then, question answered!" Cory replied in a happy voice and then asked me to play a game of darts with him. I wasn't very good at darts, but I had fun and by the end of the night I had begun to find Cory attractive. When he asked me to go to dinner with him the next night, I agreed. "Will you pick me up in that square car of yours?" I asked.

"Sure will," he replied and smiled big.

I loved his car, a teal blue 1976 AMC Pacer with tan leather bucket seats that went all the way back if you pulled a lever on the side of the seat. "My grandpa gave it to me," he told me. "He said I could sell it and use the money to pay for school, but it's such a cool car I decided to keep it."

"The AMC Pacer is the worst car ever built in America, according to my dad," I said when he picked me up to take me to dinner.

"Who's your dad?" Cory asked in a real serious tone.

I thought about it for a few seconds before I answered, "He's no one important," and then we both laughed in an uncomfortable "conversation over" way.

We'd been seeing each other for two weeks when I told Cory it was okay if he wanted to have sex me. "I don't mind if you want to do something other than missionary style. I could even get on top if you wanted. Have you noticed how your seats go all the way back?" I added as I lifted the lever and let the seat drop back until I was lying completely horizontal. I put my legs up in the air and opened them wide.

He pulled his head back and shook it from side to side a couple of times before he said, "Why would you say that, and why would you do what you just did?"

"Why not?" I grinned as I moved my hand up and slid it over his thigh to his crotch. "I'm pretty good at sex, even hand jobs."

He pushed my hand out of the way, gave me a dirty look, and said, "You talk so nasty sometimes."

"Is it nasty? I thought it was sexy," I replied.

"It's nasty! And you're being nasty," he said. His reaction made me feel dirty and stupid. I couldn't think of anything to say, and when he dropped me off at Mom's that night we didn't kiss goodnight, or even say good-bye.

● ● ●

After that, Cory didn't call me again. I never did get around to asking him to get me anything from Nick's pharmacy, but I knew he wouldn't have done it anyway. So I got a part-time weekend job in October at the other drug store in the mall. It was a big store and had a much larger pharmacy than Nick's.

After a couple of weeks working as a relief cashier, I talked one of the store pharmacy assistants into letting me help out behind the counter on Sundays, but it was hard to get my hands on much because every pill and ounce of liquid was measured, monitored, and checked. Sometimes the pharmacist would break or spill a bottle of something good, but it wasn't often I got to go home with anything.

I quit the Sunday pharmacy shift just after Thanksgiving, when I got caught taking two pills out of a filled prescription bottle. I didn't get fired, but the head pharmacist told me off pretty bad. "I see people like you all the time, people who've been on their way to AA since they were born. Do yourself and everyone else a favor and join now."

He scared me, and I thought about what he said every time I drank from then on. Sometimes I tried to limit my drinking, or I'd take a couple of pills before I started drinking so that I didn't drink too much. It rarely worked, though, and by the end of the year I was drinking way more than I meant to all the time and staying at the Hangout Bar until it closed most nights.

● ● ●

When Mom told me on New Year's Eve that Robbie and his new girlfriend were getting married, I almost laughed. It was funny to me that anyone would want to marry Robbie, and I was curious to learn more about her.

"Isn't it great that Sarah Lizbeth and Robbie found each other?" she said. "She lives just up the road, in Cypress, and her parents are paying for a big wedding, bigger than Aunt Flo's. I can't wait."

"Is Sarah a she/he, or a Navy Seal?" I joked.

"That's not funny. Don't say it again!" Mom shouted.

"I was just kidding," I replied.

"No you weren't. You do that all the time. Stop it."

Sarah Lizbeth and Robbie had been dating for just six weeks when he proposed. They sent Mom an envelope full of their engagement photos, and Mom insisted on showing them to me while we sat at the kitchen table eating. I was surprised to see that Sarah Lizbeth was a blonde, blue-eyed Barbie doll, because I expected her to look like a grease monkey, like Robbie's other girlfriends.

Robbie took a leave from work at his job in Sacramento and showed up a week later to stay for a few weeks so he could help Sarah Lizbeth with the wedding arrangements. I hated the idea of Robbie being around the house, but Mom thought it would be great to have us both home.

It was over dinner the first night that Robbie brought out a seating chart for the reception dinner and gave me a lecture about where I would sit, who I would be sitting next to, and how I needed to behave. "Don't wear any of your slutty clothes, try wearing some deodorant, and maybe you could go home after the ceremony, huh?" he said.

"I don't want to go to your wedding; it sounds boring, just like you!" I screamed as I got up and headed to my room.

The next morning Mom got all teary when she heard me and Robbie arguing in the kitchen about who would make the coffee. "I think your dad would be so proud to see us all at the wedding together," Mom said as she walked into the kitchen.

I don't think either of us agreed with her, but we both shut up, and the next day Robbie moved into Sarah's place.

Robbie and Sarah Lizbeth's engagement announcement was published in the local newspaper a few days later. It had one of those staged glamour photos with it, and Mom asked me to get a few color copies made so she could mail them to her sister and brother. That's what I was doing when I ran into Sarah Lizbeth and Robbie at the mall. Robbie was talking on his mobile phone and tried to pretend he hadn't seen me, but Sarah Lizbeth smiled and said, "Fancy meeting you here."

"I'm just going to get copies made of your engagement thing for Mom," I replied. "What are you guys doing?"

"A bit of shopping," she said as she held up two bags.

"Have fun," I replied, already turning away. I picked up my pace, and was about ten feet past them when I heard Sarah Lizbeth say, "Hey, I think it would be nice to have you in the wedding. Would you be a bridesmaid?"

I turned around just in time to see Robbie put his hand over her mouth. "She can't be in the wedding. Look at her. She's bovine-like and she'll ruin the photos," he said loud enough for anyone within twenty feet to hear.

I could feel the tears welling up in my eyes, and I knew Sarah Lizbeth saw them too. I told Robbie to fuck off and practically ran all the way to the women's bathroom.

Sarah Lizbeth called the next day to apologize for Robbie and practically begged me to come over to her apartment the next weekend to try on dresses with the five other girls she'd lined up to be bridesmaids. "I really want you in the wedding," she said.

"I'll think about it," I said before I hung up.

After I told Mom about what had happened at the mall, she said, "You have to, honey. Do it for me. Okay?"

Robbie was right. Compared with the other bridesmaids, who were all blonde and beautiful, I was a cow, and there was no way I would get into the size six dress Sarah Lizbeth had bought for me. "It only comes in size two, four, or six, and I don't think there's enough material to take it out much," Sarah Lizbeth said after I tried to get it over my head with no success.

I knew she'd figured out she'd made a big mistake asking me to be a bridesmaid, but instead of letting me off the hook, she told me I was going to join her diet group—that she and her other bridesmaids would be my diet coaches.

"I don't like to diet," I said.

"You will by the time we're done with you," she said, laughing.

The bridesmaids were excited about helping me lose weight, and it went well for the first two weeks. But after my two-week weigh in, I started sneaking food and drinking beer. I knew I shouldn't, but I couldn't stop myself. By the end of the third week, the idea that I could lose enough weight to go from a size fourteen to a size six was becoming more depressing than hopeful.

Three days before the bachelorette party (a week before the wedding), we had a weigh-in at Sarah Lizbeth's apartment, after which we were supposed to go out to a new Mexican bar. I didn't eat a thing that day in preparation for the weigh-in, which told me I was still twelve pounds short of my goal weight, and still too fat to zip up the dress. No one said a thing about my zero weight loss, and I acted like I didn't know why I hadn't lost any weight.

By the time we got to the restaurant I was starving and thirsty. When the bartender started setting up tequila shots in front of us and said if any of us could do a dozen shots they were on the house, no one wanted to try it but me. I'm sure none of them thought I could or would, but I did. And it only took me about ten minutes. Even though I had to go the bathroom to throw up, I was still able to get back up on my bar stool afterward. I even downed a couple of margaritas.

At that point, Sarah Lizbeth and her friends tried to talk me into going home, but I didn't want to go home. I was having fun and wanted to stay. But everyone complained that I was too loud and too drunk, so Sarah Lizbeth called Robbie to come and get me.

I should have just gone with him—should have kept my mouth shut—but he arrived with his bad attitude and gave me the "look," and after kissing Sarah and saying hi to everyone else, he pulled me off my barstool and tried to twist my arm so I'd go with him. That's when the words started spilling out.

"Hey Sarah, did you know Robbie likes to fuck boys? He does, he really does. I've seen it. Many times."

Sarah screamed, "You're lying, shut up!"

Robbie said something about the fact that he was going to kill me, and he twisted my arm so hard as he pushed me through the small crowd to get me out to the parking lot that I thought I heard something snap.

He drove me home and left me on the front lawn. I remember lying on the lawn and thinking I should get up and go into the house, but I must have decided to sleep instead, because that's what I did—until Mom came out and practically dragged me all the way to my room. The next day, I was officially uninvited to be a bridesmaid and demoted to guest book attendant via a long message Robbie left on our answering machine.

That was the biggest fight Mom and I ever had. "I can't believe you made up such a vicious lie about your brother. You've probably ruined his chances for a happy marriage!"

I knew I wouldn't have said it if I hadn't been so drunk, and I was sorry for upsetting Mom, but inside I felt vindicated. Robbie had it coming, and I'd been waiting for years to let him have it. Mom made me call Sarah Lizbeth and all the bridesmaids to tell them I was a compulsive liar and would be getting help for it soon.

After that, I was on my best behavior, and even helped Mom make the groom's cake, which was just a basic fruitcake cut up into little pieces and wrapped in light green foil and pink netting. I didn't get to go to the rehearsal dinner because Robbie said I didn't need to rehearse how to be a fuckup.

Mom went to the rehearsal dinner with Olive and brought home a plate of food and a piece of chocolate cake for me. I sat at the kitchen table with her and listened to her talk about how everyone looked so beautiful and happy, and how Sarah Lizbeth had given her, and her own mother, a bouquet of pink and white roses and identical gold and silver bracelets with an inscription on the inside: "We couldn't have done it without you." Mom thought it was the sweetest thing.

Cory showed up the day before the wedding at the Hangout bar to apologize for calling me nasty. I couldn't face going to the wedding alone, so when he asked if I'd consider going to a movie with him, I said, "Sure, I'll go to a movie with you next Saturday if you go with me to my brother's wedding tomorrow."

"Deal!" he replied.

I was happy that Cory was coming with me, because I knew he wouldn't let me get too drunk. I also thought he'd defend me if Robbie started yelling at me.

We didn't actually see the wedding, because there wasn't enough room in the little chapel, so we went to the reception hall, next to the chapel, early and helped get things ready. As the guests made their way from the chapel to the hall, Cory took their coats and I sat behind a little table asking people to sign the guest book and stacked their wedding gifts neatly on a table behind me. When four people from Cory's high school arrived, including a girl who seemed to know him pretty well, he helped them find their table. Turns out Cory and Sarah Lizbeth had gone to the same high school. As the night went on, Cory continued to spend time dancing with his friend, and I continued to sit at the guest book table watching them and getting pretty drunk off the bottle of Johnnie Walker Red someone had given Robbie and Sarah for a wedding present.

I was a third of the way through the bottle when I decided I couldn't take it any longer. I went into the reception hall and tried my best to persuade Cory to leave with me, but he said he'd rather stay and hang out with his friends. I kept at him until he finally excused himself and walked me to my car. When we got there he said he wasn't going anywhere with me. "You're such a lush these days. And there was no reason to be so rude to my friend," he said.

That sobered me up. And pissed me off. After he walked back to the reception hall I drove home and called Nick to see if he wanted to meet up at the condo. He was there before I arrived. I let him do whatever he wanted, on the condition that this time I got to go into the pharmacy afterward and pick out my own drugs.

CHAPTER 18

A week later, Nick showed up at the Hangout to drive me home and asked me to move back into his condo and come back to work at his store. "I'll give you all the hours, and all the pills, you want," he said. "Besides, you shouldn't be at your mom's. What if she finds out about us?"

I agreed to go back to work at his store, but I refused to move back into his condo because I'd noticed the new bed and dining table at the condo the night of Robbie's wedding, when I went to meet Nick there. They used to be at Nick and Sharon's house. When I asked Nick about it he only said, "Sharon had them delivered here because she bought new things for the house. I didn't know she had a key to the condo."

"Does she know about us?!" I screamed.

"She does not. I know that for a fact," he replied.

I hated the thought that Sharon could open the door to the condo at any time and find Nick and me there, but I did think that moving out of Mom's was a good idea. We'd been getting on each other's nerves since before Robbie's wedding. "You're twenty-two, too old to be living at home," she'd said to me one night after I walked in on her and her new boyfriend making out on the living room couch.

I wasn't too thrilled with Mom's new "downunder" boyfriend Gavin. I could barely understand a word he said, and I was pretty sure he had a stutter, but it was hard to tell. A few weeks after I interrupted them, I found him in the kitchen one night wearing Mom's bathrobe and making toast and boiling water for tea.

"Hey, I had to park my car behind Mom's because there's a tractor out there. Is it yours?" I asked.

"Right as rain," he replied.

"It's not raining," I said.

"Good as gold, mate," he replied.

I went to bed and the next morning I started looking for my own place.

Nick lent me the deposit money for a small apartment not too far from his condo. It was perfect and even had a small garage, just big enough for my Fiesta. I moved in on March 23rd, 1998, and started full time at Nick's store a few days later.

● ● ●

I was pretty happy for the next couple of months, and while I still took a few pills every day, I'd almost quit drinking by the time my twenty-third birthday rolled around.

When Nick arrived at my apartment the morning of my birthday with a dozen yellow roses and bottle of Percocet I was in the bathroom throwing up.

"You're not pregnant, are you?" he yelled out from the bedroom.

"I might be," I managed between gags.

"You're on your own with this one. I've already got a six-year-old and a four-year-old. I'm done having kids!"

"But I want it," I cried out as I pulled myself up from the bathroom floor and made my way to my bed.

Nick threw my only lamp against the wall and yelled, "Get rid of the fucking thing!" before he stomped out and slammed the door.

I knew he meant it, and I was pretty sure we were done until he showed up at my apartment a couple of nights later with a bottle of wine and three bottles of chloral hydrate capsules. We had sex, and it wasn't rough at all. Actually, he was kind of nice about it, and held me for a long time afterward. Before he gave me a card with a phone number on it, he said, "I've arranged everything with an old friend of mine who's a doctor. He's expecting you to call. I want you to take care of your little problem before it becomes my problem, okay?"

It took me a few hours to decide it was okay to have the abortion, but only about two minutes to convince myself it was okay to use the chloral hydrate. For the next two weeks I stayed home and I stayed stoned.

● ● ●

Throughout the rest of June and July, every time Nick came over, which was just about every morning, he'd ask me if I'd taken care of my problem and I'd tell him I was planning to make an appointment and it would be over soon. But I didn't get around to calling his doctor friend until August 8th, after Nick noticed how tight my smock was at work one day and followed me out to my car to tell me off.

"Will you make the goddamn appointment?" he grumbled.

"Yes, I'll make the fucking appointment!" I said before I drove off.

I knew I shouldn't have missed my first appointment on August 14th, but I was too scared and too stoned to go, and I was hoping Nick would call and beg me to keep our baby. When I finally got to the doctor's office on August 20th, his nurse questioned me about the date of my last period and took a large vial of blood from my arm. I had to stay alone in an exam room for almost two hours while I waited for the test results. I was tempted to leave, but I didn't because I knew Nick would hate me if I didn't go through with it. Besides, I had nothing left at home to make me feel better, and I knew they'd give me something after the abortion.

The doctor I had for this abortion wasn't nice like the one I'd had the last time. He was mean and had a serious look about him. He didn't even say "hi" when he came into the room.

"Any special reason for not coming in during the first trimester?" he asked.

"I wasn't sure if I was pregnant," I replied.

"Really? You don't look that dumb," he said.

"But I am," I heard myself reply as I felt the twilight anesthetic start to flow through my arm and to my head.

It didn't put me out like I hoped it would, but it felt pretty good. It made me feel like I was floating on a nice fluffy cloud somewhere far away. I didn't moan or move an inch as the doctor did what I'd come for. And I didn't open my eyes when he told me it was over and offered me free birth control.

"No thanks, I have some," I said.

"Then use it," he said as he left the room.

It only took a few minutes for the twilight to start wearing off, and when it did all I wanted to do was get out of there and get high.

After what seemed like a week, the nurse brought me a glass of orange juice and handed me two white envelopes, one with six painkillers in it and the other with antibiotics and a folder of information about taking care of myself post-surgery.

"Is someone coming to get you?" she asked.

"My fiancé is supposed to be here any minute," I said.

"That's good, because we close at 6 p.m. and it's almost 6 p.m. now," she said.

When I'd called Nick earlier that day and told him what I was doing, he'd said "It's about time" and promised to pick me from the clinic when he got off work. At 6 p.m. I walked across the road, made myself comfortable on the bus stop bench, and waited.

Nick didn't show up until after 7 p.m., but I didn't care because I'd taken all the painkillers the nurse had given me and was feeling pretty relaxed. He drove me to my mom's house because he wasn't willing to spend the night with me at my apartment.

"It's a fucking circus at my house, both the girls are sick," he said. "I can't stay with you. In fact, I think we should cool it for a while."

"I don't care about your bratty kids, and if you want to cool it that's fine with me. In fact, I'm thrilled about it!" I looked out the window so Nick wouldn't see me cry.

He stopped his car about a block from my mom's house, then reached around to his backseat and grabbed a bag. "Here, these should keep you happy for a while," he said.

Two pharmacy-size bottles of Percocet and Xanax is what I got for aborting Nick's baby. I opened the bottle of Xanax and swallowed one dry before putting both bottles in my bag. I was glad he gave me so many pills; it made me feel good to know I could stay high for a month or two.

● ● ●

Mom and Gavin were eating dinner when I arrived. "You might want to knock first instead of just walking in, huh?" Mom said. Her tone let me know that she hadn't forgiven me for what I'd said about Robbie to Lizbeth and her bridesmaids months ago.

"For the millionth time, I'm sorry for what I said. Can you just forgive me, please?" I snapped.

"I'm thinking about it," she replied in her nice voice. "Do you want to join us for dinner? Gavin's made something he's calling a cottage pie. It looks pretty good."

"I'm not hungry," I said. "Think I've got the flu. Can I stay in my old room for a few days?"

Mom looked at Gavin and then at me. "We've made your room into an office, and I got rid of the sofa bed in the den, so there's nowhere for you to sleep," she said.

"Really?" I said, my voice rising. "You just got rid of my stuff without even asking? I just moved out five months ago!"

"I'm sorry, honey. I was planning to call you and to bring some of the bedroom furniture to your apartment this weekend."

"How about a ride to my apartment, then?" I asked.

"My car is in the shop; I've been taking the bus back and forth to work all week. And Gavin hasn't bought a car yet. Has to learn to drive American-style first." Mom laughed.

I took a few things from my bedroom closet, mostly stuffed animals, and walked to the bus stop. The bus shelter was empty, so I spread my things out on the bench and lay down. By the time the bus arrived I was almost asleep and had to scramble to get my things together. I was just about to step up and onto the bus when I heard someone yell my name. When I turned around I saw the good-looking twin walking toward me. I hadn't seen him for five years, since the summer after graduation. He looked better than ever. He yelled for me to wait, so I told the bus driver I'd catch the next one.

I felt like I had to give the twin a reason for my scruffy appearance and slurry speech. "Sorry, I just had surgery—a girl thing. That's why I look like shit," I said.

"That's cool. We've all had surgery." He laughed.

I got a ride to my apartment and an invite to his big birthday party on September 18th. He even helped me into my apartment and told me he was glad I was okay.

I slept for two days before I felt good enough to take a bath and wash my hair. It took me a while, but I talked myself out of being sad and started to get excited about the idea of going to the twins' birthday party. I even thought about what I might wear and who might be there and if the good-looking twin and I might make out.

I went back to work at Nick's store five days after the abortion and worked there for three days before I asked the bartender at the Hangout for my old job back.

"You can have it back if you agree to stay away from creepy old guys," he said, laughing.

● ● ●

I'd read the post-surgery instructions they gave me at the doctor's office, so I knew I was supposed to take extra-good care of myself, finish the antibiotics, and not have sex for at least six weeks. I did take good care of myself for the month after the abortion, and I promised myself I wouldn't get wasted and I wouldn't have sex at the twins' party.

I phoned the good-looking twin a few days beforehand and told him I wanted to go but needed a ride.

"Great," he said. "I'll pick you up. I'll just honk a couple of times, okay?"

I guess I shouldn't have drunk so much of the power punch or taken the ecstasy some guy handed me when I arrived at the party, because I was out of it when I fell down and hurt my leg. I tried to find the twins' car but I got lost and passed out and didn't wake up until I felt someone slap me and heard a man's voice yelling at me to relax. That's when I realized I was in some stranger's car, and that I was having sex with some guy I'd never seen before. I tried to get him to stop but he told me to shut up and hold still or he'd make it hurt. So I did what he said. I was scared because there were two other guys in the front seat yelling at him to hurry up and finish because it was their turn. As soon as the guy finished I rolled to my side, pulled up my pants, and sat up.

"I want out, let me out!" I screamed.

The guys just laughed, but as soon as the driver slowed to turn a corner, I grabbed my purse, opened the door, and stepped out.

It's baffling to me that I thought it would be okay for me to get out of a car while it was moving. That's how I remember it, anyway: I thought I could just step out and onto the street and walk away. After I finished rolling and slammed into the curb I just stayed there, too scared to move and too weak to even try. A biker found me and called for help, and the state patrolman figured I was either pushed or fell out of a car. I let him think I was pushed.

CHAPTER 19

An ambulance took me to the hospital around 1 a.m. A doctor examined me and put a bandage on my nose and twelve stitches in the cut above my left eye, and then I was moved from the ER to a room on another floor that was very quiet and almost empty. It was scary and I wanted to leave, but I could hardly see with the eye patch they'd put on me, and the IV tube someone had taped to the back of my hand was on so tight I didn't think I could rip it off without the needle tearing my vein.

I hadn't said a word to anyone, not even the police, about being raped in the car. I didn't want to explain how I'd gotten into the car in the first place, and I didn't want an examination because then I'd have to explain my abortion. What could I say for myself?

When the night nurse came to give me a couple of Tylenol and one Ativan, I told her one Ativan wasn't going to be enough to put me to sleep.

"Why not? Do you take them often?" she asked.

I mumbled a few things about taking them for a disorder in my brain, but I could tell she didn't believe me. She didn't give me an extra pill.

I stared at the ceiling for what seemed like an hour before I began to cry. My dad was right. I was nothing.

I waited for the night nurse to close my door and turn out the hall lights before I got up to find my purse and the bottle of Valium I'd put in there before I went to the party. There were only six left. I took one and found my way to the bathroom. I wanted to see my face, and I especially wanted to get the smell of rape off me. I used every cleaner I could find to wash myself and I buried my underwear under a pile of paper towels in the garbage bin.

I thought about calling Mom to come and get me, but after I had a look at myself in the mirror, I decided not to. I knew she'd be upset and I'd be too humiliated to look at her. I crawled back into my hospital bed and prayed to Uncle Hank for help.

● ● ●

I don't know what I was thinking when I agreed to go to the Facility. It all happened so quickly. The social worker was in my room at 8 a.m. my first morning at the hospital telling me how sorry she was about my accident and how she could help me. She convinced me that I needed a break from my hectic life and I agreed.

"I know of a life-changing place that has scholarships available for young people," she said. "I'm sure you'll qualify."

By the end of the day, she'd arranged everything: called my mom, arranged for someone to drive me, and given me two sets of clean clothes from the hospital's lost and found closet, along with two ten-dollars bills. "Just in case you need anything," she said.

I used some of the medical tape from my IV to hide my last few tablets of Valium. I taped them to my left leg before I put my sock on and before I got into the backseat of a hospital car. The old guy who drove listened to a baseball game the entire time. I was grateful.

The way the social worker had gone on about the Facility

I was convinced that I was going to a glamorous Hollywood spa, but it wasn't. It was something completely different. The Facility was in the middle of nowhere, on old farmland in San Bernardino. The building was mustard yellow and huge. It reminded me of an old factory, and I could tell just by seeing it that I didn't want to stay there.

I'd only just arrived at the Facility when a woman who looked like she was in charge of the world told me to leave my things by the front door so she could have a look through them later. Then she talked without taking a breath as she escorted me to a big room full of people sitting in chairs arranged in a circle.

"You're here for thirty days and you've got a lockdown period of twenty days. No visitors, no phone calls, no exceptions. Most of the people in the room here are clients, just like you. Make a friend or two. It could save your life," she said before she left me to listen to a couple of people talk about how they would organize our daily schedule at the Facility.

I didn't make eye contact with anyone. I just sat and read the activity schedule I was handed when I arrived. My personalized schedule included seeing a nutritionist three times a week, checking in with a doctor every other day, participating in relaxation hours and lots of group therapy sessions, the first of which started at 8 a.m. the next morning.

As I looked around the room at the other twenty or so clients, it was clear to me that I was the youngest one there by a long shot. The others were old, and too many of them were red-faced, grumpy men. There were a few women, but none of them seemed very friendly. I was relieved to learn that I wouldn't have to share a room with anyone, and especially happy to hear that the women's bedrooms were located in a brand-new part of the building that had recently been painted a creamy lilac.

● ● ●

I was assigned a private room overlooking the "serenity courtyard." It was a nice room with floral wallpaper and a pink and yellow circular rug on the floor. I liked it, but I wasn't happy about the door not locking.

By nighttime I was desperate to leave but couldn't get anyone to listen to me about being admitted to the Facility by mistake. It was hard to tell if the three people I spoke to about it didn't believe me or didn't care. None of them responded with anything more than an "Is that right?" and no one would give me anything for my headache.

Every muscle in my body ached, and my swollen face throbbed to my heartbeat. It was driving me crazy and making me cry. I went to my room and lay on top of the blankets for hours, too tired to get under them but not tired enough to fall asleep.

I took one of my five Valium at 4 a.m. and fell asleep until 7:45 a.m. Before I got dressed I moved the tape and the pills from my leg to underneath my right toes, just to be sure no one found them. I had to sit alone at breakfast because the others had eaten by the time I got to the dining hall. I had a piece of toast and went outside to smoke the cigarette I'd borrowed from someone who'd left a pack on the kitchen bench. I'd almost finished smoking when I spotted an old guy walking toward me. "I'm Charlie, the day manager here, which kind of makes me the boss," he said as he sat down next to me, so close that I could smell his coffee breath.

"I'm Randall and I don't plan on being here very long, Boss." I quickly stood up and moved away from him.

"That's fine, but you're here today, so get to group," he replied.

● ● ●

I arrived at my group therapy room just in time to stand in the open doorway and listen to a guy, dressed in an old army jacket and grayish-green-colored slacks, talk about his wife and how she'd taken off with his best friend while he was in Iraq, and how he'd tried to hang himself because of it. It was kind of sad but I didn't want to care so I stopped listening, looked down, and stared at everyone's shoes. It took a few minutes before I got to the therapist's shoes and when I did, she said, "Keds," pointing to her feet, and motioned for me come in and sit in the chair next to her. The second I sat down she put her hand on my shoulder, introduced me to the group, and asked me to say a few words about myself.

I wiggled around until she got the hint and moved her hand off my shoulder. "It's Randall and I'm here because someone at the hospital made a mistake and sent me to the wrong place. I'm probably going to leave this afternoon," I said.

"How'd ya get those black eyes?" said the girl with a devil tattoo on the back of her hand.

"I was at a party and got into a fight with a bigmouth who wouldn't leave me alone. I broke a beer bottle over his head and he beat my face for a few minutes before someone pulled him off me."

I heard a few people moan, like they understood or agreed, and it made me feel okay about telling them that story instead of what really happened.

I saw the therapist reach across her desk and grab a tissue and then wipe a tear from her cheek. It made me feel weird, like I'd said too much or the wrong thing.

A few of the others spoke, including a guy named Josh who was pretty angry and wanted the therapist to sign a court slip he had with him so he could leave. I guess the therapist figured this was a good time to give her little speech. "You've all got three things, three secrets, and this is your chance to get rid of them," she said. "Write 'em down." She passed around pens and pads of paper.

"I don't have to do it, do I? I'm leaving just as soon as I can get a ride," I said.

"Until then, why not try it? It can't hurt, and it'll give you something to do while you're waiting for your ride to get here," she replied.

"I don't know what you mean by three secrets," I snapped as I moved to let a fat old guy squeeze by on his way out of the therapy room.

"Writing will help," she said.

"Writing what?"

"Start with everything you don't want me to know," she replied.

"Geez, that's a lot," I grunted.

As I stood up to leave, she asked if I'd brought any drugs with me. I froze, wondering if she'd noticed how careful I'd been walking, trying to protect the pills I'd taped under my toes that morning.

"I don't think so," I said quickly.

"Come on, everyone brings something," she said as she put her hand out, palm up.

"But I'm not staying," I replied

"Then I'll give them back when you leave," she said.

"Well, they're not in my pocket."

"I'll wait," she said.

I had to sit down on the floor to take my shoe and sock off. And it hurt a little when I ripped the piece of tape from underneath my right big toe, but not as much as having to give her my last four Valium. Three of them fell from the piece of tape onto the carpet, and she reached down and picked them up before I could. "I'll take the piece of tape too," she said as she pulled it from my fingers.

"Now what am I going to do? I need those and I'm really leaving!" I cried as I covered my face and sobbed.

"Then I'll give them back to you when you leave. But right now you're a client, and clients can't be holding. That's just the way it is," she replied.

In the next moment I felt her hand reach under my arm to help me stand up. The same way Uncle Hank used to. "I really know what I'm doing and you're going to be fine, honey, really you will," she said.

I felt calmer than I had for months as she walked me to the medical room and introduced me the nurse. "Can you have a look at Randall's eye and maybe give her a lavender wheat bag to take to bed tonight?" she said before she left me.

Later on, I thought about what a couple of women had said in group therapy that morning. I couldn't figure out why they felt okay about telling such awful things about themselves to perfect strangers. It's not like I'd never seen those TV talk shows where people spill their guts, but I'd never been in the same room with people who said they'd fuck anyone for twenty dollars or give details about beating their kids. It was weird, but kind of interesting, though I hoped they didn't expect me to tell them anything I'd done.

I heated the wheat bag in the dining hall microwave exactly the way the nurse told me to and put it on my chest that night when I got into bed. It didn't do anything for me, though, and I was awake all night staring at the cobwebs in the corner of my room.

At breakfast the next morning I was tired and poured myself two cups of black coffee (with six spoons of sugar) before I found a seat at a table with Mike, the guy from our group who bit his fingernails down to the skin like I did. "Why does she want to know three things about us?" I asked.

"That's what it's all about—to get it all out. I've been here twice before but it didn't work because I'm not willing to talk about the worst things I've ever done." He smiled and quickly bit the edge of his thumbnail.

"Really? That's what she wants to know? The worst three things I've ever done?"

"That's it, little lady. Figure it out and you win," he grinned.

"Oh god, what if I have more than three?" I asked.

"Tell her everything you've done that you hate. Why not? You're young enough to make a new life for yourself. I'm too old to change and too set in my ways to care enough to try. I'm just here because I got my sixth DUI last month and it doesn't look good for my law firm if I go to jail again."

"You're a lawyer?" I said this so loudly he cupped his hand over my mouth as he nodded his head yes and grinned a little sheepishly.

Before we got up to go to group therapy, he told me that a

few of the staff members were alcoholics and drug addicts and that he'd seen them at meetings. I was shocked, mainly because I didn't think that type of a person could have a job. I began to wonder if any of them might have something they'd be willing to share with me, because I knew it would be a lot easier for me to sit in group therapy if I was a little bit high. Something to take the edge off would help so much.

At group I confessed that alcohol was the least of my worries, that I had much bigger problems than drinking or taking a few pills now and then. Such as Nick and the child he'd made me abort the month before. The therapist asked me how I felt about Nick and the abortion.

"Of course I feel bad. It was stupid to get pregnant and more stupid to wait so long to have an abortion, but I thought Nick was going to change his mind and decide he wanted our baby, like I did." I felt my bottom lip begin to quiver.

On the afternoon of my fifth day at the Facility I told Charlie, the Boss, that I really needed to phone my mom. "It's her birthday!" I practically screamed.

"You've got five minutes, not a second more," he said.

Instead I phoned the social worker at the hospital to tell her she'd made a mistake and I wanted her to help get me out of the Facility. "I don't think I've made a mistake, Randall. I think you're exactly where you need to be," she said just before the phone went dead.

I didn't understand what she meant, but when I called her back to ask someone else answered the phone and told me she'd gone home for the weekend. I was pissed off and quickly dialed Nick's cell phone. He didn't answer so I left a message about where I was and how much I wanted him to come and get me.

I was pretty upset by the time Charlie walked up behind me telling me my time was up. I wanted to talk to him about the social worker tricking me but Charlie said I didn't have time because there was an AA meeting I had to attend. He wasn't the type of guy I could argue with so I went to my room and changed out of my sweatpants and into the purple cords I'd gotten from the hospital's lost and found. I'd never been to an AA meeting, though I'd seen a lot of them on TV shows and they always looked so corny, almost embarrassing to watch. I did see a movie once that starred Meg Ryan playing a pathetic drunk, and she went to AA meetings. I wondered if the meeting I had to go to would be like that. I hoped not because I wasn't about to walk up to a podium, say my name, and announce to everyone that I was an alcoholic.

At 6 p.m. a little yellow school van picked six of us up in front of the Facility and drove us into the city for what I assumed would be some secret place where AA meetings were held. But it turned out the meeting was in the basement hall of a Catholic church right in the middle of town. I was sure they'd brought us to the wrong place, because there must have been a hundred people there and I couldn't believe that many people would be in AA.

The others from the Facility headed to the front of the room and found seats at one of the several long tables set up with metal folding chairs around them. I stood frozen, self-conscious about the state of my face. I wished I'd brought something to cover my face, even a pair of sunglasses would have helped, but I didn't have anything and I hadn't thought to ask anyone if I could borrow something before we got on the bus.

After about ten minutes, an old bald guy with a long beard hit a mallet on a table at the front of the room and said, "Good evening everyone, welcome to the 'do it or die' meeting of Alcoholics Anonymous. My name's Dan and I am an alcoholic."

Everyone in the room yelled back, "Hi Dan!"

"Are there any newcomers here tonight? If so, can you introduce yourself by your first name only?" Dan asked.

I watched the five people I came with raise their hands. Each one said their real name, followed by, "and I'm an alcoholic," and each time the room exploded into applause. I cringed with embarrassment. *How can anyone applaud for people admitting they're alcoholics?* I wondered. I sank down into my chair, expecting someone to make me do the same thing, but no one did, and I watched Dan slide coins across the table to my fellow patients, something he called twenty-four-hour chips.

I prayed no one would ask me to talk, and I cried silently through most of the meeting, hoping one of the women sitting nearby would tell me to leave. But instead one of them handed me a Kleenex and whispered that it was going to be okay. By the time the meeting was over, and everyone stood up and moved to the outside walls of the room and started holding hands, I could feel the sweat dripping down my arms and onto my hands. I didn't want to hold anyone's hand, so I ran outside to the van.

On the drive back to the Facility all the others talked about was how excited they were about getting an AA chip (which was a brass coin the size of a fifty-cent piece with a big triangle on it and some words I couldn't read). They acted as though they'd just received an Academy Award for saying out loud, in front of a room of strangers, that they were alcoholics. For that the chips should have been solid gold. I decided right then and there that I wasn't ever going to get one.

CHAPTER 20

The day after my first AA meeting, I told my group about the call I'd made to the hospital social worker. I was so angry about it that I almost choked when I told them how she'd hung up on me after she said something about me being exactly where I was supposed to be. And I got angrier when I saw everyone in my group nod in agreement. I burst into tears when my therapist smiled at me and said, "I think she knew what she was doing. No one ever gets to a place like this by mistake."

I didn't say anything the rest of the session. I felt like a prisoner and I thought about calling Mom to come and get me but my face was still pretty messed up. That night, at an even bigger AA meeting, I told three older women seated together in the back row how I was a prisoner at the Facility.

"I was tricked by a hospital social worker. She never even asked me if I was an alcoholic. Though I could sure use a few drinks right now, " I cried.

That's all it took for all three of them to scoot in so close I thought I'd suffocate. "No one knows better than a drunk what it's like to be a prisoner. I think you should stop complaining and take what they're offering you," one of them said just before she reached into her jacket pocket and pulled out a roll of cherry Life Savers. "Here, these might help you feel better. Sometimes it's just the sugar we crave."

I finished the entire roll of Life Savers and the two cups of sugary coffee they brought me during the meeting. When it was over, I bolted out to the parking lot before any of them had a chance to hug me or ask me for my phone number.

● ● ●

I didn't do anything my group therapist recommended for the next few days. Instead I read *Flowers in the Attic*, a book I found in the bottom drawer of the little dresser in my room. I felt just like those kids. Locked up and realizing that there was no one out there who would rescue them. The story made me miss my mom and hate my dad even more. After I finished the book I cried myself to sleep, which was weird because up until then I'd hardly slept a wink.

Falling asleep had been a problem since I was a little kid. I slept fine at Uncle Hank's and Aunt Flo's, but not at home. I was anxious at bedtime, scared that my dad might barge into my room and yell at me about something, which he often did. I once put my dresser up against my door, but Dad just pushed it over and came in anyway. "If I wanted you to be able to lock this fucking door, I would've put a lock on it!" he yelled before he threw my shoes at me. The ones I'd left under the kitchen table earlier.

It was around that time I started helping myself to Mom's blue pills, and the more I did it the more I needed them. I was probably twelve when I discovered I couldn't get to sleep on my own.

A few nights after I started sleeping at the Facility, I awoke to a pounding noise coming from the room next to mine. It was almost 2 a.m., and I couldn't decide if I should let myself fall back to sleep or get up to investigate, because the woman in that room was kind of crazy and I was afraid of her. She'd only been at the Facility for five days and was in one of the other therapy groups, but everyone knew her business because she never stopped talking. I overheard two women from her group talking about her one day at lunch. One of them said she was a stripper and in the Facility for leaving her kids locked in a car for a weekend. The other one said she'd flashed her tits in group the day she arrived and almost got kicked out.

As far as I could tell she didn't need to flash her tits, because they were visible all the time. She wore only white tank tops and never a bra, probably because she couldn't get a bra to fit with the big gold rings she had hanging from her nipples.

On her first morning there, Charlie told her to put on a bra or wear a darker shirt when he saw her at breakfast wearing the smallest tank top I'd ever seen.

"It's just a little ol' wife beater," she said, laughing.

"I don't care what they call it. I call it inappropriate," he replied.

"Well, don't look at it then. Take a look at my ass instead." Then she stood up, turned her butt to face him, and jiggled it.

It was gross. Charlie marched over to her table and motioned for her to sit down. I left the dining hall with a few others after he pulled out the chair next to her, sat down, and said, "Oh my, trouble has surely arrived today."

After that, I shouldn't have been surprised to wake up and hear her and some guy going at it in the room next to me, but I was because the Facility felt like a place where people shouldn't misbehave, like church. I lay still for a few minutes, hoping they'd stop, but they just got louder and louder, and I knew I wouldn't be able to go back to sleep. I got out of bed determined to go knock on her door, but the moment I opened my door I could smell the dope, so I headed down to the lounge to tell the night manager—I didn't want anyone to think I was smoking weed in my room. They busted her for using drugs, and for fucking a new guy in her room, and kicked them both out. Boy, was she pissed off.

"You're no better than me!" she seethed at me as they

escorted her down the hall. "You'll be stripping for a drink soon, you fat bitch. You're the worst kind there is—a fucking snitch. Show your face around my club and I'll kill ya!" she screamed.

It was after 3 a.m. when I got back into my bed, and I couldn't fall asleep for the life of me. It scared me to think I'd ever end up like her. I didn't want to. I wanted a nice life and a husband like Uncle Hank. After thinking about it for a few hours I decided I'd take Mike's advice and try to figure out what my three worst things were.

I found the pad of paper and pen the therapist had passed out when I first arrived. I put the date at the top of the first page (October 5, 1998) and thought about what I was going to do next. A few moments later the title "Three Things by Randall Grange" appeared on the page and I began to write about me, my life, the people in it, stuff that happened, stuff that didn't happen, and a whole bunch of things I never should've said or done. I wrote for so long I was shocked when it was time to go to breakfast and I was still writing.

Later that morning, in group, I told everyone about how I hadn't slept without pills or booze for years. One of the guys said he had the same problem and figured he couldn't sleep because he felt guilty about all the shit he'd done. That made perfect sense to me. Thinking about my family, and especially about how Uncle Hank died, could keep me awake all night, sometimes even after I'd taken a pill or two.

Uncle Hank's accident had been 100 percent my fault and I knew it. Actually, I figured I'd killed two people by the time I was sixteen, but I'd never really felt bad about Dad dying. Probably because Dad hadn't seemed to care about me. I'd wanted him to, prayed he would, but he just hadn't liked me very much.

But Uncle Hank was a different story. He'd cared about me a lot. He was the best person I'd ever known, and I felt responsible for his accident every day. I'd replayed the scene a millions times in my head, but the ending was never any different. He was dead no matter how I sliced it, and Aunt Flo was always lying on top of his body and the ambulance people were always pulling her off and saying, "It's time to let him go. Please let him go."

Sometimes when it got so bad that I thought I couldn't stay alive for one more second I'd hear Uncle Hank's voice saying, "Be brave, or pretend to be brave—either one will do."

CHAPTER 21

By the time my eighteenth day at the Facility rolled around I'd written fifteen pages about the things I'd done and things that had happened to me, and I still hadn't figured out what my three worst were. Nor had I fully recovered from my injuries. The bruise that covered my right thigh was still purple, the stitches over my eyebrow hadn't completely dissolved, and the yellowish-green bruise around my eyes hadn't disappeared, either.

I'd gotten tired of asking the nurse if I could have something for the pain, because every time I did she'd say, "Oh no, ya know, some people will take any type of pill just to be taking something. They get relief from the process of popping something in their mouth. So let's not help that part of you, okay?"

Instead she'd offer me wheat bags or hot towels with lavender oil on them. "You're gonna feel better just as soon as it stops hurting," she said one day, a half smile, half smirk on her face.

She made me feel like I was a five-year-old with a pretend stubbed toe asking for morphine. I hated her. But I needed something to make me feel better and the hot towels did help, so I kept going to her office and I kept listening to her talk about living one day at a time and staying away from the first drink, "Or in your case, the first pill."

They didn't talk too much about pills in the Facility, but they did talk a lot about alcohol. Unlike most of the others at the Facility, I didn't get smashed every time I drank. And I told everyone who'd listen that I liked pills more than I liked booze, but no one seemed to care, and the staff continued to refer to me as an alcoholic, which continued to piss me off.

The few times things got out of hand with me and booze was only because I'd lost count of how many drinks I'd had, or because I'd forgotten to eat. The really crazy episodes I'd experienced had all happened because I'd mixed booze with pills. It was the combination that wiped me out, and I had spent years trying to figure out how much I could drink with tranquilizers or painkillers and still stay standing. Sometimes it only took one or two beers to tip me over, and other times I could drink eight beers and still be the best driver in town. And there were many times when I could have gotten legless on free booze from the Hangout but I didn't because I wasn't interested or because I had a good high going on from something else. It seemed to me that a real alcoholic wouldn't turn down a drink for any reason.

● ● ●

The more I listened to the other clients at the Facility, the more I was convinced I wasn't like them and shouldn't be there. They all had DUIs, and some of them had been in jail more than three times. On day nineteen, I decided I was going to tell my therapist that I was leaving. I was planning to tell her at the beginning of the Monday morning group session, before she had a chance to start asking her usual questions: "Do you feel like using today? Have you thought about what's right today instead of what's wrong?"

My plans went sideways when she walked into group and didn't ask any questions; instead, she just started talking. "Untreated addiction of any type gets worse, never better . . . ever,

ever, ever!" she said. "And that's true whether you're currently using or not. If you don't get honest about your relationship with drugs and alcohol, you'll likely die from this disease, or from an accident brought about by using or pursuing. In fact, statistics say that of the eight of you in this room today, only two of you will get and stay sober and clean. The rest of you will leave here, decide you know what's best, and use again. But for the two of you who've had enough of being sick and tired, I'm here to help you. So, who are you?"

No one said a thing or moved a muscle. The silence became painful, so I put my hand up. "I don't think I'm an alcoholic and I don't buy the story of it being a disease," I said as quickly as I could, then wiped the sweat from my top lip.

She smiled, lips spread tight, not showing any teeth. "Alcoholism doesn't care what you believe. It doesn't care if you're convinced you've got it or not. It doesn't care where you come from, who you are, what you look like, or what you own. It only cares about being fed. And if you continue to drink, it'll continue to whip you around and drag you down, and that will happen regardless of what you believe about it. I promise."

After that speech, I couldn't bring myself to say anything about wanting to leave. She kept talking, too, telling us how hard it is for alcoholics to have quality relationships, of any type. I think she scared everyone in the group that day, because none of us spoke for the longest time. I understood what she'd said, though, and I couldn't stop thinking about it.

Her talk made me think about my childhood best friend, Katie, and writing about her in my new journal made me sad. I cried myself to sleep that night thinking about the time in high school when I watched her walking down the street crying so hard I could see her body shaking from across the road, all because I thought it was a good idea to fuck her boyfriend.

● ● ●

When it was my turn in group the next day to read through the list of friends I used to have, and the reasons they weren't my friends any longer, everyone, including my therapist, thought it was a pretty long list for someone so young.

It made me cry, and I wasn't used to crying in front of people. It also got me thinking about other people I'd lied to, stolen from, and caused trouble for. I didn't want to be that person anymore, so I decided to pay more attention to what my therapist said from then on, especially about fixing broken relationships and not beating myself up for every mistake I'd ever made.

By day twenty-one I could feel that something inside of me was changing, though I couldn't explain what, exactly. It felt like I had a word on the tip of my tongue but couldn't say it. Even though my lockdown was over I decided not to call Nick again and to give up my plans to leave the Facility until I'd figured out what was happening to me. When I walked out of group that day, the therapist said, "It takes an awful lot of shame and despair to grow an addiction like yours. Personally, I think you've got what it takes to recover, and I'm really glad you're here."

"Really? You really think I can change?" I asked.

"You've probably got a better chance than the others in your group," she said as she smiled and waved me out of the room.

From then on I felt better, lighter, and I even went to see her later that day to tell her about the guy raping me in the car because I was worried I might have gotten some disease from him—or worse, that I might be pregnant.

She made an appointment for me and drove me to a women's clinic that same afternoon. She waited in the car for me like I'd asked.

After I filled in a bunch of paperwork I was taken to an exam room and asked to strip from the waist down. I lay on the exam table with a little paper sheet over me, praying to something that I wasn't pregnant. When the nurse came in I told her I'd been dating a guy for a few weeks who didn't use condoms and I was worried I might be pregnant or something.

"Does that something have anything to do with that new scar above your eye?" she asked.

"Oh no. I got that playing softball," I lied.

I don't know if she believed me or not but she was really nice to me as she examined me and then took several vials of blood from my arm and then gave me a plastic cup to pee in.

When I got back into the car to go back to the Facility I was so happy about not being pregnant I yelled way too loud, "I'm not knocked up!"

My therapist smiled.

" And I didn't tell them I'd been raped, okay?" I said.

"It's okay with me," she replied as she started the car.

I felt safe around her now, not scared like I had for the first couple of weeks. She was a lot older than my mom, probably more like Aunt Flo's age, and she wasn't very pretty, and she didn't giggle when she spoke like most of the women in my family did. She had a steady, calm way of speaking that made everything she said sound important. Actually, she seemed more like a man than a woman to me, but much nicer and smarter. She reminded me of Barbara Walters.

After our visit to the women's clinic, she began to pay attention to me like never before. She talked to me about my mother and brother and how I might be able to make things right with them. And she even wrote me a vitamin plan to give to the Facility's nutritionist and a note for the doctor to check my thyroid and iron levels.

● ● ●

Twenty-two days into my stay at the Facility, and things were going pretty well—until Josh snuck out and lay down on a railroad track about a mile away. We were all upset the next day, and no one knew what to say or do. That day the therapist took her usual seat, blew her nose and wiped her eyes, and said, "I'm really sorry about Josh. Sorry I didn't see it coming, and sorry for his family. I sometimes wish I had an easier job, because you guys are heartbreakers."

"I saw it coming," said Sam, the guy who'd arrived at the Facility three days after me. "Josh's wife wouldn't bring his kids to visit and she wouldn't answer his phone calls. I think he tried to call her fifty times yesterday," he said.

"Be snitches, you guys. It doesn't count in here. Tell me if you're worried about someone. I'm here to help, ya know. If you want to get well, I'll do anything I can to help you, but be warned, it's probably going to get harder before it gets easier, and there's no way to go over it, under it, or around it. You have to go through it."

I looked around the room. Everyone was crying.

"It's just another day in the world of bad news," Sam said, sighing.

The therapist passed me the box of tissues and, in a softer voice, said to us, "I wish it was the bad news, but it's just a small piece. The really bad news is that you guys have no experience dealing with problems without booze and drugs. Unless you get some new skills, you're vulnerable and likely to use again. Everything we try to teach you here is designed to help you retrain your brain, create a new internal voice. One that doesn't insist that you get shitfaced before going to a family dinner or drunk because you're paralyzed over the fact that you've gained a few pounds or lost your favorite lighter. Wouldn't it be nice to live with a head that wants you to be happy instead of miserable?"

I heard myself say "yes," and I must have said it pretty loud because everyone looked right at me.

 CHAPTER 22

Twenty-four days at the Facility and I'd been to ten AA meetings and written twenty pages of stuff. I was feeling better, and everyone said I was looking better, too.

The Facility nutritionist said I'd gotten off pretty easy for someone who'd been living on a diet of downers for so long. "I'm surprised you weren't sicker coming off all that shit," she said.

"I'm surprised I was sick at all," I replied. I never thought the pills I took were dangerous or addictive, like the drugs those TV commercials warned us about. I thought drugs meant heroin, methamphetamines, and cocaine, not pills you could get from a doctor.

I also heard from the resident manager that Nick had phoned the Facility looking for me. Charlie walked right up to me as I was getting in line for lunch and said, "A guy named Nick called the office a couple of weeks ago looking for you. You know, the day I let you use the phone to call your Mom on her *birthday*."

Charlie's tone was mean, and he emphasized "birthday" like he knew I'd lied. It was clear to me, and likely everyone in the dining hall, that he was mad.

"Sorry, Charlie, but I wanted to go home and I thought Nick would come and get me," I replied.

"Well, I just got my ass chewed out for breaking the rules. I need this job. And just so you know, you're no prisoner here. You can walk out anytime and no one will say a thing."

"I'm sorry I lied to you," I replied.

"You've used up all your lies. No more," he grumbled as he walked out of the dining room.

Mike joined me at my lunch table and told me not to be too upset. "Charlie's been working here for ten years. They're not gonna fire him," he assured me.

The news that Nick had called looking for me made me happy and kind of anxious. I bummed a cigarette from Mike and skipped the afternoon meditation class because I knew I wouldn't be able to sit still and pay attention to my breathing. I hardly slept that night, too busy wondering what I should do about Nick.

When my therapist brought up the topic of intimate relationships in group the next day, and whispered to me that she knew about Nick's phone call, I was relieved. I knew I wouldn't have brought him up on my own. How could I say that I loved a man who treated me like a sex slave? I'd decided to tell my group that I was okay about breaking up with Nick, but when it came time for me to talk I blurted out, "I just don't know if I can live without my boyfriend Nick. He's the only person who cares about me."

"That's just your lonely talking girl," Mike said under his breath.

I sobbed the rest of group time, and when it was over I stayed to talk to my therapist.

"What's your plan for Nick after you're out of here?" she asked.

I inched my chair right up to hers. "I don't know. Nick knows where I live, and I think he's got a key, and I kind of miss him," I said.

"No, you just miss the drugs he gives you. Do you really think you'd want Nick around if he couldn't or wouldn't supply you with pills?"

"Maybe? I gotta think about that."

"When you make a decision to be done with drugs, you'll be able to stay away from Nick," she said.

"It can't be that easy," I replied.

"Oh, it is." She smiled as she reached over and put two fingers under my chin and lifted it until I was looking right into her face. "You might want to think about moving out of your apartment and staying with your mom for a few months, until you get comfortable in AA meetings and find a sponsor," she said.

I rolled my eyes when she said that. "I don't like AA. It's full of weirdos and drunks. I'm thinking I'll enroll in school instead. Maybe I'll become a drug and alcohol counselor like you?" I smiled at her.

Her face turned serious, and she took my hand and held it tight. "You won't be able to stay away from drugs and alcohol— or Nick—on your own for very long. You're clever, but not clever enough to outsmart this thing. Give yourself a chance to become the person you want to be. Find an AA sponsor. Someone who'll take your calls when you're frustrated or sad, or feeling like using."

I said I would, even though I wasn't sure if I meant it.

Later that same day, during a lecture on personal responsibility, the Facility psychologist talked for almost an hour about making good choices and not blaming others for what happens to us. Then he told us about the three family information evenings the Facility would be holding in the main room, beginning the next day, Tuesday. He asked all of us to give the office manager the names and phone numbers of four family members we'd like to invite by the end of the day. I only put Mom's name down, and then later on I went back to the office and added Robbie, Aunt Flo, and my sister to my list. I didn't want the Facility people to think I didn't have anyone supporting me.

The next night, Mom showed up. I was so happy it was all I could do to stop myself from giggling out loud. And I couldn't stop looking at her. She seemed so different, happier and younger, but maybe she'd always been that way and I hadn't noticed because I'd been so stoned and miserable. When she hugged me and rubbed the back of my head I felt so ashamed and so sad I practically collapsed in her arms.

She told me the Facility manager had called and asked her to come alone the first night. "But Robbie's in town tomorrow and he said he'd drop by, and your Aunt Flo called me at work yesterday. She said she was surprised and concerned to hear about where you were and promised she'd attend the session on Thursday."

I wondered which night Tammy would attend, or whether she'd attend.

During the break, Mom told me she'd read the information the Facility had faxed her at work and that she thought I probably was an alcoholic, just like my dad had been. "You got it from him, I'm sure," she said.

I stopped myself from mentioning all the pills she took, or the times when I'd seen her drunk, sometimes even drunker than Dad, because I didn't want her to be mad at me anymore.

After the lecture was over, I got a pass to leave the Facility so I could go to dinner with Mom. She held my hand all the way to the parking lot, and boy was I surprised to see Dad's yellow Falcon parked right up front. The last time I'd seen it, it had been up on blocks in the garage, exactly as Robbie had left it after Dad's funeral. Mom said her boyfriend, Gavin, had found a set of spare keys in the garage and fixed it up for her.

I got into the passenger seat and snuggled in. It felt good to be in Dad's car again, and I checked the glove box and under the seat as Mom drove.

"What ya looking for?" Mom asked.

"Nothing really. Just looking," I replied as I grabbed Dad's car service notebook from the glove box. I flipped through the pages for a few seconds. "Ya know," I said, "he bought this car for three thousand dollars when it only had seven thousand miles on it. It's probably worth a lot of money now. I'm glad you kept it."

"Me too," Mom said, and she reached out to me and smoothed the back of my hair.

Mom parked right in front of the restaurant and insisted we find a table that would enable her to keep an eye on the Falcon. "I'd sure hate it if someone stole that car," she said as we walked through the front door. The hostess seated us at a window overlooking the parking lot.

I ordered first: a cheeseburger, onion rings, and tartar sauce. Mom got the fish and chips, and while we waited she asked me to tell her about the Facility.

"Everyone's pretty nice and my room is great," I said as the waitress arrived with my root beer and Mom's wine. I told Mom about the girl who had sex with a new guy in the room next to me and the guy from my group who killed himself the week before.

"Jesus Christ, honey, what kind of place is this?"

"It's a rehab, Mom. For drug addicts, alcoholics, and troublemakers," I whispered.

I watched Mom's face drop and turn serious before she took two big drinks and sank down deeper into her chair.

I could see she was upset so I stopped talking about the Facility and said, "I'm sorry for all the crappy things I've done. For stealing things and never saying thanks."

Mom took another big sip of her wine before she said it was okay, and then told me she hadn't been too good herself lately. "I've had lots of problems this past year. My sister and I haven't settled our parents' estate yet, and she's getting frustrated and so am I. We've been trying to sell the two rental properties they had in San Diego and deal with insurance companies. Last week we hired a lawyer to help us."

As she was talking, I suddenly remembered a message Olive had left on my phone a few months ago telling me that my grandma had just passed. "Your mom wants to go to Utah to help with the funeral," Olive had said. "Maybe you can drive her, because I can't and she shouldn't be alone." I'd listened to the message two more times before deleting it. I hadn't been interested in going to Utah or in seeing Mom. Plus, I'd been doing my best to avoid seeing anyone because I was pregnant and not dealing with it very well.

"I'm sorry I didn't go to Grandma's funeral with you. I really am. And I'm sorry about your dad, too," I said.

"Thank you," she said. "Losing Mom has been hard on me. I went to Utah for a week to help my brother and sister with her funeral. It was good for me to go alone. It gave me time to think about my life."

I watched with interest when Mom made herself stop crying and then dabbed a tissue under her eyes ever so softly, managing not to smear her makeup at all. I also watched as she finished her glass of wine and waved the waitress over and ordered another. Then she told me Robbie and Sarah Lizbeth were pregnant, and that she was looking forward to being a grandma.

I didn't say what I was thinking—that Robbie was going to be a horrible father. I just focused on my burger.

When the waitress brought Mom's second glass of wine, she took a few sips and confessed to me something that completely shocked me—that she had breast implants. "I don't know if you know this or not, but I've had silicone implants for more than twenty years and I think they've been leaking for the past fifteen. I think they're the reason I get such bad headaches and lately I've been feeling like I have the flu all the time. I'm having them removed next week," she said.

"What? They're not real?" I practically yelled. I'd never considered that implants might be responsible for Mom being so busty. I laughed a little. "God, Mom, I wished I'd known. I spent years expecting something to develop on my chest because you had so much on yours. As you can see," I said, pulling my sweater open and sticking out my chest, "I could be president of the flat-chested club."

She said she'd been small-chested like me until a year after I was born. "Your dad came home from work one day and told me all about a guy who worked with him and how he'd bought a new set of boobs for his wife. He told Dad that it had made their marriage better than ever. I wanted a better marriage, and I especially wanted your dad to stop seeing Genie, so I let him make an appointment with a plastic surgeon. I even let him choose the size because he wanted to make sure he got his money's worth. Once I get these bags of poison out of my chest, I'll join your club," she said, winking.

I was stunned, and we ate in silence for the next few minutes, until our waitress arrived and we both noticed, at the same time, her big fake boobs. We giggled quietly as she refilled our water glasses, trying to avoid looking at each other; the second she walked away, Mom leaned across the table and mouthed, "Money's worth," and I burst into laughter and practically choked on the food I was chewing.

"Will you come home and stay with me after the operation?" Mom asked, turning a bit more serious. "I don't want Gavin to be my nurse. I don't want him to see anything until I'm all healed up."

"Sure, Mom. I can do that."

I knew that Mom liked Gavin, and that he wasn't like the other men she'd dated. "He cooks a little, does the dishes, and doesn't mind one little bit if I don't show up at breakfast with makeup on," she said. "He even put up a clothesline in the backyard so he could hang out the laundry."

Mom had almost finished her second glass of wine when she told me she was in love with Gavin, felt like they were meant for each other, and was planning to move to New Zealand with him. "He's keen to get back home," she said.

I didn't know what to say. I couldn't believe she wanted to move to the other side of the world. I nodded my head like I was happy about it, because I didn't know what else to do.

We both picked at our food for a few minutes before she said, "If things work out okay with you when you leave the

Facility, maybe you can come to New Zealand and stay with us."

I said I'd think about it and then asked her about her plans for the house.

"It's for sale, and there's a young couple with two boys who've looked at it twice," she said. "I'm expecting them to make an offer any day."

"What about all our stuff?" I asked.

"You can have whatever you want, honey. Just let me know and I'll make sure you get it."

"Can I have the Falcon, and maybe Dad's jukebox?"

"I don't see why not." She smiled.

I felt instantly better, probably because of the way she said it, without one bit of hesitation and not one word about Robbie and what he might think.

"I'm only taking a few suitcases of clothes with me, so I need to get rid of a lifetime of stuff. Maybe you can help me organize a garage sale, huh?" she said. "You can have all the money from the sale, but you'll have to do most of the work."

I agreed to the plan. And I was happy to know I'd have something to do when I left the Facility. I'd be helping Mom and earning some money, too.

When the waitress arrived to take our plates away and asked if we wanted anything else, Mom started to order another glass of wine but instead looked over at me and said, "Two root beers, please." Then she reached into her purse, took out one of my old poem books, and handed it to me. She'd found it when she was cleaning out my bedroom and kept it because she liked to read my poems. I hadn't seen that notebook for a long time and tried to remember what I'd written, hoping she hadn't brought the one with my hundred poems of how to die. I could tell from the several spots of dried blood on the cover that this was a notebook from a particularly bad nail-biting period. I opened it to the first page and read to myself something I'd written a long time ago when some boy dumped me, probably after having sex with me and then deciding I was too weird to be seen with.

Over is over, end is the end.
Wanting not having, needing you when.
Done is done, no one won.
Sure wanted to, would've been nice,
could've been great.
This and not that, stupid mistake.

Mom said she loved the poem and then asked, "When did things get so screwed up with you? What could I have done?"

I told her I couldn't think of anything she could've done. I didn't say, "other than give me away for adoption," like I wanted to. "I've been trying to figure it out myself for weeks," I said. "I think I went from glad to sad and then mad after Uncle Hank died. It was around then when I started helping myself to Dad's booze and your pills."

"I always wondered about that. I thought your dad was taking my pills for sleeping. It never occurred to me it might be you until after he died."

I tried to explain how it all got a whole lot worse when I moved out on my own because I was scared of just about everyone and everything, and being stoned felt better than being straight. It wasn't the entire truth, but I wasn't prepared to tell her about my relationship with Nick and all the drugs he'd made available to me.

Later on, when she dropped me off at the front gate of the Facility, she said she'd come and get me Saturday afternoon and take me home. Then, in a real quiet voice, she said, "It's okay that you didn't like your dad. I didn't like him much, either, but it took me years to figure that out."

CHAPTER 23

The next night, Wednesday, just before the family session was scheduled to begin, the Facility psychologist told me he hadn't heard from my sister or my brother about attending. "You might be alone tonight," he said, giving me a sympathetic smile and motioning for me to find a seat.

I found a seat in the back row next to Mike, kicked my shoes off, and got comfortable for what I now knew was a long lecture about avoiding alcohol, even in everyday foods. Just as the talk was getting going, Robbie walked into the room and sat down in the front row. He was wearing a black suit with a blue and red striped tie and looked as handsome as ever. I thought about getting up from my seat to welcome him, but I was kind of scared that he might yell at me in front of everyone so I stayed put.

Robbie had only been seated a few minutes before he interrupted the speaker and began asking questions about the cost of the place and why some people were paying full price when it was pretty obvious to him that the losers he saw smoking out in front of the building didn't have a dime to their name. "So it would be me, the taxpayer, who's footing the cost?" he said. "I'm paying for those lowlifes to lounge around here smoking and whining all day?"

I wanted to die. I wanted to stand up and tell him to shut his big fat fucking mouth, but I couldn't. I knew if I did he'd let loose and tell everyone in the room some of the things I'd done before I got to the Facility, including having sex with a fourteen-year-old, which Robbie maintained was statutory rape, and taking Dad's Mustang for a spin, which he said was grand theft auto.

One of the managers stood up and said, "Sir, you can call our office in the morning and I'm sure someone will be able to answer your questions about costs. We're here tonight to talk about the family disease of addiction. Do you have any questions about that?"

"Yeah, I got a question about that. How is it that a drunk can kill someone and say in court he didn't remember doing it but never forgets where he hides his booze?" Robbie asked.

I waited for someone to answer, but no one did.

Robbie shrugged his shoulders a few times and then said, "I guess killing someone isn't as important as the booze, huh?"

When he stood up to leave I got up and followed him all the way out to his car, which was parked at the end of the parking lot. I was bursting to tell him off but he beat me to it. When he finally stopped at his car, he pulled an envelope from the inside pocket of his suit coat and handed it to me. I could see it was a legal document of some sort. "It's a restraining order," he said. "I've had enough of your shit. You're a drug addict, a drunk, and a child molester, and an embarrassment. I don't want you around me, or my family, ever!" He held the pen out for me to take.

"I'm sorry, ya know," I murmured. "I didn't mean to become any of those things." I wiped at the tears that were threatening to erupt and took the pen from his hand.

He calmed down a bit after I signed, and told me to stop crying and grow up. "My life is too important to be messed up by you," he said in the very same stern manner Dad would have said it in.

I watched Robbie get into his car, and before he drove off he rolled down his window and said, "Nice going talking Mom into letting you have Dad's Falcon. You know I've always wanted that car."

"You got Dad's Impala, El Camino, and Blazer. Why do you need the Falcon?" I asked.

"Because Dad would have wanted me to have it and you know it."

He didn't hear me say "good riddance" because he drove away too fast. And I didn't get the chance to explain anything to anyone, either, because by the time I got back to the Facility it was time to go to another AA meeting. I knew the van would be in front of the building in ten minutes, and I needed to change my clothes and splash some cold water on my face.

I was usually late, so when I was the first to arrive at the van, the driver laughed and clapped. "Miracles happen every day," he said, chuckling. I laughed too, and for some reason, the closer we got to the meeting that night, the less opposed I was to going.

● ● ●

I was getting used to the AA meetings. The older women who always sat together asked me how I was doing, and one of them, Mickey, handed me a piece of paper with her phone number on it that night. "Call me anytime, and keep coming to meetings. That's important."

I liked it when people told me to keep coming back. It made me feel special, like they cared about what happened to me.

On the drive back to the Facility after the meeting, I talked to a guy who came in the same day as me about my plan to read aloud my twenty pages of writing on Saturday, my last day at the Facility. "I've written a lot but I still don't know for sure what my three worst things are. Do you know yours?" I asked.

"It's a trick, ya know? Telling us we have three things, or secrets. They know we've got way more than three, but telling us to confess a few things doesn't scare us as much as being told to give them our entire life story. They don't want us to have any secrets left when we leave here."

I felt better about my progress after he told me that. It made sense to me suddenly. It was a clean-out exercise. Alone in my room, later that night, I read my twenty pages out loud to myself so I could hear myself say each crappy thing. It was awful. I felt sad and ashamed and eager to get rid of my three things and much, much more.

Before I went to sleep I walked down the hall to the payphone and called Tammy. I wanted to remind her about the family meeting the next night, but when her message machine came on I blurted out, "You're probably really busy, so don't bother coming to the family session. I'll call you another time."

I figured she hadn't responded to the previous invite because she wasn't interested in hearing about my problems, and I didn't want to make a big deal about it.

● ● ●

On Thursday evening, the last night of the family information series, Aunt Flo showed up alone. She sat down right next to me in the back. I don't think she understood a word of the lecture on sedativism, and neither did I, but I was sure glad she came. Afterward, we sat together on a bench in the hallway and talked.

"I lost the earrings you gave me, Aunt Flo, and I killed Uncle Hank. I'm so sorry."

"Both of them?" she asked.

"Yeah, both of them."

"Well, I've lost lots of things too. I guess that's the way it goes." She smiled as she wrapped her arm around me, squeezed me tight, and whispered in my ear, "But you didn't kill Uncle Hank, he had a heart attack. I thought you knew. I discussed it with your dad when I got the report from the medical examiner."

"Oh God, *really?* He didn't slip on the suntan oil I'd spilt on the diving board?" I was shaking hard and I was practically screaming.

"He never set foot on the diving board that day. He fell into the pool from the side when he was scooping out leaves. I had a hard time believing it myself. He was in such good shape."

We sat for the longest time, sniffling. I felt sad and good at the same time. But I had a feeling Aunt Flo wasn't feeling as good as I was, and I wanted to change the subject, so I interrupted her weeping and told her how I'd gotten myself into so much trouble that I couldn't cope and how I'd gotten to the point where I was drinking and using pills almost every day.

When I finished telling her the milder parts of my story she patted my hand and told me she'd cut way down on her drinking and that Arnold had found someone younger and divorced her. "That bastard. The only things I got out of that marriage were a lot of grief, a few nice clothes, and that stupid car!"

Aunt Flo said she'd moved back into her cottage house a month ago and had been trying to clean it up because it was a dump. "Your Uncle Bill didn't keep his promise and the place was a disaster. When Genie left him, soon after your dad died, Bill started drinking and gambling and got pretty depressed. I had to throw out half my furniture because it smelled like cigarettes and booze. I only just started working on the garden yesterday and I'm pretty sore today. I could really use your help if you have the time. I can't pay you, but your room is just waiting for you."

Suddenly I had choices of where to go after I left rehab. I didn't want to turn Aunt Flo down, because there was no place I'd rather live than the cottage, so I explained about Mom and how she needed me and asked if it would be okay if I moved in with her in a month or two, after Mom moved to New Zealand. She thought that would work. "But can you come over to help me a few days a week while you're at your mom's place?" she asked.

"I'm sure that will work out just fine."

I had a couple of things to do before I checked out of the Facility on Saturday. The first was to call my apartment manager to tell her I was sorry for being so late with my rent and that I was moving out. I phoned her Friday after group therapy and it wasn't as hard as I thought it would be. She sounded happy to hear from me and told me my mom had paid the back rent and moved all my stuff out the day before. I called Mom to tell her thanks and that I was sorry about how messy I'd left the place.

"Why so many empty prescription bottles?" she asked. "You must have been really lonely, because Gavin and I threw out about sixty empty bottles and none of them had your name on them."

"Yeah, I used the names Vera Purse and Sally Munch when I went to the doctor," I confessed.

"Oh, I would have never thought of doing that," she said, chuckling, "but I'm not the one in rehab."

I guessed I was glad Mom could joke about my situation, even though it felt a little weird. But Mom and I hadn't connected like this in years, and it felt good, like things were going to be okay.

"By the way," she said, interrupting my thoughts, "there were lots of messages on your phone, and I didn't want to lose them, so I listened to them before I unplugged the machine and packed it away."

My legs went weak at the thought of Mom hearing one of Nick's nasty sex messages. "Eight hang-ups and one message from Cory," she said, "who said he was off to Portland and hoped you were okay because he hadn't seen you around. Maybe you should call him?"

"Oh yeah, maybe I will, but maybe not." I sighed, relieved that she hadn't discovered my relationship with Nick. "I'll think about it. Anyway, I'll see you Saturday at 5 p.m., okay?"

I sat outside in the courtyard and chain smoked for the next hour, trying to calm myself down and feeling grateful for having dodged another bullet.

The last thing I needed to do before leaving the Facility

was to read my twenty pages to the group the next morning, and I was ready. I slept well that night knowing I was about to let go of a lot of garbage and regrets.

I herded my group into the therapy room early Saturday morning, right after breakfast, so we could get started. I listened to two others read their stuff and had to try hard not to interrupt and ask questions. Finally, at 10:30 a.m., it was my turn to read. I did my best not to sob too loud, or read too fast, and I looked up every so often to see if people were listening or if they'd fallen asleep.

When I finally finished reading it was almost noon and I immediately began to fold the pages up.

"Is that it—nothing else?" my therapist said.

I hesitated for a second or two before I told her I had one more thing, "It's probably not that big of a thing, and we're late for lunch already, so I'll just save it for another time," I said.

"Why don't you stop by after lunch and we'll talk about it," she said.

After lunch, when I stopped by her office, she patted the chair seat next to her and I sat down. "Here's your chance, kiddo. What do you have?"

I told her about taking money from Uncle Hank's secret box years ago to pay for an abortion and replacing it with an IOU. I hadn't even tried to pay that money back, and worse, I'd been back to the box three more times and helped myself to another fifteen hundred dollars to pay for drugs. I was so ashamed, and even though I knew confessing was the right thing to do, I also knew there was enough money in the box to help me to pay for drugs for a long time.

I also told her I'd been lying to my Mom for years about my boyfriend. "Nick used to be my Mom's boyfriend, and she was madly in love with him. She'd be really hurt if she ever found out I've been sleeping with him for the past four years," I said. "And the truth is, I don't know if I'll be able to stay away from him when I get out of here. He has a weird control over me."

My therapist didn't say anything for the longest time, and I didn't look up or try to wipe away the tears that kept rolling down my face either. I just sat, hoping I hadn't forgotten anything.

When I finally composed myself and looked up at her, she had a serious look on her face. "It's over, kid. It's all over if you want it to be. You can decide to choose recovery and you can tell the prick to fuck off and really mean it. If he hassles you, you can make a phone call and report him to the state for handing out drugs without a doctor's prescription. I'll even give you the phone number before you leave."

I almost laughed, because it sounded so simple the way she said it, and a perfect way to free myself from Nick.

"You'll need to make a decision soon about your Uncle Hank's box, though," she said. "Having access to a secret stash of anything isn't a good thing for an addict."

Later on in my room, I tore a piece of paper from my journal and wrote a letter to Nick. I told him I'd already told a few important people about all the drugs he'd given me from his pharmacy. And just to be sure I'd never call or try to see him again, I told him the hairy mole on his top lip was a super gross-out. I was shaking when I finished writing the letter, but I sure felt good.

My last day at the Facility had been hard. And now I was confused. I couldn't understand why I didn't want to leave a place I'd never wanted to be in to begin with. I sat on the bed in my safe little room for ages thinking about how comfortable I was there. When I finished packing, I took the letter I'd written to Nick to the management office and got an envelope and stamp from the secretary. I cried as I put the stamp on, and she gave me a tissue and said, "I sure will miss you, sweetheart. I hope everything goes well for you from now on." That made me cry even harder, and I continued to cry as I made the rounds to say good-bye to everyone.

My therapist arrived at my room just as I was getting ready to head to the parking lot to wait for Mom. She gave me the phone number to call if Nick ever hassled me, and a book of morning meditations. I opened it to see that she'd written her name and number on the front page and a few words: "Don't drink or drug no matter what."

Then she told me we had one more thing to do before I left, and she guided me out to the large empty field behind the building. There was a big metal pot on top of a cement block.

"I heard about this cleansing pot from Mike, but I thought he just made it up," I said.

"Oh, if this pot could talk." She smiled, handed me a lighter, and invited me to tear and burn each page I'd written. As I watched the papers burn, I said good-bye to those three things . . . and a few more.

 CHAPTER 24

Being at home with Mom and Gavin was odd—maybe because I wasn't using, or maybe because I wasn't accustomed to a man who did stuff around the house. He vacuumed my room the day I arrived and washed Mom's good clothes by hand before hanging them outside on the clothesline he'd put up in the backyard. The next night, after returning home from an AA meeting, I found him in the kitchen making cheese scones.

Mom had surgery two days after I moved in, and everything went okay. She came home from the hospital the very same day. I didn't know anything about helping someone who'd had surgery and I thought Gavin would be much better at taking care of Mom than me, but she insisted that I help her get dressed and change her bandages because she didn't want him to. It wasn't too bad. The drain tubes were the worst part, but her incisions were just a couple of inches long, and not bloody or very bruised. The hardest part for me was her medication: four prescription bottles sitting on her nightstand. Sometimes I could actually hear them talking to me, and a couple times I had to call Mickey from the AA meetings to ask if she thought it would be okay for me to hold a bottle of pills for a while.

"Your mom's pills are none of your business," she said. "If you're finding it hard to stay away from them, ask her to hide them."

From then on, every time Mom took a pill I was able to walk away, and even though I was curious about what they gave her, and why they gave her so many, I didn't look at them and I didn't ask her how it felt after she took them.

I went over to Aunt Flo's for the first time later in the week because she'd been calling to ask how Mom was and to see if I had time to help her cut back some vines that were killing her favorite trees. When I drove over that morning, I was surprised to find both O and B (Olga and Boris) sleeping out front on the garden path. I'd never thought any of the cats would still be alive; I'd forgotten they'd been kittens when Uncle Hank died. When I went out to the backyard with Aunt Flo to start the pruning, I noticed that Mayadelsa didn't have any water in her and I asked Aunt Flo about it.

"The pool filter is broken and I don't have any money to get it fixed. I found out last week that Bill didn't keep up with the property taxes, like he promised he would, and that I owe the city twelve thousand dollars. I don't have twelve thousand dollars, though, and I'm pretty sure the city will take the cottage and sell it to get their money."

She cried the entire time we were chopping away at the vines and tree branches in the backyard. "I don't have an income, other than social security, and it isn't enough to get me out of the mess I'm in. I sold my mother's wedding ring last month to an antique dealer for two thousand dollars. It was just enough to pay the electric company so they'd turn the power back on and to buy a few things for the place. The used car dealer down the road says he'll give me four thousand for my Mercedes, but then I won't have a car."

Aunt Flo told me she had other problems besides owing back property taxes. "The roof leaks, the pool is in bad shape, and most of the fences Uncle Hank put up are falling down. It's going to cost thousands to get things fixed around here, and I can't imagine where I'll ever get the money."

"What about the bank, have you gone to the bank?" I asked.

"I can't get a loan because I can't afford to make payments. I even went to a pawn shop to sell the ring Uncle Hank had made for our anniversary, but after standing in front of an old man and watching him inspect it, I decided I'd rather die homeless than live without Uncle Hank's ring on my finger."

I couldn't believe what I was hearing. I almost told her right then and there about Uncle Hank's hidden box, but I didn't because of the money I owed it. I didn't want her to find my IOU. Plus, I hadn't been into it for almost a year, and for all I knew Uncle Bill could have found it and taken everything. But if I'm being honest, I guess there was also still a piece of me that wanted to keep the box to myself. It was a lot of money, and I knew I wouldn't be seeing that kind of money again for a really long time, maybe ever.

● ● ●

I cut and chopped away at the vines for another few hours. The whole time I kept hearing my therapist's voice in my head saying, "The truth will set you free."

By the time I was done for the day, I knew I wanted Aunt Flo to have Uncle Hank's box. I wanted her to know she might not have to worry about losing the cottage ever again.

Before I drove back to Mom's that night, I spent at least an hour inspecting Mayadelsa, looking for cracks and making mental notes about missing pieces, hoping I would be able to find replacement crystals and stones in Uncle Hank's shed. When I finished, I told Aunt Flo I wanted to bring Mayadelsa back to life, and she half laughed, half cried. "It's gonna take a whole lot more than wanting."

When I got back to Mom's that night I told her and Gavin about what was happening with Aunt Flo and the cottage. They seemed surprised and worried. Gavin said they had a few weeks before they were moving to New Zealand and he wasn't doing much until then except helping me out with the garage sale. "I'd be happy as Larry to give her a hand," he said.

I wasn't sure what that meant but I gave him an air hug anyway and said thank you.

I didn't sleep very well that night. I couldn't stop thinking about Uncle Hank's box and wondering how much money was in it, and whether it would be enough to help Aunt Flo keep the cottage. The more I thought about it, the more I realized I couldn't bring myself to tell her that I'd known about the box since I was eleven. I didn't want her to open it and see the IOU I left years ago, either.

I only needed fifteen or twenty minutes alone in the shed to get my IOU out of the box, and I planned to do that as soon as possible. After the IOU was taken care of, I thought I could casually bring up the box in a conversation with Aunt Flo and we could go to the shed and discover it together. That was my plan, anyway, until I remembered the garage sale and how much money I might make—maybe even enough to put the nineteen hundred dollars I'd taken back.

I spent the next two days preparing for the garage sale, which was a big hit. I made more than thirty three hundred dollars selling everything from appliances to ugly dishes. But it was Dad's car parts and tools that brought in the most money. The day before the sale, Gavin had suggested I call Mike from Dad's car club to tell him about the parts I was planning to sell. Mike told me not to put any prices on them. "There's some great stuff there, worth lots, so let people make offers and then jack up the price fifty percent," he said. "See if they go for it."

The sale had been going for about three hours when my sister and John showed up. She said she'd gotten my messages: the one about the family evenings at the Facility, the one with my apology for being a bad sister, the one with the garage sale details, and the one with my offer for her to come over and get a few of Dad's things. I was glad to see her, even though I was a little pissed off about her ignoring me. I was about to mention it when I felt a hand on my shoulder and looked around to see John standing next to me.

"You look great, and we're so happy our prayers have been answered," he said, smiling. "The Lord works in very mysterious ways."

I didn't know how to reply, so I nodded in agreement and led them over to the workbench where I'd set aside some of Dad's photos and books, a military hat he once wore, one of his purple hearts, and some of his other medals. I told Tammy she could have it all if she wanted, but she didn't want anything except Dad's trench coat and leather gloves. Before she left, she hugged me and said she'd call me soon.

● ● ●

The Tuesday after the garage sale, I arrived at Aunt Flo's early enough to bring in the newspaper and to catch her in her nightgown (something I'd rarely seen). I'd planned to find a way to sneak into Uncle Hank's shed and take care of the box, but Aunt Flo was by my side all day. I helped her dig up weeds and cut bushes back for few hours, and when we finished Aunt Flo made me dinner and we talked about Uncle Hank until it was time for me to go to my AA meeting.

The next day I thought for sure I'd get the opportunity to go to the shed and put the nineteen hundred dollars in the box and take out my IOU, but Gavin arrived to help Aunt Flo before I had a chance and he stayed until after dinner fixing things Aunt Flo had on a list. He even put all-new elements on the stove, repaired the leaky toilet in the guest bathroom, replaced every washer on every faucet, and promised to come over the following Monday to clean gutters and repair the roof. Aunt Flo was so grateful, and she kept saying thanks as she walked him to the car.

Before I left Aunt Flo's that night I checked the shed door, but it was locked, so I told Aunt Flo I needed the key so I could look for replacement pieces for Mayadelsa. As she handed me the key she said, "I locked the shed because of the wine that's still in there. Bill drank most of it, but I noticed there were still a few bottles high up on the shelf and I remember what they said at your treatment place about being thoughtful."

"That's nice of you, but I don't like wine, so you don't have to worry." I put the key in my pocket and promised I'd be back the next day to work on Mayadelsa.

I got up extra early the next morning and drove to Aunt Flo's. I parked a block away so she wouldn't hear my car and snuck around the cottage to the backyard. I used the keys and pushed the shed door open, just enough for me to get in. The inside of Uncle Hank's shed was exactly the same as it was the last time I was in it. I walked to the back, where the steamer trunk was, and moved it to the side, away from the loose floorboard, which I lifted up with the same screwdriver Uncle Hank had used when he first showed the box to me. I picked up the box from its hiding place, opened it, and stared for a minute or two, taking a quick inventory of its contents. It was obvious that no one but me had laid a hand on it since Uncle Hank died twelve years earlier. I grabbed the IOU and stuffed it in my back pocket. I put the nineteen hundred dollars under a stack of American money. I closed the lid and said a "thank you" and a "sorry" to Uncle Hank. It only took me a few minutes to put everything back, and then I was at the front door knocking before Aunt Flo was even up.

Later that day, when I was scrubbing and polishing Mayadelsa's face and tail, Aunt Flo brought me a glass of lemonade. "Will it bother you if I have a vodka and lime?" she asked.

"Okay by me," I replied.

She took a big gulp before she sat down in a lounge chair. I climbed out of the pool so I could have a few sips of my virgin lemonade, and so I could listen to what she was telling me about the vodka bottle. "From now on I won't be keeping my vodka in the freezer, and I took those old bottles of wine out of Hank's shed this morning when you were mowing the front lawn."

"Hey," I said, seeing my opening, "speaking of Uncle

Hank's shed. What did you do with that box of money and stuff he used to keep under the floor?"

Aunt Flo jumped straight up and practically shouted, "What are you talking about? What do you know about it? I looked for that box for years after he died because he told me he had some foreign money hidden away in a toolbox, but I could never find it. Where is it?"

I put my lemonade down and walked with Aunt Flo over to the shed. She pushed the door open and I led her over to the trunk, moved it to the side, and pretended to look for something to raise the floorboard with; immediately she reached for the familiar screwdriver and handed it to me. I reached down, lifted the floorboards, picked up Uncle Hank's box, and sat it down next to her. When she opened it you could've heard the scream clear to the North Pole.

ACKNOWLEDGMENTS

THANK YOU for sharing your wisdom, kindness and encouragement Brooke Warner, Anna Rogers, Lois Ashley (Mom), Pat McGrath, Lindsay, Chelsay, Lori Ann, Wendi Ann, Juli Ann, Peter Wright and all my loving friends.

ABOUT THE AUTHOR

MODAFOTOGRAFICA

J.A. WRIGHT was raised in the Pacific Northwest and moved to New Zealand in 1990.

   With more than thirty years in recovery from drug addiction, she's been crafting this novel for years.

SELECTED TITLES FROM SHE WRITES PRESS

She Writes Press is an independent publishing company founded to serve women writers everywhere. Visit us at www.shewritespress.com.

Cleans Up Nicely by Linda Dahl. $16.95, 978-1-938314-38-4. The story of one gifted young woman's path from self-destruction to self-knowledge, set in mid-1970s Manhattan.

Beautiful Garbage by Jill DiDonato. $16.95, 978-1-938314-01-8. Talented but troubled young artist Jodi Plum leaves suburbia for the excitement of the city—and is soon swept up in the sexual politics and downtown art scene of 1980s New York.

Pieces by Maria Kostaki. $16.95, 978-1-63152-966-5. After five years of living with her grandparents in Cold War-era Moscow, Sasha finds herself suddenly living in Athens, Greece—caught between her psychologically abusive mother and violent stepfather.

Things Unsaid by Diana Y. Paul. $16.95, 978-1-63152-812-5. A family saga of three generations fighting over money and obligation—and a tale of survival, resilience, and recovery.

Fire & Water by Betsy Graziani Fasbinder. $16.95, 978-1-938314-14-8. Kate Murphy has always played by the rules—but when she meets charismatic artist Jake Bloom, she's forced to navigate the treacherous territory of passionate love, friendship, and family devotion.

Our Love Could Light the World by Anne Leigh Parrish. $15.95, 978-1-938314-44-5. Twelve stories depicting a dysfunctional and chaotic—yet lovable—family that has to band together in order to survive.